A tough, [...]
he risks h[...]
headed l[...]
of gold and he's completely...

# *At Her Service*

**A woman's fantasy...**

**The soldier or the fireman?**

**No need to choose—we've got both
in these wonderful stories from
Annette Broadrick and
Marie Ferrarella!**

Dear Reader,

Welcome to a scorching month for Silhouette Desire.

This month our first volume, **Special Delivery**, includes a tough marine who needs to dust off his baby-handling skills in *Prince Charming in Dress Blues*—the latest instalment of the ever-popular BACHELOR BATTALION mini-series by Maureen Child. The second story portrays an honourable man who's reunited with the woman he loved and the son he didn't know he had in *A Lady for Lincoln Cade* by BJ James—one of her MEN OF BELLE TERRE books.

More strong and sexy bachelors can be found in our second volume—**At Her Service**. This contains *Hard to Forget* by Annette Broadrick where ex-sweethearts meet again in most unusual circumstances, and *Tall, Strong & Cool Under Fire* by Marie Ferrarella, where a hunky fireman is about to take a walk on the family side of life.

Finally, volume three has two bachelors who are **Rugged, Ruthless and...Ready!** Jackie Merritt's *Tough to Tame* and *The Rough and Ready Rancher* by Kathie DeNosky both have heroes who thought they could resist their perfect match. How wrong they were!

Enjoy!

The Editors

# At Her Service

## ANNETTE BROADRICK
## MARIE FERRARELLA

SILHOUETTE®
DESIRE™

*Silhouette, Silhouette Desire and Colophon
are registered trademarks of Harlequin Books S.A.,
used under licence.*

*First published in Great Britain 2002
Silhouette Books, Eton House, 18-24 Paradise Road,
Richmond, Surrey TW9 1SR*

AT HER SERVICE © Harlequin Books S.A. 2002

The publisher acknowledges the copyright holders of the
individual works as follows:

Hard To Forget © Annette Broadrick 2001
Tall, Strong & Cool Under Fire © Marie Rydzynski-Ferrarella 2000

ISBN 0 373 04748 7

51-0502

*Printed and bound in Spain
by Litografia Rosés S.A., Barcelona*

# HARD TO FORGET

### by
### Annette Broadrick

## *ANNETTE BROADRICK*

believes in romance and the magic of life. Since 1984, Annette has shared her view of life and love with readers. In addition to being nominated by *Romantic Times Magazine* as one of the Best New Authors of that year, she has also won the *Romantic Times* Reviewers' Choice Award for Best in its Series; the *Romantic Times* WISH award; and the *Romantic Times Magazine* Lifetime Achievement Awards for Series Romance and Series Romantic Fantasy.

To Susan Plunkett, whose warm support and infectious sense of humour rescued me from the deep abyss of non-creativity. I miss our weekly lunches at Marie's!

# Prologue

Eighteen-year-old Joe Sanchez looked into the cheap mirror over his scarred dresser and blinked. He didn't recognize the stranger he saw. Tonight was the first time in his life that he had worn formal clothes. They were rented, of course. It had taken him weeks to earn the money to rent the tuxedo he would be wearing tonight to the Santiago High School senior prom in Santiago, Texas, a small town on the Texas-Mexico border.

He grinned at the thought and was once again startled at the image in the mirror. He couldn't remember ever seeing himself smile—either in a mirror or a photograph. He had a great deal to smile about tonight, though, because he was taking Elena Maldonado to their senior prom.

He was still amazed that she had agreed to go with him. For the past few months she had been tutoring him in English and history. Thanks to her help, he was fairly certain he'd be graduating, after all. He'd be the first of his family to get a high-school diploma.

Last year, even last fall, he wouldn't have thought that any of this would ever happen....

"Yo, Sanchez,," Coach Torres hollered at the end of football practice in late September. "Meet me in my office after you've showered."

Joe gave him a brief nod and trotted with the other team members into the locker room. He went over to his locker and pulled off his football uniform. He knew what the coach had to say to him. His teachers had already told him his grades were dropping after the first round of exams.

So what? At least he'd been able to play on the varsity football team these past two years. That was worth a lot to him. Coach Torres had made him a wide receiver because he was fast and could handle the ball. In fact, he was getting the reputation of having magnets in his hands. He usually managed to snag the ball if the quarterback got it anywhere close to him.

His teammates chattered around him, but he tuned them out as he showered and dressed once again in his faded jeans and hand-me-down shirt. He walked out of the locker room down the hall to the coach's office, knowing he was about to be dropped from the squad.

Coach Torres was on the phone when Joe walked in. Coach waved him to the chair in front of his desk. Joe slid into the chair and watched the coach, who sat with his ankles crossed on the desk. When he hung up, Coach dropped his feet and pulled his chair closer, placing his elbows on the desk.

"Tell me something, Sanchez," he said in his gruff voice. "You planning to follow in Alfredo's footsteps?"

Joe blinked. What did his older brother have to do with

anything? He eyed the coach warily. "What do you mean?"

"I understand Al was convicted of drug smuggling a couple of years after he dropped out of school. He's how old now?"

"Twenty-two."

"Uh-huh. And been in and out of jail for most of the past five years, right?"

"So?"

"Is that what you want for your life?"

Joe shrugged.

Coach Torres didn't say anything. Just looked at him. And kept looking at him.

Joe shifted in his chair, placed his foot on his opposite knee and began to pull at the sole where it was coming loose. He kept his attention on the shoe.

Finally Coach said, "I'm going to offer you an alternative to Al's life, Joe, if you're willing to consider it."

Joe looked up in surprise. Coach was still studying him. It was as though he'd never taken his eyes off him.

"You're intelligent, Joe. You learn the plays quickly. You're a natural leader. You've got every guy on the team following your lead. You've got everything it takes to make it big in the world, except the drive to do it."

"You calling me lazy?" Joe asked, his expression sullen.

Coach smiled. "Nope. You're just not motivated. And I'd like to help you to change that."

"How?"

"By getting you a scholarship to go to college next year."

Joe's foot fell off his knee and he straightened in surprise. "College? For me?"

"That's right. At the rate you're going, you're going to

be ready to play college ball in another year. If you can get your grades up, that is.''

Joe slid back down in the chair. "Yeah. Right."

"You think that's so impossible?"

He shrugged again.

"How much time do you spend on homework every day?"

He shrugged again.

Coach Torres looked down at a piece of paper in front of him. "Obviously not enough if your present grades are any indication."

Joe didn't see a need to respond to that comment, either. He went back to worrying the sole of his shoe, wondering where he was going to get the money to buy a new pair.

"You don't believe you can do it, do you?" Coach asked.

Joe shook his head without looking up.

"Then I've got more faith in you than you do. As a matter of fact, I found someone who would be willing to tutor you if you want to put some effort into bringing those grades up."

Joe looked up from beneath his brows. "Who?"

"Elena Maldonado."

Joe frowned. He'd never heard of her. He started to shrug once more when he suddenly remembered a girl in several of his classes named Elena. "Is she that skinny nerdy girl with glasses and all that hair?"

"That's the one."

Joe laughed. "She said she'd help me with my classes?"

"Yep."

"You've gotta be kidding. She don't—doesn't give any-body the time of day. She's like a mouse—creeps into class and sits there taking notes all the time."

"Well, those notes may make the difference between

your graduating from school and going on to college, or someday ending up in jail alongside your brother. Your choice, my friend.''

Joe wouldn't admit it for the world, but the thought of actually getting to go to college electrified him. A chance to get away from the poverty of his home life. A chance to make something of himself. A chance to be able to provide for his mother, who had worked all her life to support him and his brother.

"So what do you think?" Coach asked as the silence lengthened. "Are you willing to work at bringing those grades up so you can continue to play ball? Because if you are, I'll do what I can to place you in a college next year with a full scholarship. You'll have to earn it in class, though.''

Joe started to speak, but his voice broke. He cleared his throat. "If you're sure Elena won't mind, I'd like to work on getting my grades up.''

"Good choice, son," Coach Torres said with a big grin on his face. "I'll let her know. The two of you can work out the arrangements of when and where you'll work together.''

Joe left the coach's office that day feeling bewildered. He and a few of his friends spent most of their time chasing around town at night, raising hell. If he was going to start working on his grades, his time was going to be taken up with things other than hanging out with his buddies.

The thought of college made him smile. It might even be worth it.

The truth was, he was ashamed of what Al had done, even though he didn't blame him. Al had never done much in school. He'd dropped out in the middle of his sophomore year because he'd convinced his mom he would get a job. He hadn't bothered to tell her that the job wasn't exactly legal. When you lived on the border, there were all kinds of ways to make money, as long as you didn't get caught.

He waited until the end of his history class the next day to approach Elena. He'd watched her in English earlier in the day. She'd kept her head down and never looked his way. It was only after he almost ran into her in the hall and saw her blush a fiery red that he knew Coach Torres had spoken to her.

He walked up to her desk as she was placing her books into her backpack.

"Hi," he said.

She didn't look up. "Hi."

"Coach tells me you're willing to help me bring up my grades."

She nodded.

"So where do you want to do this—your place or mine?"

Her head jerked up and she stared at him, eyes wide. "I can't do it at home. My, uh, dad doesn't like it when I have anyone over."

He knew that was a crock. He'd asked around about her and found out that her dad rarely worked and spent most of his time in one of the three bars in town. She just didn't want him there if her dad came home drunk.

Not that he blamed her. But at least she *had* a father. His dad had left when he was five. He barely remembered him.

"You want to come to my place, then?" he asked, dreading the idea that she would see the shack he lived in. He knew that her home was much nicer. The Maldonados lived on the outskirts of town in a large home that her dad had inherited from his family.

"What about working here at school?" she asked. "We

could meet in the library or outside the cafeteria. There are tables and chairs there.''

They were bolted down, but they were there. "Sure," he said. "Whatever you want. When can we start?"

"Don't you have football practice?"

He nodded. "We're through at five. I could meet you after that."

She ducked her head. "Okay."

"Today?"

"Uh-huh."

It had taken him several weeks of their studying together before he broke through the wall of reserve that was always around her. He discovered that she had a delightful personality and a wonderful sense of humor. He'd fallen for her playfulness, as well as her vulnerability.

She'd been too thin, with thick riotous hair and oversize glasses perched on her nose. Somehow, though, she had a way of looking at him that had made his heart race. He'd never been able to figure out what it was that she did to him.

He couldn't remember when he first began having erotic thoughts about the girl helping him pass his classes. What would it be like to kiss her? What would she do if he tried to touch her? Would his fantasies be fulfilled if he ever had the chance to make love to her?

For the first time in his life, there was a girl that he thought about more than football or going out and raising hell with his buddies.

Now, months later, they were going out on their first date together.

He gave one last look in the mirror, then walked into the room where his mother sat mending one of his shirts.

"Oh, Joe, you look so handsome!" she said, pressing her hand to her chest. "You take my breath away."

He leaned over and gave her a kiss on the cheek. "Thanks. And thank you for getting Uncle Pete to loan me his car for the night."

She looked at him over the top of her glasses. "You'd better not let anything happen to it."

He held up his hand. "I promise. I will take very good care of it."

Of course the thing was ancient, but it was wheels, which was more than he had. He couldn't very well ask Elena to walk to the prom with him.

He drove the old Plymouth away from town, eventually turning into the lane that led to Elena's house. This was the first time he'd ever been to her home. He wasn't sure what made him more nervous—taking a decent girl out on a date, driving a borrowed car, or having to meet her parents for the first time.

He walked across the small porch and knocked on the front door. Before he could take another deep breath, the door swung open.

Elena had on a slim black dress that was held up by tiny black straps, exposing her shoulders. The dress fit her slim form as though made for her, ending at the toes of her high-heeled shoes. She had her hair piled on her head with curls framing her face. Her glasses perched on her nose.

That was when Joe realized that he was in love with Elena Maldonado.

Elena caught her breath as soon as she saw Joe standing at the door. She'd never seen him in anything but old jeans and faded shirts. She couldn't believe how different he looked tonight. Older. More sophisticated. To-die-for handsome.

"Come in," she said, stepping back from the door.

Joe walked past her and she got a whiff of an aftershave lotion she hadn't known he wore. She wasn't sure her knees would hold her up. Wouldn't she feel foolish if she collapsed in his arms before they even got out the door?

She would never forget how he looked in his rented tuxedo. The white ruffled shirt emphasized his dark skin and the suit drew attention to his wide shoulders and slender hips. She felt as though the night had cast a spell on her, and she wondered if this was all a dream.

Going to the senior prom with Joe Sanchez was very special for Elena because it was her very first date, with Joe or anyone else. Meeting him after school and discussing English and history with him certainly didn't count as dating someone.

Even when he got into the habit of meeting her between classes and walking her to her locker, she hadn't allowed herself to think he meant anything by it.

However, when he asked her to the prom, her hopes soared. She knew she wasn't pretty, not like the other girls. Even though she'd gotten her braces off two years before, she was still careful about smiling at people. She didn't know what to say to the other kids, who seemed so sure of themselves, so she just went to her classes without making eye contact and without speaking to anyone.

But during the three weeks between the time Joe had asked her to go to the prom with him and the prom itself, Elena knew that she had blossomed into another person. She felt popular and attractive for the first time in her life. She'd held her head up and smiled at classmates, who had been startled at first before they had smiled back.

She'd felt more comfortable joining a group in the cafeteria and listening to their conversation. She still didn't talk much, but she listened and smiled and nodded her head in agreement. And she'd laughed more, because she was happy.

When anyone asked if she was going to the prom, she told them she was going with Joe Sanchez just to watch the expressions of amazement on their faces. Joe had quite a reputation around school. He was known for being a little wild and therefore exciting. He didn't date girls from the school but had been seen from time to time with older girls who lived in town.

Elena and her mother had driven to San Antonio to find her the perfect gown to wear. It was midnight-black and straight, falling to her ankles with a slit to the knee so she could walk. She'd even worn two-inch heels, mostly so that she wouldn't trip over the hem of her dress. Her mother had helped her with her hair, pinning it high on her head and letting stray curls tumble around her face and neck.

Of course her glasses didn't help her glamorous image in the least, but without them she was practically blind. But not even having to wear her hated glasses could detract from her joy when Joe Sanchez saw her for the first time tonight.

He looked stunned. He acted stunned. And as the evening progressed, he didn't let her get more than two feet away from him.

The only time Elena was uncomfortable was about midway through the dance when three of his buddies came up to them and made joking comments that she didn't understand and that seemed to upset Joe. She asked him about it later when they were out on the dance floor, but he shrugged off her questions, saying his friends were too stupid to bother with.

Joe had begun to relax and enjoy the dance before the guys had shown up. He didn't know how they'd managed to be here, since they were all dropouts. These were the guys he'd considered friends until last fall when he'd changed his lifestyle by working hard to bring up his grades.

They hadn't liked that he was suddenly too busy to hang out with them. As the months passed, he'd realized what losers they were, doing stupid stuff, getting into all kinds of trouble for no other reason than they were bored.

His life was different now. Coach Torres had told him last week that he'd been approved for the scholarship to go to Texas A & M at College Station. He'd talked to him about joining the Corps, which was the military school there. All at once, Joe could see a future for himself, a chance to get away from bums like these guys.

Elena noticed that Joe had become quieter after he'd told those guys to leave them alone. When he suggested they leave the dance sometime later, she was ready to go. She wasn't used to dancing and she certainly wasn't used to dancing in high heels. As soon as they got into his car, she kicked off her shoes.

He immediately removed his tie and undid the top button of his shirt. They looked at each other and laughed.

"That was fun, Joe. Thank you so much for inviting me…and for the beautiful corsage." He'd given her a wrist corsage of gardenias, her favorite flower.

"Do you have to go home right away?" he asked, looking at his watch.

"Not anytime soon," she replied. Her mother understood that this was a once-in-a-lifetime occasion. As for her dad, she hoped he'd be asleep by the time she got home, so the later the better.

"I thought we might go out to the levee for a while…."

Her heart began to pound and she tried to remember to breathe. The levee was where the kids went to make out. Not that she'd ever been there before, but that was what they liked to talk about. Going to the levee.

It had been built many years ago to control flooding and to help direct irrigation from the Rio Grande into the canals that branched from it.

"If you don't want to, that's okay," he finally said, and she realized she'd been sitting there, unable to provide him with a coherent answer.

She gripped her hands together. "I'd like that," she said quietly.

He grinned. "Great." As though her agreement freed him in some way, he leaned over and gently kissed her. Boy, if she thought she was having trouble breathing before! She forced herself to relax and placed her hand on his chest. Only then did she discover that his heart was racing as fast as hers. She found that somehow reassuring.

When he finally straightened, he looked at her for a long time before starting the car.

Once parked, she saw why this was such a great place. It was higher than most of the land around them, and she could see the lights of Santiago, as well as those across the river in Mexico.

She wasn't surprised to find that there were several other cars parked, but Joe parked in such a way that each car had adequate privacy.

Once Joe shut off the engine, the quiet around them seemed to seep into the car. They rolled down the windows and a slight breeze wafted through.

Joe pushed the seat back, then took off his jacket. "I, uh...I've never brought anyone here before." His voice sounded forced.

She turned and looked at him. "Really? I would have

thought a football star like you would be up here every weekend.'' She was amazed that she could tease him.

He undid another button of his shirt. ''Actually football kept me really busy all fall. Since then, I've been spending most of my time on homework. How about you?''

''Homework keeps me busy, too.''

''No, I mean, have you ever been here before?''

She laughed. She couldn't help it. ''Who would bring someone like me up here?''

''What do you mean, someone like you?''

She shrugged. ''You may not have noticed, but I'm not one of the popular girls in school.''

''You could be.''

''What do you mean?''

''I mean, if you'd relax a little more and join in. Actually I've noticed you with some of the girls in the cafeteria lately. They all seem to like you just fine.''

She hadn't given their response to her much thought. ''I guess so.''

He slid his arm around her shoulders. ''I'm glad I've gotten to know you this year, Elena. You've helped me to look at life in a whole new way. I mean, you have all this ambition—you plan to go to college and do something with your life.''

''You mean work my way through college.''

''Well, we all have to do that. I hadn't really believed I had a chance to go to college until Coach started urging me to fill out applications and you and I became friends. I just found out that I've been accepted at A & M for next year.''

''Oh, Joe, that's wonderful!''

''I wouldn't have considered it before. I guess I figured I would stay here and find something to do with my time like everyone else.''

"I'm glad you're looking at the bigger picture." She lightly touched his jaw with her finger. "I'm also glad you consider me a friend."

He took her hand and kissed the tips of her fingers. "How about you? Do you know what you're going to do after graduation?"

"I've been accepted at George Washington University in D.C. I've been offered a scholarship and a couple of grants. Mom says she has some money put away that I can use, as well."

He framed her face with his hands and looked at her with a serious expression on his face. "I want to be much more than just friends, Elena," he finally whispered.

"You do?" She could scarcely get her breath.

"Uh-huh," he replied, kissing her with a lot more assurance and passion than he'd allowed himself during their first kiss.

She'd never felt like this before. She couldn't get enough of his touch. Her brain shut down and all she could do was to feel. She knew that the scent of his aftershave would always bring this magical night to mind. When the kiss ended, they were both breathing rapidly. The night was too dark for her to see his face, but she knew by his breathing and the racing of his heart beneath her palm that he was equally affected by what they had just shared.

"There's not much room up here with the steering wheel and all. Do you want to move into the back seat?"

She nodded, and somehow he must have been able to see that. Since the car was a two-door, he pulled one of the seats forward and helped her crawl into the back. Then he followed her.

He stretched out the width of the car as far as possible, then pulled her down on top of him.

She'd never been so close to anyone before. Her dress

had a halter top that now fell open. She was grateful that it was too dark for him to see anything.

Soon she no longer cared. As he kissed and caressed her and encouraged her to do the same to him, his shirt and the top of her dress became hindrances. He unfastened the back of her dress while she rapidly undid the buttons on his shirt and pulled it off him. Clumsily he unfastened her strapless bra so that there was nothing between them. Just bare skin, touching.

She stopped breathing when he touched her breast. He was so gentle, so caring, that all she wanted was to have him touch her again and again. She could feel how aroused he was through the thin material of her dress and his trousers.

His next kiss set her on fire. When he slid his hand along her thigh and through the slit of her dress to her panties, she pushed into his hand, wanting to feel more of the magic.

She heard the zipper of his pants in the silence between their labored breathing and knew that if she didn't stop him, they were going to make love now. She realized that she didn't care. At that point, all she wanted was to continue being close to him. He shoved her panties down and off her, then lifted her slightly so that his hard flesh was pushing against her.

She moved slightly, opening herself so that he could enter her. The sudden invasion and size startled, then hurt her, and she clamped her legs together, trying to stop him. But it was too late. He lifted his hips in a strong surge, holding her against him with such strength she couldn't move. Why had she thought she wanted him to make love to her? It hurt. He was too big. She tried to pull away from him, but he kept his hands on her hips as he pumped into her until he made one final lunge and fell back onto the seat, his hands dropping away from her.

As soon as he released her, she scrambled to get away, pulling herself up and off him. The top of her dress was around her waist; the rest of it was twisted around her hips and legs. She struggled to lift herself off the dress so she could pull it around and cover herself.

It was then that three large flashlights appeared at the windows. She heard male laughter and hateful humiliating remarks.

"Way to go, dude. We knew you could do it!"

"Damn. Looks like we're going to have to pay up on that bet, after all. You always bragged you could score with her, given the chance. Guess you were right!"

"Who woulda believed you'd get this far with her on a first date! That beats all your records. Gotta hand it to you, buddy."

At the first sign of the flashlights, Joe jackknifed into a sitting position and reached for Elena, but not before the boys had seen her bare breasts. They hooted and hollered, laughed and made obscene jokes while he helped her refasten her dress.

He quickly covered himself, then pushed the seat forward and jumped out of the car. The boys took off running with Joe in hot pursuit.

Elena was numb with shock and humiliation. There was a bet? He had gone out with her...he'd made love to her...because of a bet?

She crawled back into the front seat and huddled against the door, waiting for him to return to the car and take her home. If she could live through this horrible night, she would never, ever speak to him again.

Eventually he returned to the car. When he jerked open the door, the overhead light flashed on. She turned her head so she wouldn't have to look at him, but she didn't miss his disheveled appearance and the scrape on his cheek.

He closed the door but didn't start the car right away. She could hear his harsh breathing. Finally he sighed and said, "I can't believe those guys did that. I am so sorry, Elena. They've been drinking and they're angry at me for leaving the group. I guess they thought they'd pay me back this way, but it wasn't fair to you. For what it's worth, I told them what I think of them. I can't believe I ever considered them friends."

"Please take me home," she whispered.

"Of course." He started the car. "I'm so sorry our evening had to end this way."

She didn't say anything. She couldn't. It took all her concentration not to burst into tears and further humiliate herself. As soon as they reached the end of her driveway, she said, "Please stop here."

He pulled in and stopped. "Let me take you up to the—"

That was all she heard before she pushed on the door and got out, then slammed it. She clutched her purse in one hand and her shoes in the other, her skirt dragging in the dirt. She grabbed it with a couple of her fingers and sprinted to the house, not looking back.

Joe watched her, feeling helpless. He'd never been in this kind of situation before. Sure, he'd had sex with a few girls, but tonight was the first time he'd made love with anyone. He'd had no control with her. He knew he'd hurt her, knew this must have been her first time.

Those stupid bums had ruined everything. If he'd had more time, he could have explained that his lack of control was because of the way he felt about her. He could have told her that she was very special to him.

He would wait until Monday and talk to her. Maybe by
then she would be calmer and willing to listen to him.

Unfortunately Joe never had a chance to talk to Elena
again.

# One

*Eleven Years Later*

**T**he staccato sound of her heels striking the polished floor echoed down the hallway, causing Elena to wince. She felt the need to tiptoe as she followed the directions she'd been given to attend a nine-o'clock meeting at the Quantico, Virginia, headquarters of the FBI.

This was not the part of the building where she'd worked as an intelligence analyst for the past seven years, and so the area was unfamiliar to her. She had no idea why she'd been requested to attend a meeting here with Douglas Wilder and his group. If nothing else, her curiosity had been aroused.

She glanced at her watch and decided she had time to stop at the women's restroom to make certain she looked as professional and competent as possible when she met with Wilder.

Special Agent Wilder headed a team of field agents, people who had trained intensively to work with and around the public. She, on the other hand, was more comfortable working with facts, figures and raw data. She'd made it through the academy all right and had been relieved when she was assigned her current position.

Elena had discovered a long time ago that she was more comfortable being an observer than a participant in life. She enjoyed searching through information to find patterns, to make sense out of various bits and pieces of information and to put it together to explain what illegal activities might be going on in the country. She was used to working alone. Since receiving the phone call at home last night, she'd been unable to come up with any idea why Special Agent Wilder would want her to be in today's meeting.

She pushed open the restroom door. Ceramic tile covered the floor, as well as the lower half of the gray walls. A frosted-glass window allowed natural light to flood the area. The small room, with its three stalls and four sinks, was empty. She sighed with relief. She wasn't ready yet to see anyone this early in the morning.

Elena took a deep breath and forced herself to release the air in her lungs in a slow calm manner. *You can handle this,* she reminded herself. Maybe there was something in one of her reports that needed further explanation in person. There was no reason to panic. She was competent in her job. She just wasn't used to working in a group.

She ran cool water over her hands and wrists, then carefully dried them on a paper towel from a nearby dispenser. She stared into the mirror that ran the length of the sinks, inspecting her image one last time.

After she straightened the collar of her white blouse, she

adjusted the belt of her black slacks. Her lightweight cotton jacket matched her slacks.

Only her hair detracted from the professional and competent look she wanted. The thick wavy mass had always been the bane of her existence. Today she had forced it into a not-so-tidy knot at the nape of her neck. Unfortunately there were strands already escaping and curling around her ears. She felt a trickle of nervous perspiration slide down her spine.

Elena peered into her green eyes, deliberately narrowing them in an effort to look tougher. Her long thick lashes were no help at all. She'd been told that she had sultry eyes. Sultry! That was the last thing she wanted to hear from anyone.

Another glance at her watch told her she needed to get to the meeting. She tucked a curl behind her ear and made certain there was no smudge of lipstick on her teeth. With another deep breath she opened the door into the hallway and proceeded to the room where the meeting would be held.

She paused in the open doorway and looked around. She counted seven agents—all men—only one of whom she recognized. Chris Simmons. He glanced up from the coffee machine where he was filling a cup and saw her standing there. He smiled with an obvious look of surprise. He filled a second cup, then walked over to where she stood, greeting her with a big grin.

"Well, hello, stranger. Welcome to our little part of the world," he said, offering her one of the cups he held.

So he remembered her strong dependency on coffee to get her day started. Today of all days, his offer was greatly appreciated. She'd skipped her second cup of coffee this morning for fear she'd be late.

She returned his smile. "Thanks, Chris," she said. The

aromatic brew was just what she needed to settle her jumping nerves. She inhaled the lovely fragrance and took a hasty sip.

He nodded. "You're quite welcome. It's good to see you. It's been a while. Come on in and find a place to sit."

She followed him into the room and looked around. It looked like every other government conference room she'd been in, with its large oblong table in the middle, surrounded by unpadded wooden chairs.

"So what brings you to our neck of the woods?" Chris asked. "I thought they liked to keep you and the other brains away from the rest of us poor working slobs."

Since Chris had aced all his tests at the academy, she wasn't buying into his "dumb me" act.

"I have no idea," she replied with a shrug. "I was told to show up this morning, so here I am." She glanced around the room. The other agents were either in the process of getting coffee or already sipping from their cups. They milled around the table until they each claimed a chair and laid out their pads and pens. With a hint of hesitancy she added, "I just found out last night that I was to be here."

Chris motioned for her to sit, then took the chair next to her.

They had been friends since they'd graduated from the academy together. They'd dated for several months back then before recognizing that they enjoyed each other's company but weren't interested in pursuing a more intimate relationship, which might come between them and their careers. Elena had never been sorry about that decision.

She enjoyed Chris's blond good looks and the fact that, although he took his profession seriously, he never took *himself* seriously. He had been one of the few men in their class who had actively supported her efforts during their training.

He leaned back in his chair. "You know, seeing you again reminds me that we haven't gotten together in months. How about catching a movie tonight?"

She nodded. "I'd like that, unless this meeting has to do with an assignment and you'll be sent out of town right away." Since Chris spent most of his time away from headquarters, she knew the odds were good that he wouldn't be here for long.

Before Chris had an opportunity to respond, Douglas Wilder walked into the room carrying a thick file. He sat down at the head of the table. The two agents still standing quickly found seats.

Doug Wilder was in his midfifties, tall, unabashedly gray-haired and all business. He glanced around the table, and when he spotted Elena, he said, "Thank you for coming this morning, Ms. Maldonado. I know you were given short notice." He quickly made introductions around the table.

She nodded to each of the agents before returning her attention to Wilder.

"Okay, here's what we're dealing with, people," Wilder began. "The Immigration and Naturalization Service has asked for our help to resolve a delicate situation going on along the Texas-Mexico border."

As one, the male agents burst into laughter. One of them asked if today was April Fool's Day. In truth, it was the middle of May.

Elena knew that the fierce rivalry between various government agencies made the idea of asking for help appear ludicrous. The last thing any agency wanted to admit was that they couldn't handle a situation without outside help.

Wilder's furrowed brow eased somewhat, and Elena could almost imagine she saw the hint of a smile on his narrowed lips.

"Glad I can provide so much entertainment for you this early in the morning." He flipped open the file and began to pass around stapled pages to each of them. "Just for that, you're going to get a brief history lesson so that you'll understand what the government is up against in that region."

The agents settled back into their chairs. Elena knew enough of Wilder's reputation to know that he wasn't one to waste his breath. Whenever he chose to talk, everyone around him stopped to listen. Today was no exception.

"There has been an upsurge of traffic these past few years from Mexico into the United States along our shared borders from Texas to California. Despite the beefed-up patrol of the border, too many illegal drugs and aliens are moving into the United States.

"We understand the problems in their country—the devaluation of the peso, the continued drought that has affected Mexico, as well as our Southwestern states. However, we cannot ignore the problem in hopes it will go away."

As Doug continued to review the present situation, Elena reviewed what he was saying. She knew all too well what he was talking about. Santiago had originally been a farming community. When she was small, the migrant workers moved there early in the growing season and continued northward as the season progressed. The last time she'd gone home to visit her mother, Sara had mentioned the problems the area was having with illegal drugs and aliens being brought across the border. What she was hearing wasn't new to Elena.

Wilder continued. "The high incidence of drugs and

aliens successfully crossing the Texas-Mexico border in the past eight months or so has become a black eye for the Border Patrol, the local arm of the INS and the Drug Enforcement Agency working that particular area.''

From the back of the room Sam Walters asked, ''And they think we can do their job better?''

Wilder looked at Sam from beneath his bushy brows. ''We've been asked to join a task force to find out why those two agencies are not making more arrests. The word is that some of the agents may be taking money to look the other way. I received word late yesterday that we need new faces to work the area, people who are unknown to either of the two agencies. None of us likes to think about an agent who has turned, but it happens. I have handpicked each of you to work on this. We're going to find out if any INS or DEA agents are on the take, and if they are, we're going to remove them.''

He looked around the room to make certain everyone understood. Then he nodded at the papers lying in front of each one of them. ''What I've handed out here is general background material on what has been done by the two agencies up until now. Here's the plan. I requested a list of possible suspects who may be involved in the smuggling operations—people who were arrested and let go for lack of evidence, people whose behavior is suspicious, people who need to be watched by agents who can be trusted.''

For the first time since he had introduced her to the group, Wilder looked at Elena. ''I'm sure you're wondering why you've been chosen for this team.''

She tensed, recognizing that the knot in the pit of her stomach had been forming as she slowly realized that she wasn't there to interpret information. Douglas Wilder intended to use her on this assignment. She smiled, hoping to cover her nervousness. "Yes, sir. The thought did cross my mind."

"If you'll look at page fourteen of the handout, you'll notice that a significant increase in activity has been narrowed to an area in and around Santiago, Texas. Santiago is located between Rio Grande City and Laredo right on the Texas-Mexico border. A new bridge was opened there about eighteen months ago to facilitate the movement of factory products from Mexico into the United States. Several suspects listed in these handouts live near there." He glanced around the room. "Fortunately I believe we've discovered a secret weapon right here in our own agency, gentlemen. You see, Santiago happens to be Elena's hometown."

Elena quickly turned to the page in question and began to read in order not to make eye contact with the other agents.

Wilder continued, "As soon as I discovered that we had a trained agent from that area, I knew we were already ahead of the game. We've got an agent familiar with the area who will be able to mingle with the locals without causing any suspicion."

He looked around the room. "Are there any questions so far?"

No one spoke.

"All of you will be working undercover. Elena, obviously, will be our insider, feeding us as much information as she can while we work the other border towns in that general vicinity. Our plan is to have Elena spend the next few months getting reacquainted with old friends, neighbors and schoolmates and collecting as much local information as possible. We're counting on her being able to get close to some of the people we think might be masterminding these runs. We'll also be working on finding out which U.S. agents are feeding the smugglers information that keeps them from being discovered.''

One of the agents raised his hand. ''But won't those people know she works for the government?''

Elena answered with the information Wilder already knew about her from reading her personnel file. ''When I first came to work here, I decided not to tell anyone back home who I worked for. Instead, I told them that I'm an accountant for a small firm in Maryland.''

Wilder went on, ''Her cover will be that her firm was bought out and she was let go with a generous severance packet. There would be nothing unusual in her choosing to go back home for a while before she decides where to apply for her next job.''

He looked at Elena as though to confirm that this scenario would work for her. She nodded, unable to come up with an alternative.

Wilder said to the group at large, ''Study the workup on the list of suspected smugglers. They live in towns from Brownsville to Laredo. I want you to learn their history and get to know as much about them as you know about your own brother. Or sister. You'll see there are some women on the list.''

He waited while the agents scanned the pages. Elena spotted some familiar names. ''How do you want this handled, sir? If I'm working inside, I won't be able to communicate much with the others.''

''Sam Walters will be heading up the group down there, reporting directly to me. Chris Simmons will be your immediate contact. My suggestion is that you make regular shopping trips into San Antonio where you'll meet with Chris for status reports. He, in turn, will stay in touch with Sam.''

Wilder looked at the others. ''What we're hoping is that

you'll hear or see something that might hint at a coming shipment. You'll be doing utility work—electric, cable, gas, telephone—in order to have a reason to be in rural areas at odd times of day and night.

"Do what you have to do to blend in and become a part of the various small communities in the area. Each of you will have a different area to cover, some south of Santiago, others north. The main thing is not to have any run-ins with the local authorities, because you won't be able to tell them why you're there. Keep your noses clean and your eyes and ears open." He paused and looked around at each of them. "Any more questions?"

Wilder's voice faded into the background when Elena flipped to a new page and saw the name listed at the top. A photo, a detailed description and background check were all there, but she couldn't get past the name and photo.

For a moment she thought she was hallucinating. This couldn't be real.

Joseph Sanchez. Joe Sanchez lived in Santiago now? Since when? She couldn't believe what she was seeing. He was listed as one of the suspects.

She scanned the report. Twenty-nine years old. Received an honorable discharge from the army as a major. Currently residing in Santiago, Texas.

His black eyes stared out of the photo without expression. His hair was much shorter than she remembered, but the stubborn jaw, the dent in the chin, the slight scowl that drew his black eyebrows to a V were very much the same. There was no mistaking him.

His shoulders appeared wider and more heavily muscled than she remembered, which wasn't surprising. She knew *she* had changed considerably in the past eleven years. Her changes had been more than physical.

Someone asked a question; then others added their queries. Their words washed over her without making any sense. She tried to focus on the discussion, but all she could do was stare at the photograph, aware of her heart pounding heavily in her chest.

She hadn't thought of Joe Sanchez in years. She hadn't seen him since they'd graduated from high school. It had been her devout hope at that time that she would never ever see him again.

Joe Sanchez was a horrible reminder of the most humiliating time in her life. She'd been so shy around boys while she was growing up, not at all certain she could trust them. She'd seen how her father's behavior—his drinking and the accompanying lies he'd told with charming sincerity—had so often upset her mother. She'd grown up not trusting anything her father said.

Joe had seemed very different from her father. In the months she'd gotten to know him, she'd learned to trust him, to believe that not every male was like her father. Joe had betrayed her in so many ways the night of their senior prom that she had determined never to allow another man the opportunity to get close enough to hurt her again.

Instead, she had focused on her career. She knew that this assignment was the biggest test she'd been given since she joined the bureau. She was returning to her hometown and would have to pretend it was because she'd lost her job, which would certainly put a dent in her ego.

In addition, she was being assigned to get close to Joseph Sanchez, who was suspected of drug smuggling, to find out all his secrets and betray him.

How ironic was that?

Finally Wilder said, "Okay, that should take care of everything I wanted to cover during this meeting." He glanced at her and said, "Elena, I need to speak with you for a few minutes."

After the last agent left the room, Wilder closed the door and turned to her. "Sorry to spring this one on you like that." He sat down in the chair that Chris had vacated and faced her. "I would have discussed it with you last night when I called, but I couldn't take a chance that someone might get wind of my decision to use you in the field and try to get around it. I know this is a dangerous assignment, but I also believe from everything I've heard about you that you can handle it. I hope you agree."

Elena pushed her chair away from the table so that she was facing him. She nodded to him and said, "Yes, sir. I do. I appreciate your faith in my abilities."

"I want to stress that no one outside our group will know you're working with us. No other agency will have your name. We're doing everything we can to protect you."

"I appreciate that."

"We noted that one of the suspects graduated from Santiago High School with you. Is that correct?"

"Yes, sir."

"How well did you know him?"

She thought of several responses to that, but chose to be circumspect. "It was a relatively small school. I knew everyone in the class."

He nodded. "Then you don't think you'll have any trouble making contact with him?"

*Trouble?* That wasn't the word that came to mind. "I don't think so."

Wilder stood and Elena followed his lead. "How soon can you leave?" he asked.

She rubbed her forehead, where a steady pulsating throb was already working itself into a full-fledged headache. "Probably tomorrow. Possibly the day after. I'll need to contact my mother and prepare her for my moving back home.'' She glanced at Wilder. ''Do you really think this will take months?''

''At the very least.''

She sighed, kneading her temples.

''Is this going to present personal problems for you?''

Her mind flashed to Joseph Sanchez, ex-military.

''No, sir,'' she lied without a qualm. She would deal with the situation because she was a professional.

Wilder held out his hand and she shook it. ''Good luck,'' he said gravely.

''Thank you, sir.''

They left the conference room together.

She needed to go pack. She needed to contact her mother. And yes, she needed all the good luck she could get.

In the coming months she would use all her skills to investigate the man who had caused her so much pain. If what was suspected about him was true, she would be a part of the team that brought him down.

Several sayings flew through her mind as she retraced her steps down the hallway and returned to her own department. Two in particular kept circling.

Revenge is sweet.

Paybacks are hell.

Well, she and ex-army major Joe Sanchez were about to find out if those sayings were true.

# Two

A week later Elena sat at the end of the bar in a small smoke-filled cantina in Santiago, Texas, watching the locals at the other end of the bar indulge in their daily ritual of drinking and discussing their day with friends and neighbors.

She'd arrived in town five days ago, and already she was suffering from serious signs of emotional claustrophobia.

Elena had forgotten what life was like in a small town, where everybody knew everything about you and your family and didn't mind asking personal questions. No matter how she might attempt to sidestep such questions, she found it impossible without appearing to be rude or disrespectful.

Her mother kept reminding her that people asked about her life because they cared.

Elena could do without so much caring.

In the days since she'd arrived, she must have explained to every resident of the town, all fifteen hundred or so…

Why she was back in town visiting her mother.

Why she had chosen to return home after losing her job.

What she'd been doing all these years.

Why she wasn't married.

And whether she intended her return home to be permanent.

As if that wasn't enough, after five days of putting up with intensive interrogations from her mother's friends, who made law-enforcement officials appear timid and soft, she'd seen no sign of Joe Sanchez.

However, she'd heard about the new factories that had been opened right across the border from Santiago and how the economy of the town had been helped by residents of Mexico crossing the border to shop in Santiago stores.

She'd sat in the local café and listened as town members complained about the big trucks rumbling through the town at all hours of the night, moving product northward.

This was the second night in a row she'd sat in the bar, watching and listening. Once the locals had placed her, they had pretty much ignored her presence, which was exactly what she—and Wilder—had counted on.

What she didn't hear was anything about illegal trafficking along the border. Wilder had been right. This case wasn't going to be handled quickly.

She'd traded in her tailored slacks for well-worn jeans, her silk blouses and jackets for T-shirts, her dark leather shoes for sandals. She'd been forced to carry her weapon in her purse because she could not conceal it on her body unless she wore a jacket, and even in May, the weather didn't call for any kind of jacket.

She'd lucked out last night when she walked into the cantina for the first time since she'd come to Texas to discover Chico Morales tending bar. She'd gone to school with Chico. So far he offered her the best opportunity she'd had since she'd arrived in Santiago to ask casually about other former classmates, including Joe Sanchez.

Chico had been embarrassingly excited to see her, going on and on about how good she looked and how no one would guess she would be thirty on her next birthday.

She couldn't really say the same about Chico. He'd obviously married a good cook. Either that or he'd spent the past few years knocking back several bottles of his favorite brew on a daily basis.

He'd pulled out photos of his children, three boys and a little girl who was a real cutie. She must take after her mother, Elena thought.

After listening to him reminisce about his life since high school, she had gradually eased the conversation around to other class members. He'd been obliging, filling her in on who had married whom and who was running around with whose wife.

She'd listened and smiled, joked about her own lack of a love life and encouraged him to fill her in on what had been happening in Santiago since she'd left school.

Eventually Chico mentioned Joe and how surprised everyone was when he left the military and moved back to Santiago a few months ago.

Exactly her reaction. He must have had a strong reason to come back here after getting a chance to see how the rest of the world lived. Elena gave no indication that Joe was the person she'd been waiting for. She had nodded and made comments similar to the ones she'd made about others they had known way back when.

She felt she'd made definite progress when Chico mentioned that Joe came into the cantina once in a while, but he wasn't a regular like the group at the other end of the bar. Most of them came in every night after work, sometimes forgetting to go home until the place closed down.

According to Chico, Joe traveled a lot, but he couldn't quite remember what it was Joe did when he was away. When he was in town, he worked out of his garage on people's cars. Folks were surprised to discover he was such a good mechanic.

Then he reminisced about what a great wide receiver Joe had been in high school, what an outstanding team they'd had their senior year when they went to the finals before losing out to some school up north. Up north in Texas, that is. Few people in their circle ever left Texas.

While Chico had been pouring her second beer the previous evening, he'd asked, "So whatever happened to you, Elena? You seemed to disappear as soon as we graduated. Now you say you've been working in Maryland?" He made the place sound as though it was located on an asteroid in another galaxy.

She shrugged. "It seemed like a good idea at the time. But it didn't really work out."

Most of her classmates had been content to stay in Santiago once they finished school. She, on the other hand, had counted first the years, then the months and finally the days until she could leave the dusty streets of the small border town. Once gone, she'd never looked back. To paraphrase the title of an old country song, happiness to her was seeing Santiago, Texas, in the rearview mirror.

Elena would have been content never to return here for more than brief visits with her mother. So where was she sent for her first and probably only field assignment?

Santiago, Texas.

The irony of the situation was inescapable.

Elena glanced at her watch. It was after ten o'clock. She supposed she had gathered enough information for one day. She wondered how Chris and the other men were doing with their assignments. She was supposed to meet Chris in San Antonio the day after tomorrow for her first debriefing. She hadn't done badly in gathering general information, but she had nothing specific to report, which irked her.

Oh, well. She might as well go home, visit with her mom for a while and get to bed. Another exciting day in Santiago was drawing to a close.

A couple of the men at the bar said their goodbyes and headed toward the front door. When it swung open, a man stepped inside, moving out of their way and greeting them with a smile and a few words.

Elena glanced up, her glass halfway to her mouth, then stared.

She recognized him immediately. She straightened on the barstool and watched as he sauntered across the small area cleared for dancing as if he owned the place.

*Joe Sanchez, as I live and breathe,* she thought sarcastically. Her next thought was, *It's about time.*

Thank God he'd shown up. Her patience had been rewarded. She hadn't been forced to go looking for him. At least now their meeting would be construed as accidental.

Oh, if the powers that be only knew how much she hated having to pretend to be friendly toward this guy, they would nominate her for a medal for serving her country above and beyond the call of duty. Much, much beyond.

She watched him in the mirror mounted behind the bar.

Joe paused at the jukebox at the other end of the bar and made several selections before walking to the middle of the bar and ordering a drink. Several of the men clustered at the other end turned and greeted him, keeping him in conversation. Now she had to decide how to handle this first encounter.

She'd studied his file and looked at his photo until she had it memorized, but she still wasn't prepared to see how the added inches in height and the extra pounds that were part of his vital statistics made him even more attractive than he had been eleven years ago.

Whatever he'd done in the army had given him a physique most women would sigh for.

Not her, of course.

She knew the person inside. She knew him for the piece of cow dung he was, but she had to admit that he managed to fill out a pair of jeans just fine.

Oh, my, yes. He certainly did.

She hadn't missed the glances he'd received from the other women in the place as soon as he walked in and while he'd studied the titles on the jukebox. In those snug jeans he wore, he was a walking advertisement for buns of steel. His feminine audience was definitely appreciative. She could practically hear the lip smacking going on.

She sipped her beer and mentally made a face at the taste. Maybe tonight would be the last time she would have to order that particular beverage. A good white wine was her drink of choice, but she shuddered to think what she might have been served if she'd dared to order wine here.

Elena knew that her thoughts were going in six different directions. What difference did it make what she was drinking or what the other women thought of Joe Sanchez? She had to focus on what was important, why she was here. She had to figure out a way to cause him to notice her without making it obvious.

Eventually he glanced into the mirror and caught her gaze.

*Oh, that's not obvious, Maldonado. Staring at the guy like some lovelorn soul until he catches you.*

Rather than pretend he hadn't caught her staring at him,

she held his gaze for a long moment before she tilted her glass toward him in a slight—a very slight—salute. She took a sip without dropping her gaze.

He turned his head and looked squarely at her, his forearms resting on the bar so that his carefully sculpted butt stood out in relief. She had no doubt he knew exactly the effect he had on most women.

Just not her.

Never her.

She put her suddenly racing pulse down to the fact that she had finally made contact with her quarry.

She deliberately glanced at her watch, then drank some more from her beer without looking directly at him again. From the corner of her eye she watched as he called Chico over and said something to him. Between the music blaring from the jukebox and the lively discussions going on around her, she couldn't hear what he said. However, it didn't take a brain surgeon to guess that he was asking Chico about her.

She saw the shocked look on his face when Chico answered him and almost smiled. *Yeah, Sanchez, I imagine I'm the last person you'd expect to find here in Santiago.*

He straightened without taking his eyes off her. After tilting the bottle to his mouth and letting the golden liquid flow down his throat, Joe ambled along the bar until he came to the short arm of the L where she sat.

He leaned his elbow on the bar as he continued to look at her.

She didn't move, but kept her hand lightly wrapped around her almost empty glass.

Up close she could see the lines that bracketed his mouth, as well as the sun lines radiating from the corners of his eyes. The dent in his chin appeared to be more pronounced. She'd grown used to looking at the photograph of him staring at the camera without expression. Now his eyes showed their shock and a warmth that surprised her.

"I don't believe it," he said softly, his gaze taking in each of her features as though mentally comparing them with earlier memories. He spoke below the blaring music and boisterous conversations so that she heard his words as clearly as if he'd whispered them in her ear. "I'm out of town for a few days and look who I find is here when I return."

She suppressed the shiver that ran through her body. She'd forgotten how his deep voice had always had such a strong effect on her. In a flash she was that shy teenager again, reacting to his good looks and blatant charm.

*Somebody help me, I'm drowning in memories here,* she thought in panic.

"Hello, Joe," she said quietly, then quickly picked up her glass and drained it.

He immediately signaled Chico to bring her another as he sat down on the stool at the elbow of the bar, so that they were almost facing each other. She was thankful she'd chosen to sit next to the wall. Now she turned on the stool and casually braced herself against the wall, hoping to look relaxed and totally at ease with this meeting, thankful for the three barstools that separated them.

"Elena Maldonado," he let the syllables of her name roll off his tongue as though savoring each one. "I would never have recognized you if Chico hadn't told me it was you hiding over here in the shadows." His voice was filled with admiration and pleasure.

Chico arrived with her drink, wearing a grin. "What do you say, man? She's looking pretty good, don't you think?"

Chico's presence gave her the time she needed to get a

grip on her emotions. She'd known for a week that her ultimate goal was to make contact with Joe in a believable manner.

So far, so good.

Elena gave each of them a slow sensuous smile. "Thank you both," she replied. Once Chico left, she tilted her glass and carefully refilled it from the new bottle before she glanced at Joe and said, "I believe Chico mentioned that you still lived around here. It *is* Joe Sanchez, isn't it?" she asked casually, determined not to let him know how much she was affected by this encounter.

She was a professional. She could do this.

His smile flashed white in his darkly tanned face. "That's right. I'm surprised you remembered."

She lifted one shoulder. "Oh, you really haven't changed all that much since you were our high-school football hero." She fluttered her lashes at him mockingly and sipped from her full glass.

Interesting. He actually flushed.

"What did you do after we finished high school?" she asked, as though she couldn't recite to him everything she'd found in his dossier about the past eleven years. At least what he had done legally. He had no criminal record. Yet. She hoped to change that before all this was over.

He looked down at his drink as though surprised to see it in front of him. "I got that scholarship to go to A & M. Opted to go into the army once I graduated." He paused, then cleared his throat. "I was discharged three months ago."

She lifted an eyebrow and smiled. "Decided not to reenlist?"

He looked away and her gaze followed his to two couples dancing. She thought he wasn't going to answer her before he finally turned back to her and said, "I needed to come home."

*I just bet you did.*

He leaned forward. "No kidding, I can't believe how great you look these days. No glasses, that long hair cut off—" he leaned to the side so that he could see more of her "—and you've filled out in all the right places."

She could have said the same thing about him.

But she didn't.

"I wear contacts now," she replied. She ran her fingers through her shoulder-length hair. "I wanted an easy-to-keep hairdo and this certainly fits the description. As for my weight, I guess I eat more or something."

He smiled. A slow seductive mind-numbing smile that packed so much sexual invitation in it that she had to remind herself to swallow before she forgot herself and drooled. "It isn't the weight, honey. It's the distribution that makes all the difference."

*You win that round,* she silently told him. *When it comes to flirting, I can't begin to compete in your league.*

Instead of answering him, she held up her glass and said, "Thanks for the drink."

Joe sat there watching the woman across from him in shocked wonder. He was having trouble dealing with the sudden appearance of one of the people from his past he'd never expected to see again.

He was also having trouble adjusting his previous image of her with this confident, sophisticated and very sexy woman who watched him with an amused expression on her face.

"My pleasure," he acknowledged before asking the question that had nagged at him since he'd discovered who she was. "So, what are you doing back in Santiago?"

She pursed her lips slightly, calling his attention to the

provocative pout that had kept the youth he once was in a state of perpetual semiarousal. Youth or not, he still reacted to that sultry combination of pouty oh-so-kissable mouth, high cheekbones and slightly slanted eyes with their thick lashes playing peekaboo with him.

She was responding to his question and he'd already forgotten what he'd asked. He forced himself to concentrate on her words, instead of her mouth.

"I'm currently unemployed," she said. "I haven't been home in a while, so I thought I'd check to see how my mom was doing, catch up on the news around here, maybe look for something to do in this area."

He was remembering so much about her now that she was here in front of him, things he thought he'd forgotten...

Her luminescent green eyes that used to mirror her every thought and mood but now revealed nothing.

Her fair skin that felt as soft beneath his callused palms as it looked, causing a boy to crave the sensation of touching her.

Memories of Elena had haunted him for years. His erotic dreams had been filled with visions of a young girl who looked like the woman sitting across from him now.

He had to keep his mind on their conversation, he reminded himself. She'd mentioned coming home again because she was unemployed. If the woman had half the pride of the girl he'd known, she must hate the idea that someone might think she'd failed at whatever goal she'd set for herself.

"How are things at home?" he asked, and saw a flash of emotion in her eyes that was quickly gone. He regretted the loss of the girl who hadn't guarded her responses. Although now that he thought about it, she had never talked much about her family back then.

Only now did he wonder why.

"My dad died a few years ago. My mother is coping as well as can be expected," she finally replied.

"So," he said, "tell me what you've been doing since we graduated."

She gave him another one of those indecipherable looks of hers. Damn, but she was even more fascinating and exotic now than she'd been as a girl. He glanced at her hands and noticed that she wore no rings. How could she have stayed single all this time?

He reminded himself that he'd been too busy to settle down. Maybe she was the same.

He waited, but she didn't answer him right away. Instead, she sipped her beer, then set it down on the bar and drew circles in the condensation with the bottom of the glass. Finally she lifted her head and looked at him.

"Let's see," she said, her voice sounding husky and more than a little erotic. "As soon as I graduated, I hitched my way out to Los Angeles, where I managed to get a job as a topless dancer in one of those places not far from the airport. The hourly pay wasn't all that great, but the tips were good. And I met a lot of people out there. Men, mostly. Eventually I was offered a chance to be in the movies—the pornographic ones—and the rest, as they say, is history."

He stared at her in complete and total shock.

Elena rather enjoyed the look on his face while she recited all that. Dead silence greeted her last words. She took another sip of her beer and barely restrained herself from humming. She stared into the amber depths of her drink and decided she was finally getting used to the taste of the stuff. She wasn't sure if that was good or bad.

The continued look of shocked horror on his face was

priceless, but no more than he deserved. She gazed at him through her lashes and smiled.

Finally he managed to say, "You've got to be kidding me, right?" in a gruff voice.

"Yes," she immediately answered.

He propped his elbows on the bar and let his face drop into his hands. "You had me going there for a minute."

"Are those songs playing still your choices?" she asked, deliberately changing the subject.

As though coming out of a fog, he glanced around at the people on the dance floor and talking at the bar as though he'd forgotten where he was. He listened for a moment, then smiled. "Yeah, I think so." He looked at her. "It's a little loud to talk over, though. What do you say we go somewhere else?"

"Why?" she asked starkly.

He looked startled for a moment, then grinned. "Damn, I never know what you're going to say next! That was direct enough, I suppose. I just want to talk, catch up on what you've been doing all these years. We used to be—"

"If you dare use *friends* as your next word, you'll be wearing this glass of beer."

His smile disappeared, leaving his face looking older than his years. "Yeah," he finally said, "I hear you." He picked up his drink and drained the bottle. "Do you think we could go somewhere and talk about what happened between us back then?"

Now it was her turn to be shocked. Of all the things she might have expected from Joe Sanchez once she found him, his desire to discuss their past was certainly not one of them. She had counted on the fact that he would be too ashamed ever to refer to what had happened, and she certainly hadn't intended to broach that painful subject.

"What earthly good would that do?" she finally asked,

caught between the need to encourage him and her personal desire to run away from any mention of the past.

"I owe you an explanation. You never gave me a chance to explain back then."

"An explanation? You think that something you might say could possibly make a difference to me now?"

She'd blurted out her gut reaction without taking into consideration her need to pretend to like him if she intended to become a part of Joe Sanchez's daily life, to learn all his secrets and to use any and everything she learned about him to destroy him.

Luckily he wasn't surprised by her response. If he had an ounce of sense, he would have expected it, she supposed.

Okay, so maybe this was the best way to go. Let him talk. Let him explain. Hey, let him throw in an apology or two if that was what it took. What she had to remember was that all of that was in her far-distant past. None of it could hurt her now. She'd made something of her life. She had a good job, a well-established career. Most important, she reminded herself, she was now the one in control. Only, he didn't happen to know that.

"I just think we might be able to find common ground," he said mildly. "We're adults now. Kids make stupid mistakes, but we get over them."

A mistake, he called it. What an interesting spin to put on the most traumatic time of her life.

She deliberately leaned back against the wall and looked at him. Then, as though she was reluctantly drawn to him and unable to resist, she shrugged and said, "Why not? You're right. We can't talk in here."

"Great!" His surprise at her acceptance showed. She'd have to watch her step or she would blow her first contact

with him by sending him wildly mixed messages. How
would *that* look in her report?

He reached into his back pocket and pulled out his billfold. She could have sworn that nothing more than a slip
of paper could have had room back there. He placed some
bills on the bar and stood, holding his hand out to her.

Chico gave them a big grin and a knowing look as she
allowed Joe to help her off the stool and lead her through
the crowd to the door. She gave Chico a brief wave and a
smile, then followed her assignment outside to the graveled
parking lot.

# Three

The night air felt good after the smoke-filled cantina. Elena took a deep breath and exhaled, looking up at the sky. There was no moon in evidence, and the sky was a bright canopy of stars that looked close enough to touch.

Elena stretched in an effort to relax the tense muscles in her shoulders. Her investigation was moving forward—she'd made contact with one of her assigned suspects. The fact that he affected her more strongly than she had anticipated wasn't going to throw her.

She reminded herself that she was a professional. She could handle all phases of this investigation, including spending time with Joe Sanchez.

Joe touched her elbow, making her jump.

"I didn't mean to startle you. My truck is over here."

She glanced around the parking lot. "Why don't I just follow you in my Jeep? Where do you want to meet?"

A bright light was mounted over the front door of the

cantina, bathing them in its glow. He glanced at his watch. "It's too late for Rosie's Café to be open. I would invite you over to my place but..." He let his voice dwindle away. Then he grinned, causing him to look more like the boy she remembered. "It seems to me we had this same problem when we were in school."

Only, she wasn't going to suggest any of the places where they used to hang out and talk for hours. She was no longer that shy young bookworm of a girl, thrilled to have caught the interest of one of the most intriguing boys in school.

What a naive idiot she'd been back then. No more. Not ever again.

"We can go to my mom's if you'd like. She has a big backyard with lawn furniture arranged beneath a large tree. It's very peaceful and we won't be disturbed. She's probably already asleep."

"Are you sure it will be okay with her?"

"As long as we don't come rolling in honking our horns and singing at the top of our lungs, we'll be fine."

"Lead the way," he said, giving her a wave before he headed toward his truck.

She walked over to her white Jeep. Her mother had been surprised by her mode of transportation, but Elena enjoyed driving in the open vehicle. Besides, it was good on rough terrain.

Traffic was light at this time of night. She pulled onto the highway and watched until Joe's lights appeared behind her. Then she headed toward home.

The house was several miles past the town limits. When she was a little girl, the house had been surrounded by farmland that had been part of the property. Over the years her father had sold off parcels until now there were maybe three acres left.

He'd never been much of a farmer, even though he'd convinced her mother when they first married that if she'd leave her hometown of Dallas and move to his hometown, he would provide her with everything her heart desired. It hadn't turned out that way, but she had seldom heard her mother complain. Despite his chronic drinking and aimless existence, her mother's eyes still glowed whenever she talked about how Trini Maldonado had swept into her life and swept her off her feet thirty years ago. He'd been an exotic Latino who'd made the other men Sara Grayson dated seem dull.

Sara's heart had been broken when Trini died suddenly of an aneurysm five years ago.

Elena had always thought her father had let her mother down. He'd been more of a dreamer than a provider. Charming, yes. Dependable? Not very.

So what had Elena done, with her parents' relationship as a guideline? Fallen for another charming and feckless Latino before she was out of high school. She certainly hadn't learned much from her mother's experience, that was certain.

Elena pulled into the narrow lane that led to the house. Her mother had left on a light for her. She continued past the house and parked behind the shed, which listed rather dramatically, as though a strong wind would blow it the rest of the way down. The darn thing was stronger than it looked, since it had looked as though it was going to collapse for as long as she could remember.

She turned off the ignition and hopped out, watching Joe's headlights approach. He drove a battered pickup truck that looked as though it was held together with glue, wire, spit and generous amounts of prayer. Of course, he wouldn't want to show up in Santiago in a flashy new car, either. No reason to cause suspicion among the natives.

He parked several yards away from where she stood waiting for him. She was amused that he'd turned around and parked heading out, as though prepared for a quick getaway.

*The man was smarter than she gave him credit for.* The thought made her smile.

"I'd forgotten what a nice place this is," he said, walking over to her. "I bet you enjoyed having room to run and play as a kid."

She turned and walked across the grassy yard. "I suppose." She looked around at him. She was surprised to see how much light there was just from the stars. Although she couldn't see his eyes, his face was clear enough. Her eyes were drawn to his mouth. She shivered. *Don't go there,* she warned herself.

"We used to live in a small rental place not far from the river. The houses were built close together. About the only place we had to play was in the street." Glancing up, he said, "I'd forgotten how beautiful the night sky is. When I was in the army, I used to spend time studying navigation by the stars."

"Did you enjoy your stay in the service?" she asked, leading the way to the lone stately tree that stood like a sentinel at the back of their property. She picked up one of the chairs and moved it out from under the shadows made by the tree limbs. He followed her example. When he positioned his chair, she placed hers across from him so that she sat facing him.

"Actually I did," he replied. "I liked the structure and the discipline. I also appreciated the opportunity to see something of the world. It certainly changed my perspective about who I was and what I could accomplish with my life."

She eyed him for a long moment before she said, "Then

I'm surprised you left the service. Living here can't be nearly as exciting as being in the service.'' She was careful not to reveal that she knew he'd reached the rank of major, which told her he'd been quite good at what he did.

He shrugged and looked away. Obviously he didn't want to talk about his reasons for being in Santiago. She couldn't help but believe that it strengthened the suspicion surrounding him.

Why would he be living here now unless he thought there was something in it for him?

''I noticed a light on in your house,'' he said into the silence. ''Someone must still be up.''

''Not necessarily. My mother leaves a light on for me whenever I'm out.''

''Ah.''

She waited for Joe to say whatever he'd decided needed to be said to her. She braced herself not to let whatever he said upset her.

''This is nice,'' he said after a long silence. ''I can't remember the last time I was able to kick back and relax. Thank you for inviting me over tonight.''

Nice opening. She could pretend there was nothing between them, and yet he had said there were things he wanted to discuss. She mulled over possible responses before she quietly said, ''You said you wanted to talk.''

''It's been eleven years, Elena. I never expected to see you again, so you can imagine my surprise to find you living here in Santiago after all this time.''

''I could say the same thing about you.''

Silence fell between them. ''I suppose that's true,'' he finally said. ''I still remember how hard I tried to talk to you the week after the prom, but you refused to listen to anything I attempted to say to you. Believe me, I know

you had every right to be upset with me and I wanted to
explain what happened—''

"There was no need for explanations, Joe," she said,
interrupting his rush of words. "You see, your buddies
were only too eager to tell me about the bet you made with
them where I was concerned. Once everything was explained to me, there really wasn't anything more I needed
to hear."

He sat up in his chair. "What bet? What are you talking
about?"

*Stay calm,* she reminded herself. This was ancient history.

"Having a little selective amnesia, are you? The bet you
made the fall of our senior year when you bragged to your
friends that you could get a date with any girl in the class.
So they suggested me, the nerd in glasses who'd never had
a date, just to see if you'd really do it. You were known
never to back down from a dare. I can see why you might
decide I was a challenge. Of course we both know I was
anything but."

He leaned forward in his chair as though he was going
to reach out to her. She'd made certain they were far
enough away from each other that he couldn't actually
touch her. She congratulated herself for the foresight.

"That's not how it happened. Wow! No wonder you
wouldn't talk to me after the prom! You thought—''

"No, I *knew,* Joe. They dared you to take me to the
prom. I never did ask what you won from your friends. It
was obvious what you got from me. It was quite a big
night for you, wasn't it?"

"Damn, Elena—! You've got it all wrong." He rose
from his chair and glared down at her. "Do you honestly
think that the only reason I took you to the prom was
because of some kind of bet?"

She stared up at him with a deep feeling of contempt. "Absolutely."

He took a couple of steps away from her, then spun and faced her. "That's absolutely not true! I never discussed you with anyone. I don't care what anyone said. Those guys had nothing to do with you and me. Nothing. They were angry at me because I'd quit hanging around with them. They wanted to embarrass me. No doubt that's why they told you all those lies."

She forced herself to relax back into her chair. "If you say so." She knew her disbelief showed in her tone of voice.

He returned to his chair and moved it closer, so that when he sat down again, their knees were touching. He reached for her hands, gripping them firmly. "Listen to me, Elena. Asking you to help me get my grades up had nothing to do with anyone. The coach told me that I had a chance for a scholarship if I managed to pass my classes. I told you that at the time."

"Ah, yes. You asked me to tutor you. I recall that quite clearly. That was the only reason we spent any time together that spring."

She'd been such an idiot back then. Dazzled by his request. Thrilled to get to spend some time with him. If only she had realized what was really going on, she wouldn't have allowed her silly daydreams to be filled with the possibilities of a future with him.

Joe shook her hands lightly in his as though to gain her attention. "At first, maybe that was true. You were acing the exams and I was flunking. If I didn't pass that semester, I didn't graduate. There wouldn't have been a scholarship. I wouldn't have had a chance of getting out of this place without it. You saved my butt, if you recall."

"Glad I could help out," she said quietly.

He released her hands and leaned back in his chair as though relieved by her response. After a moment he chuckled and said, "We had some fun times together back then, remember? I always enjoyed being around you, catching hell from you for not paying closer attention in class, for not taking better notes, for being too impatient to read the assigned books. You were fun to be with, I remember that quite clearly. I recall you could always make me laugh. I enjoyed being with you."

Maybe that was what he remembered, but he had never asked her out on a date. Not once during those last few months of school when they had studied together. Not until he asked her to go with him to the senior prom.

She'd been overjoyed. She couldn't remember a time in her life when she'd been so happy. Not only was she attending her senior prom when she'd been afraid she'd never be asked, but she was going with one of the most fascinating boys in school. At the time she'd thought that nothing could be more perfect than finally having a date with Joe Sanchez.

She'd been too naive to question his motives. She'd been too thrilled to wonder why he would take *her* when he could have chosen one of the most popular girls in school.

Up until the night of the prom, they had spent time together by meeting immediately after school. She had drilled him on grammar and literature, using her copious notes. She'd quizzed him on history. His teasing and good humor had eventually eased her shyness with him until she had learned to tease him right back.

He was right. They had spent a lot of time laughing together. During that time, she had developed a huge crush on him. No doubt it had been obvious to him. In fact, it couldn't have worked out more perfectly for him.

Oh, yes. For a few months that year she'd floated in a bubble of fantasy that she alone created.

Their conversation had stopped and the silence of the night surrounded them. Finally Joe spoke once again.

"I'm sorry they told you those lies. You must have thought I was horrible if you thought I was only pretending to like you. The truth was—"

"Please, Joe. Let's just drop it, okay?" She stood up. "I no longer want to wander down memory lane with you, do you understand? I don't want to hear anything you might want to say about that night. I would think that was obvious even back then." She paused and carefully enunciated the words, "I...do...not...want...to...discuss...it. I don't want to even think about it." She stuck out her hand. "It was nice seeing you again. Thanks for stopping by."

When he just sat there and stared at her hand as though she'd aimed a gun at him, she dropped it with an impatient sigh, then spun on her heel and marched off, leaving him sitting there alone in the dark.

*Well, Elena, you certainly handled that one well,* she told herself as she strode toward the house. *That's going to really help with your plan to get closer to him.*

She was almost to the house when she heard his truck start up. She watched as his lights swung over her, spotlighting her by the back door. Then he was past, and she listened as the sound of his engine grew faint and then it was gone, leaving her once again in the silence of the night.

She shook her head. "Let's face it, you screwed up," she muttered. "Now you're going to have to go look him up tomorrow and apologize for being rude."

Apologize to Joe Sanchez. Wasn't that just dandy!

"Elena, is that you?" she heard her mother call in a low voice when she let herself in through the back door of the house a few minutes later.

"Yes, Mom," she replied patiently. She peeked into the kitchen and saw her mother sitting at the table with a cup of steaming liquid in front of her. Elena came in and sat down across from her.

"I made some hot chocolate, if you'd like some," Sara said, pointing to the stove.

She was a tiny birdlike woman with bright doll-button green eyes that had always made Elena feel that no matter what happened, she was safe as long as her mother was there. She'd felt a pang of shame that she hadn't come home more often after her father had died, leaving her mother to cope with his loss alone.

The problem had been that Elena was dealing with her own feelings about the loss of her father. She'd felt guilty that she'd never been closer to him, that she'd had so little respect for him as a father, a husband and a provider.

"I'm fine, Mom. What are you doing up so late?"

Sara shook her head. "Hot flashes. I guess I'm going to have to see about taking something to help."

"I was afraid we might have disturbed you."

Her mother glanced up from contemplating the steam rising from her cup. "We?"

"I ran into an old schoolmate tonight. We sat out back and were catching up on the news about our lives. Ever since I returned home, I feel as though I'm back for some kind of reunion."

"Who was here?"

"My senior prom date—Joe Sanchez."

Her mother made a face. "You want to steer clear of him. I remember that you liked him when you were in school, but that was a long time ago. He's nothing but trouble."

Her ears perked up. "Really? What's wrong with him?"

"There's talk about him...and his family."

"Oh?" Elena eased out of her chair and crossed to the stove, where she poured herself a cup of hot chocolate in order to keep the conversation going. "Tell me more," she said with her back to her mother.

"His cousin Tina married some guy who's not from around here. I'm not sure where he's from, but he's got money and no visible means of support, if you know what I mean."

Elena sat down again and tentatively tasted her drink. It brought back so many memories of times like this when she'd sat and talked with her mother. At least it got rid of the stale beer taste in her mouth. "You think he's smuggling?"

"He's doing something illegal. There's talk about the whole Sanchez family, which is too bad. Remember Joe's older brother was sent to prison before Joe ever finished high school. I don't know what ever happened to him. It was all so sad. And now! Conchita wouldn't have tolerated such goings-on if she were still alive. She took Tina to raise when the girl was barely old enough for school."

"Conchita?"

"Conchita Perez. She was Joe and Tina's grandmother. She and your father's mother were best friends. She took care of your grandmother during her last illness."

"I never knew that."

"Why should you? You weren't even born back then." She took a sip of her chocolate. "There's been talk that Joe has been involved with some of Tina's group."

"Thanks for warning me, Mom. I promise I won't get involved."

Which was a promise she had no intention of keeping.

Her biggest hope was that she would get right in the middle of whatever was going on in Santiago.

The sooner the better. She wasn't sure how much she was going to be able to handle if the past was going to keep coming up in her face. The important thing was that she had survived it. That had to count for something.

It was only later that night as she tossed restlessly in bed that she focused on Joe's remarks about their last night together. If he'd been telling her the truth, the evening had been as embarrassing and humiliating for him as it had been for her, which gave her a whole new perspective of the matter.

All these years she'd been wallowing in her own pain without giving much thought to how he might have felt about that night.

She also realized that, despite the months they had spent together when she had gotten to know him, she'd been quick to accept the worst possible motives for his behavior.

She'd been a kid back then, unsure of herself, distrustful of the male gender. What was her excuse now?

# Four

Joe pulled out of Elena's driveway and headed to his house. He'd much prefer going back to the bar and spending the rest of the night numbing his feelings with alcohol. The problem with that was twofold—he would have to face Chico's questions about leaving the place with Elena and showing up there again within the hour, and he didn't relish the hangover that would follow an evening of heavy drinking. Sooner or later he knew he'd have to face what seeing Elena again was doing to him.

It was eating him alive.

How could he have forgotten what a strong effect she had on him? It didn't matter whether he was eighteen or twenty-nine. Hearing her voice, watching her and wanting to touch and taste her once again made a mockery out of his belief that he'd forgotten her.

He'd made a fool of himself tonight with his fumbling attempts at an apology for what had happened back when they were in high school. He'd always been embarrassed by what had happened, not only because his so-called friends ambushed them, but also because he hadn't been able to control his own response to her. Because of his heightened emotions he'd rushed their lovemaking, no doubt ruining her first intimate experience, without having the chance to show her that he could bring her to experience the same mind-blowing pleasure he'd felt.

He realized while being with her tonight that he wanted a second chance with her. Unfortunately, she couldn't have turned up in his life at a worse time.

Who would have believed when he volunteered for this undercover assignment to return to his hometown that he would run into his first love, the one who'd gotten away?

The question was, what he could do about it now? She was here. So was he. Ignoring her would look more suspicious than trying to renew a relationship with her.

The problem was, he didn't have the time or energy for a relationship.

As a member of army intelligence, he was directly responsible for assisting in the recovery of a large shipment of arms that was stolen from one of their overseas military bases last year. His unit had spent months tracing the movement of the arms, waiting to see which of their enemies had stolen them.

When it became apparent that the stolen equipment was headed for a town in Mexico south of Santiago, his superior officer decided to place him here to monitor what was coming across the border.

Of course it made sense to place a native in the small town. Because of his brother's reputation, no one was surprised that another Sanchez had returned home with his tail between his legs, unable to make it out there in the big world.

He often wondered if his brother would have made it out in the world without falling back into his illegal activities. Since his brother had been killed in a knife fight in prison four years ago, no one would ever know how he might have turned out.

Joe had been prepared to use his mother's failing health and his need to look after her as his excuse for leaving the army, but no one had bothered to ask. The local folks figured he couldn't do the work required by the army satisfactorily. He did nothing to change their opinion.

However, he was making progress. He'd been checking out leads for weeks, and some of them were beginning to pay off. He reminded himself that he needed to keep his focus on his assignment, not on how Elena Maldonado could make his body respond.

He was no longer an inexperienced kid with out-of-control hormones. Now all he needed to do was convince a certain unruly part of his anatomy of that.

Joe pulled into his driveway and parked by the back door, which opened into the kitchen. He entered the house, walked over to the refrigerator and snagged a beer, which he took to his bedroom. He had a hunch he was going to need some help getting to sleep tonight.

Hours later, Joe felt as though he had just fallen asleep when the phone on his bedside table rang. He fumbled for the offending instrument.

"Sanchez," he muttered.

"Joe, I'm sorry to bother you so late…"

He sat up in bed and reached for the light. "It's okay, Mom, what's wrong?" It was almost three o'clock in the morning according to the small clock by the phone.

He heard his mother sigh. "It's Tina again. She called me earlier because she expected Francisco home by now, but he hasn't returned from his latest trip. I've been here since about ten o'clock and I can't get her to settle down. I hate to bother you, but I'm at my wit's end trying to deal with her.''

He shook his head in disgust. ''You shouldn't have to deal with her, Mom. I take it she's gone off her medication.''

''She won't say. She just keeps repeating that she knows something must have happened to him or he would be home by now.''

He sat up and reached for his jeans. ''This is getting ridiculous, you know. I want you to go home and get some rest. I'll come over and see what I can do.''

''I can't leave her alone, but it would help if you could be here.''

''Sure, Mom. I'll be right there.''

He hung up the phone and shook his head. Tina was getting worse. He wished his mother didn't feel obligated to hold her hand through these episodes.

When his mother first told him that Tina had married a wealthy entrepreneur, Francisco Delgado, he'd hoped for his mother's sake that Tina's mood swings would stabilize. Losing their grandmother had been especially hard on Tina. Their *abuelita* had been the closest thing to a mother she'd had.

According to his mother, marrying Cisco and planning their large hacienda overlooking the Rio Grande had given her life purpose once again. Then she had miscarried several months ago and depression had again set in.

The problem was, his mother didn't need the worry and she was the one Tina continued to call. But what the hell. He was home now and he'd gotten fairly good at calming her down when she got hysterical.

He just wished that her husband would give her a

thought once in a while. Cisco no doubt had been mesmerized by Tina's elfin beauty and had ignored the signs of her delicate emotional state. But after a few years of marriage, Francisco had learned to ignore the outbursts and the crying, the accusations and the tantrums.

His trips grew more frequent, no doubt to get away from her. It wasn't a good situation, and Joe didn't know how to make it any better. Maybe he'd have a talk with Cisco once the man got home.

He finished putting on his jeans and grabbed a clean T-shirt before stuffing his feet into his boots and palming his keys and billfold.

He stepped outside the house and looked up at the sky. He figured he'd probably gotten three, maybe four hours of sleep. He shook his head. He already knew that tomorrow—today, actually—was going to be a rough one with too much to do and not enough hours in which to get it done.

One of the reasons he was willing to get involved with Tina was that he had suspicions about her husband, who owned several factories in Mexico that shipped their products north into the States.

So far, he'd never caught Francisco Delgado doing anything improper, much less illegal. There was always the chance that one of his employees might be using Delgado's trucks as a way to move items across the border without detection.

Joe had made himself available to help out his relative by occasionally filling in when Cisco was shorthanded and needed more drivers. As far as Cisco was concerned, Joe was just another one of his wife's poor relatives, looking for extra money. His trips back and forth across the border gave Joe a perfect opportunity to sniff out illegal activities.

Of course he knew he had to be careful. If Delgado was

the conduit through which stolen weapons and other con-
traband were being smuggled across the border, and if he
got a hint that Joe was anything more than a relative of
his neurotic wife's, Joe knew his life would be worth nothing.

So he played a part, hanging around the Delgado man-
sion, looking after Tina and trying to keep his mother from
being overtaxed. The doctors had warned her that her heart
wasn't in very good shape. Joe believed it was his mission
to nag her into taking better care of herself.

As he drove out of town on his way to Tina's home, he
wearily shook his head. He certainly had enough to deal
with without the added distraction of Elena Maldonado.

Joe sat in the back booth of the local café finishing a
late lunch a little after two o'clock that afternoon. The
regular lunch crowd had cleared out by now. Rosie was
busy wiping down the lunch counter when the bell over
the door signaled another customer.

Joe was on the verge of taking another sip of coffee
when he spotted Elena cross over to the counter and sit
down. He froze, the cup halfway to his mouth.

Damn, but she looked good. Her faded jeans lovingly
clung to every curve of hip and thigh, and the thin T-shirt
she wore showed off her lithe body.

He brought the cup to his lips, still watching her. Rosie
had just refilled his cup, and he almost burned his mouth
because he wasn't paying enough attention to what he was
doing. He set the coffee down with a muttered curse, then
pushed his empty plate away.

He hadn't managed to get back to bed last night. It was
after six by the time he'd arrived home from Tina's place.
He had three jobs waiting for him that he'd promised to
get out today, so he'd scrounged around in his kitchen for

something to eat, made a mental note to get some groceries as soon as possible and gone to work.

He'd lucked out during the morning and discovered that the Ford pickup needed a new fuel pump, which he'd managed to replace with one in stock. Since he carried very few spare parts, he knew that his luck had changed for the better with that find.

The old Chevy Nova, his second job, needed a complete engine overhaul, but he knew Mrs. Salinas couldn't afford one, much less a newer vehicle. So he'd done what he could and had driven it to her home a little after one. He'd been walking back to the shop when he passed the café and on impulse decided to stop in for some of Rosie's great cooking.

He glanced at Elena. Even though she had her back to him, he could see she was tense. It was in the way she held her shoulders. Whatever she was discussing with Rosie wasn't going well. He wondered if she was trying to find work.

It wasn't any of his business. He'd made a hash out of trying to apologize last night. There was very little he could do at this late date to make things better between them. Besides, it was best that he not have much contact with her. She was definitely a distraction he didn't need in his life at the moment.

He continued to watch her talk to Rosie. Then she stood, nodded in response to something Rosie was saying and started toward the door.

Joe called out her name before he had a chance to talk himself out of it. "Elena, do you have a minute?"

She turned around and looked at him with surprise, obviously unaware until that moment that he was in the café. He could read her body language quite clearly. She wasn't overly thrilled to see him.

Slowly she approached the booth.

"Do you have time for a cup of coffee or maybe some iced tea?" he asked, deliberately smiling at her in hopes of appearing perfectly harmless, when in truth he felt more like the big bad wolf luring Little Red Riding Hood closer.

She eyed him for a moment, no doubt debating the wisdom of accepting his invitation, then reluctantly nodded. She glanced over her shoulder at Rosie and said, "Iced tea, please."

"Sure thing, honey," Rosie replied with a grin, bustling behind the counter to fill the order.

Joe almost groaned out loud. By evening every one in Santiago who hadn't seen or heard about them leaving the bar together last night would be talking about their meeting at the café today. By the end of the week, there would probably be talk of a wedding.

Elena slid across the bench seat opposite him and rested her folded arms on the table. Now that she was there, he wasn't sure what to say to her. Feeling like a fool, he took another sip of his coffee, grateful that it had cooled down enough for him to drink it.

Elena was the first to speak.

"I...uh, I'm glad I ran into you," she said when the silence had stretched between them to an unbearable degree. Her tone sounded anything but glad.

Joe almost laughed.

"Really?" he replied, draining his cup and carefully replacing it on the table. "Your enthusiasm is overwhelming, I must admit," he added dryly.

Her smile was rueful. "All right, so I'm not all that glad, but only because I promised myself that the next time I saw you, I'd apologize. Truthfully I was hoping to have a few days' grace before actually having to do it."

He raised his brows. "Apologize?"

She sighed, shoved a piece of hair behind her ear and said, "Yes. I was rude last night, refusing to accept your explanations about something that happened almost half a lifetime ago. And I'm sorry." She paused and gazed at him steadily. "I really am. So. If it's all right with you, I'd like to start over and see if my manners have improved." She reached out her hand as though to shake his. "Why, Joe Sanchez, as I live and breathe," she said in a breathless excited voice that was totally and quite deliberately false. "I haven't seen you in years and years! How have you been? What are you doing these days? How's your family?" She batted her lashes for good measure.

He took her hand, then relaxed against the back of his padded bench seat and grinned, shaking his head. "You know, I've never known another woman who could keep me off-balance the way you do. Regardless of my age, I still feel like an awkward teenager around you. How do you manage that?"

Her grin became natural as she replied, "Just part of my charm, I suppose."

Once again Joe felt ambushed by the strong feelings she evoked in him after all this time. He couldn't seem to adjust to the changes that made her even more attractive than he remembered.

Now that she wasn't hiding behind those godawful glasses she could never keep up on her nose, he could better see her eyes, which seemed to gaze deep into his soul. And that delectably kissable mouth of hers. How could he have forgotten that, even after all these years?

She eased her hand away from his, forcing him to let go. This woman made his head swim. She had him half-aroused and all she had done was touch his hand—that, and look at him with those mesmerizing eyes. Had her lashes always been so long and so thick?

In a more natural tone she said, "So, Joe, what have you been doing with yourself since getting out of the army?" as though she'd just met him a few minutes ago and was eager to catch up with everything that had happened to him.

He forced himself to concentrate on what she was saying rather than what his body was doing. He was glad that he was seated and that the table concealed his lower half. Somehow he was going to have to gain some control over his reactions to her before he walked out of here.

Joe cleared his throat. "Actually I managed to accidentally turn a hobby into a full-time job."

She leaned forward, showing sincere interest. "Really? What's that?"

"As a teenager I always enjoyed working on cars. When I got back here, I decided to find my own place to live, so I rented a house with an oversize garage. I hadn't been home long before I noticed that Mom's car wasn't running right, so I worked on it for her. Then one of my neighbors asked if I could look at his pickup truck, and before I knew it, I was putting in sixty-hour weeks and running a full-time garage."

"Good for you." She nodded, as though impressed with his career choice.

He made a face. "It certainly isn't how I want to spend the rest of my life, but for now I make enough to live on while I look after my mom. I keep reminding myself about a saying I once heard—life is what happens to you while you're making plans. I'd hate to think this is what I'll be doing thirty years from now."

She smiled sympathetically. "I can certainly relate to that. Who would have thought I'd end up back here myself?"

"Actually," he said, wondering how he could suggest

this without making her defensive, "I…uh, I was hoping maybe you might want to come to work for me."

She blinked as though startled by his suggestion, but she didn't appear to be offended. She tilted her head and eyed him warily. Not that he could blame her. He was kidding himself, thinking she'd want to spend time around him, but now that he'd started this crazy conversation, he'd better explain.

"The thing is, the business has grown bigger than I expected, too big for me to handle."

She shook her head slowly. "As much as I'd like to help, I'm afraid I don't know anything about cars."

He threw back his head and laughed. It felt good to find something amusing about his present situation. The idea of Elena under the hood of a car…

"No," he finally said, "that's not what I'm asking. The paperwork is killing me. There's the accounts to keep up with, payments to be recorded. Hardly anyone has the money to pay me all at once, and I'm struggling to keep up with who owes me how much. Then there's the auto-parts invoices that I need to make sure are paid on time." He shook his head. "I hate all that stuff."

She narrowed her eyes. In a careful voice she said, "Let's see if I understand what you're saying here. You want me to take care of your books?"

"Yeah." He gave her a grateful smile. "I remember you were always good with stuff like that in school. Maybe if you could get me organized, show me how to keep up with everything once you've set up a system… I mean, I'm sure you'll find something better suited to what you want to do on a permanent basis, but I was thinking that, as a temporary measure, you could really help me out."

"You aren't just feeling sorry for me, losing my job and having to come back home, are you?"

He raised his brows. "Is that why you're back here? You neglected to mention it last night, you know. I tell you what—why don't you come back with me right now and I'll show you exactly what I'm talking about, then you can decide who I'm feeling sorry for here."

She accepted the glass of tea from Rosie and immediately drank half of it without stopping. After she paused and carefully blotted her mouth with a paper napkin, she nodded.

"I could do that. I did some accounting in school actually. I was always good in math."

"Yeah, I know. Math, history, English. You aced them all."

She shrugged. "I didn't have much else to do with my time."

"Until I started hanging around," he reminded her.

She gave him another of those long looks that had him wondering what she was thinking. Then she nodded again. "I still managed to keep up with my grades, even with you as a distraction."

He reached over and took her hand, determined to learn how to be around her without feeling this sensual draw. "I'm really pleased you've come back to Santiago. My life has been very dull since I came back home. I have a hunch you're going to add a great deal to it."

She carefully removed her hand from his and looked away for a moment. When she glanced back at him, she smiled. "I guess we'll have to see, won't we."

Joe knew he was taking a chance that he would be distracted by Elena, but he didn't care. He was good at his job. Besides, he had a right to a personal life while he worked his assignment. There was no reason he couldn't enjoy Elena's return. Seeing her would even enhance his cover. What could be more natural?

Joe was pleased with his conclusions as they left the café.

Elena tried to keep up with Joe's long strides as they headed toward his house.

She couldn't believe her stroke of luck. Her mother had sent her in to talk to Rosie about helping with the planning of the church bazaar. Unfortunately, Rosie felt she had too many other commitments, so Elena realized she herself was probably going to have to volunteer to help out, something she wasn't looking forward to.

Now here was a bona fide job offer to work for one of the people she'd come to Santiago to watch. What could be better than that? Joe had handed her a perfect excuse not to help out with the bazaar, as well as a way to further her own professional agenda.

She took a skipping step about every fourth step and finally said, "Do you have to walk so fast?"

He glanced at her in surprise. "Sorry. I was just thinking about what I've got to do this afternoon. I'm really getting backed up."

She almost smiled. So much for believing that he might be thinking about her going through his papers, worrying about what she might find. But then, he might be covering up what he was really thinking.

They turned down another block that led into an older part of town. There were vacant lots and some old boarded-up houses. The street ended at a cattle fence that enclosed several acres for grazing on the other side.

Joe strode across the yard of the last house, heading for the steps leading up to a covered porch.

The house was old. It had probably been built in the forties, but someone had either kept it in shape or put it back into shape. She wondered if that had been Joe.

There was a new roof, as well as a fresh coat of white

paint trimmed in dark green. The steps looked new. They
were stained the same color as the porch. The screen door
also looked new.

"Is this place yours?"

He held the screen door open for her. The wooden door
stood open, even though he had been out. There wasn't
much crime in the area, she supposed.

"No, but I'm thinking about buying it. It belongs to one
of my uncles. I told him I'd fix the house and garage up
in lieu of rent."

"He got a good deal, it seems to me." The front door
opened into a living room. She could see a dining room
and a kitchen from where she stood. A door opened off
the living room; she guessed it led to a bedroom.

"The house was basically sound. Uncle Alejandro took
good care of it until he was hurt on the job a few years
ago. Now he draws disability and is living with one of his
sisters. So the house was just sitting empty when I came
home from the army."

She wandered into the dining room and stopped, ap-
palled by the mess of papers scattered over a large oak
table. He followed her into the room. "Now do you see
what I mean? I know I've got some invoices to pay and
some statements that need to be sent. But by the time I
stop for the night, I'm too tired to think."

She shook her head at the mess. "I don't suppose you
have a computer, do you?"

He looked at her blankly.

She sighed. "I didn't think so."

"That's a great idea!" he said with a rush of enthusiasm.

She folded her arms and studied the table. "It would be
a lot of work, but once all of this is entered into a business
software program, you'll be free of the mess." She looked

at him. "I have to go into San Antonio tomorrow. If you want, I can look around for you and see what I can find."

"Better yet, I'll go with you. That way, if you find what you think we need, I can get it right then."

She caught her breath, trying to hide her dismay at his suggestion. Of course it made sense for him to suggest such a thing. Since she'd already volunteered the information that she was going, she had no good reason to turn him down. So now what? She would be meeting with Chris at the Marriott Hotel downtown. She could just see showing up at her meeting with one of their suspects!

"Sure," she finally replied, praying she sounded casual enough not to arouse any suspicions. If she was willing to work for him, she didn't want to give him the impression that she hoped to avoid him.

Working for him was too good a chance to miss.

After another pause, she added, "I've got several errands to run, but we can each go our own way and meet somewhere later—whenever and wherever it's convenient."

He looked at the table, then back at her. "Once again you've come to my rescue. You helped me pass my classes so I could graduate way back when. Now you're going to save me from drowning in paperwork."

He really did look relieved. He showed no sign of being nervous that she might find something incriminating in all that mess.

She waved her hand toward his garage and said, "Why don't you go ahead and do whatever it is that's so pressing out there while I see if I can bring some order to this chaos?"

He grabbed her waist and swung her around the room. "You've saved me, woman," he said with a laugh. "I'll never forget this!"

His sudden movement caught her off guard, and before she knew it, her feet had left the floor and she was being whirled in a circle. When he finally put her down, she gripped his arms to keep from falling over.

While she was trying to find her balance, he leaned down and gave her an exuberant kiss, his mouth shaping itself to hers so effortlessly she was stunned at the sense of familiarity.

This man hadn't kissed her in eleven years, but she was briefly flung back in time by the mere touch of his lips.

Elena jerked away, unnerved by her strong reaction to him. "A simple thank-you is quite adequate, you know," she said a little breathlessly.

His wicked glance told her that he knew he'd rattled her and was glad. "Actually you're going to get more than a simple thank-you," he said, thoughtfully. He absently pulled on his earlobe. "I'm not really sure how much I can pay you, but for now, can we say ten dollars an hour? I know that isn't much, but—"

"Ten dollars is fine. I don't have many expenses. My car is paid for and I'm living at home. Besides, you have no idea how many hours it will take me to make some sense out of all of this." She looked at the table with some dismay and hoped she wasn't taking on more than she could handle. But she couldn't resist the golden opportunity to be this close to Joe and whatever he was doing.

"Fine. Then I'll talk to you later," he said jauntily, and continued through the house to the kitchen, leaving her standing in the middle of his dining room. She heard the back screen door slam.

She followed him to the door and watched as he strode to a combination shed/garage that sat behind and to the side of the house. Two cars were sitting in the driveway next to his battered truck. He got into one of the cars and

drove it into the garage. Within minutes she could hear
loud music coming from a radio, together with his whistle.

She was obviously on her own.

Well. She turned around and looked at the kitchen. He
hadn't done much in the way of renovation here. The stove
looked to be at least thirty years old. The refrigerator was
no doubt equally old. But, the place was clean enough.
There was some coffee left in the pot on the counter, but
the light was off, so it was probably cold.

An open door off the side of the kitchen led into a bedroom that didn't look as though it was used for much more
than storage, although there was a bed and dresser peeking
out from beneath boxes.

She walked through the bedroom into a large bathroom.
An old-fashioned clawfoot tub took up one side of the
wall. A cabinet with a sink and mirror was on the other
side, and the commode was next to the tub. A faint hint
of aftershave reminded her of the man who still had the
ability to make her heart beat double time.

Almost everything in the room seemed to have been
placed there when the house was first built. A shower may
have been added at a later date. The shower curtain hung
from a circular pipe directly above the tub.

A couple of towels hung crookedly from towel racks,
and shaving gear cluttered the cabinet, but the place wasn't
dirty, which meant that someone came in and cleaned for
him, or Mr. Sanchez was fastidious enough to keep it up
himself.

Two doors opened into the bathroom. Elena opened the
door opposite to the one through which she had come in
and found that it opened into the front bedroom, which
was obviously the one Joe used.

She could feel his presence in the room so strongly it
made her knees weak. Not a good sign. If she reacted this

way to an empty room, how was she going to handle being here in his house with him?

She shivered, looking around the area. The bed was unmade and there were clothes tossed on the floor. He obviously hadn't been expecting company, but again, there was no sign of dust or grime.

She forced herself to leave the intimacy of his bedroom and returned to the living room. She'd made a complete circuit of the house. If she were to make a guess, she would say all the furniture was left over from the time when his uncle had lived there. There was nothing expensive. Everything looked well used, but comfortable.

There was no sign that any money had been spent to make the place more lavish. A roof that didn't leak and new paint on the outside didn't seem to be extravagant.

She glanced through the wide arch between the living and dining rooms. It certainly didn't seem that there was anything here he didn't want her to find.

The dining-room table beckoned. The truth was, Elena loved to organize things. She'd been that way all of her life. A shrink would probably explain it as her need to bring control and order to some part of her life. For whatever reason, Joe couldn't have suggested a job she would find more appealing.

Not only that, but this job would allow her to keep close tabs on him. If only she didn't have such a strong reaction to his presence, she would be ecstatic over this opportunity to do the job she had been sent to do.

She pulled up a chair and was soon immersed in deciding how best to set up different categories. She had no idea how long she'd been there sorting papers when she heard the back door slam. She glanced up from a handful of invoices marked paid just as Joe appeared in the kitchen doorway. He looked hot and he had a smear of grease on his cheek. He rested his arm high on the doorjamb and said, "So what do you think? Am I paying slave wages here?"

"Not at all."

"What were you making at your last job?"

Think fast, she reminded herself. With a slight shrug, she said, "About the same."

He straightened after a long silent moment, then grinned. "Well, I guess it's better than working in a strip joint." He turned away, disappearing into the kitchen. "You want something to drink?" he called. "I forgot to mention I keep the fridge stocked with soft drinks and beer. Just help yourself."

She could feel the trickle of perspiration move down her spine. She had no idea what the going rate was for a good assistant of any sort. It had never occurred to her that she might need that information for her cover.

She closed her eyes and took a few calming breaths. What did it matter what he thought about her and how she made a living?

"Yes or no?" he called out.

"Oh! Yes, thank you. Whatever soda you have will be fine."

He came back in with a popular cola and handed it to her. "As you can see, I'm not much for formality here. But if you want that in a glass with ice, I can—"

"No, this is fine. Thank you."

He studied her for a moment in silence. "Let's wait and see how much time this is going to take you before you're stuck with accepting a low wage. I promise to be fair with you, okay?"

She nodded.

After another long silence, he turned and went back outside. Only then did Elena realize she'd been holding her breath.

The tension seemed to have heightened since their kiss. It was as if each of them was remembering...comparing...and wondering what they might have started by the decision to work together.

Elena knew she had no choice but to go on with this. Her feelings did not count here. They never had, really. Until she could prove otherwise, Joe Sanchez was a suspect, and she needed to treat him as such. Too bad she still found him so attractive.

Her strong reaction to him just made the task a little more difficult than she'd originally expected.

# Five

---

Elena drove into Joe's driveway early the next morning after spending a very restless night. Because she'd forgotten that she'd left her Jeep at the café yesterday, she'd had to walk back to get it before going home last night.

She didn't like how he could so easily rattle her.

The fact that she would be meeting Chris in San Antonio with her first report on this assignment should be the focus of her attention. Unfortunately it wasn't.

She'd also had this inexplicable desire to look good today. Joe had seen her in jeans. She'd wondered what his reaction would be if she decided to dress up. Just a little, of course.

Finally she had chosen a coral sleeveless cotton dress that buttoned down the front. She'd been told she looked good in red. Right now she needed all the confidence she could muster. Trying to appear interested in Joe for the sake of her assignment was one thing. Recognizing that she actually cared what he thought of her was another.

She walked up the back steps and tapped on the screen door, even though she could see that the wooden door stood open.

"Come on in, it's open," Joe called from another part of the house. She stepped into the kitchen and looked around. "Coffee's made. Help yourself," he added.

The heavenly smell of freshly brewed coffee had already informed her of that. She heard water running. Joe must be shaving. She opened a couple of cabinets before she found the cups, then poured herself one. In her ridiculous concern over her choice of clothes this morning, she'd left her mother's house without her morning jolt of caffeine.

She leaned against the cabinet and sipped the coffee with appreciation.

"Mind pouring me a cup? I'm running a little late this morning."

Elena glanced up to see Joe standing in the doorway of the back bedroom. He had on a pair of jeans and was towel-drying his hair. She tried not to stare at the sculpted look of his tanned chest and the way the jeans lovingly molded his blatant masculinity.

She immediately turned away and put her cup down. As she reached up into the cabinet for another cup, she heard Joe make a growling sound deep in his throat. Startled, she glanced over her shoulder, then wished she hadn't. He now leaned against the doorjamb and was staring at her like a starving man at a multicourse meal.

"You look like dynamite, honey. Red is definitely your color."

With as much dignity as possible she retrieved the cup and filled it with coffee, hoping he couldn't see how his words had affected her.

"Thank you," she mumbled, handing him the steaming cup without looking at him.

"Thank *you*," he replied with a grin as he took a couple of steps into the kitchen and accepted the coffee. After a quick sip he said, "I'm sorry to hold you up. I'll be ready in another five minutes."

She concentrated on the cup in her hand. "There's no rush, really. I thought we might go early enough to avoid some of the heat."

He laughed. "Obviously you haven't been back in Texas long enough or you'd know there's no way to avoid it." He retraced his steps. When he returned he had a shirt and a pair of boots in one hand while he continued to drink from his cup.

He sat in one of the kitchen chairs and began to put on his socks. "Do you want something to eat before we leave?"

She shook her head. "I had some toast. That will hold me until lunch."

"I need to get groceries. I seem to be out of everything."

She wondered if he was expecting her to volunteer to do that little chore, as well as sort through his business papers. Since grocery shopping wasn't one of her favorite chores for herself, she would keep quiet.

He slipped his arms into the sleeves of his shirt and absently buttoned it. Then he slid first one foot, then the other, into his boots. He stood and stamped, pulling on the top to ease each foot deep into the boot. When he straightened, he said, "I'm ready."

Only then did she realize that she'd been staring at him, scrutinizing every move, as though mesmerized.

She nodded, unable to trust her voice not to sound hoarse. She walked to the back door and was about to open it when she heard a pounding at the front door and a woman's voice calling Joe's name.

She turned, looking through the three rooms—kitchen, dining and living rooms—to the front door. A young gorgeous brunette stood there. She was small and had long curly hair tumbling over her shoulders. She wore a white halter top that bared a fat-free midriff and snug white shorts that showed off a pair of very shapely legs.

"Joe? Are you here?" the woman was saying, cupping her hands and peering through the screen.

Elena glanced at Joe. He gave her a rueful smile and shrugged as if to say, *So much for keeping a schedule,* before he strode to the front door.

"I'm here, Tina. What are you doing up so early?" He pushed open the door and Tina leaped into his arms, wrapping her arms and legs around him. "Oh, Joe! I'm so happy. I couldn't wait to tell you!"

"I take it that Cisco is home safe and sound, right?" he asked, carefully unwrapping her arms from around his neck and her legs from around his waist before lowering her to the floor.

"Yes, but I just found out that I'm definitely pregnant! Isn't that wonderful? I can't believe it! The doctor told me I wouldn't have a problem getting pregnant again, and I didn't know whether to believe him or not. But he was right!"

Elena watched the scene as objectively as possible. Of course Joe would have a girlfriend. He was young, healthy and darned good-looking. His love life had absolutely nothing to do with her assignment. Any reaction she had to the woman was merely surprise that she would discuss such intimate matters in front of a stranger, that was all.

Elena watched as Joe escorted the woman back to the kitchen where she stood watching them.

"Elena, let me introduce you to my cousin, Tina Delgado. Tina, this is Elena Maldonado. She's kindly helping me out with what I laughingly call my accounting system."

Elena told herself that it didn't really matter that Tina was related to Joe and that what she was feeling was not relief. Objectivity was the key, of course.

Tina's eyes had widened when she spotted Elena. She bounced over to her and grabbed her hand. "I'm so pleased to meet you. Joe has needed help for a while. I would have offered, but I would have really messed things up for him."

"That's for sure," Joe agreed with a fervent nod.

Tina made a face at him, then looked back at Elena. "Do you live here in Santiago? I don't remember seeing you before."

"I grew up here but was away for a long time. I just moved back."

"Oh! Well, Joe will have to bring you to the party tonight so you can meet new people. We're going to have so much fun and—"

"What party?" Joe asked, interrupting his chattering cousin.

"Frankie said I could have a party tonight so we can celebrate the news with our friends."

*Frankie? Could she be talking about Francisco Delgado?* Elena wondered. He was another one of the suspects on their list. Of course. The briefing reports had mentioned that there was a family tie between the two men. Delgado was married to Joe's cousin! Elena had trouble not showing her excitement at the prospect of meeting yet another person she was assigned to watch.

"I would love to come to your party, Tina," she said as calmly as possible. "Thank you for asking."

Joe said, "That's fine, but we're going into San Antonio first, and if we expect to get back in time to attend your party, we need to hit the road, Tina." He started toward the front door. "Come on, I'll walk you to your car."

So here was an interesting development to her situation, Elena thought. She mentally reviewed what she'd read about Francisco Delgado. He owned several factories south of the border that shipped goods to the United States. The report made it clear that his operations had been carefully watched for months without a hint of anything illegal going on. She wondered why he was still considered a suspect.

When Joe returned to the kitchen where she waited, he was shaking his head. "Sorry about the delay. If I hadn't walked her out of here, she would have spent the entire day chattering away. She has no sense of time passing. She's family, but a little of her goes a long way."

Elena stepped out on the back steps while he closed and locked the door behind them. "She's very vivacious."

"That's one of her moods—yes. Then she falls into a morose mood where she swears that Chicken Little is right—the sky is falling and we're all doomed."

"There's medication for mood swings like that," Elena said.

Joe nodded. "I know. I've talked to Cisco about the possibility of getting her help. The problem is that he indulges her whims, then when she gets impossibly demanding, he conveniently stays away because of business, which means that my mother has to deal with her. Mama has enough to deal with, so I try to play buffer. I have to admit it gets old at times.

"If you don't mind going in my truck, I'll be glad to drive," he said, pausing beside his truck.

"If you don't mind driving, that's fine with me."

He helped her inside.

"I know this thing looks like a junk heap, but it runs," he said, starting the engine. Elena listened to it purr like a big cat. Joe's vehicle was the best advertisement for his skill as a mechanic.

She smiled, but didn't comment. Their transportation to San Antonio was the least of her concerns.

Once on the road, they didn't talk much.

By the end of the first hour on the road, Joe knew beyond a doubt that he'd made a serious error in judgment thinking that he could spend the day with Elena in the close confines of his truck and not be gnashing his teeth in sexual frustration.

He'd forced himself to focus on other subjects—such as the national economy, the environment, the Euro dollar, the next election, what he planned to have for lunch. He tried to concentrate on anything other than the scent of Elena's perfume, the silky sound of her clothing whenever she shifted on the bench seat, the way her dress fell upon at the bottom button and revealed a hint of thigh.

He adjusted the air-conditioning vent so that the cool air blew directly into his face. Unfortunately that wasn't the part of his anatomy heating up. If he was reacting this way after an hour of being in her presence, how in the world was he going to survive the rest of the day, including Tina's party tonight?

The idea didn't bear thinking about!

He'd placed his sunshades over his eyes as soon as they headed east, thankful they wrapped around his face enough so that she wasn't aware of how often he glanced at her. She had settled back against the seat, looking relaxed, and had eventually closed her eyes.

He still couldn't get over how the young and coltish girl

he knew in high school had turned into a sophisticated and extremely sexy woman. His youthful hormones had hummed whenever he'd been around her back then. His more mature hormones wanted to break out into an eight-part harmony of the "Hallelujah Chorus." Forget about all the self-control he'd learned in the past several years. For some unknown reason, he couldn't fight his reaction to this particular woman.

The question was, what was he going to do about it?

He'd hired her to work for him, which was a really stupid move, considering his need to keep focused on this assignment. However, he really did need help with his books if he was going to survive as a small-town mechanic. She was available to help; thus his decision was simple.

Nevertheless, it meant he had to dredge up some much-needed self-control. Otherwise, he was going to be grabbing her and kissing her at the least provocation. Not a wise move. That would be like taking a small bite from a favorite food and pushing the plate away without having more.

He wanted a great deal more than kisses from Elena. He wanted another chance to make love to her, to bring her a pleasure so intense she would experience the same mind-numbing joy he'd felt that first time.

But making love to Elena was not part of his assignment. Nor could he allow her to distract him from doing his job. He had no idea how he was going to reconcile the conflict between his duty and his desires.

Elena pretended to sleep as she fought to gain control over her heightened reactions to being with Joe Sanchez. His freshly shaved jaw taunted her, with its smooth eminently kissable surface. His dark glasses hid his expression, and he appeared to be totally unaware of her.

She wished she could say the same about herself. Instead, her silly thoughts kept drifting back to that night so many years ago when he'd made love to her.

They'd been a couple of inexperienced kids back then. She had never before been sexually aroused and didn't have a clue about stopping what eventually happened. She'd thought they would park and maybe do some light petting. She'd been totally unprepared for the strong desire that had swept through her, washing away any doubts about what was happening.

She had never told him to stop. She had no way of knowing if he would have, but the fact was, she'd never asked. Up until the time his friends had shown up, she had wanted to be with him, to explore her own newly aroused sensuality. Once aroused, she'd wanted Joe to make love to her, and then he'd actually done so. She hadn't expected the awkwardness and discomfort. The reality of the act had snapped her out of her fantasy-based idea of what lovemaking was like.

She'd decided that the act of lovemaking was greatly overrated. Sex wasn't at all the way it was portrayed in books and movies. She could certainly do without it—and had—without missing it.

Because of what had happened immediately afterward, whenever she thought of the incident later, she blamed Joe for everything—for making love to her, for the pain she'd experienced and, most of all, for the humiliation caused by his friends.

In fact, that evening with Joe had caused her to look at her life and her future in an entirely new way. She'd decided that she would never allow another man to take advantage of her.

Over the ensuing years, she knew there had been talk about her lack of a love life, with the usual speculations as to why, but she didn't care.

She'd put all her energy into getting through school with the best grades possible. Because of her single-minded focus on her career, she'd been able to move ahead without distraction.

Even when she'd recognized Joe's photograph, she'd believed that he would no longer have any effect on her.

Now it seemed as if her life had come full circle. She was once again in Santiago and once again spending her time with Joe. The most unsettling aspect of the situation was that she'd discovered that she still reacted to him on a sexual level, something that didn't happen with other men.

No matter how much she worked to convince herself that she was no longer attracted to him, she knew she was kidding herself. The sight of him made her heart race. His smile caused her knees to weaken. Her palms itched with the need to stroke his muscled chest and arms.

What in the world was the matter with her? This was the man she thought she had hated for the past eleven years. This was the same man who had turned her completely off sex. So why had she been salivating over him ever since he'd walked into the cantina the night before last?

She wasn't a love-starved teenager. She was a mature successful adult on a very important assignment. She didn't need to be distracted by one of the people she'd been assigned to watch and possibly have arrested.

Did that mean that Joe was the only man who could make her want to experience lovemaking? Despite everything that had happened back then, she couldn't stop her mind from creating all kinds of erotic scenarios involving her and Joe. Her dreams these past two nights had caused her to wake up shaking and aroused.

She wasn't sure what was going to happen next with the two of them. All she knew was that whatever it was, she could not allow their present circumstances to reflect on the job she'd been assigned to do. Somehow she had to get a grip on her emotions.

Elena was thankful she would be seeing Chris in a few hours. He'd be able to help regain her perspective.

"You've been awfully quiet," Joe said after another hour on the road. He turned his head slightly, to glance at her.

"Just enjoying the ride," she replied, wondering what he would think if he knew what she'd really been thinking.

"We should be in San Antonio in another half hour. Where do you want to go first?"

She'd already thought how she could handle this part of their trip. "Why don't you drop me off at the mall? I'm sure you have things you can do besides follow me around shopping. As well as what I was going to look for, Mom gave me a list of things."

"Okay. I need to pick up some supplies for the shop. I may check out a couple of the auto-parts stores here, so I can do some competitive pricing." He tugged one of his earlobes and made a face. "And I suppose I'd better look for something to wear to Tina's party tonight. I doubt she'll want me there in jeans."

"That's another thing I'll need to add to my list." She glanced at her watch. "We should be there by eleven-thirty. Why don't we meet at two-thirty? That should give us time to look at computers. Once you decide how much you're willing to spend, it should be easy enough to find what you want."

The calm in her voice surprised her since her nerves

were jumping at the prospect of her first meeting with Chris. This assignment was too important to mess up. She'd taken a risk coming to San Antonio with Joe. Why hadn't she told Joe no, made up some reason why she needed to make the trip alone? She knew the answer. She had to be careful not to arouse his suspicions, of course. As far as he knew, she'd planned a day of shopping. Oh, great. He would expect to see her with an assortment of bags and packages by the end of her trip. Now she had really painted herself into a corner.

She could only hope that the meeting with Chris wouldn't take long. She focused on relaxing. After all, her report to Chris would be positive. Everything about this assignment was moving forward in a timely manner.

Only her strong reaction to Joe was out of control. Unfortunately she had no idea how she was going to deal with the strong feelings he stirred within her.

# Six

They were on the outskirts of town when she yawned. "Sorry," she said. "I stayed up too late last night reading." She certainly wasn't going to admit that she'd had a restless night because of him.

He gave her a sideways glance through his sunshades. "As I recall, you were always a bookworm."

"True. I generally preferred the lives I read about to mine." As soon as she made that statement, she wished she'd kept her mouth shut. What was it about this man that caused her to blurt out her most intimate thoughts?

"I'm really surprised that you decided to return to Santiago. I remember you talked as though you could hardly wait to leave."

"Well, those feathers you see at the corners of my mouth are the remains of the crow I had to eat. The truth is, I didn't know where else to go when I was laid off. I know that something in my field will turn up eventually."

She glanced at him. "What made you choose to come back?"

Joe thought about that for a moment, then said, "I always knew that I'd end up coming back as long as my mother was alive. Someone needed to be around to look after her, although she's too independent to allow anyone to hover. I try to drop in every day or two without being obvious and check to make sure everything is okay."

*This guy is too good to be true,* she thought. If he was making extra money by smuggling, he sure wasn't keeping the money for himself, from the looks of his place. She might learn more after going through his paperwork, but she doubted she would find anything incriminating or he wouldn't be so willing to hire her.

But that didn't mean that he wasn't looking after his mother and any other relatives with the extra cash. Regardless of motive, if he was doing something illegal, she intended to prove it, regardless of any feelings she might harbor for him.

The problem was that she wasn't feeling quite as eager as she had at first. That was the trouble with knowing a suspect too well. Human beings were multifaceted creatures. No one was totally good or totally bad. Well, maybe there was true evil lurking in some, but she didn't see it in Joe.

For his sake and for his mother's sake, she sincerely hoped he was playing by all the rules. Unfortunately the fact that he was related to another suspect in this case made it more likely that he was involved in whatever was going on.

Traffic around the downtown mall was heavy. By the time Joe dropped her off near there, it was almost twelve o'clock, an hour later than the time she'd chosen to meet

Chris. As if she wasn't nervous enough about this trip, now she was late for their first meeting. She hurried the few blocks to the Marriott Hotel on the River Walk and strode into the lobby.

She spotted the house phones down a hallway that housed several boutiques. By now the lunch crowd was beginning to congregate near the restaurant off the lobby. There were also tables arranged outside for those who preferred to be closer to the river.

She made her way through a knot of people and stopped at the bank of phones. She glanced around before she asked for his room.

He answered on the first ring.

"Hi," she said quietly.

"You're late," he responded, sounding impatient.

She rolled her eyes at the obvious comment. Determined to hide her nerves, she said lightly, "Guess you'll have to dock my pay. Or…you can give me your room number and I can make my abject apologies in person."

He laughed. "Sorry. Room 312. Time seems to crawl when there's not much to do but sit."

"Uh-huh. And you've never done a stakeout, I'm sure."

He groaned. "I hate those things!"

"I'll see you in a few minutes." She hung up and went over to the elevators. One arrived with quiet efficiency. Several people stepped off, and she got on and went to the third floor.

She paused in front of the room marked 312 and took a calming breath. With a confidence she was far from feeling, she knocked on the door. It immediately swung open.

Chris bowed low. "Please enter and share your many pearls of wisdom with me, oh, beauteous one."

"Yeah, right," she replied with a chuckle. She stepped inside and surveyed the room. A king-size bed took up about half the space. There was the regular collection of hotel furniture, including a mini bar.

"I ordered lunch," he said, nodding toward the table where there were two plates with sandwiches and a pitcher of iced tea.

"Great plan," she said, heading toward the table, which was in front of the sliding glass doors to the small balcony. She peered out. "A view of the water, I see. All the comforts of home."

Chris followed her and took the other chair. "I wish. I thought you said you'd be here at eleven."

She nodded, pouring herself some tea. "That was my plan, but Joe was running late and by the time we left, it was—"

He held up his hand like a traffic cop. "Whoa, whoa, wait a minute. Are you talking about Joe Sanchez, one of the men you're supposed to be watching?"

"The very one. We rode to town together."

He stared at her without expression. "Have you lost your mind?" he finally asked before taking a bite out of his club sandwich.

"It gets better," she said, slipping off her shoes and propping her feet on the edge of the bed. "He's hired me to work for him." She took a big bite from her sandwich, only now realizing how hungry she was.

"Well, how cozy. Are you going into the smuggling business with him, too?"

She laughed, feeling better now that she'd made contact with Chris. This was her real life. Not Santiago. Not Joe Sanchez.

"No. He's running a garage and needs help with the paperwork. He just hired me yesterday. When I explained that I needed to come to San Antonio today, he offered to bring me so that we could look for a computer. I told him

I'd input all his records, which gives me the perfect opportunity to look at his financial situation. I asked for a couple of hours on my own because I had some shopping to do.'' She batted her lashes at him. ''Isn't that what all women have on their minds?''

''You said it. Not me.''

They quickly finished their meal. ''So. That's most of my news. What's happening with the others?'' she asked, refilling her glass.

''Everyone is in place. The INS gave Wilder more names to check out for them, which Walters received early this morning. That will definitely keep us busy, but I think we've spotted some possible means of transport the smugglers may be using. There's been an increase in border crossings in the past three days. The word is that sometimes when there's a flurry like that, the smugglers think they'll be watched less closely. All I know is, we're out there on the back roads taking down license plates and having every one of them checked out.''

Elena nodded. ''One of the reasons we were late getting away this morning was because Joe's cousin dropped by to invite him to a party tonight. Because I was there I got an invitation, as well. You may recall from our briefing that Joe had a family connection with Francisco Delgado. Well, this is it. His cousin is married to Delgado.''

That certainly got Chris's attention. He sat up in his chair and stared at her. ''And you've been invited to his home tonight? Good work, Elena.''

She laughed. ''I lucked out by being there when she dropped by with the invitation, that's all. Of course, this means I need to get out of here and truly do some shopping.''

Chris grinned and shook his head.

''I'll see you next week,'' Elena continued. ''It's going

to be a little tricky, figuring out what to say to Joe about needing time off every week. But I'll think of something.''

"Sounds like the two of you are already living in each other's pockets.''

"You need to remember that I've known this guy forever. We went through school together, graduated the same year. I can't pretend to be a stranger to him.''

"I don't recall you mentioning that before.''

She shrugged. "Guess I forgot.''

"Uh-huh.''

She'd gone to the mirror and was putting on lipstick. She looked around at him. "What's that supposed to mean?''

"I'm just wondering how you feel about possibly putting an old classmate behind bars.''

She tilted her head slightly and looked at him. "If he's guilty, that's where he belongs.''

"But you're not sure he's guilty, is that it?''

"After little more than a week? Hardly. But you can count on the fact that I'm looking for evidence. If he's involved, I'll find out. The same for Delgado.''

"Be careful, Elena. If you run into a problem you can't handle, don't hesitate to contact me.''

"You can count on it. But Wilder was right. I was able to convince everyone that I'd come back home for a long visit, so nobody thinks anything of my being in the area.'' She glanced at her watch again. "That's all I have to report this time. I've got to run.'' She glanced around. "Do you intend to stay overnight?''

Chris nodded. "I've got a couple of things to check out while I'm in town, so I figured it would be just as easy to get a good night's rest and head out first thing in the morning.''

"Okay. I'll see you next week, unless we get a break before then and somebody confesses."

They both laughed as she left.

She hurried back to the mall. Since her so-called shopping trip had been planned before she received her invitation, Elena knew she had to buy more than the dress for tonight's gathering or Joe would be suspicious. Unfortunately she didn't have long to look for items and, as far as he knew, she needed to be careful with her money.

With that in mind, she went to the kitchenware department and bought her mother a few things, then checked out the blouses, once again for her mother, who rarely spent money on herself.

By the time she left the store, her hands were suitably full of packages.

Next she went to a small dress shop and found something she hoped would be suitable for herself. It was green and brought out the color of her eyes. It had a belted waist and a full short skirt. More importantly it looked festive without being too ornate.

As soon as she'd purchased the dress, she went back to the corner where Joe had let her off and watched for him.

Fifteen minutes passed before he showed up. He pulled over and helped her into the truck, stowing her packages behind the seat. "I'm so sorry. I kept getting caught in traffic jams. I hope you didn't have to wait long."

"No, I'm fine." She pulled out a folded piece of paper from her purse. "I saw this ad for computers in a flyer while I was looking around the mall. The store is on the north side of town, but it looks like you could get a decent machine for a reasonable price."

He grinned. "I'll take your word for it. You navigate and I'll drive."

By the time they were headed out of town sometime

later, they had accomplished a great deal. Joe was the proud owner of a new computer and printer. Plus they had bought paper and other supplies. Elena was surprised at how easy he was to shop with.

She and the salesman explained the various options he might want, and he had followed her advice without showing any concern about cost. She wasn't certain why his trust in her made her uncomfortable. Maybe it was because she didn't have the same feelings about him.

The truth was, she didn't know the man he was today. She wasn't sure she ever had, but certainly the past eleven years had shaped him into the person he was now, just as those years had shaped her.

However, he seemed willing to accept her without qualification. She wished their situation was as simple as that.

Once they got away from the city, traffic eased and Joe was able to pick up speed.

He glanced at her and smiled. She returned his smile and he focused on the road once more—until a few minutes later when he looked over at her again.

"What?" she asked. "Do I have something on my face?"

"Not really, although I've got to tell you, that elusive smile of yours can sure do wonders."

She frowned. "What are you talking about?"

He shrugged. "Nothing. I just remember how seldom you smiled when we were kids. Since you've been back, I've seen it flash a few times. Now I find myself watching for it." He reached over and touched her hand. "I want to see you happy. I'm sorry you lost your job. I know the loss has been hard on you, yet you never mention it, never complain. I wish there was something I could do."

Darn. Why did he have to say things like that? She didn't need him sympathizing with her over her nonexistent loss. With a lightness she didn't feel, she replied, "You have. You've given me a job. You're buying me equipment to make that job easier. What more could anyone ask?"

He drove without comment for several miles before he said, "I don't know what someone else might ask. What would *you* ask for if all your wishes and dreams could be fulfilled?"

She closed her eyes for a moment in order not to be distracted by his penetrating gaze. Traffic was almost nonexistent now, so he had very little to distract him. Why couldn't he be as silent on the way home as he'd been on the way out?

Finally she opened her eyes and looked at him. "Peace on earth, good will toward men."

He sighed. "I was serious."

She relaxed against the seat, propping her elbow on the back to hold her head while she faced him. "So was I. I would like to see people settle their disagreements amicably and with good will, rather than with guns. I would like our country to focus on health and education, rather than spending so much of our resources playing policeman for the rest of the world."

"And where do you fit into all that?"

For just a second she found herself wanting to tell him how different her life would be if there was no necessity to enforce the laws of the land. That she would be out of a job and she would be happy if that was the case.

Instead, she said, "Oh, I would be happy with a home and healthy children to raise."

He frowned. "You say that as though there's no possibility of that ever happening."

"Okay, so maybe one day it will happen. Satisfied?"

The look he gave her made her pulse raise. "Not even close," he replied with a drawl.

By the time they returned to his house, it was dark. "I'll pick you up at your place in about an hour. Will that give you enough time to get ready?" he asked as they transferred her packages to her Jeep.

"That will be fine."

"Meanwhile, I'll see what I can do about getting the computer set up."

"Or you can wait and let me help tomorrow."

He laughed. "That's a much better plan." He took her hand and squeezed it. "I've enjoyed today. It's rare for me to have a day off. I didn't realize what a rut I was in until I was able to get away from the place for a few hours."

She pulled her hand away and gave a little wave. "I need to get home. I'll be ready in about an hour."

As soon as she got into the Jeep she found herself trembling. What was it about this one man out of all the men she knew in her life? How could he affect her so when it was the very last thing she wanted...or needed? He was a suspect, of all things. Why couldn't she control her responses to him?

She had no answer.

"Wow!" Elena said softly later that evening as they turned into the driveway of a palatial home with extensive grounds. The tall wrought-iron gate stood open between massive pillars at the entrance to the place. The same wrought iron formed an equally tall fence that disappeared into the distance on either side. "I had no idea there was any place near Santiago that looked like this."

Joe drove between the open gates toward the house,

which was lit up like a giant Christmas tree. The architecture was Mediterranean style, with wide terraces and a tiled roof. Cars were parked in an area that looked like a public parking lot.

Joe pulled up in front and two men in valet jackets opened the doors to the truck as if it was a BMW. After Joe handed one of them the keys, he walked around the truck to where Elena stood, staring at the splendor all around them.

The driveway curved around a large pond with a fountain in the middle. Lush gardens framed the house, the driveway and, Elena suspected, the rear of the place, as well.

"I can't imagine the cost of keeping up with all of this," she said when he laced his fingers between hers and started up the steps that led to the massive front doors.

Joe shook his head. "Cisco indulges Tina far too much. She needed a project, he decided, so he told her to plan a home for them. This is the result."

"Not many husbands would be so doting."

He pulled her closer to him and said, "Oh, I don't know. Depends on who they're hoping to please."

"Are you saying you'd allow a wife to plan something like this?"

"On my budget?" He laughed. "I'm afraid not. But then, Cisco can afford it."

"How? What does he do?" She felt the question was perfectly natural under the circumstances.

"He has business holdings in Mexico—some factories, as well as warehouses and offices that he owns and rents out."

"I had no idea there was so much profit in businesses like that."

"I'm afraid I don't know all that much about it. He

seems to have a great amount of influence with politicians on both sides of the border. He was very pleased when NAFTA was approved and he could move products into the United States without the scrutiny he'd had in the past.''

They reached the top of the steps, and the doors swung open as though connected to a magic eye. Elena immediately recognized Tina, who was still dressed in white, but this dress was obviously couture. It floated around her as though it had a life of its own, clinging to her curves before drifting away. She looked like a fairy sprite.

Standing next to her was a slim man wearing an equally expensive and obviously custom-made suit that subtly called attention to his graceful build. She could almost see him with a fencing weapon in his hand. His skin was much darker than Tina's, his eyes a fathomless black. A thin carefully manicured mustache adorned his upper lip.

"Ah, Joe. It's good to see you, *compadre*," he said, clapping Joe on the back. He was at least half a head shorter than Joe, but his presence almost made Joe appear to be too tall and clumsy by comparison. Elena wasn't certain how the man managed that.

"It's been a while, Cisco," Joe replied genially. He slipped his arm around Elena's waist. "I want you to meet a very dear friend of mine, Elena Maldonado. Elena, this is our host, Francisco Delgado."

Tina clasped each of their hands and said, "Oh, I am *so* glad you came. This celebration wouldn't be the same without you, Joe. You look so distinguished in your suit." She smiled at Elena. "You have a strong effect on my cousin, it seems. No other woman has ever managed to get him to dress up and come to one of my parties. I congratulate you."

Elena glanced at Joe who still held her snugly by his side. He winked at her.

Cisco spoke. "We need to wait here to welcome a few more of our guests. Please go on in and make yourselves comfortable. There's plenty of food and drink, and we have a band playing on the lower terrace in back if you care to dance."

Once they were out of earshot, Elena whispered, "I've never met anyone who radiated such a powerful presence. I wasn't certain whether to shake his hand, bow or lie prostrate at his feet!"

Joe threw back his head and laughed. "Ah, Elena. I've missed you and your sense of humor. Thank God you came back home."

As the evening progressed, Elena met more and more people. Some she remembered from when she'd lived here before. Others were new faces. The one thing they all seemed to have in common was an abundance of wealth, if their apparel and jewels were any indication.

The food was amazing, and her glass of champagne was never empty. As the night progressed, she found herself relaxing and enjoying herself. More specifically, she was enjoying being with Joe.

When he led her out to the dance area and took her in his arms, she was reminded of their senior prom.

"This certainly brings back memories," she said almost under her breath. But there were differences, as well. His grip was more firm, his guidance more experienced.

"I hope they're good memories," he replied, holding her closer than necessary, so close, in fact, that she became aware of his arousal.

She looked up at him and smiled. "Now that you mention it, some of those memories *were* good, I guess. Maybe I've spent too many years remembering the wrong ones."

They danced in silence through two songs before he said, "You know, this probably isn't the time or the place, but I have a confession to make."

He sounded so serious that she raised her head from where it rested on his shoulder and looked at him. "What kind of confession?"

Her first thought was that he knew why she was here before she realized that there was no way he could know. So what other confession could he have?

"The reason I was such a lousy lover way back then and probably put you off sex forever is that I'd had very little experience. I'd never wanted anyone like I did you, and my feelings overwhelmed me, which made me less than a decent partner."

A series of shocks were going through her body at his words—that he had brought up what had happened after she had thought they had put that incident behind them, that he actually mentioned her obvious lack of enjoyment of the act and that he hadn't had much more experience than she'd had. He was confessing that he had really cared about her back then. That what had happened had been as important to him as it had been to her.

Had he actually guessed that she had never had another sexual experience since? She was jolted by the thought. Was it that obvious?

She stopped dancing. He quickly moved her out of the way of another couple and led her to the terrace railing. "See? I told you it wasn't the time or the place."

"You lost control?" she asked, breathless with all the implications of what he was admitting to her.

He kept his gaze steady on hers. "Uh-huh. I've spent many a sleepless night reliving what I did and how it all happened. If we hadn't been interrupted, maybe I would have had sense enough to make it better for you the next

time, but who knows? What I knew back then about plea-
suring a woman was next to nothing.''

''You've learned since then, is that what you're saying?'' she asked, smiling.

He looked away, then down at their hands, still clasped,
resting on the railing. ''I haven't had all that much experience, but yeah, I've learned enough to know what a dis-
service I did you—and that was before those apes showed
up with the stupid flashlights. I never could reconcile how
an evening that started off so well could have ended so
badly.''

She, too, looked away, but she could think of nothing
to say.

Finally he said, ''I've always wanted to make it up to
you.''

His words caused another flurry of electrical currents to
ricochet through her body.

''And how, exactly, did you intend to do that?''

He turned so that he was facing her and leaned his hip
against the railing. His gaze seemed to caress her, heating
her body, before he said, ''I would like to take you to a
private place where there would be no possibility of being
interrupted. It would have a bed that had plenty of room
so that we would be comfortable, and we'd have all the
time we needed to explore each other, to find out what
each other likes. I would like to pleasure you, Elena, in
every way I can think of. I would like to kiss and caress
every inch of your body until we were both too weak to
continue.''

His words captured her heart and her imagination. She
could see the room, the bed and them lying on it. The
image weakened her knees so that she could scarcely
stand.

''I don't know what to say,'' she finally whispered.

"Say yes and we'll be out of here right now," he replied.

"Excuse me."

They both spun around as though they'd been caught doing something illegal. And to Elena, that was an apt description of what she was thinking.

Cisco looked at them quizzically and said, "I'm so sorry to have interrupted you, but I was wondering if I could speak to you in private for a few short moments, Joe." He smiled at Elena. "I promise not to keep him long."

Joe began to protest and Elena smiled. "Of course I don't mind," she said. "I didn't mean to monopolize him all evening."

Cisco strode away, taking for granted that Joe would follow him.

Once they disappeared inside, Elena let out her breath. She wasn't certain if she'd been rescued or not. She glanced down at her glass. She certainly needed to lay off the expensive bubbly and try to clear her head before she made a really stupid mistake.

"What happened to Joe?" Tina asked, suddenly materializing at her elbow. "Every time I got a glimpse of him tonight, he was gazing adoringly into your eyes."

Elena chuckled. "I don't think he's all that enamored of me, Tina, but thank you."

Tina's mischievous smile faded and she looked at her with a depth and sincerity that caught Elena off guard. "Joe is in love with you, Elena. Surely you must know that."

"You've just met me. How could you possibly know that?"

"Yes. I've just met you. But I have known my cousin for many years. He keeps to himself. In all the years I've known him, he's shown very little interest in a girl. His mother once told me about a girl Joe knew when he was in school. She said he spent most of his time with her and that he seemed happier during that time than she'd ever seen him. Then something happened and he spent his time at home, never went anywhere, not even with his buddies, and she said he grieved, although she could never find out why.

"I think that girl was you, Elena. I think you knew him in school. I think he loved you then and he loves you now."

Elena didn't know what to say. She couldn't think straight at the moment. Her body was still tingling from her reaction to what Joe had said. Now Tina was telling her that Joe might be in love with her. Might be? She was insisting that he was.

"How do you know so much about his feelings?" she finally asked.

Tina looked into her glass of club soda. "Joe is one of the special ones, Elena. He understands things without being told. He's a listener. He heals people, as well as machines. But he spends his time alone. I watch him and I wonder about him. I know he considers me a flake, but he is very patient with me, regardless. I have watched him tonight and I am seeing a man I never knew existed. A man with a light deep inside of him that has suddenly been turned on. Whenever he looks at you, he glows. And he has seldom taken his eyes off you tonight. That's how I know."

Tina reached out and touched Elena's arm. "Please do not hurt him again. Maybe it was your leaving here that did it before. I don't know. Just be careful with him, will you please?"

Elena heard Cisco talking as he and Joe approached them. She turned and smiled at the men.

"How are you holding up, *carina?*" Cisco asked Tina. "We don't want you becoming exhausted." With a gentle touch, he smoothed his fingers over his wife's flat stomach, and Elena realized that he truly loved his wife. Somehow, that gave him more humanity than anything she had seen since she'd first laid eyes on him.

"How about you?" Joe asked, looking at Elena. "Are you ready to head back to town?"

The question sounded innocuous enough, but Elena felt that her answer could very well change the course of her life. She held his gaze for a long moment before she nodded and said, "Yes, I believe I am."

# Seven

He took her hand and they both thanked the host and hostess for their invitations to the party. Then they left the terrace and walked into the house without looking at or speaking to each other.

Once inside, several people stopped them and made conversation. Elena no longer cared what was being said. She let the comments and the laughter sweep over her.

Finally they were outside once again. One of the men working as a valet brought the truck to them. Joe helped her into the passenger seat, tipped the man and walked around to get in on the other side.

He started the truck and they slowly drove down the long winding driveway and onto the highway. He accelerated to the speed limit but no more as they made their way to town in silence.

Elena sat with her hands clasped in her lap and waited almost numbly to see if he would continue through town the few miles out to her mother's house. Or…would he turn at the light and go to his home, instead?

She couldn't look at him. She wasn't even sure what she was thinking at the moment. If he knew how completely he had seduced her with his words, he wouldn't worry that she would turn him down if he suggested that they go to his house. If his words hadn't been enough, then Tina's remarks would certainly have done it.

The one time they had made love, they had both been a couple of kids who didn't know what they were doing. At long last she could truly accept that. The ensuing eleven years since then had disappeared this evening. She felt the same way she had after they had left the prom.

She saw a light blinking in the distance. Traffic was so light this late at night in Santiago that the light became a four-way stop signal after ten o'clock.

Joe smoothly braked and brought the truck to a complete stop. He waited. She glanced at him and saw that he was staring straight ahead, both hands on the steering wheel. She looked closer. His hands gripped the steering wheel so tightly that his knuckles had turned white.

Slowly she turned her head and looked fully at him. They had been sitting there for some time without moving. When he moved his head ever so slowly to look at her, she saw the emotion, the fear of rejection, in his face. The tension that had been building within her eased, and she reached out and lightly placed her hand on his thigh. He jerked as though he'd been electrocuted, then dropped his hand over hers and squeezed.

He reached for the gearshift and moved it into first, turned the wheel and headed toward his house.

He turned into the driveway but did not continue to the garage. Instead, he parked near the front porch. Moving slowly, he walked around and opened her door, took her hand and eased her out of the truck. Still holding her hand, he led her up the front steps and across the covered porch; then he flipped through his keys until he found the right one.

He'd left a small lamp on in the living room, and it gave them light when they stepped inside. He didn't pause once inside the house except to lock the door behind them. Then he led her into his bedroom.

Once again the bed was unmade. He leaned over and pulled the top sheet back and smoothed the other sheet, all with one hand. His other hand still gripped hers as though afraid to let go.

Finally he turned and looked at her. "I know this isn't very fancy," he began, but she stopped him with her fingers across his lips. She reached up and pushed his suit jacket away from his shoulders. When he shrugged, she slid it off his arms and carefully draped it over the back of a chair.

While she had her back to him, he reached for the fastener to her dress and carefully unzipped the dress until it fell away from her upper body—the belt the only thing holding it in place.

She unfastened the belt and let the dress fall to the floor. This, too, she placed over the chair.

"You are so beautiful," he whispered, his voice shaking, when she turned and faced him. "I think I must be dreaming." He smoothed his thumb across her shoulder to her neck. "I've imagined this so many times that it would be easy to think I'm imagining it now."

She quickly loosened his tie, then his shirt, before reaching for his belt. "I'm real, Joe. Very real."

He quickly toed off his dress shoes and stepped out of the rest of his clothing. Elena just as quickly removed her fragile underwear along with her heeled sandals.

Then she waited.

The light from the other room gave off enough illumination for her to see him and for him to see her. He reached out and touched the tip of her breast, causing it to form a tight pebble, then he leaned down and touched it ever so lightly with his tongue.

She whimpered and reached for him. He picked her up and placed her on the bed, stretching out beside her. She could see him in the soft light—the firm muscles of his chest and arms, the ripple of his abs, the intensity of his arousal. He waited, watching her, as she carefully traced a trail with her finger down the middle of his chest, then his abdomen. She paused briefly before she encircled him lightly, moving her fingers down the solid length of him, causing him to gasp.

"Well," she said with a smile, "what exactly did you have in mind once we were alone and comfortable?"

His grin flashed white in his dark face. "I, uh, seem to have lost my concentration. Let's see," he mused, leaning over her. "I believe I was going to do some exploring…" He matched his words with a light caress across each of her breasts, before he leaned down and covered one of the tips with his mouth.

The sensation was indescribable. No one had ever done this to her before. She could smell his aftershave and shampoo as his tongue played over first one, then the other nipple. She could hear his labored breathing as he fought for control, which reminded her that she was holding her breath. Telling herself to breathe, she reached up and touched his cheek, then pushed her fingers through his hair.

He lifted his head and found her lips with his.

The kiss went on and on while his hands explored her

body. She touched the tip of her tongue to his, teasing him while his hands worked their magic on her body.

By the time he paused for breath, she was whimpering with need. She wanted him to do more, much more, no matter how painful it might be. She tugged at his shoulders, silently imploring him to make love to her.

As soon as he moved over her, she lifted her knees, giving him room, even as she felt his hard flesh nudging against her. A flashback of the pain made her stiffen briefly, but then she forced herself to relax and lifted her hips to meet his.

He teased her by barely moving into her before he pulled away. She grabbed his buttocks and lunged upward, forcing him deep within her. Her eyes flashed open at the exquisite sensation of having him there once again. There was no pain. Only pleasure. When he once again began to move away, she held him tightly, moving her legs up around his waist to anchor him to her.

With a groan, he gave up resisting her and began a hard and fast rhythm that soon sent her soaring into a whole new realm of experience. With one final lunge, Joe let out a cry and held on to her as he reached his climax seconds behind her.

She clung to him, finally understanding what all the books she'd read were talking about. This was what it felt like to become one with another person. She moved her hands up and across his back, then back again, feeling the moisture from his exertion dampen her palms.

When he finally lifted his head to look at her, she smiled at him. His frown eased and he gave her a short hard kiss before easing over onto his side.

"That wasn't quite the plan of leisurely making love to you I had in mind," he rasped out, taking deep breaths between his words.

"Do you hear me complaining?" she asked with a hint of laughter in her voice.

"I guess I still don't have much control where you're concerned."

"I can understand that it's tougher for you because you have to stay in control of your responses."

He sighed and rubbed his hand over her arm. "It would have helped me considerably if I hadn't been in an aroused state since the first night I saw you. I haven't been involved with anyone in a long while, so the combination pretty well did me in."

She leaned up on her elbow and looked at him. "I keep hearing you apologize, but I don't understand why. However, if you feel you want to improve on anything that happened just now, be my guest."

He choked, then started laughing. He pulled her down to him and placed her head on his shoulder. "You should know by now that men need a little time to recuperate."

"I should know that, huh," she replied sleepily. "Okay."

After a moment he said, "I figure that you've had at least a couple of serious relationships during these last few years."

She shook her head, not looking at him. He placed his palm at the back of her head and nudged her to look at him.

"What are you telling me here?" he asked.

"I haven't said a word."

"What is it you aren't telling me, then?"

"That it's time for me to get home before my mother is convinced I've been in a wreck, maybe?"

He stared at her for the longest time. She made herself meet his gaze. After all, she had nothing to be ashamed of, nor did she have anything to hide. If she'd chosen not to have another relationship after the first time with him, that was her choice.

Finally he shook his head. "I never even asked if you were on any kind of birth control. If you're not saying what I think you're not saying, you've had no reason to be on any, have you?"

She shook her head.

He'd brought his head off the pillow with his question, and when he saw her response, he dropped it back with a muffled oath. "Way to go, Sanchez," he muttered. "The only protection I have is in my billfold, and I'm not sure it's any good." He glanced at her. "But if you're still interested, we could check it out to see."

She grinned and nodded. He bounded off the bed and found his wallet in his pants pocket. When he returned to the bed, he gripped the foil package in his hand like a medal.

During the next few minutes Elena learned yet another lesson in her sadly neglected sex education.

She came awake with a start. Joe was sound asleep beside her, his arm and leg across her as though afraid she might leave.

"Joe?"

"Mmph?"

"I really have to go home."

He yawned and turned over onto his back. "I know," he admitted.

As soon as he freed her, she got out of bed and quickly dressed. When she turned around, he was wearing his jeans, a T-shirt and his work boots.

He helped her into the truck and in moments backed out of the driveway. Without turning on his lights, he drove to the end of the block, then turned them on when he reached a busier street.

"No reason to alert the neighbors that I'm out and about," he said sleepily.

"This has been quite a day," she replied, "since I arrived to go to San Antonio this morning."

He draped his arm around her and pulled her to his side. "We were planning to put that computer together tomorrow, but we'll have to postpone that little task for a few days."

"Why?"

"Oh. Guess I forgot to tell you. Cisco asked me to fill in for one of his truck drivers for the next couple of weeks. He doesn't want to replace him permanently because he has a wife and several kids. But the man's too sick to work right now."

Her heart gave a lurch. "You're going to work for Francisco Delgado?"

He glanced at her with a puzzled expression on his face. "Well, yeah. I fill in for him from time to time. Why do you ask?"

*Keep calm,* she reminded herself. "I'm just surprised, that's all. You seem to have more than enough to keep you busy right here."

"Tell me about it. I'll have to get on the phone in the morning and call a few people about postponing the work they want done on their vehicles." He tapped the steering wheel lightly with the palm of his hand. "Man, oh, man. The very last thing I want to do is leave town now."

"Now?"

He gave her a quick glance. "I don't want to give you time to build another thick wall between us."

She smiled and leaned her head against his shoulder. "I

don't think you need to worry about that." After a moment she said, "You know, I could put your computer together. I managed to put mine together without much difficulty. That way, I could start working on your accounts while you're gone—that is, if it's all right with you."

"Are you sure?"

"Positive. I'll just need a key to your place."

"The extra one's at home. I'll leave the back door unlocked for you and the key on the table. I really appreciate this, honey. You must know I'll work to get back as soon as I can."

He pulled into her driveway and followed the lane up to the house, once again cutting off the headlights after he left the highway. He walked her to the door and made certain she was inside before giving her a final wave.

She watched from the darkened living room until he pulled out onto the highway, then she slowly walked to her room.

She needed to think about how all of this affected her and the job she was sent to do. She knew that Joe couldn't possibly be involved in anything illegal. She just knew it. But she still had to turn up evidence on whomever was behind the smuggling that was going on. Maybe it wasn't anyone from Santiago. There were other suspects scattered up and down the river. She was just keeping tabs on this particular site.

She thought of Tina tonight and how happy she had been. She thought about the baby and what a difference it might make in Tina's life.

A baby. There was a chance that she herself might be pregnant as a result of tonight. She couldn't quite take in the idea. She'd never been sexually active. Therefore, the possibility had never before come up. She wasn't sure how she felt about it. In fact, she wasn't sure how she felt about anything just now.

She'd think about all of it tomorrow.


"I never heard you come in last night, Elena," Sara said to her daughter when Elena finally entered the kitchen late the next morning.

Elena shuffled over to the coffeepot and poured herself a cup of the steaming brew. "It was really late, Mama." She opened a couple of cabinet doors. "Where do you keep the aspirin?"

Sara hopped up from her chair and crossed to the side of the kitchen opposite from where Elena stood, holding her head. "I take it the party was a success?" she asked dryly, handing her daughter the bottle of tablets.

Elena quickly washed down a couple of aspirin with a glass of water before sitting down at the table. "I guess you could say that."

"So? What did you think of all that? Didn't I tell you? No self-respecting people would live like that. One of these days the authorities will figure out that something is going on out there that isn't legal. You just make sure you don't get involved."

Elena continued to hold her head and mutely reminded herself never, ever, to drink champagne again.

"I know, Mama. You mentioned that yesterday when I told you where I was going."

"It's a fancy place, isn't it?"

"Very."

"Did you have a good time?"

Oh, if her mother only knew, but there were some things you couldn't discuss with your parent, no matter how much of an adult you'd become. "It was interesting to see how people live with unlimited resources at their disposal."

"I thought Joe looked quite nice when he picked you up."

Elena smiled to herself, remembering her shock at seeing him in his dark suit. He reminded her so much of how he had looked years before in formal wear. He'd looked even better last night out of that suit.

"Now that's a dreamy smile on your face if ever I saw one," Sara said in a mellow tone. "If I didn't know better, I'd think you were falling for this guy."

"Maybe I am, Mama. Would that be so bad?"

*What about your career?* She mentally answered her own question with another one guaranteed to chase any dreams out of her head.

Sara joined her at the table. "Well, one good thing would be that you'd not be running off again looking for happiness elsewhere."

*I have to, Mama. I can't live here, no matter how this assignment turns out.*

"Didn't you say you were going to be working for him?" Sara asked when Elena didn't comment on her last statement. Sara glanced up at the kitchen clock, a cuckoo clock that had kept Elena awake the first couple of nights she'd been home. Now she never heard it. "He's not going to be very impressed with you showing up this late for work."

"Lucky for me he had to go out of town early this morning. He wasn't sure when he'd be back. Once I get there, I'll see what I can do to get his books organized."

Sara pushed herself up from her chair. "Let me make you some breakfast, honey. It will help you, I promise."

Elena nodded mutely. The thought of food was repugnant, but she knew she needed something on her stomach to get her started.

Hours later she was grateful that her mother had known

just what to feed a queasy stomach. Then again, she'd probably had a great deal of practice over the years feeding Elena's father.

Once she'd gotten the computer set up and running and installed the proper programs, she was able to set up several accounts for Joe.

Her only moment of emotional turmoil was when she walked into the bedroom later that day. The telltale rumpled sheets and the indentations on both pillows testified to what had happened there the night before, forcing her to face her own actions in the clear light of day and without alcohol in her system.

She'd made love with one of the suspects in her case. Had she jeopardized her assignment? At the time she had felt that making love with Joe was more important than anything else. The irony of her situation didn't escape her. She could well remember her attitude toward the men she'd worked with over the years, wondering why their sex life was such an important topic of conversation. She realized that until last night, where any discussion about the joys of a healthy sex life was concerned, she'd been like a person who was tone deaf, wondering what all the excitement was about during a symphony.

Well, now she could understand. Oh, boy, could she ever. She was already wondering when Joe would return and how long after that before they would be back in this bed. There were so many things she wanted to do with him, so many ways she wanted to experience him, so many ways she wanted to give him pleasure.

So what did that make her? A hypocrite at the very least. And a definite late bloomer in this area.

Elena quickly stripped the bed and made it with fresh sheets she found in the linen closet. She dumped the dirty sheets into the washing machine in the alcove off the kitchen and, in a fit of atonement, went through every room of the house using the professional techniques she'd been taught looking for any evidence that might help to incriminate Joe.

When she turned up nothing, she felt such a profound sense of relief that she was almost giddy with it. Joe couldn't be involved. Hadn't she known that on some level?

With a renewed sense of well-being, she went back to work on the computer, carefully posting everything she found, including his checkbook and bank statements for the past several months.

By the end of the day, she was caught up with everything that she could post without getting some clarification from Joe.

That night she went home, fell asleep early and dreamed about making love to Joe.

"So you don't think Joe Sanchez has anything to hide," Chris repeated the following week during their regularly scheduled meeting.

They were seated across from each other at a small table in an anonymous room of another major hotel in San Antonio.

"The only thing I've come up with is his connection to Cisco Delgado. A person can't be held responsible for the behavior of a relative. At least I hope not," she added, thinking of some of the things her father used to do and say.

"Well, the trucks coming through during the past week were all Delgado's and, despite intensive searches, we haven't been able to turn up a thing," Chris said with real disgust. "If he's smuggling, he's got us all stumped as to how he's doing it. We've practically torn his trucks apart, unloaded merchandise, checked for concealed doors, false roofs and floorings. It looks as though he is what he says he is.''

"Did you spot Joe Sanchez on any of those runs?"

Chris nodded. "Yep. I didn't let him see me. He was searched. He even helped the Border Patrol unload his truck without complaint."

They looked at each other. "What do you suppose this means?" she finally asked.

"You want my theory?" Chris said, finishing off a can of soda. She nodded. "I think we've proved that somebody in the Border Patrol or DEA knows exactly what shipments to concentrate on and which ones to ignore."

If an employee of one of the law-enforcement agencies was taking bribes, it wouldn't be the first time, but it was really tough on the rest of them. The lure of large amounts of cash could be tempting to some, irresistible to others. No matter how closely people were monitored, there would always be a way to get away with accepting bribes. At least for a while.

"Nobody said this job was going to be easy," Elena said, staring out the window.

"Well, I have a plan," Chris said with a grin. "I've filled my boring days and nights coming up with different scenarios of how I'd do it if I were working this operation."

"And—?"

"I'd have everyone tied up at one particular border crossing checking each and every truck coming across. Meanwhile, I'd have a much smaller load going across upriver somewhere, say, there in Santiago."

"Is there a way we could watch the smaller places on the border without being spotted by either the Mexican authorities or a possible Border Patrol agent who's work-ing with the smugglers?''

He grinned. ''How about having your boyfriend—me—show up unexpectedly to visit, and you show him around your hometown? It would give me a reason to be there, and I could be the typical nosy tourist going into Mexico for souvenirs.''

''I suppose that might work,'' she said slowly, wonder-ing how she would explain Chris's presence to Joe.

''I've already run the idea past Sam, and he thinks it's worth trying. He told me to coordinate the details with you. So you'll need to let me know when and how to show up.''

On her way back to Santiago from San Antonio, Elena wrestled with her conscience over what needed to be done to get this particular assignment concluded.

If they could catch the smugglers in the act and she could prove that Joe had nothing to do with any of it, then she would feel justified in keeping all this from him. She couldn't jeopardize the work being done or the lives of the men involved by letting him know her real reason for be-ing in Texas. Therefore the sooner they caught the smug-glers the better.

She had hoped that Joe would be back by now, but when she drove by his house on her way home, his truck wasn't there. There was nothing more she could do at his home until he returned. Restless, she turned around in his drive-way and went home.

Ten days later Joe let himself into his house. The neigh-borhood was quiet at two in the morning. He hoped it would stay that way. He was beat.

He flipped on the kitchen light and looked around. The place was spotless, much cleaner than when he'd left. He

checked the dining room and found that it had been turned
into an office. There was a small filing cabinet in the corner that hadn't been there earlier. The computer had its
own desk and chair now. The printer sat ready, its tray
filled with paper.

He walked over and picked up a file lying beside the
computer. Inside were various statements and invoices
with self-sticking notes attached, various questions scrib-
bled on them, all starting with "ask Joe."

When he walked into the bedroom, he stopped and
stared. There were new prints hanging on his formerly bare
walls, a new bedspread with matching curtains at the window and a small throw rug beside the bed.

She'd turned the room into a comfortable restful place
in which to sleep.

He sat down on the chair and untied his boots, tossing
them into the corner of the room. Then he stripped and
went into the bathroom. A new shower curtain greeted
him, and there was a matching set of rugs by the side of
the tub and around the commode.

Joe stood under the stinging spray of the shower, trying
to wash off the bone-tiredness that he felt after more than
two weeks away from home.

He squeezed his burning eyes shut, knowing that lack
of sleep had caused them to be bloodshot. He'd spent a
lot of sleepless nights while he was away. He was eaten
up with guilt.

He'd vowed that he wouldn't get involved with anyone
while he was here. The last thing he needed was to welcome Elena back into his life just now.

However, spending an entire day with her had made him
lose sight of his ultimate goal, and he'd succumbed to his
dreams of making love to her as an adult, rather than a
randy teenager.

Unfortunately making love to her hadn't helped his concentration in the least. He found himself reliving that night with her no matter where he was or what he was doing.

Coming home to find that she had added some much-needed feminine touches to his bachelor existence made him realize that he had placed himself in an untenable situation. This was not the time in his life when he could work on a relationship. Getting involved with Elena could jeopardize everything he was doing.

He hated the fact that he was lying to her, that he was pretending to be something he wasn't. He couldn't help but wonder what she might do if and when she found out the truth.

# Eight

Joe woke up the next morning to the smell of fresh coffee. He felt as though he'd been pulled from some deep and dark place by the enticing aroma, irresistibly luring him to consciousness much too soon. He groaned and sat up in bed, holding his head with both hands.

The shades and new draperies had kept the light from coming into his bedroom. When he looked at his bedside digital clock, the red numbers showed that it was after ten o'clock.

He reached for his jeans and pulled them on, went into the bathroom to splash water on his face, then continued into the kitchen. Sure enough, a full pot of coffee sat on the kitchen counter, beckoning to him.

He poured himself a cup and was just turning away from the counter when he heard Elena's voice.

"So you're awake at last."

He almost spilled his coffee, jerking around to see her.

She stood in the doorway to the dining room, wearing a pair of cutoffs and a sleeveless shirt that hung almost to the hems of the cutoffs. He was suddenly reminded that he hadn't bothered to fasten his jeans, letting the zipper hold them together just enough to be barely decent.

"You should have gotten me up," he said, wondering if she noticed that just the sight of her had brought his body to full alert.

"You looked tired when I peeked in on you earlier," she said with a sweet smile.

"And you look wonderful," he muttered, no longer interested in his coffee. He placed the cup on the counter and in a few strides was across the room. He gathered her into his arms and kissed her with all the passion and intensity that had been stored up since he'd left.

Her open response was all he needed to slide his hands beneath her bottom and walk them toward his bedroom, her feet dangling several inches from the floor, without breaking the kiss.

He released her over the bed and, by the time she'd stopped bouncing slightly, he had shucked his jeans and was lying between her legs, pulling at her shorts. She was laughing breathlessly at his eagerness, and her eyes widened when he paused long enough to reach into the drawer of the bedside table and pull out a new box of condoms.

He fished one out of the box and she helped him remove the foil. A few seconds later he was imbedded deep inside her.

He rested on his elbows and looked down at her. "Did I remember to say good morning?" he asked softly before kissing her deeply once again, his body setting up a lazy rhythm of its own.

He closed his eyes. This was where he wanted to spend the rest of his life. If only life was so simple.

When he lifted his head so that they could draw breath, she replied, "It certainly is a good morning. I'm very pleased to see you back."

He quickly unfastened her shirt and whisked off the bra beneath it, then nuzzled her breasts with a sigh of pleasure. He licked first one tip, then the other. He loved to feel her response when he touched her. Her face was flushed a rosy hue, her eyes sparkling. If he hadn't admitted it to himself before, Joe now knew that he loved this woman more than he could have thought possible.

He fought to hang on until he felt the first convulsive spasms that signaled her climax before he allowed himself to go over the edge into the sensual free fall of his own completion.

They lay there in bed for several minutes, calming their breathing, before she said, "I left the back door open. I hope you aren't expecting company anytime soon."

"If anyone shows up, I'll tell them to come back later—much later," he replied, his hands moving over her, exploring every curve and indentation, already feeling himself grow hard once again. He couldn't seem to get enough of her.

This woman would be the death of him.

Several hours later his stomach growled insistently. They both laughed.

"I doubt there's any food in there," he said. "Why don't we go over to Rosie's for something to eat? At least we won't have to worry about running into the lunch crowd at this hour."

He rolled off the bed and walked into the bathroom. After turning on the shower, he went back to the bedroom and hauled her out of bed. "Come on, we can save time and shower together before I keel over from hunger. You've made me weak-kneed, woman."

"I doubt that," she said, looking him up and down spec-ulatively. She patted a particularly sensitive part of his anatomy. "I'm pleased that all of you was so eager to see me." She sauntered into the bathroom and stepped into the tub without looking at him.

Her light touch performed a miracle. A part of him that he'd have thought beyond recovery had sprung to life once again. He shook his head in wonderment before following her into the shower.

By the time they were seated at Rosie's, he was certain that what he was feeling was far beyond lust. For an instant he imagined himself proposing to her—before he reminded himself that he wasn't in a position to marry anyone, even the love of his life.

They were halfway through their meal when she said, "You're awfully quiet. Did I really exhaust you that much?"

He shook his head and smiled. "Not you. Just the sched-ule I've been on. Cisco has kept me really busy, but at least he pays well." He took another bite of his steak.

"Oh? I wouldn't think a driver would make very much."

He shrugged. "He knows that I have my own business to take care of, so he compensates me for that, as well. Of course I couldn't retire on what he pays, but he's more than fair."

She waited until they were indulging themselves with some of Rosie's fantastic lemon meringue pie before Elena said, "There's something I need to discuss with you."

Now that he had some food inside him, Joe was feeling much better. Not quite so desperate. More willing to let things happen as they needed to.

"You've found another job," he guessed, taking a sip of coffee.

"No. Although actually I don't have much to do for you now. Maybe when you've opened the accumulated mail, there'll be some bills to pay and money to deposit."

"Okay, I give up. What do you need to discuss with me?"

He was very pleased with his world right now. He doubted there was anything she could tell him that would disturb his sense of well-being, unless... He carefully set his cup down before he leaned forward and murmured, "You're pregnant, aren't you?" Why hadn't he thought to ask her first thing? How could he have let the idea sink into the background of his thoughts until now?

She shook her head. "No, I'm not. I found out last week, but of course there was no way to let you know." She flushed and he realized that she was suddenly ill at ease.

"Then what is it?" he asked in a low voice, reaching for her hand.

"This is really awkward for me, Joe. I want you to know that there's really nothing between us—we're just friends—I mean we've been friends for years and..."

He felt a constriction in his chest at her words. "Are you talking about you and me?"

She blinked in surprise. "No! I'm talking about Chris Simmons."

"Who the hell is Chris Simmons!" He fought not to raise his voice and cause the other customers to notice them.

She frowned. "I just told you. He's a friend of mine. I've known him a long time and, well, he's in town visiting me," she finished in a rush.

"He's here? In Santiago? When did he get here?"

"A few days ago. I don't remember when exactly." Her face was still flushed and she wouldn't meet his eyes.

"He's staying at the hotel downtown. That should keep his stay short," she added, working to make a joke out of this new development in their relationship.

"I see," he finally replied. "Any particular reason he chose to come here—that is, since you're just friends and all?"

"I didn't ask him. Believe me, I was just as surprised as you when he called from San Antonio and said he'd gotten my number from mutual friends in Maryland and decided to look me up. He said he's never been to Texas before. So I've been showing him around the area, doing the tourist thing with him."

He eyed her for a couple of minutes without speaking. He could feel his animosity toward a complete stranger grow. What was the matter with him, anyway? Did he think she'd spent all these years without making friends?

"Where is he today?" he finally asked.

"I'm not sure. He said something about going over to Mexico and doing some shopping for souvenirs to take back home with him."

"Then it was just a coincidence that you happened to be at the house this morning when I woke up."

She shook her head. "Actually it wasn't. I've been driving over every day to see if your truck was back. When I saw you were there this morning, I figured you might have something for me to do." Her face went red once again.

He grinned. "And you were right. See what a good assistant you've turned out to be?"

Rosie walked over to the table and asked, "Is there anything else I can get for you, folks?"

Elena laughed. "Maybe some assistance to get me out of this booth. If I keep eating your cooking, I'm not going to be able to get into my clothes for much longer."

Rosie laughed and took their empty plates away after refilling their cups with coffee.

"So when am I going to meet this guy?" he asked after Rosie walked away.

She shrugged. "I don't know. I'm not sure how much longer he'll be here."

"The next time he calls you, why don't you bring him over?"

She nodded. "Sure."

They stood and Joe pulled out his wallet. He threw some bills on the table as a tip, then walked over to the cash register at the end of the counter. Elena didn't follow him. Instead, she waited for him outside the door.

*So this is what jealousy feels like,* he thought, feeling a little sheepish. What would cause a mature male who had no claim on a woman to feel so possessive of her? He paid for lunch and turned toward the door. She was peering off into the distance, looking pensive. He paused as though seeing her for the first time.

Maybe it was a trick of his imagination, but she looked totally alone, as though her life had been spent that way. Despite how she responded to him or how happy she appeared to be about his return, he suddenly realized that there was something about her he couldn't quite figure out.

It wasn't a wall, exactly, certainly not like the one he'd slammed into the first night he'd seen her back in Santiago. He shook his head. He must be imagining things.

He pushed open the door and stepped outside. "Ready to get back to the house?"

She turned and smiled, but the smile never reached her eyes. "Sure. I've got some questions for you."

He draped his arm around her shoulders and amiably replied, "I've got all kinds of answers. Pick whichever one you want."

\* \* \*

Elena tapped lightly on the hotel door late that evening. Chris opened it and she stepped inside without a word. This room was smaller than the ones they'd used in San Antonio. The hotel was much older than the new ones built along the River Walk.

She sat down on the edge of the bed and looked at him. "Find anything?"

He sprawled in the only chair. "Maybe. I'm not sure."

She sighed. "Sanchez is back."

He nodded.

"He wants to meet you."

"Me?" He looked at her, puzzled. "How does he know about me?"

"I told you that I'd have to explain your presence here before someone happened to mention seeing me around town with you while he was gone. You've forgotten how quickly news travels in a small town like this."

"Do you think he'd introduce me to Delgado?"

Her laugh showed no amusement. "Somehow I doubt it. He didn't seem too pleased that you'd come to visit me."

He raised his brow. "Really? Is he getting a little possessive of his new help?"

"Possibly."

"Or is it more than that?"

She stared at him. "What's that supposed to mean?"

"You seem different somehow. I can't put my finger on it. In D.C. you were always so goal-oriented. Here you seem softer and—" he looked at her shorts and shirt "—a hell of a lot sexier. First time I've had a chance to admire those legs of yours, Maldonado. Is this your secret weapon?"

"Very funny."

"Is this assignment getting to you?" he asked quietly.

She looked away. "I'm dealing with it, but yeah, I'll be glad to have it over. I don't like lying to my mother about why I'm here. She's making plans as if she thinks I'll end up getting married and living here for the rest of my life."

"Getting married? To Sanchez?"

"I suppose. She knows I spend time with him. I'm not seeing anyone else. She's managed to put two and two together to get five." She pushed her fingers through her hair. "She keeps dropping these not-so-subtle hints about grandchildren, for Pete's sake."

Chris laughed. "Mothers have a tendency to do that, you know."

"Yours, too?"

He nodded. "Yeah, but I told her that since I knew you'd never marry me, I'd never find another woman who would be able to take your place in my life." He attempted to look soulfully rejected, but didn't quite manage to pull it off.

She sprung off the bed as though propelled. "You did what?"

He was laughing so hard at her immediate and strong reaction that he doubled over. "I'm kidding! I'm kidding!" he managed to say. "I've never seen you so touchy in all my life, Elena. Lighten up a little, okay?"

She shook her head in disgust and sank back onto the bed. "You've got a weird sense of humor, Simmons, you know that?"

"But you love me, anyway, right?"

"Please. Enough already."

His smile faded and he said, "I am concerned about you, though. I've seen the strain you've been under. I don't think Wilder had any idea what he was sending you into when he assigned this case to you."

"I'm handling it."

"But not without a struggle. Okay. That's all I'm going to say." He picked up a folder from the small table beside him. "Since I've been in town, here's what I've seen going on at the bridge." He began to describe how the shifts on either side of the bridge worked, how many personnel worked each side and the amount of traffic that passed through between midnight and six o'clock in the morning. "Coordinating that information with the reports from the other agents on the main road, I would say that at least one vehicle crossed here two nights ago that was not checked. There was a seven-minute window—both sides just happened to be looking the other way—when an unmarked truck came through."

"Did you have the truck stopped?"

"Yep, about fifteen miles north of here, but the truck was clean and the driver was alone. We think he'd already made his drop by the time he got to us."

"What makes you think this one was different?"

"The driver's surprise that he was stopped. He kept asking who we were, what authority we had to stop him. He wouldn't give us any information about the owner of the truck or what he was doing coming across with nothing in his truck."

"Did he see you?"

"No. The rest of our team was there. Since I wanted to stay here for a while longer, I figured it would be better if no one recognized me."

"Is he one of Delgado's men?"

"The truck was registered to one of Delgado's companies."

"Did you take the driver into custody?"

"Couldn't. We had no reason. His papers checked out. We let him go, but I also think we scared him into believing that their backup plan wasn't working as well as they'd hoped. I think we're making them nervous. In that case, they may mess up."

"It will only take once and we'll get them," she said. "I hope it's soon."

"Yeah. Your late-spring weather is getting a little too warm for me."

She grinned. "Haven't you heard? When a Texan dies and there's a chance he might go to hell, he packs an overcoat to make sure he's comfortable down there."

She stood and stretched. "I've got to get some sleep. Keep me posted. I'll make plans for you to meet Joe at the local café in the next couple of days if that's okay with you."

"Sure, whatever you say."

She nodded and quietly left the room. The lobby was deserted when she got off the creaking elevator, which was just as well. Being seen leaving the hotel by one of the locals wouldn't do her reputation much good.

Once on the street, she walked the half block to where her Jeep was parked, got in and headed out of town.

She didn't see Joe sitting in his truck on the side street nearest the hotel when she pulled away.

# Nine

Elena finished posting the current week's receipts and invoices into the computer and leaned back in her chair with a sigh of satisfaction.

Joe had been home for three weeks. During that time she'd done her job of keeping the postings up-to-date during the day. Her evenings and part of each night she spent in his bed.

She'd also arranged a meeting between Chris and Joe. Both men were polite, but there was a tension in the air that she decided was probably her imagination. Chris left a few days later.

Elena noticed that since meeting Chris, Joe's lovemaking had been more intense, more possessive, almost frenzied at times, as though he wanted to claim her as his. She concentrated her energies on him when they were together, but whenever they weren't, she was filled with despair.

She knew very well that this relationship could go nowhere, even if Joe wasn't a part of her investigation. She had lied to him. She had made him believe that she had moved to Santiago permanently. Everything about her was a lie, except for the fact that she was in love with him.

He was the first man she'd ever loved, or at least been infatuated with. Once she left, she knew she would not allow herself to become involved with anyone else.

She'd known for the past several days that there was no longer any reason for her to stay in Santiago. She'd filed her report setting out everything she'd done to find evidence to prove Joe was involved with smuggling. Her written conclusion was that he was doing nothing illegal.

Chris and the other agents were following leads that looked promising, and she needed to join them now that her work was finished here. The problem was that she hadn't been able to tell Joe she was leaving.

Immediately after breaking the news to her mother that morning that she'd accepted another position in the East, she had arrived at Joe's with the intention of giving him the same news. The first problem had been that he was already under a truck working on it. Then he'd had some problems and left to go to the auto-parts store.

Finally she'd decided to wait and see how the rest of the day developed before attempting to make any decisions. She still didn't know how she was going to explain to Joe that, despite everything they had shared, she was going off in pursuit of her career goals.

It was true that he had never told her he loved her. Nor had he ever hinted that he wanted their relationship to become permanent. And yet she knew that what they shared was important to him. Maybe it was better that neither of them had revealed their feelings to the other.

Perhaps they would both look back someday and be grateful for the time they'd spent exploring their sensuous natures. She knew that she had learned a great deal about herself from this time with Joe.

She'd learned that she would never want another man to touch her.

She'd learned that she would never love another man.

She also knew that her commitment to her chosen profession came before her personal feelings. That was the toughest lesson of all to acknowledge to herself.

During the time she'd been with him, she'd discovered a lot about Joe that he probably wouldn't want others to know. However, there was nothing illegal about anything she had learned.

For example, she'd found out that half the people in town owed him money, but that if they were having a difficult time making ends meet, he would have her hold their invoice, saying he would send it later. Sometimes he told her to cancel a debt.

He had one sixteen-year-old, a distant relative of his, doing his yard work to pay for the rear-end work Joe had done on the teenager's wreck of a car.

She shook her head with a smile. She was thinking about nominating him for sainthood any day now.

No wonder the Border Patrol found him to be suspicious, she thought with a touch of cynicism. This guy could be making big bucks working in a large city, so what was he doing living in this sorry excuse for a town?

His excuse that he was looking after his mother was commendable. She had learned that it was also accurate.

He generally took a break sometime around the middle of the morning and went into town. When he came back with mail from the post office, he usually had some home-baked goods from his mom, which meant he found a reason to check on her every day.

She was staring blindly at the computer when she heard

the back screen door slam and the sound of boots crossing the kitchen floor. She smiled to herself as she heard the refrigerator door open, close and then the sound of a can of soda hissing as the top was popped open.

She wasn't surprised when Joe appeared in the doorway between the two rooms and leaned against the doorjamb. He looked hot, dirty and disgusted.

"Having a bad morning?" she asked with tenderness.

He rubbed his arm across his forehead, leaving another streak of grease across his face.

He ignored her question to ask one of his own. "How are you doing in here?"

She spread her hands. "I'm finished. So if you want me to knock off for the rest of the day, I don't mind."

"Now that's the best idea I've heard in a long while," he said, tilting the can and letting the cold cola pour into his mouth.

Well, that was certainly to the point. This was obviously the time to tell him that he no longer needed her help. The timing couldn't have been more perfect. She leaned over and picked up her purse.

"Then I'll get out of here," she said.

He straightened and gave her an annoyed look. "You don't have to leave. You've just talked me into taking the rest of the day off. So why don't you come with me?"

She paused in feeling for her shoes with her toes. She knew her shoes were under the desk somewhere. "Come with you where?"

He grinned. "A place I know about that is cool and isolated and guaranteed to smooth the wrinkles of your day."

She eyed him warily. "Have you been drinking?"

He shook his head. "Nope. I've just been pushing to get caught up since I got back, and I'm tired of all this.

The great thing about being the boss is I can choose to take a day off once in a while. We'll swing by your place for your swimsuit, stop at Rosie's and grab something to take with us and run away together—at least for the afternoon.''

She could always say no. She could tell him what she'd arrived there earlier in the day prepared to say. But his offer was tempting. Perhaps after getting away for a few hours, he wouldn't think that she'd deserted him.

So she nodded and with a lightness she didn't feel said, ''I've got to admit that anything that might cool me off would be a priority today.''

He nodded without smiling. ''Then let's go.''

He walked past her and disappeared, heading toward his bedroom.

She turned off the computer, covered it and gave a last look around. It would be easy enough for him to pick up from where she had last posted. She'd made careful notes, explaining each step.

This was going to be tough for her in so many ways. But at least she could leave knowing that he was not involved in anything illegal.

She went through the kitchen and was at the back door when he reappeared, holding towels.

''Do you want to follow me so I can leave the Jeep at Mom's?''

''Sure,'' he said, walking out behind her.

''I'll see you at my place, then,'' she said.

The weather had certainly gotten hot this past week. Every time she spoke to Chris he gave her a hard time about the weather in her native state.

As she drove to her mother's place, she talked to her guilty conscience. She deserved one more day with Joe before she walked away from the love of her life. They would have a few more hours together, then she would find the strength to tell him that she was leaving.

By the time they were on the road out of town it was almost one o'clock. Rosie had packed a cardboard box full of food. The delectable aromas that filled the truck made Elena's mouth water with anticipation.

She glanced over at Joe. "I hope this place isn't too much farther. I didn't realize I was hungry until you got into the truck with the food. Whatever she put in there smells wonderful."

Joe must have washed up at Rosie's while she packed their food because his face was no longer decorated with streaks of oil and grease. He also looked considerably more relaxed now that they were headed out of town.

"This was a great idea," he said with a grin. "I'm glad you thought of it."

"Me?" she looked at him in surprise.

"Sure. When you said you had no reason to work today, I realized that I didn't have to, either." He glanced around at her. "You've been a tremendous help since you reappeared in my life. Have I remembered to mention that to you?"

She chuckled. "Only every day. I have to admit those first few days were fairly strenuous. Now that I have everything posted to your computer, though, you should do just fine without me."

"Is that your subtle way of quitting?"

She didn't respond right away. When she did speak, it was without directly answering him. "I don't like taking your money when I'm not doing much anymore."

There. She had planted the seed. Even though he'd given her the opportunity she'd been looking for all day, she knew that today was important to both of them. He had been putting in long hours and deserved a rest, and she wanted to spend one more day with him before she had to end their relationship.

He made no response and they rode along the highway in silence.

She wished that she could tell him the truth about why she'd come to Santiago and why she had to leave, but she couldn't. At least she could console herself with the fact that she had managed to clear his name. Removing him from suspicion was the secret gift she had been able to give him, although he would never know about it.

"Hang on," he said, interrupting her thoughts. "I'm going to be turning off the pavement shortly. From there on, it's going to be a rough road."

"Where are you taking me, anyway?" she asked, looking around. They had driven twenty or more miles from town.

"It's a place I stumbled across when I was a kid. I don't know who owns it or if it's part of state lands. I've never seen anyone around, so I've more or less adopted it as my own. If I had the money, I'd probably try to find out who holds the title and see if I could buy it. At the moment, though, coming out here once in a while works for me."

She was glad he had warned her about the road once they turned off the highway. Actually she thought he was being generous calling the cow path they were attempting to follow a road. She wouldn't dignify it by calling it a lane.

"Did you say no one else knows about this place?" she asked.

"I have no idea. I've never seen anyone else here. And you're the only person I've ever brought with me."

She continued to brace herself as they bounced along. When he finally pulled beneath a shade tree and stopped the truck, Elena gave a relieved sigh and looked around. There was a narrow stream of water flowing nearby, but she lost sight of it as it meandered around a hill to the left of them.

He got out and picked up the box of food. "Grab the towels and the rest of our things and follow me."

"Oh, boy, just what I wanted to do on a hot afternoon— go on a hiking expedition," she teased.

He was already striding away, following the stream. "You got it," he said without hesitating. "This is one time you're definitely going to earn your meal."

She ended up with her arms full of towels and the bag she'd brought containing her swimsuit and sunscreen, so she didn't spend much time looking at the scenery. She was too busy trying to keep up with his long strides and watching where she stepped.

She had no idea how far they'd walked when he paused and looked back at her. "How are you doing? We're almost there."

She looked ahead of them and saw a bluff that appeared to block their path. When she paused beside Joe, she saw, upon closer inspection, a trail that followed the stream into a cave. The entrance was grown over with sagebrush. Once inside, she had to duck to keep from hitting her head on the low ceiling. She could see light through a tunnel and moved forward.

"I can't believe you ever managed to find this place. No wonder no one ever comes here," she said, moving carefully.

Feeling a little like Alice in Wonderland, she continued until she stepped out of the cave and found that the path widened as it continued to follow the water. Then, just ahead of them was a grassy glade with a large pool of water formed by a waterfall cascading from the top of the bluff that extended around the glade.

"Oh, Joe, this is beautiful," she said softly. "It's like a miniature Eden."

He took the lead once again and within minutes he found the spot where he wanted them to stop. A huge shade tree was near the deep pool. He placed a large blanket on the grass beneath the tree, then sat down and began to unload the box of food.

Elena helped. She laughed as she saw how much Rosie had put in there. They had enough for three meals. There were two thermoses, one with water, another with lemonade. There was fried chicken, potato salad, coleslaw, pickles, and two huge chunks of chocolate cake.

"If I ate even a part of that, I'd be so heavy I'd sink to the bottom of the pool," she said.

"Then let's swim first, cool off, then eat and maybe nap a little."

Elena glanced around. Because of the bluffs and the foliage the place was secluded. She turned away to slip into her two-piece swimsuit. When she glanced around she saw that Joe was already in the water, swimming away from her in long powerful strokes that revealed the well-developed muscles in his shoulders. He reached the other side of the pool and flipped over onto his back. He floated with his eyes closed, a blissful expression on his face.

With a smile, Elena slipped into the water, finding it refreshingly cool. She shivered as the water caressed her too-warm skin. She swam away from Joe and headed toward the waterfall, which filled the area with a wonderfully refreshing mist.

"Was it worth the rough ride and long hike to get here?" she heard him ask when she finally came to a rest, treading water.

She laughed. "You know, you're always full of surprises. But yes, this is definitely worth it. I feel as though we're the only people who've ever been here."

"Yeah, that's how I always feel whenever I take the time to come out here. I have to admit it's been a long time. I'm glad nothing's changed."

He swam lazily toward her, causing her breath to hitch in her chest. There was something so predatory, so very male about him. She'd made love to him enough in the past few weeks to recognize that particular look on his face.

"You didn't wear a suit today, did you?" she asked, grinning at him.

"Nope."

"And yet you allowed me to be modest."

"I thought it better to be safe, just in case someone had stumbled across my private Eden. Besides, you look sexy as hell in that suit."

She slid her arms around his shoulders and hugged him. "Thank you for bringing me here."

"I would have done it sooner if I'd thought about it," he replied, letting his feet sink to the bottom of the pool. The water was chest high. She wrapped her legs around his waist, fully aware that the thin strip of material between her thighs was the only thing separating them.

He reached down and nudged it aside, then gently moved her down on him until he was fully inside her. She closed her eyes, not wanting to let him see how much his casual taking of her touched her to the very depths of her soul. They were so comfortable with each other. She was amazed at how close they'd become since she'd arrived.

She pulled herself up, the water helping her body's buoyancy, then slid down over him once again.

"Mmm," he said, nibbling her neck.

"At least that," she whispered, doing it again. She tightened her crossed ankles at his back and increased her pace until he took over, holding her as he rapidly moved deep within her. They both cried out at the same time and clung to each other for several minutes until she slipped away from him, moving closer to the waterfall. She hoped he would think any moisture on her face came from the mist.

"That wasn't too smart," he said a few minutes later, joining her under the cooling spray.

"What?"

"We've been so careful to use protection since that first time." He waved his hand at the blanket spread out on the shore. "I brought some with me, but once we were in the water I never gave it a thought."

He pulled her close and kissed her. When he raised his head, he said, "The thing is, Elena, I almost hope you do get pregnant."

"I, uh...maybe it won't happen," she replied, unable to believe that she could have forgotten something so important, as well. "I mean, this isn't the best time for me to get pregnant."

He kissed her again, then said, "Let's get something to eat, okay?"

She followed him out of the water, admiring his bare buns that were several shades lighter than the rest of his tanned body.

She watched him pick up a towel and quickly dry off before he pulled on his jeans. He sat down next to the food. She willingly joined him.

They were both sleepy by the time they'd eaten their fill. Joe lay down and patted his shoulder. She stretched out beside him and closed her eyes with a sigh. She'd grown used to falling asleep next to him at night. She wondered how she was going to face the rest of her life without him.

He woke her some time later when he stirred. She sat up and sleepily looked around. The sun was far into the western sky.

"I'm sorry to disturb you, but my arm had gone to sleep and was tingling," he said, rubbing his shoulder.

"No wonder. We must have been asleep a couple of hours or more."

He rolled over and tugged her back down beside him, then draped his arm and leg across her. "Are you in a hurry to get home?"

"I think we'd want daylight to help us find our way out of here."

"Or we could just stay here forever and forget about the rest of the world," he suggested softly.

"That sounds nice, doesn't it?"

"But not very practical." He smoothed her hair away from her face. "So tell me," he finally said.

She turned her head and looked at him. "Tell you what?"

"Whatever it is you've been avoiding discussing with me since you arrived this morning. I spent the whole morning thinking of different scenarios, not liking any of them. My concentration was shot and I kept skinning my knuckles. I finally decided to get the hell away from stubborn engines for a while and find out what's going on with you."

"Am I that obvious?" she finally asked.

"There was a sadness in your eyes I haven't seen before when you arrived this morning. So just tell me."

She took a couple of deep breaths before she said, "I've

accepted a job back East. I really couldn't turn them down. The problem is that they need me right away."

"So you really *were* telling me that you were quitting, weren't you?" he said after a long pause.

She closed her eyes and put her arms around him, burying her head in his shoulder.

"I don't really guess I'm all that surprised," he finally said. "You'd never be content living here all the time. I've always known that on some level."

"I wish I could explain," she said.

"You don't have to. I'm just glad that I've had this time with you. I'll never forget it."

She swallowed the tears that threatened to choke her. He wasn't trying to talk her into staying—not that she could, but he didn't know that—and he wasn't asking her to marry him. Maybe he'd never thought of her in that way.

He released her and sat up. "You're right. We'd better head back so we don't get lost in the dark."

They put the food away in silence. Elena folded the blanket and towels, and they started their trek away from their beautiful little spot without saying anything more.

*It's better this way,* she told herself several times on the way back. He'd taken it better than she had hoped. Maybe—secretly—she'd hoped he would protest more.

Once in the truck, he pulled her closer to him even though he needed both hands on the steering wheel to control the truck over the rough trail. It was completely dark by the time they reached the highway. He put his arm around her and held her until they reached her mother's house.

It was after he pulled up in front of her house and turned off the headlights that he turned to her and said, "There's no reason to lie to me, you know. I've never asked any more of you than you were willing to give. I've never tried to make a claim on you.''

"What do you mean, lie to you?" she said, her heart leaping in her chest.

"I know why you're leaving, Elena. I'm not that stupid.''

His words sent a wave of panic over her. He couldn't possibly know. There was no way anyone could have told him. Finally she said, "I'm afraid I don't know what you're talking about.''

He sighed. "You don't think I'm capable of connecting the dots? Everything was fine with you until your so-called friend, Chris, showed up. Now you suddenly have a job that will take you back to him. You see, I know you were with him while he was here. I saw you come out of his hotel a couple of times after you had been with me.''

"You followed me?"

He nodded. "I needed to know. I waited for you to tell me, and then I realized you had no intention of mentioning it. I finally figured out that this was your way of paying me back for what happened when we were kids. You thought I led you on because of some kind of stupid bet. When you saw an opportunity to get back at me, you took it.''

She stared at him in disbelief. "Is that what you think?"

"Yeah, that's what I know.''

"And you continued to make love with me, believing that?''

"At first, I kept expecting you to confess. In fact, I was hoping that was what you intended to tell me today, but as soon as I saw your face when I asked if you were quitting, I began to think it was more than admitting you've been using me ever since you got here.''

"It's not like that at all, Joe.''

"Then tell me what it is like."

She stared at him and knew that the pain she was feeling was her heart splintering into little pieces. "I can't," she finally said.

"Then you don't mind if I draw my own conclusions, I hope?" he asked, opening his door and walking around to help her out.

"Joe," she said, once they were at the front door. "You never answered me. If you didn't trust me, why did you continue to make love to me?"

He looked at her for a long while before his lips finally formed a half smile. "It was worth it."

He turned around and walked away.

# Ten

*Four Months Later*

**"D**amn, Elena," Chris complained, "I'll be glad when this case is finished and we're back in Washington. I've never seen you so depressed."

They were sitting in her Jeep on some deserted road not far from the Rio Grande. If their information was correct, tonight they were going to get the evidence they'd been working so hard to obtain for the past six months.

"I'm not depressed," she said, lying through her teeth. "I'm just tired. I know Wilder expected us to take this long, but I'd hoped to be able to be through in no more than three months. If we pull this off tonight, maybe we'll be home in time for Thanksgiving."

"Do you plan to spend the holiday with your mother?"

She shook her head. "No. She thinks I'm back in Maryland. I told her I couldn't get away so soon after starting a new job.''

''Getting tired of the lies, aren't you?''

She shook her head. ''It's all part of the job. I just need a vacation, that's all.''

''Sounds good. If you had the time, where would you go?''

Before she could answer, her hand-held radio crackled. ''Here they come,'' Sam Walters said softly.

She and Chris left the Jeep where it was parked and started moving on foot toward the road through the mesquite, sagebrush and cacti.

Elena was proud of the work they'd done on this assignment. They had proof that three agents were taking bribes, keeping the other side fully informed of what was happening along the border. In addition, they'd been able to trace the payoffs to high in the INS office. What they hoped to get tonight was the evidence needed to prove their case.

Now they understood why cargo was moving across undetected. The authorities had been fed the wrong information to keep them away from the actual places where trucks were crossing.

It was a well-thought-out plan. The smugglers had gotten to key personnel. As far as they knew, no one north of the border had any idea of the route being taken tonight.

Two of Sam Walters's team had managed to get close enough to employees of the two suspected factories in Mexico to find out when they intended to come north. They'd signaled the rest of the team several hours ago that the trucks were en route.

Because of the need for secrecy, no other authorities had been notified. They weren't sure at this point whom they could trust. Once the leaders were arrested, they would call

for backup and reinforcement, but for now, their team was
on its own.

The two men in Mexico had waited until the trucks were
headed north, then beat them to the border by a couple of
hours. At least the whole crew was here, ready for action.

She could hear the rumble of the trucks coming toward
them. Adrenaline had taken over. She could feel the fear
seeping out her pores. This was considerably different
from working in the office with her computer every day.

The first driver wouldn't see the roadblock until he
swung around the sharp curve. By that time, the third and
last truck would be in place so that a roadblock could be
quickly put in place behind them, preventing possible escape.

They were all wearing bulletproof vests and reinforced
helmets to gain as much protection as possible. There
should be two men in the cab of each truck.

According to Chris, Sam had asked the local police to
be on standby, explaining that there might be a problem
with capturing the men they were looking for. He hadn't
explained who they were or that the suspects would be
coming from Mexico. It was the only way to protect
sources and not have information leaking to dirty cops.

She and Chris waited in the brush beside the road. They
could see two of the other men across the way. The roadblock would look like an accident at first, a pile of brush
that could have fallen off a truck or been blown into the
road.

Sure enough, as soon as the first truck came around the
bend, the driver saw the barrier in the road even though
he was traveling without headlights. She heard the driver's
exclamation as he stopped the truck. There was a brief
conversation before he and another man got out. The second truck was now stopped and the third one slowing

down. She knew the second roadblock was quickly being moved into place.

Then everything seemed to happen at once.

Bright lights and a bullhorn sounded from the road ahead of them. She spun around in time to see trucks filled with soldiers driving through the brush from several directions, headed directly toward them.

"What the hell?" Chris said incredulously. "Who the hell are these people?"

The man on the bullhorn was saying, "Get out of the trucks with your hands up. Move carefully and nobody will be hurt. Move carefully—"

That's when she heard the first shot. It was immediately followed by a fusillade of bullets.

She and Chris dropped to the ground and rolled toward cover, their weapons in their hands. With the sounds of screams, shots and yelling all around them, she never expected to get out alive. Her only fleeting thought was of Joe. She wished she had told him that her love for him had never been a lie.

Within minutes the area was secured, the firing stopped. The men still standing by the trucks were being rounded up. She heard Sam demanding to know who was in charge of the soldiers.

A lieutenant colonel in camouflage stepped forward. "Colonel Grady Davis. What in the world are you people doing out here tonight?"

Sam showed him his credentials. "I could ask you the same thing, sir!" Sam replied. "We've been working this case for months. They're moving drugs, as well as aliens, across the border and we've managed to catch them in the act."

"Begging your pardon, sir, but that isn't the only thing they've been moving. They've been using this route to smuggle arms banned in the U.S. into the country, most of which were stolen from our military.'' He motioned with his head. ''See for yourself.''

She turned and watched as the back doors of the trucks were opened. Soldiers were handing down wooden crates. One of them was opened and she spotted assault weapons.

''Too bad we weren't able to work together on this, Colonel,'' she heard Sam say. ''We had no way of knowing you were in the area.''

''I think we're both a little too good at our jobs. Because we hadn't received any sign that you were here, either.''

Chris came running up to her. ''Elena, you'd better come with me.''

She spun around. ''Oh, no. Did one of our men get hit?'' she asked, racing after him as he headed back toward the trucks.

''Actually, two of them, but neither is life-threatening. Johnson was hit in the leg, Farnsworth in the arm. But that's not the problem.'' He slowed to a walk and nodded to where several soldiers were working over someone lying on the ground. ''One of the truck drivers got hit. He's in pretty bad shape.''

''I'm sorry to hear about it, Chris, but we had no control over the firing. Maybe he was the one who started shooting first. Whoever started it set off a mini war there for a few minutes.''

Chris stopped and grabbed her arm. ''It's Joe Sanchez, Elena. I thought you'd want to know.''

She stared at him numbly. A part of her was screaming, *No, no, it can't be. Not Joe. He wouldn't be here. I cleared him. He's no longer a suspect. It can't be Joe.*

She reached the group and discovered that there were several men down. Medics were moving among them, cleaning wounds, bandaging, starting drips and preparing to load them into one of the army trucks to be taken to the nearest hospital.

She fell to her knees beside Joe. Despite all the medics could do, he continued to bleed from a wound in his chest. He lay there with his eyes closed, unaware of anything around him.

*I was wrong all along* was all she could think. Joe had been working with Delgado on the shipment of weapons, as well as drugs. She'd let her feelings for him blind her to the truth.

She'd never guessed, even after he'd left to work for Delgado that time. Hadn't Chris said something about his being part of a group that had been stopped? But they hadn't found anything then.

She'd never found anything, either. There had been no sign of unusual wealth. No sign of any illegal activity.

But he was here. That was all the evidence that was needed.

She couldn't stop the tears. She no longer cared what her group or the soldiers thought of her. They'd been successful in catching the smugglers in the act. She knew that as soon as the area had been secured, Sam Walters had contacted Wilder in Washington to arrest the men who'd been under surveillance for the past few months.

Francisco Delgado would be picked up, as well.

The mission had been a success.

Elena knelt in the dirt beside Joe. The calls, the shouts, the conversations all faded from around her. She was there with Joe, who had turned out to be one of the enemy, after all.

Someone had covered him with a blanket and propped his head with a jacket. They'd ripped off his shirt to work on his wound, and they already had an IV drip going into his arm.

She picked up his hand and held it. "Oh, Joe," she whispered, "I'm so sorry."

From the headlights of the army trucks, she saw his lashes flicker, and then he opened his eyes. He stared into the night sky before focusing on her face.

"'Lena," he said in a slurred voice. "Wha'... doin'...?"

"I could ask you the same thing. Oh, Joe, what made you do it? I thought you'd be safe."

He closed his eyes.

Her tears fell faster.

"Pardon me, ma'am. We need to get him into the truck." She looked up and saw two soldiers with a stretcher. She stepped back and watched them lift him onto the stretcher, carefully moving him to the truck. Within minutes all the wounded were loaded and the truck pulled away.

When she stood and looked around, Elena saw that the local police were now on the scene. They were taking the uninjured drivers to vans and placing them inside, while the soldiers loaded box after box of weapons and ammunition into their trucks.

She heard Sam speak to the chief of police. "It looks like we did pretty well tonight, Chief Crossett. Thank you for your help."

"Hell, Agent Walters, you didn't need my help. You got half the U.S. Army crawling all over the place." He stood with his hands on his hips, looking around the area and shaking his head.

"We had no idea they were bringing up weapons from the interior, Chief," Sam said. "They must have been on the trucks when they arrived at the factories, because our agents never saw any sign of them. From what I can gather, the army's been working its own operation independently. This was a case where the right hand didn't know what the left hand was doing.''

"Who started the shooting?" Crossett asked.

"I don't know. Maybe one of the men in the trucks. For a time I wondered if we were going to have a massacre out here."

"Well, we'll have the drivers ready for the feds to pick up first thing tomorrow."

"Thank you."

"Did you get the ringleaders you were hoping to find?"

Sam nodded. "I was radioed that they picked up Delgado without incident. He was home asleep. Hope the judge knows to hold him without bail, or we'll never see him again."

"How about the others?"

"I understand a couple members of the Border Patrol didn't take too kindly to being picked up. They're both in the hospital under guard."

Elena could no longer stay quiet. "What about the ones taken to the hospital from here?"

The chief spoke up. "Two of my men led the army truck to the nearest hospital. We'll make certain nobody leaves."

"I need to know what hospital. I knew one of those men," she said.

"Really? Now there's a coincidence."

"Not really. I grew up in Santiago and went to school with him."

"That's a shame. It's always harder when you happen to know them."

She stared off down the road that was now emptying of all vehicles. "Yes, sir, it certainly is."

Elena finally managed to get to the hospital the morning of the second day after the successful raid. She'd spent

most of the previous day helping with the paperwork and
working with Sam, who was busy soothing the feelings of
agencies that had been left out of the informational loop.

Sam had assigned her some of the duty explaining that
out of fear of a leak, their group had been ordered not to
share information with any other agency. She left unsaid
that after all this time, it was their small group that had
managed to get the hard evidence needed to put the smugglers behind bars.

She wasn't looking forward to seeing Joe behind bars.
Nor did she feel particularly proud that she had helped to
put him there.

*We all have choices,* she reminded herself. Joe had made
his for reasons she would probably never understand. She
thought back to that last afternoon they had spent together.
She had been so tempted to tell him the truth about her
reason for being there. She'd come so close to throwing
her career away by exposing a covert operation to a civil-
ian.

If she had, Delgado would have been warned and their
entire operation during these past several months would
have ended up a waste of time, energy and money.

She pulled up in front of the hospital in Corpus Christi,
where the more seriously wounded had been airlifted
within hours of the shootings.

She walked into the cool building, glad to be out of the
sun. Spotting the information desk, she walked over and
asked where she could find Joe Sanchez. The young volunteer checked her screen, then shook her head. "I'm
sorry. No one by that name is listed under admissions."

"They might not have admitted him, yet. He was
brought in sometime yesterday. A shooting victim. Perhaps
he's in ICU?"

"You could check with them on that floor if you'd like."

Elena was so tired she wondered how she could stay on her feet. But she had to know that Joe was going to be all right. Only then would she check into a hotel and sleep around the clock.

When she stepped off the elevator into the ICU, she was immediately stopped at the nurses' station.

"I'm sorry, but we don't allow visitors here," one of the nurses said.

"I'm trying to locate a shooting victim who was flown in last night. There may have been more than one."

"What's the name?"

"Joe Sanchez."

The nurse went over to one of the boards and checked names. She turned away and returned to the desk. "Are you kin to Mr. Sanchez?"

Elena shook her head. "A friend. I was there when he was shot."

The nurse gave her a sympathetic look. "I'm afraid Mr. Sanchez didn't make it, ma'am. He never regained consciousness. I'm sorry."

# Eleven

Elena sat on the patio outside her rented beach cottage and listlessly watched the waves roll into the lagoon before eventually washing up onto the white sand of the beach.

It was hard to believe that it was the middle of December. Back in the States an early winter storm had covered large portions of the nation with ice and snow. Here in the West Indies it was perpetual summer.

She glanced down at her lightly tanned body. She'd been living in shorts and halters for more than a couple of weeks now, wearing her sunscreen constantly so that she wouldn't end up with melanoma. It seemed funny, somehow, to be worrying about dying of cancer. People died all the time, regardless of what they ate or didn't eat, whether they smoked or ran marathons, whether they exercised or became permanent couch potatoes.

People died, and there wasn't anything she could do about it.

People relied on modern medicine to make everything better, to solve any and all health problems. Who was to blame when none of it worked? Everybody had done what could be done to save him.

Besides, he'd been one of the smugglers. One of the bad guys, although she would never be able to see him that way.

Instead, she chose to remember him the way he looked the night of Tina's party, in his charcoal-gray suit and startling white shirt, holding her close, smiling down at her, letting her feel how much he wanted to make love to her.

Or later that night when he had made love to her, showing her for the first time what a sensual woman she was. But only with him.

She pictured him swimming in the pool by the waterfall, the sunlight glinting off his bronzed skin.

Whenever she pictured him, she saw him whole and healthy, not with a bullet wound in his chest, his life's blood draining away faster than they could replace it.

She'd never told him she loved him, something she would always regret.

He'd never told her that he loved her, either, but she knew that he had. He'd given himself away in so many ways.

They'd only been together a few weeks. A few very short weeks. In the end, she had contributed to his death. Somehow she had to figure out a way to live with that knowledge.

She didn't have a single photograph of him.

She would never have his baby.

Elena had talked to her mother by phone before she'd asked for a leave of absence. Sara told her that she had attended the memorial service for Joe and that the church had been full to overflowing with friends and family. A week later Joe's mother had a massive coronary and died before they could get her to the hospital.

Francisco Delgado had been moved to a maximum-security facility somewhere unknown to await trial. Elena knew that the government hoped he would give them information in exchange for leniency, but he didn't strike her as a person who would do that.

She'd asked her mother about Tina. The word wasn't good. Tina had retreated into her home, refusing to see any visitors. The doctors were worried about her and about her pregnancy.

Elena hoped that, eventually, Tina would pull herself together for the sake of her unborn child.

She wished that she had a baby to hold and care for—a joyful reminder of the man she loved.

Her stomach growled. She needed to eat something. A woman came in each day and filled her refrigerator with food. All she had to do was eat it, but sometimes she forgot, unless her stomach complained, as it was doing now.

She pushed herself out of her lounge chair and turned to go inside when a figure walking on the beach caught her eye. She paused and shaded her eyes. It was a man, but he was too far away for her to recognize.

He looked out of place on the beach, for he was wearing long dark pants and a long-sleeved white shirt, with a suit jacket slung over one shoulder. His shoes must be full of sand by now. But there was something about him that looked familiar.

And then he lifted his hand and waved.

She stood without moving and watched as he approached her cottage. He waited until he stepped up on the patio before he spoke.

"It's good to see you again, Elena."

She nodded. "Hello, Chris. I was just going in for something to eat. Would you like to join me?"

"Sure. You look like you could use a few more meals. You've lost a few pounds since I last saw you."

She held the door open for him to come inside.

The cottage had one large bedroom and an equally large bath. The kitchen was part of the living room, separated by a waist-high bar. She motioned for him to sit at the bar while she moved dishes from the refrigerator to the bar.

"I eat a lot of salads and fruits," she explained. "It's too hot to cook."

Chris sat on one of the stools and looked around. "This is nice. Does it have air-conditioning?"

"No. Most of the time the breeze off the water is enough to keep it cool. I keep all the windows open and the paddle fans on."

She poured them both glasses of fruit punch, then sat down beside him.

"You don't seem surprised to see me," he said after a few minutes. "I expected to answer all kinds of questions about why I'm here."

"I'm sorry. I can't seem to think of any questions right now. Maybe later."

"I like your hair loose like that. I'm used to seeing it pulled back," he said after a moment.

She touched her hair, which was now past her shoulders. "I don't bother with it much."

"It's obvious you've been spending your time in the sun. Your tan makes your eyes glow like emeralds."

"What a poetic thing to say, Chris. Thank you." They finished eating and she poured them each another glass of fruit punch. "Would you like to sit outside, or are you more comfortable in here?"

"I'm not exactly dressed for the sun. I'd like to stay in here where it's a little cooler."

"Suit yourself." She motioned to one of the rattan chairs and seated herself in the other one. She sipped on her drink and waited.

"Wilder's worried about you, Elena," Chris said awkwardly. "Hell, we're *all* worried about you. I guess he's feeling guilty about having you in on this assignment, although you did an excellent job, as I know he told you. He understands that you took Joe's death hard. You had time coming, anyway, and no one blames you for taking some time off now. It's just that the bureau wants to know when you intend to come back to work."

"I don't know."

"I don't think it's good for you to spend so much time alone. You need to be around people, get back to your former routine. Wilder said that he could use you in the field more often if you were interested. He was quite impressed with the way you handled yourself on the Texas case."

"That's funny, don't you think? I did everything wrong and I'm being praised for it."

"What are you talking about? We nailed them. We had to work around all kinds of crooked agents to track them down, but we did it."

"Uh-huh, but I never had a clue about Joe. It's a wonder we didn't all get shot and killed that night with the bumbling and stumbling around that took place."

"Nobody's blaming you."

She didn't respond.

"Are *you* blaming you? Is that what all this is about?"

"Maybe. I don't know. Everything happened so fast. It was sheer luck that we didn't end up shooting at the soldiers and them shooting at us while the three trucks got away.''

Chris grinned. ''Wouldn't that have been a mess to explain.''

''It could easily have happened. We're just lucky it didn't, so I don't want to hear about any so-called praise I might have received.''

''It wasn't your fault that Joe was killed, Elena.''

''I feel as if it was.''

Chris sat up straighter in his chair. ''I get the distinct impression that you don't really care much about anything anymore.''

''That's probably a true statement.''

''You need to come out of this depression, Elena.''

She lifted her brow. ''Do I? Since when have you become the expert?''

''I can't make it all go away for you. I would if I could. It's obvious that something was going on between you and Sanchez, or you wouldn't be taking this so hard.''

''Did I ever tell you that Joe Sanchez was my first lover?'' she asked idly, as though discussing the weather.

He frowned. ''You know you didn't. You've never discussed your personal life with me.''

She leaned her head against the cushioned back of her chair and closed her eyes. ''I'm tired. No matter how much I sleep, I'm still tired. It's an effort to get out of bed, to walk, to move at all.''

''That's depression, Elena. And I'm not going to let you wallow in whatever it is you're wallowing in, whether it's guilt or self-pity or what. Do you hear me?''

She didn't bother to open her eyes. ''Everybody on the island probably hears you.''

''Well, for your information, your friend Joe lied to you.''

Her lips twitched. "Tell me something I don't know. Remember? I'm the one who took him off our suspect list. He was a damned good liar, I'll give him that."

"Hell, Elena, he never lied about smuggling because the subject never came up between you. You told me that when I was there. I'm talking about his real job. He lied about leaving the army. He was still in the army when he died, did you know that?"

She sat up and stared at him. "He was what?"

"You heard me. He was living in Santiago on a mission for the United States Army. He was part of a military covert intelligence operation. You met his commanding officer, the colonel in charge the night of the raid. How do you think the army knew where they were going to be? Joe had been feeding them information. That's why he was working for Delgado. He was gathering evidence about the arms smuggling."

She started laughing. "You can't be serious. So all the while I'm pretending to be the unemployed loser of all time, he's pretending to be a poor-as-dirt mechanic, and we're both working for the government! Didn't we make a pair?" She continued to laugh until her laughter turned to sobs.

Chris put his arms around her.

"I thought it might help you to know he really *was* one of the good guys."

"But it doesn't make him any less dead," she cried.

He held her until her sobs eventually turned into gasps, hiccups and short sighs. He mopped her face with his handkerchief, and when she was finally quiet, he said, "Come back with me, Elena. Don't do this to yourself. The only thing that's going to help is time. Meanwhile, you've got to get on with your life. Let your friends help you. Will you let us do that, please?"

She finally raised her head and looked at him through swollen eyes. "I can't, Chris. Not yet. I need more time. I appreciate what you're saying. I appreciate your taking the time to come find me, but I've got to work through all of this. Thank you for telling me about Joe. It explains a lot of things that I didn't really understand. In a way, it's given me some closure. I'm going to be all right now. I know that. But I need some more time."

He studied her face for a long while before he finally nodded. "All right. I'll make a deal with you. I'll be back to get you in another week. Today's December twelfth. I'll be back on the nineteenth. I will expect to find you packed and ready to return with me. Agreed? If you don't want to go back to Texas for Christmas, we'll plan a gathering in Washington. You can do this. I know you can."

She thought about his offer and knew that he was making sense. Finally she said, "Deal."

"Atta girl." He picked up his glass and finished his drink. "In that case, I'm headed back to town and the hotel there. I can get a flight out tomorrow. Now promise me that you'll start eating before you waste completely away and all I find in another week is a bag of bones and a hank of hair."

She knew her smile wobbled, but she tried. "I'll do my best." She stood and faced him.

He hugged her. "Please take care of yourself. Joe would hate to see you grieving like this."

"Are you kidding? He wouldn't believe it. He thinks everything I did was to pay him back for what happened when we were kids."

"Or maybe that's what he wanted you to believe."

"Meaning?"

Chris shrugged. "Remember, he had his own cover story. He had to make it seem realistic. Even if he'd wanted to marry you, he couldn't very well ask under the circumstances. So you really don't know how he felt about you or whether he believed you or not.''

''I know he spied on me when I went to the hotel to see you—because he told me.''

''No kidding? Then I was lucky not to be shot by a jealous boyfriend. Why don't you give the guy the benefit of the doubt? It was obvious to me that he loved you. Just look at it from his point of view. He had to ignore his feelings and do his job.''

''The same as me.''

''Exactly.''

She took a deep breath, then slowly let the air leave her lungs. After several of those she asked, ''You really think he loved me?''

''Oh, yeah. No question about it.''

She smiled. ''Thanks, Chris.''

''Don't mention it.'' He walked over to the door. ''I'll see you next week. You'd better be packed.''


Elena woke up the morning of December eighteenth and knew that she'd be ready to go back to the States tomorrow.

She was grateful that Chris had given her another week without much argument. She'd been able to use the time constructively, reviewing everything that had happened between her and Joe from the time she first saw him in that cantina until she found him lying in the dirt on a forgotten rural road.

No wonder he'd been in such great physical shape. The new information Chris had brought her gave new meaning to everything Joe had said to her. Even more importantly, to everything he hadn't said to her.

She had known the truth when he'd made love to her.

Neither one of them had been able to hide their true feelings at that time, regardless of their chosen roles. She was fiercely glad to have the memories she had of him.

Once she got back to Washington, she would contact Colonel Davis to see if she could obtain a photograph of Joe. Not that she would ever forget him, but she knew that it would help her to see his face each day.

So today was her last full day on the island. She would make the most of it. After all, it wouldn't take her long to pack. She changed into her bikini and adjusted the ties. She had gained a couple of pounds this past week. She knew it was only a matter of time before she reached her normal weight. There might come a time in her life when she would look back to this time and yearn for her slender figure.

For now, she intended to go swim in the lagoon and store up memories for the cold winter days ahead of her. She'd begun to think about work once again. She was going back to being an analyst; she wasn't cut out for fieldwork. Her work was a challenge and would keep her thoughts from straying to Joe.

It was time to rejoin the living. Chris was right. Joe would not have wanted her to grieve for long. If she'd been the one who had died, she would have wanted him to go on with his life and to be happy.

She wasn't certain she could pull off the happy part, but she'd give it her best shot.

She stopped in the kitchen area to gather some fruit and pick up a bottle of water. She put them in a bag, picked up her towel and sunglasses and walked outside.

The water was so blue it appeared to be artificially colored, and the sand looked as if it had been freshly bleached. It was still early morning. The sun hadn't been up more than a couple of hours.

She placed her things in the shade of one of the many palm trees and strode to the water. It felt like satin brushing against her feet. She took a few deep breaths and filled her lungs with the fresh morning air, then continued walking into the water until it was deep enough for her to swim.

In the past week she had started to take long walks to build up her strength. She'd also been swimming every day. The daily exercise had helped her to rest better at night, as well. There would be no reason for anyone to say that she'd allowed herself to get out of shape while she'd been on leave.

So she swam, then floated, then swam some more. She went out to the coral reef and watched the teeming sea life. Eventually, though, she decided to head back to shore.

As she touched bottom and began walking out of the water, the sun had come up high enough to shine right in her face. She squinted, wishing for the sunglasses she'd left with her towel and bag.

She'd come out at a slightly different angle from where she'd gone in. She turned and headed toward the palm tree only to see a vague figure of someone sprawled on the beach near where she'd left her things.

She shaded her eyes with her hand and tried to make out the figure. As she drew nearer, she realized it was a man. He wasn't just near her things, he was actually sprawled on her towel and eating a piece of her fruit.

She grinned and called out, "Hey, you're early. You weren't supposed to show up until tomorrow, you rat."

He didn't respond, just watched her intently as she approached.

"I'm practically blind out in this sun without my glasses," she said, moving closer to him. "I'll be glad to have my sunshades on to help me…" Her words faded as she stared at the man watching her.

"No," she whispered, shaking her head slowly back and forth. "I know this can't be real. I..." Her knees gave way and she fell to her knees in the sand.

He quickly moved over to her and knelt beside her. "I'm real, all right. Seeing you again makes everything I've gone through these past few weeks worthwhile."

Joe gathered her in his arms and rocked her back and forth while she clung to him and wept.

# Twelve

She clung to him, afraid to let go, afraid to open her eyes for fear that she might be dreaming. If that was the case, she never wanted to wake up.

"You're the most solid ghost I've ever encountered," she whispered into his shoulder.

She could hear the amusement in his voice when he said, "The report of my death was only slightly exaggerated. I'm still here."

Opening her eyes, she looked deeply into his. They told of the suffering and pain he'd gone through, but all she could think about was the fact that he was alive.

"I can't believe it. Why did they tell me you had died?"

"Because the army told them what to say, and I wasn't in any condition to argue with anybody for the next several days. I understand they flew me immediately to Washington to a military hospital. I barely remember what happened during that time. I was in surgery at one point. They told me I was luckier than I deserved. Outside of a punctured lung, nothing vital had been hit.

"All I could think about while I was recuperating was that I was determined to get back to you. For weeks I dreamed that I saw you the night of the raid among all the soldiers that swarmed the place. It was only last week that I spoke to Agent Wilder of the FBI, who not only told me that you really had been there that night, but why. He also told me how to find you." He glanced around the area and shook his head. "When you decide to vacation, you certainly know how to do it, I'll give you that."

"Let's go inside," she said. "If my legs will carry me."

"I hope so. I'm not sure I'd be able to do it at the moment," he admitted ruefully.

They stood and she got a good look at him. He'd lost weight and his tan had faded a little, but oh! he looked wonderful to her. The shorts he wore revealed his strong muscled legs.

She took his hand and went over to where she'd left her towel and bag. Slipping the sunshades onto her nose, she said, "I'm sorry. I got you all wet." She touched his shirt. "Are you still wearing bandages?"

They turned and headed toward the cottage. "No. They finally came off last week. I'm still not on active duty. I've got to rebuild my strength." He glanced at her beneath his lashes. "I was hoping I could spend some time recuperating here with you."

They reached the cottage door and she stepped inside, motioning for him to come in. "Have a seat while I get us something cold to drink," she said.

Elena couldn't stop smiling. She felt as though her mouth was now carved into a permanent smile on her face. She watched him even while she went to the refrigerator for their drinks, almost afraid if she looked away for a minute he might disappear.

Joe sat on one end of her small sofa. He looked wonderful. She walked over and handed him the glass, then sat down beside him. She placed her hand on his bare thigh, giving in to the need to touch him.

"I wish we could stay, but Chris is supposed to be here tomorrow to pick me up. That's who I thought you were when I saw you waiting for me on the beach."

He reached into his shirt pocket and pulled out a multifolded paper. He handed it to her. Puzzled, she started unfolding the many pieces. When it was finally open and flat, she read:

I've authorized an additional thirty days for you for much-needed R&R. You deserve it. Thanks again for your help.

Doug Wilder

"How did you find Wilder?" she asked. "He's a very secretive man and hard to locate when he doesn't want to be found."

"Actually he found me. I guess your friend Chris told him what had happened, and he figured he needed to get more particulars on me. Colonel Davis filled him in. I understand the two of them had quite a session comparing notes on how they'd managed to keep their agents' identities and locations secret from one another." He grinned. "Your commander made it clear that I must be good at what I do if you didn't stumble onto my real assignment. He considers you a fine agent."

She shook her head. "I never had a clue."

"Me, neither, darlin'. You had me totally convinced you were down on your luck and forced to return home."

She could only sit and stare at the miracle beside her. It was a shock to see him again. A good shock, of course, but her body, mind and emotions were still reeling.

"Did they find out who shot you?"

"I know who did. The bodyguard riding with me. The moment he saw the army, he was smart enough to put it together and know I was the one who'd betrayed them. He waited until we got out of the truck before he turned and shot me. I didn't have a chance to protect myself."

"Dear God. I don't know how you managed to survive being shot point-blank."

"I probably wouldn't have, but I did manage an evasive maneuver just as he aimed at me. Otherwise, he would have hit my heart. Even so, the loss of blood made things a little dicey there for a while."

She reached for his hand and folded her hands over it. "I was so sorry to hear about your mother."

"Yeah, that was tough. I didn't hear about it until after the funeral, but I wasn't all that surprised. She'd had a couple of smaller attacks after you'd left. Until a few days before that run I'd been staying at her place, taking care of her. When I wasn't around, one of her sisters stayed with her. She knew her heart was weak. Hearing the news that I'd been killed was too much of a shock for her."

"I still don't know why the army lied about that."

"Because of Delgado. If he'd known that I'd survived, he'd have had a contract out on me. So I'm going to have to stay dead, for all practical purposes. I'm lucky my name is such a common one, although it has been suggested that I leave the army in case someone decides to check up on me. In fact, I've been offered a new job."

"Doing what?" she asked.

"Agent Wilder has suggested I join the bureau and work

for his department. He feels that my background and experience are uniquely suited to what his group does.''

''And you said?''

''That I had to talk it over with you first. From here on in, you're my number-one priority. I hope that's all right with you.''

She leaned over and lightly kissed him. ''That's only fair, since you became my number-one priority as soon as I discovered you're still alive.''

They smiled at each other.

Finally he said, ''You'll never be able to let anyone in Santiago know about us. Just as I can never go back.''

She thought about her mother. It would be difficult not to let Sara know that she had a life Sara could never know about. However, that was nothing new. ''I can live with that,'' she finally said.

''Does that mean that you'll marry me?''

''Absolutely.''

He sighed and briefly closed his eyes. ''You don't know how hard that was for me to ask.''

She leaned over and kissed him. ''Oh, sure. When you know how much you mean to me.''

He ducked his head for a moment and actually looked embarrassed. ''Well, until I spoke with Chris, I had no idea how you felt about me. I was coming to find you, anyway, because I wanted some answers from you. Until Chris talked to me, I really believed that you were deliberately getting close to me as payback for that night on the levee.''

She looked at him for a long moment before she said, ''If you weren't recovering from major injuries to your body, I'd be tempted to inflict some of my own. I would never have made love to you if I hadn't come to terms with what had happened to us back then. Nor could I have made love to you without being in love with you.''

He grinned. ''Well, in that case...'' He allowed his expression to speak for him. She laughed and grabbed his hand, pulling him to his feet. Without a word, she led him into her bedroom. A small bag sat on the floor beside the bed.

He leaned over and picked it up, opened it and dumped the contents onto the bed. She spotted several pair of shorts and some wildly printed shirts, along with shaving gear, underwear and a large box of condoms.

She almost laughed at the sight of his optimistic hope for his stay on the island. With economical movements, she put his clothing in drawers, pushed the covers on the bed away and coaxed him into lying down.

''Guess I'm not fully up to speed yet,'' he said with a rueful smile. ''This bed feels good.''

She took her time undressing him, as well as herself, then found the lotion she kept handy. After pouring some of the lotion into her palm, she carefully massaged his battered body, careful not to put pressure on his chest.

He would always carry the scars from the bullet wound, as well as the surgery he'd gone through. To her, the scars were as distinguished as a Congressional Medal of Honor.

She continued to massage his body, working down to the muscles in his thighs and calves. Kneading and massaging, she paused when she heard him make a small sound.

She immediately jerked her hands back. ''I'm sorry. I didn't mean to hurt you.''

He gave a painful chuckle. ''It wasn't that kind of hurt, honey.'' That was when she noticed that he had a strong and healthy-looking arousal only inches from her hands. ''There were times when I never thought I'd see that kind of reaction again," he murmured, peering down his body at her. "From the looks of things, my recovery is progressing quite satisfactorily."

With a mischievous grin, she leaned over and gently kissed him there. His whole body jerked in reaction, but he didn't seem to mind her touch. She adjusted where she sat and continued to kiss and caress him until he was gripping the sheet beneath him with both hands.

At last she carefully straddled him and slid down on top of his full length, capturing him as he reached an explosive climax, his body jerking and shuddering beneath her. She just as carefully moved away after a few minutes and stretched out beside him.

"You keep tempting fate, honey. If you aren't careful, you're going to end up pregnant before this month is over."

She kissed him and said, "If I don't, I'm going to be extremely disappointed. I'm afraid all those condoms you brought are going to go to waste."

With a lingering kiss, he held her close to his side and quickly fell into a deep sleep. Elena placed her hand over his heart, finding comfort in the steady beat beneath her palm. She would never take that wonderful knowledge for granted.

*   *   *   *   *

# TALL, STRONG & COOL
# UNDER FIRE

by
**Marie Ferrarella**

To all the firefighters in my city, for taking such good care of all of us and making us safe every year.

Thank you.

Come closer still
to Silhouette with
a FREE book and
a welcome gift

# How to claim your
# FREE book
# and welcome gift

If you've enjoyed reading this new book, then this is your opportunity to get ev
closer still to Silhouette Desire® and enjoy another free book and a welcome g
This is all you have to do.

1. **Peel off the free gifts seal** from the front cover. Place it in the spa
   provided to the right. This automatically entitles you to receive one free bo
   and a lovely Austrian crystal necklace.

2. **Complete your details** on the card, detach it along the dotted line, and pe
   it back to us. No stamp needed. We'll then send you a selected romance fro
   the Silhouette Desire series, yours to keep absolutely FREE.

3. **Enjoy the read.** We hope that after receiving your free book you
   want to remain a subscriber. But the choice is yours – to continue
   cancel, any time at all! So why not accept our no risk invitatio
   You'll be glad you did.

# Your satisfaction is guaranteed

You are under no obligation to buy anything. We charge you nothing
for your introductory parcel. And you don't have to make any
minimum number of purchases – not even one! Thousands of
readers have already discovered that the Reader Service™ is the
most convenient way of enjoying the latest new romance novels
before they are available in the shops. Of course, post and packing
to your home is completely FREE.

*Jane Nicholls*

Detach and keep your complimentary bookmark

# Yours FREE...
## when you reply today

You'll love this exquisite gold-plated necklace with its 46cm (18") cobra linked chain and multi-faceted Austrian crystal which sparkles just like a diamond. It's the perfect accessory to dress up any outfit, casual or formal. RESPOND TODAY AND IT'S YOURS FREE.

Not actual size

# YES. Please send me my FREE book and welcome gift

PLACE
FREE GIFTS
SEAL HERE

YES. I have placed my free gift seal in the space provided above. Please send me my free book and welcome gift. I understand that I am under no obligation to purchase any books, as explained on the back and on the opposite page. I am over 18 years of age.

BLOCK CAPITALS                                                          D2EI

Ms/Mrs/Miss/Mr                              Initials

Surname

Address

                                            Postcode

*Thank you!*

Detach and keep your complimentary bookmark ▶

Detach along the dotted lines and post this card today. No stamp needed.

# How The Silhouette® Reader Service™ works

Accepting the free book and gift places you under no obligation to buy anything. You may keep the book and gift and return the despatch note marked "cancel". If we don't hear from you, about a month later we will send you two new novels and invoice you for just £4.99* each. That's the complete price – there is no extra charge for postage and packing. You may cancel at any time, otherwise every month we'll send you two more books which you may purchase or return – the choice is yours.

*Terms and prices subject to change without notice.

SILHOUETTE READER SERVICE
FREE BOOK OFFER
FREEPOST CN81
CROYDON
CR9 3WZ

NO
STAMP
NEEDED

# Chapter One

"Are you a fireman?"

The high, exuberant voice caught him by surprise, lifting him out of his realm of preoccupation. Turning away from the newly washed fire truck he was facing, Bryce Walker saw her. All three foot one of her. Completely adorable and most assuredly completely out of place.

The glib response on his lips, reserved for ladies far older than this little blond visitor obviously was, died away unspoken. Instead he smiled at her.

The little girl, decked out in soft pink coveralls with white daisies scattered throughout the body of the fabric, stood on the threshold of the fire station, obviously accepting the silent invitation the wide-open doorway extended to wayward travelers. She rocked slightly forward on the balls of her feet, her small hands shoved into her pockets like someone intent on doing nothing more with her morning than shooting the breeze. Her eyes watched him expectantly, waiting for an answer.

"Why yes, I am."

Amused, Bryce crossed to her and then got down on one knee in an attempt to lessen the huge difference in their heights. He glanced to either side of the little girl, expecting to see a parent or at least an older sibling hanging back somewhere in the near vicinity.

But there was no one close by, not even any stragglers coming out of the library located directly to the right of the fire station, or eagerly flowing out of the summer school classes being given at the high school located in the center of the long block.

His visitor was apparently alone and very obviously fearless.

On occasion, Bryce gave talks on fire safety at the various local elementary schools located in Bedford, California. The little girl before him looked too young to be attending school. Bryce guessed her to be around four, or perhaps a very small five, though he doubted it. Intelligence shone in her cornflower-blue eyes, opened as wide as the daisies she had on her rompers.

The way she was regarding him told Bryce she thought of him as her equal in every way but height and opportunity. Her eyes darted past him to the truck that was just behind. "Do they let you drive the truck?"

He heard the hopeful note in her voice mingled with a touch of hero worship. The appeal of fire trucks had long since crossed the gender line. Bryce bit back a laugh, thinking of Alex. With three years seniority, the firefighter acted as if the truck was his own private property and would sooner walk over hot coals than allow someone else to touch the steering wheel.

"No, I'm afraid not."

The little girl nodded her head in a commiserating manner that seemed far older than her obvious tender years. "Mommy won't let me drive, either."

It seemed to Bryce the perfect opportunity to initiate a reunion between the wayward child and her mother. "And where is Mommy?"

Leaving him in her wake, the little girl made her way to the fire truck in small, cautious steps, as if the truck wasn't simply metal and gears, but a living, breathing thing that could be frightened into running off at any second if she wasn't careful.

"At home."

Bryce had a feeling that his unannounced visitor was going to be a fetching challenge when she got a little older. He wished any man who lost his heart to her luck. They were going to need it.

Getting up, he followed her slow progress around the vehicle. "And where's home?"

Pausing, she looked over her shoulder, her expression momentarily sad, as if she was mourning something that had been lost. "Not Dallas anymore."

He'd thought he'd detected a slight twang to her voice. But knowing her origins didn't exactly help him at the moment. "And why's that?"

The sigh she released was enormous. Slowly she made her way around the perimeter of the truck, studying every detail more closely than the fire chief during an impromptu inspection. "We moved."

She was too young to be coy, though that would have been the word he would have used had she been a teenager. Bryce began to feel as if he was trapped in a children's program. "To where?"

The little girl ran her hand along the front of the truck and he got the distinct impression she was petting it. "Here."

Playing along, Bryce looked around, pretending to be mystified at the information. "You live here? In my fire station?"

He was rewarded with a giggle that was so infectious, he had a hard time not laughing along with her. She turned to look at him, her eyes crinkled with humor. "No, silly. In Bedford."

He'd assumed as much, but it was nice to receive confirmation. At least she wasn't visiting from out of town. It looked as if he just might finally be getting somewhere. "Do you know where in Bedford?"

She paused, considering his question. "Our house, of course," she told him as if it were silly to think that there could be any other answer. "Mommy's and G-mama's and mine. Mommy said it belongs to all three of us. Equally." She wrapped her tongue around the last word very slowly, as if careful to get it right.

Bryce noticed she didn't mention a father and wondered if that meant that Missing Mommy was divorced, or possibly widowed. Or if she'd never been married in the first place. He doubted if the omission was an oversight. The little girl seemed to have an almost incredible grasp of her situation. He knew adults who were less aware of their surroundings than she appeared to be.

Following her as she made her way back to the side of the truck, he tried again. "Do you know your address?"

This time, the expression that met his question was a pint-size composition of frustration. The little girl shook her head. "No. It's new."

She seemed so upset that she couldn't remember it, Bryce felt it best to gloss over the detail. No sense dwelling on it. If Mommy didn't show up soon to claim her, he had friends on the police force who could help track her down.

"Sometimes," he commented, "new things are hard to remember." Holding her hand, he helped her up the steps of the fire truck so that she could get a closer look inside the cab. "Do you know your name?"

She looked at him with just a touch of impatience bringing her small, wheat-colored brows together in a puckered furrow. "Of course I do. My name's not new. It's as old as I am."

"I see." He pretended to nod his agreement. "My name is Bryce Walker. What is your name?"

She tossed her head, sending soft swirls of blond hair bouncing back and forth. "CeCe Billings. I was named after my G-mama. The first part."

"The first part," he repeated, not quite sure that he followed her.

"Yes. CeCe." She held her arms out for him to help her down. "Except her name's really Cecilia.

Mine is, too, but Mommy calls me CeCe so she doesn't mix G-mama and me up.''

Bryce set her down on the ground again. "I see.'' Though it didn't actually have anything to do with finding her mother or her home, he couldn't resist gleaning just a little more information about this diminutive blonde chatterbox who had wandered into his station. "And what does your daddy call you?''

"Nothing,'' she told him with a matter-of-fact air worthy of someone five or six times her age. "I don't have a daddy. Mommy says we're doing just fine without one.''

"Uh-huh.'' Mommy was obviously rather adamant about the subject, he thought, given the verve he heard in CeCe's voice. "Well, I don't think she's doing just fine right now,'' he speculated, more to himself than to the tiny intruder. "She's probably out looking for you right now.''

His visitor shook her head with feeling, sending her blond curls flying back and forth again. "I don't think so. Mommy's busy.''

"Doing what?'' He had a very low opinion of a mother who was too busy to notice her child was missing. In his mind, he envisioned a woman neglecting her child for any one of a half-dozen reasons, none of which were acceptable.

Like someone on a deliberate, savored odyssey, CeCe's inspection of the fire truck was taking her to the rear of the vehicle. "She's gotta tell all those men what to do. They're all confused.''

They weren't the only ones, Bryce thought. "What men?''

"The men who are helping her." She frowned. "You're not listening. Mommy told G-mama men don't listen."

"Oh, she did, did she?" Mommy obviously didn't have a very high opinion of men. Which made them equal, because he didn't have a high opinion of women who misplaced their children.

But, in the absence of the appearance of a frantic woman searching for her wandering gypsy of a child, he had no recourse but to keep the little girl occupied. On a hunch, he tapped her on the shoulder and when she turned around to look at him, he extended his hand to her. "Would you like a tour of the fire station while we try to figure out how to find your mommy?"

CeCe took his hand readily, but she cocked her head and looked at him, as if that would help her understand his meaning better. "Why? Mommy's not lost."

He smiled at her. If he had chosen a different path for himself, a child like Cece might have been his by now. But that was all water under a bridge he had crossed over voluntarily a long time ago.

"No, but you are."

"No, I'm not." The smile that came to her lips was so bright, Bryce found himself instantly charmed and very firmly captivated. How could anyone not notice that a little doll like this was missing? "I'm right here. With you."

He found he had a difficult time arguing with that, so he didn't even try.

* * *

Lisa Billings felt as if she had taken exhaustion to a new high. Or low, depending on the point of view.

All she knew was that right at this moment, she felt more drained than a riverbed during a prolonged draught. For the last six months she had been flying between her former home in Dallas and the city she had decided to resettle her family in, trying to find the perfect locale for both her store and her new home. A new home where she intended to make a new life for herself and her daughter. The appeal of a fresh start was strong.

Her requirements weren't many, but they were nonnegotiable. She wanted someplace that was bright and clean and safe, somewhere with a wonderful school system that would benefit a daughter as bright and eager to learn as CeCe was. The hundred and twenty some-odd details that went into making the transition had finally led her to Bedford, which was as near-perfect as she could hope for.

Looking back, she couldn't remember a time in the last six months when she hadn't been busy enough for two people. As busy as she was, she couldn't spend too much time thinking and that was a blessing. She didn't like to have too much time to think, or reflect.

But somehow, amid all that busy-ness that was taking place, she had just about "busied" herself out and lost sight of the most important thing of all. CeCe. CeCe, the reason she had undertaken owning and running a toy store that catered to a child's fertile imagination and not to noise, chaos and the advertis-

ing toy craze of the moment. CeCe, who was, quite
simply, the reason she drew breath every day.

Somehow, amid the rush of movers who were bent
on testing the durability of every breakable item she
owned and the confusion of getting everything re-
organized again, she had misplaced her daughter.

One minute, CeCe was playing in the new front
yard, doing her best not to get underfoot. The next,
when Lisa looked back to check on her, CeCe was
gone. A quick search of the area told Lisa that her
daughter wasn't in the front yard, or the back. Or
anywhere else in the house, either. Tired of exploring
it, CeCe had obviously gone on to conquer other areas.

Lisa tried very hard not to give in to the panic that
was swiftly filling all the empty spaces left inside of
her. Praying she had somehow missed seeing her,
Lisa made another, faster pass through the two-story
house, looking behind boxes and any place CeCe
might have decided to turn into a temporary play
area.

When this go-round proved to be as fruitless as
the first, she hurried out to the front yard again. There
she found her mother. Cecilia Dombrowski was di-
recting the movers like one of the field marshals who
had existed in her family tree.

One look at her daughter's face had Cecilia halting
in midcommand. "What is it?"

Years of taking on too much, of trying to be in-
vincible, had brought Lisa to the brink of collapse
and had her tottering there now. She felt herself very
close to crumbling and hated herself for having the

feeling. "I can't find her anywhere, Mother. I can't find CeCe."

The older woman set her mouth grimly. Moving quickly, Cecilia did an about-face and placed herself in the center of the movers. Raising her hands, she immediately captured their attention.

"My granddaughter is missing. You all know what she looks like. Please stop what you are doing and look for her. Now." The movers, four burly men of varying heights, looked at one another, somewhat bewildered and confused. "Now," Cecilia repeated. She pointed first to the left of the house and then to the right. "There are houses on both sides of this one. Knock on doors. Ask. She was here a few minutes ago and her legs are short. She could not have gone far. Your legs are much longer, you can cover more distance. Please."

The last word was issued as more of a command than a plea. Cecilia's look was unwavering as her eyes swept over the four men's faces.

The men quickly scattered, doing as she asked. The furniture could wait.

With a semisatisfied sigh, Cecilia turned to her daughter. She placed hands on Lisa's shoulders and Lisa could feel warmth and encouragement in the very contact.

"You do the same. Go. Look. We will find her. You know that we will."

There were times Lisa felt that even God wouldn't argue with her mother and she certainly wasn't about to. Just hearing Cecilia's reassurances that this would all be resolved shortly and satisfactorily heartened her and gave her something to cling to. Never mind that it was intangible.

"Yes," Lisa answered with more conviction than she felt. "We will."

"Good, I will remain here, in case she returns home on her own. You know how CeCe is," Cecilia said, smiling.

Lisa blew out a breath, telling herself she was just overreacting. CeCe knew better than to go far.

Then where was she? she demanded silently.

Nodding at her mother's words, Lisa began to walk to the house on the left, the last one on the corner of the development. A car passed by on its way out, its windshield catching the sun and instantly flashing it all around like a sunburst intent on illuminating the immediate surrounding area.

The glare hurt her eyes. Shading them with her hand, Lisa squinted.

And that was when she saw it.

The fire station across the street on the corner. She'd only paid marginal attention to it when she'd driven past it before, taking notice of it the way she had the library and the high school beyond, as part of the scenery, nothing more.

Now it registered with glaring lights. A fire station.

It wasn't as if it was immediately accessible. Between the house and the fire station was a wide street with three lanes of traffic going in either direction and a small island in between for pedestrians who weren't quick enough to take advantage of the traffic signal.

CeCe loved fire trucks.

*Oh, please, let her be there.*

Her heart in her throat, not waiting to tell her
mother her hunch, Lisa paused only to glance at the
flow of immediate oncoming traffic and to take in
the traffic light that was, for at least this moment,
green. Taking advantage of it, Lisa sprinted across
the street like the high school track and field team
member she'd once been.

She made it across the entire street, eschewing the
island, before the yellow light had a chance to slip
into red.

He didn't know exactly what made him turn just
then. Maybe he'd been half waiting for the approach
of a frantic parent, maybe it was nothing more than
chance that had made him look through the window
facing the street just then. Whatever the reason, he
caught the motion out of the corner of his eye and
then found himself mesmerized as he watched the
woman sprint from one corner to the next.

The woman moved like a gazelle.

She moved, he realized, the way the wind would,
if it had taken on the form of a young, shapely
woman with hair the color of sunshine just after sun-
rise. Dressed in white, cuffed shorts that brushed
against her upper thighs as she moved and in what
could only be termed as a skimpy red tank top that
clung to the swell of her breasts with each breath she
took, she was definitely a sight to behold. He was
surprised that some of the other firefighters on duty
weren't hanging out of the upper story window,
cheering her on.

Bryce sobered as she made it to the opposite corner. This had to be CeCe's mother. The concerned look was a dead giveaway.

"Honey," he said to the little girl who was holding his hand as if they were old friends, "I think I just spotted your mommy."

CeCe pressed her lips together in deep concentration, as if she was trying to remember something or reconcile a new fact with the ever-growing data base that was expanding in her mind. "Mommy doesn't like spots on her. She's very clean."

He bit back a laugh. "Right now, I'd say she was very angry." He drew CeCe over to the doorway just as the woman ran up the walk.

"Excuse me," Lisa called out the instant she saw Bryce's movement, "have you seen a little girl go—CeCe!"

CeCe looked mystified by both Bryce's observation and by the strange look on her mother's face. She thought she saw tears shining in her mother's eyes. Tears made her feel sad.

Mommy didn't cry very often, but when she did, CeCe always felt that there should be something she could do to make her mother feel happy again.

CeCe put on her brightest smile. Mommy always said she liked seeing her smile. "Hi, Mommy. Are you okay?"

"I am now."

There had been very few times in Lisa's life when she had felt like laughing and crying at the same time. This was one of them. Fears she had refused to allow loose were now throbbing in her head like so many explosive puffs of steam expanding within a pressure cooker.

Completely ignoring the man with her daughter, Lisa dropped to her knees and wrapped her arms around CeCe. Pulling her close to her, Lisa hugged her daughter while fighting a losing battle with her overwrought emotions. It took everything she had not to burst into tears and sob her relief.

Only after she had assured herself that her daughter was real, safe and unharmed did Lisa lean back and, still holding on to her, look at the small face. "Oh God, CeCe, how could you do this to me? How could you run off like that?"

The answer seemed perfectly logical to the four-year-old. "He has a fire truck. A real one." She pointed to the vehicle in question behind her.

But Lisa wasn't looking at the fire truck.

She had suddenly become aware of the fact that she was on her knees in front of a very tall, very blond man wearing a navy blue fireman's uniform. Moreover, she was kneeling before a man who was looking at her as if he'd just come off an enforced seven-week fast and she was a piece of fried chicken prepared just the way he always liked it.

# Chapter Two

"Look, Mommy, it's just like the fire truck you had in your store." A hint of an impatient pout graced CeCe's small mouth when her mother didn't look at the object of her affections.

Lisa lowered her eyes to her daughter's face, trying to ignore the fact that she felt as if she were being slowly appraised and measured by the man standing behind CeCe. Instead she focused on the reason her heart had all but stopped beating earlier. Things could have turned out a great deal worse and she knew it. In light of that, being surveyed by a good-looking man didn't seem like such a terrible price to pay in exchange for finding CeCe safe and sound.

Holding her by both small shoulders, Lisa looked at the little girl who had been the joy of her life even before she'd been born. From the moment she'd learned that she was pregnant, Lisa had crafted her life carefully around the promise of a child and the kind of life that would follow once the child was born. She couldn't afford to remain unfocused any longer. Children needed things.

Most of all, they needed mothers who were there for them, to hold them and love them the way hers had. It gave Lisa a purpose to her life she was grateful for and that she had never lost sight of.

Even if she had lost sight of CeCe for the last ten minutes.

Hiding her relief, Lisa attempted to look stern. She didn't want this happening ever again.

"Now listen to me, young lady. I don't care if you saw an entire fleet of fire trucks, or if there was a great big yellow dragon sitting in its place," she said, referring to CeCe's favorite cartoon program, "you know better than to run off without telling either G-mama or me where you were going. And you know something else, too, don't you?" Deliberately narrowing her eyes, she pinned the little girl with a look.

CeCe sighed, squirming uncomfortably before she nodded her head. As her mother began reciting the one rule she was strict about enforcing, CeCe joined in, parroting words that had been drummed into her head ever since she had been able to string two words together.

"Don't ever talk to strangers."

Then, sucking in air as if she intended to launch into a rebuttal that left no room for her mother to voice her opinion, CeCe grabbed the firefighter's hand and pulled him forward as she protested with feeling.

"But he's not a stranger, Mommy. I know his

name. It's Bryce Walker and he's my new best friend. And he's a firefighter, Mommy. That's like a policeman, right, except nobody shoots at him. You said if I was ever lost, to only talk to a policeman or a police lady. Remember? Well, I couldn't find a policeman, but I found him.''

Lisa closed her eyes. There was no arguing with CeCe once she got started. She took after her grandmother that way—except worse. Lisa learned by experience to wait until the torrent of words subsided.

When she opened her eyes again, she saw her daughter's new best friend looking at her. She supposed he did deserve an apology.

Rising Lisa brushed her hands against her shorts, a tingle of nerves unaccountably zigzagging through her. She wasn't accustomed to thinking of herself as anything except CeCe's mother. The firefighter wasn't looking at her as if he thought of her as anyone's mother.

Lisa cleared her throat, nodding toward CeCe. ''I'm sorry if she was any trouble.''

She looked flustered, Bryce thought. He liked the slight tinge of pink that came into her cheeks. Looking down at his talkative new friend who had an iron grip on his hand, he grinned.

''CeCe? No, she wasn't any trouble at all. I was just about to give your daughter a tour of the fire station.'' His grin extended to include CeCe's mother as well. ''I'm sure the tour group could be expanded by one if you're interested.''

''Thank you, but no.'' Lisa saw CeCe's face fall. Though she was completely right in turning down the invitation for more than one reason, Lisa still felt guilty. She always did whenever she denied CeCe anything. Wanting to give her daughter the world, the guilt that accompanied any refusal was something she continually had to wrestle with.

"But Mommy—" CeCe began to protest.

Lisa remained firm. She had to. "We're in the middle of moving in and everything's a big mess. I can't spare the time right now, honey. Besides—" she suddenly remembered "—I have the movers all combing the neighborhood for you."

Confusion puckered the small brow. "Why do they want to comb me, Mommy?"

Bryce bit back a laugh. "It's just an expression, honey." Very gently, he withdrew his hand from the small grasping fingers then raised his eyes to Lisa. "I can put the tour on hold, if you'd like. Consider it a raincheck." He saw her open her mouth to protest. "Everyone should get to know their neighborhood firehouse. We're not just for fires anymore." He winked at CeCe, clearly winning her heart by becoming a coconspirator. "And on rare occasions, we even offer baby-sitting—um, big girl sitting services," he amended seeing her small brows rise in indignation.

CeCe Billings was, he thought, what his grandfather had been wont to call "a pistol." He wished the old man was still around to meet the little girl. On second thought, his grandfather would have probably attempted to make a play for CeCe's mom. The man had retained a twinkle in his eye until the day he died at age ninety-three.

Bryce hoped the condition was hereditary and that he'd be half as spry when he got to that age.

Lisa wished she had on something other than a tank top and shorts, but she had a feeling the man would make her aware of his gaze even if she were wearing sack cloth and ashes. She raised her chin, determined to retreat as quickly as possible.

"That's comforting to know, but I'm sure we won't be bothering you again, Mr.—um—"

"Walker." He put out his hand to her. "Bryce Walker."

"I already told you, Mommy," CeCe reminded her.

Lisa hesitated, not wanting to waste any more precious time. Across the street, her mother and the movers were undoubtedly still searching for CeCe. She had to get back before her mother decided to call the police. Her mother had never believed in taking the slow approach to anything and was a firm believer in getting the system to work for her any way it could.

But the firefighter was being awfully nice about having CeCe bend his ear and he *had* looked after the little girl for her. She didn't want to think about what could have happened if CeCe had just continued to wander off on her own.

So, with one foot out the door, holding her daughter firmly by the hand, Lisa extended her free one and slipped it into his. His grip was firm, hard. Warm. And his eyes were definitely unsettling, reminding her just how long it had been since she'd looked at any man as something other than a customer.

"I'm Lisa Billings." Her throat felt inordinately dry. She had to remember to stop and drink something once in a while, she told herself. All morning long, she'd worked like a whirling dervish, trying to get the new house organized. She had a limited amount of time before she had to get back to working on the store. The opening day was close. "Thank you for minding CeCe."

"It was a pleasure."

He was still holding her hand. And her attention. Fighting self-consciousness, she withdrew her hand from his. Uncoupled, she saw that he was nonetheless following her, step for step as she began to edge away.

"CeCe says you're new to the city."

She gave CeCe a reproving look. She was going to have to see about getting her daughter to be a little less forthcoming.

"We are."

He wondered if it was his imagination that made him think she looked a little uneasy, talking to him. "And the state."

"That, too." She glanced at her daughter again, making it across the threshold this time. Just how much did CeCe tell this man about them?

He was still on duty until this evening, so he couldn't very well take off with her, although there was something about her that tempted him to do just that.

So instead, Bryce lingered in the doorway. "Well,

since I seem to be one of the first citizens of Bedford you've encountered—and you'll probably be too tired to cook after the movers leave—maybe you'd like to have some dinner?''

"I'm sure I'll have some dinner." Lisa tossed her answer over her shoulder, turning away with CeCe.

"I mean, with me," he added.

She never broke her stride as she looked at him. "I wouldn't dream of putting you out."

"You wouldn't be," he called after her.

But she was already hurrying across the street, her hand firmly wrapped around CeCe's, leaving him to stand in the doorway of the station, feeling a little confused, rather like an adolescent who had just been rejected by the prom queen. It wasn't anything he knew from firsthand experience.

"First time for everything, eh, Walker?"

He thought he was alone on the floor, having left the others in a hot poker game in the main room upstairs. Surprised, he turned around and saw Jack Riley standing next to the truck, laughter in his eyes. He and Riley went way back to a time when both their voices were higher and their permanent teeth hadn't come in yet.

He might have known this would amuse Riley.

"Though I'd never thought I'd see the day when a woman would turn you down." Jack laughed to himself, coming forward. "Hell, my mother would go out with you if you just showed a little interest."

Closer than brothers, they had trained together and signed on for the same station when the time came.

Bryce hooked his thumbs in his belt loops, still watching Lisa and CeCe.

"No offense, but I'm really not interested in having my neck separated from shoulders by your father." There was no disguising the affection he bore for both of Riley's parents. Riley's father had been his own father's best friend, and had willingly taken on the role of surrogate father to Bryce and his younger brother when they'd needed one.

Joining him in the doorway, Riley studied the departing form that had caught his friend's attention. "Doesn't look like your usual type."

Bryce raised a brow. "Meaning?"

"Well, for one thing, she's got a kid." Riley knew better than anyone how Bryce felt about family. He paused, taking a different route than the obvious. "How do you know she's not married?"

CeCe turned at the island and waved at Bryce. He waved back. "Her daughter didn't mention a father."

Riley shrugged carelessly. "Doesn't mean one doesn't exist, Walker. Maybe she's just mad at him."

Bryce merely shook his head. He watched as, reaching the opposite street, Lisa and CeCe make their way to the second house from the end of the block. Funny how he'd missed the moving truck earlier. Now that he was aware of it, it was as obvious as an elephant standing in a front yard.

"You had to be there," he told his friend.

"Sorry I wasn't." Riley leaned over a little farther as the woman waved over four burly men in beige coveralls. The latter came trotting over obediently. He would, too, Riley thought. "Nice rear view."

Bryce knew Riley meant nothing by the comment. Riley was all talk and as honorable as the day was long when it came to women's feelings. Still, he couldn't help the rejoinder that came to his lips. "You kiss your mother with that mouth?"

Riley grinned. "Only when she insists on it. Do I detect a chivalrous note coming through?"

Bryce saw another woman hurrying to Lisa, her arms outstretched. CeCe leaped into them. That had to be G-Mama, he decided. "No more than usual."

"Oh, but this one's a little different than usual," Riley observed. "Like I said, she doesn't seem to be your type."

The reunion over, the three women went into the house. Bryce turned away. "And my type being?"

"Stringless. Absolutely stringless." Riley nodded toward the house. "In case you didn't notice, this one looks like she's full of strings."

Maybe he had been paying a little too much attention just now. Bryce laughed it off. "Hey, don't get carried away, Riley. As you so delicately pointed out, the lady doesn't even want to have dinner with me."

Riley knew Bryce better than that. There wasn't a time he could remember Bryce being easily put off. "Do I detect the call of a challenge?"

It was time to change the subject. Bryce indicated the rooms upstairs. "No, but I can see the dinner bell going off and ten hungry firefighters deciding to string you up because you didn't make dinner when it was your turn to cook." He flicked his thumb and forefinger at the date on the calendar that graced the

side wall. Riley's name was written in in the appro-
priate space.

Riley dragged his hand through his wayward
chestnut-colored hair. "Hell, I forgot about that." He
caught his lower lip between his teeth as he looked
up at his friend. "The refrigerator still empty?"

Bryce looked at him innocently, as if he didn't
know what was coming. As if they hadn't danced
this dance before a number of times. "Last I
looked."

Riley raised his eyes hopefully to Bryce's face.
The latter's expression was deadpan. "You wouldn't
want to take my turn, would you?"

"I took your turn," Bryce reminded him. "Last
time, remember? And the time before that," he
added before Riley could protest. "The men are beginning to think you can't cook."

Riley sighed. He knew his limitations. "The men
are right."

Riley's mother ran a restaurant and her cooking
attracted people in droves. How this talent hadn't
been passed on was beyond Bryce. Even he had
picked up a considerable number of pointers during
the years he and his brother had lived with the Rileys. Riley, however, was just slightly beyond the
boiling-water-without-burning-it-stage with no progress in sight. "No time like the present to learn,"
Bryce commented.

Riley gave him a dark look. "That's not what
you'll say when you're at the hospital, having your
stomach pumped."

Bryce glanced over his shoulder toward the doorway, impulse pushing forward an idea. "Tell you what, I've got a few things to pick up at the grocery store myself. I'll do the shopping for tonight. But then you've got to do the rest."

It was only fair, he knew, the men each taking turns. But Riley really wished they'd give the assignment to someone who was better at it than he was. "Get something simple."

"You read my mind."

Riley watched his friend leave and thought of the expression he'd seen on Bryce's face when the woman had turned down his offer.

"Only part of it, Walker," he murmured to himself. "Only part of it."

Bryce tucked the coloring book that was beginning to slip back more securely under his arm.

It wasn't like him to go where he wasn't wanted so he wasn't altogether certain just exactly what he was doing here, standing on Lisa Billings's doorstep, ringing her doorbell, flowers in one hand, a bag with a loaf of bread in the other and a coloring book tucked under his arm. There was also a broom leaning against the wall where he'd rested it.

He had a number of excuses ready to offer her when she asked, but explaining it to himself was a whole different matter. He wasn't sure if he could.

It wasn't as if he lacked female companionship. Now or ever. As Riley enjoyed ribbing him, he had more than his fair share of women ready to make themselves available to him.

There was no conceit involved. Bryce figured that

women were attracted to the uniform and to resistance, both of which he possessed. He'd been a firefighter for eight years and as for the other, that had been an ongoing thing from the very first time he ever kissed a woman. He wasn't interested in commitments and forever. He was already committed to his work and because of that, it precluded any other long-term relationships that might be headed to the altar. Any woman he ever went out with knew he was not the marrying kind. Not from any desire to remain free or to sample as many women as he could, but from a very humane standpoint. He'd been thirteen years old when his father died in the line of duty, sacrificing his life while trying to save two children from being burned to death. And then Bryce had watched, day in, day out, what that sacrifice had done to his mother. It took away the laughter from her eyes and for a while, had sent her into a depression so deep, nothing and no one could reach her.

Even when she recovered, she was never the same after his father died.

To him, marriage was a pledge in which two people promised to live the rest of their lives together. It was only natural to assume that life would be for as long a time as could possibly be managed. That didn't mean taking on burning buildings on a regular basis, which was what he did for a living. A firefighter risked his life every day, risked the happiness of those he loved every day, pitting his life against a force of nature. And sometimes, he lost. The way his father had.

The tears Bryce saw in his mother's eyes for a full

year following his father's death at the age of thirty-four made him silently vow never to put anyone through what his mother had suffered.

Since his heart had been set on being a firefighter from the very first time his father had brought him down to the station, Bryce thought it only right to make a choice. A home and family, or a career, but not both. So he followed one dream and gave up the other. Most of the time, it seemed like a fair trade-off.

But every so often, he caught himself wondering what it would have been like if he had followed the other path. If he'd gone into engineering homes instead of saving them, or harnessing nature instead of battling it.

Talking to CeCe had made him wonder again. But he told himself that it was only a passing thing and that coming here this evening, after he'd gone off duty, was merely motivated out of a sense of neighborliness.

He rang the doorbell and waited. There was no response on the other side of the door, no music coming through an open window, no sound of shuffling. Maybe they'd gone out to get something to eat, he speculated. The moving van and its four men was gone.

Deciding to give it one last try, Bryce reached for the bell again when the door abruptly opened. Instead of Lisa, he found himself looking down at a woman who could have been mistaken for a slightly older version of the woman. Rather than shorts, she had on a sundress and her short, stylishly cut dark blond hair had a ribbon of gray running through it.

But she looked up at him with Lisa and CeCe's blue eyes. "Yes?"

"I'm not sure if I have the right house, but do Lisa Billings and her daughter, CeCe, live here?" Even if he hadn't been certain that he had the right house, one look at the woman would have assured him that he did. Still, it seemed a good enough way to begin.

Cecilia took swift measure of the handsome young man at the front door. She made decisions quickly. In her life, there hadn't always been much time for debating.

She liked his mouth. The lines around it indicated that he was given to smiling frequently. It was a good trait. And his eyes were kind. You could tell a great deal about a man by his eyes. Her husband had had kind eyes. CeCe's father hadn't, but she'd found it a difficult thing to convey to Lisa at the time. You had to let your children make their own mistakes, no matter how much it pained you to watch.

"Yes." Cecilia saw the broom leaning against the wall. The young man seemed to come with an odd assortment of things. He was holding flowers in his hand and there was some sort of thin book held flat against his side by his arm. She couldn't begin to guess what he had in the bag. "You are selling brooms, perhaps?"

Bryce shifted his weight. It wasn't often he felt self-conscious. "No, I—"

Curious who her mother was talking to, Lisa hurried over to the open door. "Who is it, Mother?" Peering around the door, she stopped short. "Oh God, it's you."

Intrigued, Cecilia stepped back from the doorway, allowing the visitor better access. "You know him?"

She hadn't expected him to actually come over, Lisa thought. He must have watched her leave with CeCe. "It's the fireman I told you about, the one who I found with CeCe."

Interest transformed into something akin to pleasure. A smile bloomed on Cecilia's face as she took hold of his wrist, drawing him into the house. "Ah, please come in, yes?"

Lisa's immediate response was, "No," but it was already too late. Her mother was shutting the door, after pulling the firefighter inside.

# Chapter Three

There'd only been just enough time for him to grab the broom before Bryce had found himself being pulled into the house by the diminutive woman who had clamped her hands around his wrist. She was surprisingly strong, given her size.

"Yes, ma'am," he said obediently, trying not to laugh. Obviously her mother and her daughter were a lot freer spirits than Lisa Billings was.

Out of the corner of his eye, Bryce saw CeCe come running into the room. The moment she saw him, she clapped her hands together in pure delight. Her grin was wide and welcoming.

Unlike, he noted, her mother's expression. Nobody had to tell him that Lisa wasn't happy about this turn of events, or the lack of immediate support she had.

CeCe fairly bounced in front of him, her eyes shining. "Hi, Bryce."

Lisa didn't want CeCe getting too friendly with

the intrusive firefighter, even if this was just a one-time visit.

"Mr. Walker," she corrected.

A little of the sunlight in CeCe's eyes abated. Bryce was quick to wave Lisa's admonishment aside. Too many children called him by his first name for CeCe to be singled out this way.

"That's too much of a mouthful for someone her size, Lisa. Bryce is fine."

Lisa didn't like him calling her by her first name. It made this conversation entirely too personal. Besides, she had the feeling that he was conveying more to her than just a name preference when he said that Bryce was fine, but there was no way she was about to allow herself to be drawn into any sort of word-play over that.

In the larger scheme of things, it was all a moot point. It wasn't as if the man was going to be someone they interacted with on a regular basis. As soon as she managed to usher him on his way, she didn't expect to ever see Bryce Walker again, barring a fire somewhere in the immediate area.

But before she could say anything, her mother was taking charge of the situation.

"Well, then, Bryce," Cecilia said, smiling at him, "we were just about to sit down to dinner. Perhaps you will join us?"

For a second, the air left her lungs. Lisa felt completely outflanked. She knew from experience that sending her mother a glaring look would be utterly wasted on the woman, so she didn't even bother—as much as she wanted to.

Instead she drew herself up and sent the withering look in Bryce's direction. The last thing she needed at the tail end of a trying day was an invasion by an unwanted guest, no matter how handsome he was.

"I'm sure Mr. Walker has to be somewhere else, Mother."

He returned the withering look with a long, slow appraisal that started at the top of her head and wound its way down to her bare toes. Lisa felt as if she suddenly had nothing on and felt all the hotter for it.

"No," he assured her quietly, "as a matter of fact, I don't."

Triumphant, Cecilia hooked her arm through Bryce's. She looked back at her daughter. "See?"

A thread of satisfaction wound through her words that she didn't bother to hide. As far as Cecilia was concerned, Lisa had been hiding behind her work and her family in an effort to barricade herself away from the rest of the world and deny the fact that she had a heart that could still be hurt. If nothing was risked, nothing was gained.

Cecilia glanced at the broom Bryce was still holding. "By the way, what is all this you bring with you?"

"Yes," Lisa seconded the question, her eyes sweeping over the bag he held in his other hand. "Just why are you dragging a broom around? Are you moonlighting as a broom salesman?" Maybe if she insulted him, he'd go away.

But instead of being insulted, he flashed a grin at her. "You and your mother think alike."

*Not hardly,* Lisa thought, swallowing a groan. To
her surprise, he presented the broom to her.

"It's for you. A housewarming gift," he explained
when she only stared at it.

She raised her eyes to his face, wondering what
he was up to. "I already have a broom. And a vac-
uum cleaner," she added, in case he had one waiting
in his car.

"Lisa, if the man wants to give you a broom, you
must be polite and take it," Cecilia told her kindly,
taking the broom from Bryce as if he had just presented her with the crown jewels of England.

Bryce couldn't read Lisa's expression, but he figured he could take a calculated guess what was going
on in her mind. Being a firefighter made him sensitive to highly volatile situations.

Time to defuse the moment, he thought. "Actually
it's an old tradition." Lisa looked at him blankly.
"The broom's symbolic," he told her. "You give
someone moving into a new home a broom to sweep
away any evil spirits that might still be lurking
around, left over from the old tenants. And the loaf
of bread—" he handed the bag he'd brought to Lisa
"—is so that you never go hungry."

She vaguely remembered hearing or reading about
the tradition. But Bryce didn't strike her as the kind
of person who went in for old-fashioned customs.
Looking at him uncertainly, she glanced inside the
bag. It was a loaf of bread all right. Closing it, she
looked at the bouquet he was still holding.

"And the flowers? What are they for?"

This part was a last-minute inspiration. As her

mother watched approvingly, he offered the flowers to Lisa with a flourish. "To make you smile."

"Oh." It was a simple bouquet of daisies, but it left her flustered and at a loss for words. Her mouth curved slightly without her even realizing it as she accepted the bouquet and looked down at the clustered, bouncy petals. Daisies, to pick apart one by one, murmuring "he loves me, he loves me not." "I see."

"It works!" CeCe announced with enthusiasm, grinning broadly. Then the grin began to fade away as she looked skeptically at the broom her grandmother was holding. She lowered her voice in a hushed whisper, inclining her head toward Bryce. "Does that mean we have evil spirits to sweep away?"

He saw the beginning of fear in her eyes. He'd meant to charm the mother, not frighten the daughter.

"They're all gone already," he told her solemnly. "It's the fire department's job to send any evil spirits packing a whole month before anyone new moves in. This—" he tapped the handle with his finger "—is just to remind them to stay away. Forever."

"Oh." Relieved, CeCe released a sigh that seemed twice as large as she was.

"Hey, I almost forgot. This is for you." With a gesture every bit as grand as the flourish he'd used to present the flowers to Lisa, he awarded the coloring book he had tucked under his arm to CeCe. "It's all about different fire trucks." He winked at her. "Something the department keeps around for Bedford's future taxpayers."

She hugged the thin booklet to her, pleased to be remembered. "Mommy, where are my crayons?"

"We'll find them after dinner." Otherwise, Lisa knew that there would be no prying CeCe away from the coloring book until she was finished.

It suddenly occurred to Bryce that he hadn't brought anything to give Lisa's mother. Admittedly, the woman had not been on his mind when he was planning his strategy. He turned to her now a tad sheepishly. "I'm sorry, I didn't bring anything for you."

"Oh, but you did, Bryce," Cecilia replied with a soft smile he could only wish would grace her daughter's lips. The smile filtered into her eyes, putting him completely at ease. "You brought me your company. Now, how do you feel about pierogi?"

Unfamiliar with the word, he could only shake his head. "I'm afraid I don't have any feelings about it one way or another."

"You will," Cecilia promised, patting his arm. "In time." She gestured toward what looked to be the dining area. "Now, you and Lisa go sit and wait. CeCe and I will bring the food. You are in for a treat." Cecilia winked, then taking the bag with the loaf of bread from her daughter, she commandeered her granddaughter's attention. With a nod of her head, she led the way into the kitchen. Leaving Bryce and Lisa alone.

Awkwardness descended immediately, draping itself heavily on her shoulders. Lisa wished her mother had let her be the one to bring in the meal, but she knew better. This whole scene couldn't have been playing itself out any better than if her mother had written it all out with specific stage directions.

Taking a deep breath, Lisa told herself she'd get through this. Abruptly she turned toward Bryce. "My mother worked at an embassy overseas when she was younger, she never completely got over ordering people around."

"I think she's great," Bryce said. Cecilia reminded him a little of Riley's mother, a woman who had been closer to him in his adolescent years than his own mother had been.

Lisa nodded, acknowledging the compliment. "Most people do," she remarked. "You really don't have to stay, you know."

He studied her face, trying to sort out her signals and his own wishful thinking. "Is that your polite way of saying get lost?"

She caught her tongue between her teeth, fighting the urge to tell him just that. She didn't need a bone-meltingly good-looking man putting ideas into her mother's head just by his very presence. Her mother was incorrigible enough as it was, ceaselessly promoting the idea that she should get back out there amid the sharks and swim until she found someone special to swim through life with.

As if that was ever going to happen.

To find someone she had to be looking. And she wasn't. Having her heart kicked in once was more than enough to teach her the pitfalls of wearing her heart on her sleeve. Of loving one man to distraction and placing all her faith, all her hopes and dreams into his careless hands.

She had loved Kyle, but he had loved his freedom even more. Watching him walk away, walk away from her and the promise of the family that was to be, was something she knew would remain with her for the rest of her life. She wasn't about to put herself into the position of experiencing that again even in the remotest sense.

Still, since Bryce had been exceptionally kind to her daughter and mother, it wouldn't kill her to be nice, she reasoned. Besides, if she sent him away now, before dinner, she knew her mother would never let her hear the end of it.

So Lisa resigned herself to suffering through the next hour or so. ''If I wanted you to get lost,'' she informed him tersely, ''I would say so.''

''Glad to hear it.'' He waited until she walked into the dining room, then followed behind her. ''So, what's this pier—pier—'' Fumbling for the word he hadn't quite grasped, he looked at her for help. Amusement curved her mouth. He had a feeling she liked him at a disadvantage. ''Help me out, here.''

''Pierogi. It's the Polish answer to ravioli,'' she elaborated.

He pulled out a chair for her. ''You're Polish?''

''Yes, anything wrong with that?'' She sat down and allowed him to push the chair in for her. The next moment, she felt her pulse scrambling as he lowered his face next to hers. She could have sworn she felt his breath along her cheek.

''Not  a thing.'' He saw the pulse in her throat jump as her jaw tightened. Bryce smiled to himself as he straightened again. Nice to know a graceful body like hers wasn't entirely sculpted out of ice. "It's just that Billings doesn't sound very Polish."

Her eyes were cold as he rounded the table to sit down.

"Billings was my married name." She'd toyed with changing it back to her maiden name, but there was CeCe to think of. The little girl was incredibly bright, but she was still a four-year-old with a four-year-old's emotions. Having a different name than her mother might be too confusing for her at this point.

"Was," he echoed. So his guess had been right. But he pushed the envelope a tiny bit further. "As in—I'm not stepping on anyone's toes by being here?"

His eyes were just a little too green, a little too warm for her. "Would you care?" Lisa asked.

He had his principles and that included never cutting in on another man's territory once it was staked out. "Very much so."

Honor was not the first word she thought of when Lisa thought of men in general. She'd learned the hard way that men like her father didn't exist anymore. They were far too practical. "Why? Because it would get you into a confrontational situation?"

She was the one who was looking for a confrontational situation, he thought. "Because I socialize with married women in a different way than I socialize with unmarried women," he told her amiably. And then he leaned forward and asked, "Do you find it gives you a backache?"

Her brows narrowed. She had no idea what he was talking about. ''What does?''

Bryce nodded toward her shoulders. ''That huge chip you're carrying around on your shoulder. I'd imagine it might make you stoop a lot less if you weren't lugging it around into every conversation.''

He'd never seen blue lightning flash before. He did now, in her eyes as she drew herself up, a pugnacious tilt to her head. ''I don't have a chip on my shoulder. I'm just careful. And suspicious.''

Something stirred within him and Bryce knew that Riley had been right. He did love a challenge. Any challenge, but particularly one that came dressed in white cuffed shorts and a tank top made for stirring up erotic fantasies in his mind. He leaned in closer to her. ''Of people in general, men specifically, or just me?''

Her gaze never wavered as she met his head-on. Only her stomach did a minor flip-flop, but that was for her to know and him not to find out, she thought. ''No, maybe and yes.''

He was game. ''Why me?''

She would have thought that easy enough to see. ''Why are you here?''

He repeated the offer he'd made earlier, in the fire station. ''I thought that since you were new in the neighborhood, I'd offer my services.''

Lisa had to concentrate to keep her skin from feeling as if it were tingling, responding to the way his eyes seemed to caress her—while an all-too-knowing smile graced his lips. ''What kind of services?''

''Any kind you'd like.'' Sitting here in her dining

room, it occurred to Bryce that he would very much like to discover what kissing her would be like. He had more than a hunch that the lady wasn't nearly as cool as she was trying to pretend. "I'm handy with my hands."

She tossed her head, needing to do something to keep from sinking, knee deep, into the look in his eyes. "I just bet you are."

"Bet he is what?"

Lisa's head snapped up, whirling in the direction her mother's voice was coming from. She hadn't even heard either her mother or her daughter enter the room. CeCe was right behind Cecilia carrying another place setting for the table. Her mother had her hands full, bringing in a huge platter of pierogi. It was still steaming, with whiffs of heat rising up from the melting pats of butter.

It occurred to Bryce that both mother and grandmother were placing a great deal of faith in the child's equilibrium. Rising, he quickly crossed to the little girl, reaching for the place setting. "Thanks, CeCe. I'll take it from here."

CeCe surrendered the plate and silverware without a word. But the look in her eyes said it all. It was obvious to Lisa that her daughter was completely smitten with Bryce.

Lisa didn't like what she was seeing here. Her mother was taking all this in and, from the look in her eyes, giving Bryce points. And it was clear that CeCe was already crazy about him. That made it two against one if he decided to make another appearance on her doorstep anytime soon.

Blowing out a long breath, all Lisa could do was hope that she could put him off from trying.

"Bet he is what?" CeCe repeated, looking from her mother to Bryce.

The kid was a sponge, Bryce thought. And probably part bull terrier. He'd be willing to bet that once she latched on to something, she didn't give up until she got what she was after.

"Handy with my hands," he told her.

"Like how?" CeCe asked eagerly. She was quick to take the place right beside him at the table. "Can you do tricks?"

"I don't know about tricks," he confided even as he produced a coin from behind her ear and then presented it to her. "But I can pretty much repair anything that needs fixing."

Her eyes as big as saucers, CeCe took the coin from him, staring at it as if he'd just handed her magic in a solid form.

"Wow." Clutching the coin to her, afraid it might disappear, she looked at her mother. "Did you see that, Mommy?"

Lisa cocked her head, studying their guest. Wondering just how much more there was to Bryce Walker than met the eye. She still had no idea why he'd planted himself on her doorstep. It wasn't as if she'd encouraged him in any way. The girl within her who had flirted and taken life at face value had long since died. Reality had done that. Reality and Kyle.

She felt CeCe's eager eyes on her, waiting for an answer. She didn't want her daughter falling for this man's tricks, but it seemed almost a foregone conclusion.

"I certainly did." Reaching for the bowl her mother had placed in the center of the table, she offered it to Bryce. "That'd be a handy trick to have if I'm ever overdrawn at the bank."

Taking the bowl from her, he helped himself to two fairly large serving spoons, depositing things that looked like triangular ravioli, sans sauce, onto his place. "I'm at your beck and call."

She passed the bowl to her mother. "I wasn't aware that I had becked or called," Lisa said.

Cecilia ladled out three large pierogi onto CeCe's plate, her eyes on Bryce. "You must forgive my daughter, Bryce. She is tired after a long day of ordering the movers around."

He was prudent enough to hide the smile that came to his lips. So instead, he turned his attention to his surroundings. There were still boxes nestled here and there, but for the most part, it appeared as if the two women had gotten a good start in turning the house into a real home.

"Apparently she did a great job of it." His expression the picture of geniality, he looked at Lisa. "When I moved into my place, it seemed like months before I got the last of the boxes cleared out. And I didn't have all that much to begin with." The van, he'd noticed from his vantage point in the fire station, had unloaded a great many crates and boxes onto the lawn.

"Perhaps if you were organized…" Lisa let her voice drift off as she began eating. She heard her mother clear her throat. Sorry, Mother, this is one match that isn't going to take.

"Do you live near here?" CeCe asked.

"Yes, I do," Bryce managed to say between bites, "when I'm not at the station."

CeCe cocked her head, far more interested in what Bryce had to say than in what was on her plate. "You live at the fire station?"

He nodded, reaching for the glass of water Cecilia had brought in. "Every two days."

Her small face puckered as she tried to make sense of this eccentric lifestyle. "Why?"

She looked so cute trying to puzzle out his words, Bryce thought. "Because that's when I'm on duty. It's a lot easier to answer an alarm if I'm right there than if they have to call me at my apartment."

CeCe was clearly in awe. "Do you slide down the pole and everything?"

"Sometimes." He preferred taking the flight of stairs down, but he had a feeling that CeCe appreciated the more glamorous image. It was anyone's guess what her mother preferred, he thought, glancing at Lisa to see if she was taking this in.

But CeCe wasn't about to relinquish his attention just yet. "Can I?"

He'd probably have to clear it with the chief first. He had a feeling that CeCe wasn't the type to be satisfied with just one quick spin down the pole. "We'll see."

"CeCe, let the man eat." Realizing that her voice had been a little sharp, Lisa offered her daughter a smile, then raised her eyes to his. Damning Bryce for creating that unsettling feeling within her. "She has a tendency to ask a lot of questions."

But Bryce merely waved away the reproval. "How else can she learn?" He looked at the little girl.

"Right, CeCe?" He was rewarded with a firm nod of her head and a wide smile that did more than hint at the way she felt about him. He couldn't resist satisfying his curiosity. "How old are you, CeCe?"

To his surprise, she lifted her chin just the way he'd seen her mother do. "It's not nice to ask a lady her age."

Bryce nearly choked, laughing.

Lisa was on her feet instantly, ready to help him. "Are you all right?"

He held up his hand, trying to catch his breath. "Sorry, that went down the wrong way." Cecilia was urging a glass of water at him. He took it, drinking half before saying anything more. Setting the glass down, he grinned at CeCe. "You have yourself a gem here."

"We try not to say that around her so she doesn't get a swelled head," Lisa told him. She couldn't quite manage to keep the pride out of her voice. "And to answer your question, she's four, going on fifty."

It looked as if the way to the lady's good side was her daughter. No hardship there, Bryce thought. He'd always had a weakness for kids.

"That I can readily believe. She's extremely well spoken for four."

Never one to be left out of the conversation for long, CeCe put in her own two cents. "G-mama says I take after Mommy. Mommy talked when she was six months old."

"I can believe that, too," he confided to CeCe, slanting a glance toward Lisa.

# Chapter Four

He was overstaying his welcome.

Not that, Lisa thought, she could be accused of exactly welcoming his presence in the first place. But even if she had, he'd gone way beyond the boundaries. Dinner had come and gone, as had the dishes that went with it. They had all been collected, washed and put away and still he was here. Here charming the shoes and socks right off her family, making her feel antsy and isolated.

And completely unarmed.

It was, she felt, like standing on the sidelines, watching an accident happen in slow motion and being unable to do anything about it.

Any attempts she'd made to usher Bryce out had gone unnoticed, certainly unheeded. Her mother and CeCe were far too busy enjoying his company. Anyone coming in would have thought that they and

Bryce had been friends for ages, instead of knowing each other for just a few hours.

Lisa peered out of the kitchen into the living room where the others were sitting. She was really surprised at her mother. Granted, Cecilia Dombrowski was one of the warmest, most outgoing human beings on the face of the earth and there wasn't a person alive who didn't like her, but she'd never seen her mother take to someone *this* quickly.

Okay, her mother was friendly, but she wasn't a pushover for heaven's sake. She could usually spot a phony at thirty paces. Her mother had tried to warn her about Kyle in the beginning, but Lisa had been too blindly in love with him to listen.

But if Cecilia was so insightful, why was her mother sitting on the sofa watching home videos with Bryce and CeCe and taking turns narrating them with her granddaughter? To make matters worse, Bryce was acting as if he was really enjoying himself.

As if his prime reason in coming here in the first place hadn't been to get somewhere with her.

She frowned, withdrawing.

*Listen to yourself, Lisa. If you don't sound like the most conceited thing to walk the earth, I don't know what does.*

She sighed, dragging her hand through her hair. Maybe she was being too hard on him. Maybe he was exactly what he seemed. A nice guy. Someone who'd taken a shine to her daughter. Someone who just wanted, as he said, to welcome her into the neighborhood.

Yeah, right, Lisa laughed shortly to herself. And

if she bought into that, then there was a bridge located in the middle of the Big Apple someone was just dying to sell her. Well, she wasn't in the market for bridges. Or for men, either.

"How is that popcorn coming, Lisa?" Cecilia called out from the living room. "Do you need some help?"

Yes, she needed help, Lisa thought, opening the microwave oven door, but it wasn't with the popcorn. It was with the Pied Piper sitting in her living room, regaling her mother and her daughter.

Placing the rectangular bag seal side down in the oven, she closed the door again and set the timer.

"No, that's okay. It'll be just a few more minutes." She pushed the Start button. "It's already in the micro—"

She tensed, sensing that he'd come in behind her. Whirling around, she saw him. Something instinctive made her back up against the counter.

He grinned easily at her, wondering why she was so skittish. He hadn't given her any reason to act as if he was about to pounce on her. "Don't worry, I'm not here to steal your popcorn."

The best defense was a good offense, she knew that, doing her best to look disdainful. "Who says you were?"

"You did. By the look you just gave me. I figured that kind of look was reserved for hulking Neanderthals coming out at you in dark alleys at the stroke of midnight."

She hated the way he was just presuming things about her. The way he was making himself at home.

In *her* home. "I don't hang around dark alleys at the stroke of midnight."

"Smart lady." The grin slid into a softer, warmer smile that was that much more deadly for its seeming compassion. "You don't have anything to be afraid of, you know."

Just what gave him the right to make that kind of assumption about her, that she was afraid of him? "I know," she snapped, making the assertion much too quickly.

"Do you?" Studying her expression, he wasn't so sure. No matter what she said, she seemed afraid of him. Or maybe leery was a better word. He didn't want her to be either. "You're a beautiful woman and I just want to spend a little time with you."

Nothing was as simple as that. "And my mother and daughter?"

His eyes smiled at her even before he did. "And your mother and daughter."

Did he actually think that she believed him? That she didn't know he was just playing up to her mother and daughter to get on her good side?

"Let me get this straight. You're one of those rare human beings who actually likes watching someone else's home videos."

Did she know that when she became flippant, her eyes threw off little sparks of blue that were utterly fascinating? Bryce found himself being drawn closer. "If the subject is right, sure."

They were playing words games, she knew that, but she heard herself asking, "And it is?"

There was a wayward wisp of hair, just at her temple, and he gently tucked it behind her ear. His fingertips trailed along her cheek, his eyes on hers. "You're in every scene."

The breath stopped in her lungs. She anticipated his next move. She could almost feel his lips on hers.

The microwave bell went off.

Lisa silently blessed it as she quickly turned away from Bryce and the kiss she saw coming straight toward her. She only hoped he wouldn't hear her heart pounding madly.

The picture on the screen faded out, signaling the end of the video tape. Sitting on the chair adjacent to the sofa, Lisa breathed a sigh of relief. Her trial by fire was almost over.

Her relief was not shared by the other females in her family. Cecilia rose to her feet. "Well, it has been a very nice evening, Bryce, but now I must go and put my namesake to bed."

CeCe had been nodding off for the last part of the home video, but now her eyes flew wide-open in protest. "Ah, G-Mama…"

Cecilia smiled at her warmly. "This is when she is most like a four-year-old," the woman confided to Bryce.

"Why don't you see your friend to the door, Mother?" Lisa suggested sweetly, circumventing Bryce as she got on the other side of her mother and took her daughter's hand. "I'll put CeCe to bed."

But CeCe had her own ideas on who she wanted accompanying her to her room. "Can't Bryce do it?"

she asked eagerly, wedging her little fingers into his hand. "He can read me a story."

She was going to have to have a long, stern talk with her daughter tomorrow. For now, Lisa merely admonished, "CeCe, you don't ask a guest to read you a story at bedtime."

It was apparent that CeCe saw no reason for the rule. "Why not, Mommy?" Instead of waiting for an answer from her mother, she looked up at Bryce for help.

She was going to be a heartbreaker, he decided, no doubt about it. Just like her mother, he assumed. The innocent look he gave CeCe was accompanied by a baffled shrug. "Beats me."

That was all CeCe was waiting to hear. "Then you will?"

He slanted a glance toward Lisa. "If your mom gives her permission."

Oh, no, she wasn't about to be cast as the heavy in this drama no matter how much she was anticipating his departure. Besides, Lisa thought, a smile beginning to curve her mouth, it would serve him right if she agreed.

Lisa raised her eyes to his. "You don't know what you're letting yourself in for."

Bryce didn't see the need for a warning. He'd read stories to kids before. "Why? Are her books all written in Old English?"

"No, but—" She wasn't going to say anymore, she decided. Let him find out on his own just what bedtime with CeCe was like. Lisa inclined her head, seemingly surrendering. "Okay, you asked for this."

That wasn't strictly true. He hadn't "asked" for this, CeCe had. He had just seen nothing wrong in agreeing to read the little girl a bedtime story before she fell asleep. What he hadn't counted on was reading to a night owl. He'd been pressed into reading bedtime stories before, most notably to his niece and nephew. But Lanie and Ethan only required a few pages before they'd each drift off to sleep. Rarely had he ever even finished whatever story he was reading. It had certainly never turned into a marathon experience before.

It was one now.

Bryce found himself reading one tale after another, albeit short ones, in a book of bedtime stories that seemed to go on forever. Just like CeCe's attention span.

It was as if she hung on every word in the story. He'd never come across anyone quite like CeCe before. Which, he supposed, glancing up at her mother's smug expression as he began yet another story, was only natural since he'd never run into anyone exactly like Lisa before, either.

For a while, it seemed as if CeCe became more and more wide-awake with each page he turned. But finally, as yet another story came to an end, he looked over toward the little girl and saw that her eyes had finally closed.

The kid looked like an angel, he caught himself thinking, even if she was a taxing one. With relief, he closed the book and slowly eased himself to his feet, careful not to make any noise.

Lisa had to admit she was surprised. She would

have bet anything that the pushy firefighter would have thrown in the towel after one story. Surely after two. That he hadn't, that he'd gone on to placate CeCe, reading each and every one of the stories the child eagerly selected, undermined the things she'd first thought about him. She was impressed by his tenacity, his patience. And his kindness. Though she'd probably listened just as intently as CeCe had, but for different reasons, she'd never once detected the slightest annoyance in his voice, even when he began the last story.

Maybe there was more to the man than she'd originally given him credit for.

Silently following him into the hallway, she quietly eased the door closed behind them. The small light she left on in CeCe's room, to scare away the monsters that occasionally popped out of the little girl's fertile imagination, crept softly out, squeezing itself through from beneath the doorsill.

A tiny sliver of guilt found its way through Lisa as she looked at Bryce. Even she had to grant that his effort was far over and above the call of duty. "How's your throat?"

He would have laughed at the question if he could, but right now that wasn't possible. His whole mouth felt like a used sandbox. "Dry."

He noticed the smile that came to her lips. But rather than looking smug, he thought it seemed almost empathetic. And grateful. Maybe he'd scored a few points after all.

"I tried to warn you," she reminded him. After

hesitating for a moment, she nodded toward the kitchen. "Come with me."

Her mother had been in the kitchen when they'd taken CeCe to bed. When she'd been growing up, it seemed to Lisa that her mother spent most of her free time there. The memory of heavenly scents wafting from the oven and permeating the room still lingered in the recess of her mind.

But Cecilia Dombrowski was nowhere to be found when she walked into the kitchen now. It figured. Lisa had had a hunch that her mother would pull a disappearing act the first chance she got.

Her mother was an incurable romantic, but then, she'd married the man she'd fallen in love with at first sight and lived happily with him for almost thirty years. Things like that didn't happen anymore.

Going straight to the sink, Lisa ran the water until it was sufficiently cold enough, then filled a glass and offered it to her guest.

Bryce figured his best bet was to drain the whole glass before attempting to say anything. If he didn't, he had a sneaking feeling his voice would emerge high-pitched and squeaking, not unlike a popular daytime cartoon character his niece was fond of.

Setting the empty glass on the drain board, he turned to look at Lisa. There was new admiration in his eyes. "You do this every night? Read to her until she drops off?" If she did, he took his hat off to her.

She held back a laugh, but wasn't entirely successful. "I know how to say no to her," she answered. "You could have, too, you know. After three stories, you were more than within your rights."

They had a difference of opinion here, he thought, shaking his head in response.

"Rights are one thing, but those big blue eyes of hers pleading with me are another. I would have felt awful telling her I wasn't going to read any more." He shrugged philosophically. "Besides, there are worse ways to spend an hour."

She didn't have to look at her watch to know he was wrong. Dusk was beginning to sweep long strokes through the terrain outside the window. "More like an hour and a half," she corrected.

"Time flies by when I'm surrounded by beautiful women."

Nerves began to play hopscotch through Lisa again. She would have thought she could keep the lid securely down on them by now, she told herself, annoyed. She tried to sound brazen. "Does that happen often to you? Being surrounded by beautiful women?"

"Not often." When she turned away from him, he decided that it might be interesting to get in her way again. So he did. "Just this evening, actually."

She sidestepped him to get to the refrigerator. She suddenly needed something cold to drink. Shifting a few things aside, she reached for a can of cola. "Do you rehearse all this?"

Reaching over, he took hold of the hand with the can in it, held it steady and popped the top for her. "Comes naturally when I have the right inspiration."

She had no idea why the quick, soft spray of carbonated fizz wetting her fingers as it emerged from the can felt so erotic. Or why the look in his eyes made her feel as if she were melting. But they did.

She struggled not to sound breathless. "You sure you're a firefighter and not a salesman?"

His eyes never left her face. "What would I be selling?"

She took a quick swig from the can before answering. "You."

"Hmm." She wasn't sure if she heard the sound coming from him, or just imagined it. But she felt the heat of his smile as it slowly slipped over her. "And how'm I doing?"

With effort, she pulled back, reminding herself that the first time she had seen Kyle, her knees had threatened to buckle. The look in his eyes had seemed endless, too. But it had all been shallow.

The memory helped. Lisa straightened slightly. "I never impulse-buy," she told him. "When I want to buy something, I put it back, walk around the store, maybe even leave the store and think about it some more before I ever make the decision to bring something home with me."

The more she resisted, the more he found himself tempted to discover just what it was she was holding back. Just what her lips tasted like. Just how soft her skin felt.

"People like you could bring the economy down to its knees." He drew closer. "Or maybe only the salesmen," he corrected.

There was nowhere for her to retreat. The refrigerator was at her back, with the counter on one side and somehow, Bryce had managed to have the rest of the territory covered. The bravado she clung to was beginning to falter. "Don't firefighters have to be in bed by a certain time?"

His smile went right through her bones. "Why? Are you offering to tuck me in?"

If she screamed, her mother would be down in two minutes no matter where she was in the house. Hopefully to come to her aid, not Bryce's.

She licked her lips without being completely conscious of it. "No, I'm offering you the door."

The light glistened on her moistened lips. She couldn't have done anything more enticing if she tried. "I've seen it," he told her softly. "Not interested."

It wasn't easy sounding indignant when her voice was fading. "I don't care what you're interested in, Mr. Walker."

He inclined his head, as if he were taking every word to heart. "Aren't you?"

He was standing awfully close to her, she thought, panic refreshing itself. So close that she could feel her breath mingling with his. So close that she thought he could hear her heart pounding in her chest, giving her away.

Last time he'd been this close, on the verge of kissing her, the microwave bell had gone off, coming to her rescue.

But there was no bell to mercifully intervene this time.

The prickly feeling of panic grew, washing over her at the same time that anticipation heightened the ante, making her breath short and her skin tingle even before their lips met.

And then he framed her face with his hands, bringing his mouth down to hers. Lisa knew she should run. Run, laugh, talk, something. Anything. Anything but play into his hands and kiss him.

She couldn't move.

It was as if every bone in her body had completely frozen, become utterly paralyzed. The only thing that worked was her heart and it was swiftly inching its way out of double-time, into triple-time.

And then it happened.

The meeting of his lips with hers was soft, luxurious, not unlike slipping into a bubble bath she'd been looking forward to for a long time. Longer than she'd possibly been aware of anticipating. Even as warm pleasure wrapped itself around her, it stole her breath away. And made her pulse accelerate to speeds that were completely unclockable by mere mortal inventions created in an attempt to track such things.

She had absolutely no recollection of leaning into Bryce, or of falling headlong into the kiss that was growing hotter by the microsecond. All she knew was that somehow, the paralysis that had held her captive only a moment ago was gone, and with it, the rigidity of her body. She was almost completely liquid now. In danger of pouring out onto the floor without a vessel to hold her.

She could have sworn she heard a moan, too deep to be her, too high to be him, but it vibrated all through her, resonating in her throat, echoing in her body where it subsequently and immediately burned to a crisp.

She tasted of honey and something forbidding that he couldn't place. All he knew was that he wanted more. And that she was, even though he'd thought he was prepared, a complete surprise. A complete revelation. And someone he knew, even as his lips were sealed to hers, that he wanted to kiss again. And again.

She was someone who he wanted. Pure and simple.

The thought sent alarms through him, but he disregarded them. He'd always been able to handle alarms before and there was no reason to believe that he wouldn't be able to now.

Drawing back he smiled at her. "Maybe I'd better go home."

"Maybe," she echoed in agreement. Because something within her whispered to him "stay," and she knew that was a very dangerous sign.

# Chapter Five

"So? How was it?"

Lisa jumped, swinging around from her window to see her mother standing in her doorway, an amused expression on her face.

Was it that obvious? she wondered.

She hardly remembered closing the front door after Bryce had left, barely two heartbeats after he'd kissed her almost completely senseless. Well, maybe not senseless, but certainly draining her of the ability to string abrupt thoughts together to make any sort of a coherent whole. She knew she didn't remember how she got to her own room, to stand behind her curtain and look out across the street to where the fire station stood like some vigilant guard, keeping them all safe and allowing them to sleep soundly in their beds, secure in the knowledge that they were being looked after.

Not hardly, she thought. At least, not tonight. If

she got ten minutes of uninterrupted sleep tonight, she'd be the first one to be surprised.

Leaving the window, she gave her mother what she hoped was a properly mystified look. "How was what?"

Cecilia's smile only deepened. As if her daughter could ever fool her. There were hardly any thoughts that came to Lisa that Cecilia didn't share in some way on some level. Which was why she completely understood the heartache her daughter had suffered because of Kyle and she wanted her to work her way beyond it.

"The kiss," Cecilia replied.

There were times Lisa could swear her mother could read her mind. But because she wanted to forestall any idea her mother had to promote any sort of a relationship between her and the firefighter, Lisa tossed her head and tried to sound nonchalant. "What makes you think he kissed me?"

Cecilia came to her then, pretending to study the face she knew better than her own. "Well, either he kissed you, my love, or someone has been leaning on your lips." Her eyes shone. "Was it wonderful?"

Lisa half committed to a shrug that died away at inception. "Unexpected."

"But wonderful," Cecilia pressed, moving so that she could better see her daughter's face.

"Mother—"

Cecilia cut through the note of protest in her daughter's voice. "Why won't you admit that he stirred something inside you?"

Cecilia had never been one of those mothers too

busy in her own life to take an interest in hers. She used to think that was a good thing, but right now, Lisa wanted to be left alone so that she could rebuild the foundations that Bryce and his hot lips had shaken and put into jeopardy.

Frustrated, Lisa perched her hands on her hips in a time-worn pose. "Why do you insist that he did?"

Cecilia knew that stance. It was the one Lisa took when she was trying to make her back off so that she could convince herself of something she didn't believe. *Not this time, my darling.*

"Because that man would stir the insides of a statue. And because I want you to learn to open up again." Taking her daughter's face in her hand, she forced Lisa to look at her. "You used to laugh all the time, Lisa. You do not laugh anymore."

Lisa pulled her head back. "Yes, I do. Sometimes." The protest felt flat on her lips. She could never lie to her mother, no matter how hard she tried or how much she wanted to. "Life's just gotten complicated in the last four years, that's all."

Cecilia shook her head, unwilling to be put off. "People with complicated lives laugh." Her eyes held her daughter's. "People who hurt, do not."

Frustrated, Lisa drew away and began to pace restlessly through the room. She had no idea why she felt so restless and had, since the moment she had seen the way Bryce Walker had looked at her. Like a woman. A woman with desires and needs. She'd done her best to ignore that woman, to bury her. But one evening with him threatened to undo all her hard work.

"Don't you understand?" she pleaded. "That's exactly what I'm trying to avoid, Mother, being hurt."

"I do understand." Aching to take her daughter into her arms to make everything all right, Cecilia held herself in check. She couldn't make things all right, she knew that. All she could do was pray that her judgment was correct. "I understand that by being so on your guard, you are avoiding so many wonderful feelings. Like being kissed again. Like having your heart take wing." Cecilia sat down on the bed, patting the place next to her. After a moment, Lisa sighed and sank down beside her mother. "Your father was not my first love."

This was something she'd never heard before. Lisa had just assumed, from everything she'd witnessed growing up, and from what she'd been privy to, that each of her parents had been the other's first as well as one and only loves. To learn differently now, after all these years, completely stunned her.

She stared at her mother in utter amazement. "He wasn't?"

Cecilia shook her head, her eyes softening. "No, my first love was Vincent." She closed her eyes, remembering. "Vincent gave me my first kiss. He was tall and blond and, oh so very sweet." She looked at Lisa, wanting to share this with her after all this time. "I loved him more than I could possibly put into words. My family did not approve. Vincent was even poorer than we were, a poor student studying at the university. Only lint in his pockets. None of that mattered." She sighed, thinking of the naiveté

of youth. "We were going to run away together and
live on love."

Lisa could picture that, picture her mother trusting
to God and fate and giving her heart freely. It was
the kind of person her mother was. "What happened?"

A long, heartfelt sigh escaped Cecilia's lips. "Vincent was killed in a student protest." She smiled
sadly, covering Lisa's hand with her own. "Freedom
was not a word tolerated kindly by the authorities in
my country when I was a young girl. I cried for
weeks." Rousing herself, she cupped her palm on
Lisa's cheek. "The point is, I went on with my life
and found your father. He was a truly wonderful man
and we had a wonderful life together. And we had
you."

Lisa knew where she was going with this. Knew,
too, that the lesson didn't apply. She rose. "The difference being that your first love was wonderful,
Mother. Mine didn't exactly turn out that way."

Getting to her feet, Cecilia followed Lisa to the
closet. "All the more reason for you to look again.
Your perfect love is out there but it will not come
knocking on your door, looking for you. Well," she
amended, thinking of Bryce and his unexpected visit,
"perhaps it did, but it won't always be so accom-
modating. Not without encouragement," she said
pointedly.

Lisa took her nightgown out of the bureau drawer.
This could go on for hours. There was no way she
could convince her mother to see her side of it and
she wasn't about to capitulate. "You are a romantic,
Mother, and I am very tired."

With a sigh, Cecilia relented. "No, I am a realist and you are very stubborn, but for tonight, I will let you rest." Beginning to cross the doorway, she suddenly stopped and looked at her daughter. And then smiled.

Closing the drawer again, Lisa saw her expression and paused. "What?"

There'd been something in her daughter's eyes just then, something unguarded and fleeting that she had witnessed. "It was good, wasn't it?"

There was no point in lying or attempting to hide the truth. Only to water it down. Lisa shrugged, pretending indifference. "It was all right."

But Cecilia knew better. "You have your father's gift for understatement. But you have my eyes." She leaned over and kissed her daughter on the forehead. "Pleasant dreams, my love."

With that she walked out, leaving Lisa to spend the rest of her night with her thoughts and specters of things she both wanted and didn't want to come.

The tiny bell she'd mounted in lieu of the electronic surveillance system she had yet to hook up sounded, signaling that someone had entered the shop.

Exhausted, she wondered irritably why people didn't stop to read signs. The one in her window announced that the grand opening of Dreams and Toyland was still a week away. She should have locked the door after the delivery men left, but she'd been too busy looking over what they'd brought.

Fixing a smile she could only pray didn't look phony, she turned around from the counter littered with different toys she was only now beginning to sort out. "I'm afraid that we're not opened yet."

The smile on her lips faded as surprise, disbelief, wariness and more than just a touch of nerves came in its place, freezing her expression.

Bryce slowly ambled in, his hands shoved into the back pockets of a worn pair of jeans that had long since decided to lovingly showcase the contours they adhered to. He was wearing a sleeveless T-shirt that she vaguely remembered hearing referred to as a muscle shirt and it was displaying just that. Muscle. Lots of it.

He was looking around as he approached. She couldn't begin to guess what he was thinking but something protective rose up in her, ready to field any criticism.

"I was hoping you might make an exception, seeing our connection and all."

She'd thought that, surely here, she'd have some respite. Annoyed, she rounded the counter and crossed to him, meeting him by a stack of unopened boxes containing large trains originating from Germany.

He'd asked her what she did for a living, but she hadn't expected him to come searching for her to check the premises out for himself. Especially when she'd been so deliberately vague about where the store was.

"What are you doing here?"

He glanced around, wondering if she was attempting to do this all by herself or if there was an assistant lurking somewhere. "Your mother told me where the store was located."

Cecilia had told him when he'd dropped by their house this morning that Lisa had only just begun to put the store in order. The woman had obviously been working like a demon, he decided. There were open boxes everywhere and she'd begun making headway on one of the shelves on the back wall. He made a mental note to clean up his place if he ever decided to have her over.

Trust her mother to be on the misguided side of cupid. Though she didn't relish confrontation, there was no other way to handle this except bluntly. "Why are you following me?"

"I'm not," he told her quickly, then decided that wasn't entirely true. "Not exactly." Funny, he'd never had trouble speaking his mind before, but his tongue felt a little thick in his mouth right now. Had to be the way she looked at him, he decided. Making him lose his train of thought. "Actually—" he glanced around the shop "—I've come looking for a toy."

Yes, she just bet he did. A five-foot-plus toy. Well, it wasn't going to be her. Or any reasonable facsimile thereof. "Sorry, we don't carry any life-size dolls to play with."

He grinned at her rejoinder. He supposed he couldn't fault her for the image she had of him. Though she didn't know him, he had to admit that wasn't entirely without foundation. "It's not for me, it's for Lanie."

She stopped sorting through the clutter on the counter. "Girlfriend?"

He grinned. When she was a very little girl, no older than CeCe, Lanie had informed him in no uncertain terms that she was going to marry him—until she'd gotten a crush on a boy in her kindergarten class. "Not exactly, although she did win my heart the very first time I held her in my arms." He saw Lisa's eyes narrow as she looked at him. "She looked up at me with those big blue eyes of hers and I just melted."

Was he going to preen and parade his conquests before her, thinking she was going to be impressed how in demand he was? Irritated, she turned away. "Spare me the details."

"Why?" He came around to the counter. Leaning on it with his elbow, he bent over and peered into her face. "I thought you liked kids."

"I do—" Since he wasn't moving, she stopped trying to work. And then, like an instant replay at a sporting event, his words hit her. "What does this have to do with kids?"

"Everything, although Lanie doesn't think of herself as one. At ten, she thinks she is a young woman. But, young woman or not, she still loves stuffed animals." He liked the way surprise, mingled with what he took to be embarrassment, filtered into Lisa's eyes. It gave her a very desirable look. "She has about a couple hundred, a lot of them from me. Unfortunately, Lanie keeps most of them on her bed, something her mother holds me accountable for.

"But it's Lanie's birthday next week and I'm trying to find an exotic stuffed animal she doesn't have yet." He straightened. "As you've probably guessed, this gets to be more and more of a challenge."

Lisa was trying to sort out all the fragments of

information coming at her. "Is Lanie your daughter?"

He shook his head. "My niece. I don't have any kids, but I've got squatter's rights to my niece and nephew." He raised one teasing brow. "Does that make me a semigood person in your eyes?"

She moved back, determined not to repeat last night's mistake. If he couldn't get close to her, he couldn't kiss her. Couldn't send her into another night of sleeplessness.

And for that matter, she wasn't about to get drawn into any kind of an intimate conversation, either. "All my eyes see is a man."

He laughed softly to himself. "Well, that's a healthy start at any rate. So—" he looked slowly around, wondering just where to start in this sea of unopened shipping cartons "—do you have any exotic stuffed animals in your inventory?" Seeing what looked like a cluster of stuffed animals peering out of one box, he made his way over to the side of the store where she had begun stocking the shelves earlier.

It was against her better judgment, but she followed him. A sale was a sale. "You're serious then?"

He picked up a gorilla with particularly soulful eyes. Lanie already had a gorilla, but not one with eyes like this. In a pinch, if he didn't find anything else, this would do.

Holding the gorilla before him, he turned around. "I never joke about stuffed animals." He saw her lower lip curve slightly and considered it a break-through. "Hey, you can smile before noon."

Lisa figured it was safer not to comment. Instead she began taking out animals she had packed earlier in the week and placing them on the bottom shelf. She was a sucker for stuffed animals herself, but there was no reason to tell him that. "Just how exotic were you thinking?"

The question evoked a smile as, looking at her, he put an entirely different spin on the word. He saw a blush creeping up her cheek that he found strangely endearing. In general, his taste ran to far more worldly, experienced women. They were the kind who didn't ask for commitments and expected none. But there was just something about Lisa...

He figured maybe it was just the novelty. "Why don't you run some things by me and I'll let you know?"

Wetting her lips, she turned away and dug through the box, inadvertently giving him a stirring view to occupy his mind while he waited. Finding what she was looking for, she held up a rather realistic, yet cuddly looking grizzly bear. "How's this?"

He shook his head. He'd given Lanie the exact same one for an outstanding report card. "She already has it."

Lanie, it quickly became apparent, also had the elephant, the ostrich, the six-foot brown snake and the emu she produced. Impressed at the extent of his niece's collection, Lisa placed the stuffed cheetah she was holding on display and contemplated the contents of the box. She had other unusual stuffed animals, but they were somewhere in the back, in the boxes she had yet to open.

"You weren't kidding when you said your niece had unusual stuffed animals."

"It's what she loves," he told her. "I always try to accommodate a lovely lady."

Before she could make a cryptic comment, Bryce surveyed the store's interior with a discerning eye. The sign outside said that she was opening in a week. That probably meant she was going to work herself into a frenzy to be ready on time. Most of the displays were empty and there were shelves lying on the floor that had to go up. His schedule was such that he worked two days and then was off two days—which gave him the time to help her out if she was interested.

He knew he was.

Bryce turned back to her, tucking his hands back into his pockets. "Say, you need a hand with all this?"

That's all she needed, to have him talk his way into staying.

Ignoring him, she turned away and went back to work. The story about trying to find an unusual stuffed animal was probably just a ruse, anyway. "I can manage, thank you."

At first glance, he thought, she didn't particularly look like a stubborn woman. Just went to show how deceptive appearances could be. "Yes, but two can manage faster than one."

She spared him a quick glance. "Not if one of the two keeps getting in the way."

Presenting himself before her, he spread his hands wide. "Then order me around. I'm obedient. House-broken, too."

She paused, wondering what she had done to merit this onslaught of attention. Maybe he liked being discouraged. "Why are you so determined to help?"

The shrug was innocent—and unconvincing from where she stood. "I'm a frustrated Good Samaritan."

The line about cutting her nose to spite her face occurred to her. She couldn't afford to hire anyone when she wasn't bringing in any income. And there were a lot of boxes to lug out.

With a heartfelt sigh, she surrendered. "As long as you're not a frustrated anything else, I guess I could use some muscle."

"Muscle at your service." To underscore his statement, he struck a typical body builder pose and made a muscle with his right arm.

She was going to say something flippant, but for the life of her, she couldn't remember what. The words flew completely out of her head the second she looked at him.

The man was built like a rock, a gorgeous rock. When he flexed his arm like that, his entire upper torso transformed into a body that heretofore she'd only seen in a museum of art in New York.

It took her a minute to find her tongue and another minute to remember how to use it. The fact that it had gone dry didn't help matters any. "There're some boxes with trains in the storeroom. Bring them out."

"And?" he prodded when she didn't continue. "I

can actually remember two-step instructions on occasions. Try me.''

Try me. Why did that sound like such a tempting invitation instead of just a line said in jest? She waved him on his way, wishing that the air-conditioning system was hooked up. She was suddenly incredibly warm. ''Just bring them out.''

He saluted, winked and went to do her bidding. Leaving her stomach suddenly constricting and transforming itself into a pretzel.

In Bryce's estimation, the view from where he found himself standing at the moment more than made up for the discomfort of hauling around inventory in a store where the air-conditioning system had yet to be turned on and the temperature was hovering somewhere between dreadful and fully roasted.

The woman had legs worth killing for.

Turning around to ask a question about where the next box of electric trains was to be displayed, he saw Lisa perched at the third from the top rung of the mobile ladder. The ladder was leaning against the back wall shelves and she was stubbornly intent on stacking extra boxes of Molly Twinkle and her entire entourage. The tan shorts she was wearing were hiking up on her thigh to a dangerous, mouthwatering level and had him remembering fragments of an old poem some English teacher whose name he'd long since forgotten had tried to drum into his head. The woman he was looking at was a thing of beauty.

Especially when she reached up like that, making

her cotton candy pink tank top strain against her small, firm breasts.

He had to remind himself to breathe.

The firefighter in him, the part that dealt with people who took spills or found themselves trapped in awkward places, stopped admiring the view and snapped to attention.

"Careful," he called out as he crossed to her.

But it was already too late. The instant he issued the warning, Lisa turned in his direction and lost her balance.

He didn't remember how he managed to cross the rest of the way in less than a second, but he did. He was able to catch her just as she tumbled from the ladder before it crashed to the ground. The resulting jolt went right through his entire body. He knew what he experienced couldn't all be attributed to catching her free-falling body. Some of it came from feeling that body slam against his.

She clung to him a second too long, startled by the fall and by the heat ignited in its wake the second she found herself pressed against him.

Flushed, her heart pounding, Lisa loosened her arms from around his neck. Had he not caught her in time, that could have been one nasty fall, putting her out of commission for who knew how long. And putting a temporary hold on any income the store could provide. He'd saved her.

But he'd been the one to cause her to fall in the first place.

Lisa glared at him. "You've got to stop sneaking up on me like that."

"Calling out a warning from across the length of the store is hardly sneaking," he pointed out. She looked winded. And scared. "You okay?"

Her annoyance abated. After all, he *did* catch her. "All except for my dignity."

She certainly *felt* okay from where he was standing. He raised a shoulder, letting it fall. "Dignity is highly overrated, anyway," Bryce said.

Some very unsettling things were going on inside her and she didn't like them. She had neither the desire nor the time to cover ground she'd crossed before, no matter what her mother's philosophy was. "Don't you have a fire to put out or something?"

His eyes touched her face, lingering. Making her want things she didn't want to want. "I'm working on it."

The way he said it definitely scrambled all circuits she was trying so desperately to keep untangled. She took a deep breath, but it didn't help. "You can put me down now."

He laughed, gamely setting her down. "Spoilsport." Running his hand through his damp hair, he looked at her. "I'm ready for a break, how about you?"

She paused, looking around the store. He'd been right. With his help, she was making tremendous progress. So much so that she could safely make the date marked on the placard hung in the window with perhaps even time to spare. At the very least, it would give her more time to be with CeCe.

"Okay," she allowed. "What did you have in mind?"

This time, his laugh was deeper. Sexier. She had to struggle not to blush though she couldn't have explained why she felt the inclination.

"Never give a man a leading line like that." Leaning into her, Bryce lowered his voice. "He just might tell you."

Embarrassed, she frowned. "I meant as in food."

He let her off the hook. "I saw a pizza place at the other end of the mall." It was one of a popular chain. "We could go there or have them deliver."

"Deliver." When he passed his hand over her hair, she nearly jumped. Pulling back, she stared at him. "What are you doing?"

She couldn't have jumped more than if he'd threatened her with a hot poker. What was she afraid of? It couldn't be him. He was being as easygoing as he knew how.

"You have a cobweb in your hair," he told her. Showing her the residue on his fingers, he added, "Just getting it out."

He had to think she was an idiot, she upbraided herself. Not that it mattered what he thought, of course. Annoyed, she took another step back from him. "I wish you wouldn't keep touching me."

To make her feel a little more at ease, he slipped his hands back into his pockets. But he wasn't about to lie. His eyes continued to linger on her.

"Well, there we seem to have a problem, because I'm a touching kind of guy—and I like touching you, Lisa," he told her honestly. "Besides, I haven't figured out how to catch a falling body without using my hands."

"I guess I'm just a little wired, that's all." And he was the reason why, she added silently. Still, it wasn't something she wanted him to know. "Sorry."

He inclined his head. "Apology accepted. You've had a lot to deal with lately, what with moving, CeCe disappearing on you and trying to get your store in shape. You've got the right to get a little crazy."

When something seemed too good to be true, it usually was. It was an old rule of thumb she'd learned the hard way. She applied it to him now. "Are you going out of your way to seem incredibly nice?"

"Not out of my way exactly, but…" His voice trailed off, his eyes amused. "How'm I doing?"

That she wasn't about to tell him, either. She gestured at the phone. That, at least, *was* working. "Why don't you see about ordering that pizza?"

"I've got a better idea." He took her hand in his.

For a second, she was too surprised to pull it away. "What are you doing?"

"It's called holding your hand. It's acceptable behavior in most cultures, hardly ever punishable by death these days." But when she pulled her hand away, he made no move to take it again. "I think you just need to get away from the dust and the work for a little while. I'll even treat."

The protest on her tongue just didn't seem to find its way past her lips and when he led the way out of the store, she followed.

# Chapter Six

She insisted on paying for lunch, telling him to put his money away when the pizza arrived. The adamant way she said it left no room for argument. After a beat, Bryce surrendered amiably, returning his wallet to his back pocket and they took slices from opposite ends of the large pie.

"I don't believe in wrestling with a lady—in public," he added with what she could have sworn was a twinkle in his eye, but was probably just a result of the rather sporadically arranged lighting fixtures in the small restaurant. "But I really would have felt better if you'd let me take care of the bill."

"You're helping me in the store, the least I can do is pay for lunch." The gleam in his eye seemed to get brighter. She wasn't so sure about it being a trick of lighting anymore. To be on the safe side, she amended her statement. "Let me rephrase that, the only thing I can and will do is pay for lunch."

She wasn't afraid of him, exactly, he thought, but he had a definite feeling she was afraid of something. Bryce reached for a napkin before washing the pizza slice down with some of his beer. "Not a very trusting soul, are you?"

She drew herself up, wondering if he was going to analyze her. "Not when it comes to men, no."

Bryce paused a moment before selecting a second slice. "Did he hurt you badly?"

For some reason, the question didn't rankle her. Maybe because she'd been trying so hard to put distance between herself and what had happened. Or maybe because some of it had become somewhat muted over the last five years.

"Not that it's any business of yours, but, yes, he did." She nibbled thoughtfully on the edge of her slice, remembering. "He promised me forever. The only way it could have been forever was if he'd been a fruit fly. He left the minute he knew I was going to go through with my pregnancy."

Bryce stopped eating. The taste in his mouth had suddenly turned bad. The beer didn't help. "He wanted you to have an abortion?"

Even now, Lisa couldn't get herself to wrap her tongue around the word. The idea of sweeping away a life that she had shared in creating in the first place was completely alien to her. And reprehensible. Knowing that Kyle held the opposite view had been the beginning of her awakening. And the end of her love.

"He wanted us to remain 'unencumbered.'" She used Kyle's word for it. Lisa picked up her slice again. "What he wanted was to remain free to do whatever he wanted whenever he wanted." The smile that rose to her lips was self-mocking. How could she have been so blind? "I thought I was marrying Mr. Wonderful and what I got was Peter Pan, which would have been fine if I had been Tinker Bell, but I wasn't. I was Wendy and I had to grow up. I *wanted* to grow up. He didn't and wouldn't."

Surprised at the unexpected revelation, Bryce decided to press her a little more. "How long have you been divorced?"

There was a time she'd known exactly down to the day, but just in the past year, she had begun to let go. "Since before CeCe was born."

He wondered if this ex-husband had been the reason for her move out here. "Did he come around often?"

Lisa pretended to think before answering. "Let me see… There has to be a 'once' in an 'often,' doesn't there?"

Bryce wasn't sure just where she was going with this. "Yes," he allowed, cautious.

The laugh was short, dismissive and entirely without humor. "Then no, he didn't."

She made it sound so final. He thought of the little girl with the heartbreaker eyes. How could anyone willingly ignore a daughter? Or any child for that matter? He didn't begin to understand it, even though in his line of work he'd been given evidence of just that more than once or twice. "He's never even come by to see her?"

Lisa shook her head, aching not for herself, but for

CeCe. With all her heart, she wished she could have given the little girl a better father than the one she had. "I sent him an announcement, and then a photograph. He never responded."

It was hard for Bryce to fathom. "Maybe he never got it."

"We lived in Mesa, just outside of Dallas. It was a town small enough for people to know everyone's business. Besides, I had a friend who worked in the post office. Kyle got the announcement. And the photograph. He just wasn't interested. There was someone new in his life, someone he could call baby without having the term really apply." That was when Lisa knew she'd have to leave town. She didn't want to take a chance on running into her ex-husband and his girlfriend.

A shrug punctuated her words as she turned away so that Bryce wouldn't see that there were tears gathering in her eyes. Not tears because she missed Kyle, but tears because she'd been so stupid as to give her heart away to someone who didn't really deserve it.

Bryce knew she wouldn't appreciate his commenting on what she'd told him, so he kept most of the feelings to himself. But he couldn't help saying, "He shouldn't have married you if he didn't want kids."

She toyed with her second piece, noticing that Bryce was on his way to having his fourth. "Yeah well, according to what he said to me the night it all blew up, he kind of thought that part was understood." Bryce cocked his head, silently urging her to continue when she paused. "That we had something good going that he didn't want to change."

He reached for his glass again. "And did you?"

She didn't follow him. "Did I what?"

Bryce looked at her eyes. "Have something good going?"

"I thought we did." She wondered if admitting that made her a fool. Perhaps in a way, it did. She told him anyway. Talking about it, after having kept it inside for so long, felt oddly therapeutic. "Trouble was, I thought I had it going with a person I only thought was there. Kyle didn't turn out to be the person I thought I was marrying. He wasn't boyishly charming, he was selfish and irresponsible. He liked being taken care of." Her smile was rueful. "I thought it was because he needed me, not because he was lazy." She blew out a breath. She'd said far more than she'd intended to. "You live, you learn, right?"

He reached over and, just for a second, placed his hand over his. She looked at him in surprise, but didn't pull back. "Some things a person shouldn't have to learn."

Lisa feigned interest in the slice that still remained on her plate. "Speaking of learning, you seemed to have pulled a great deal more out of me than I wanted to volunteer." She raised her eyes to his. "What's your story?"

The shrug Bryce gave her was dismissive rather than calculating or coy. "Not much of a story. Son of a firefighter who becomes a firefighter."

She frowned. "That's it?"

His eyes met hers to show that he wasn't attempting to hold anything back. The way he saw it, there wasn't anything of interest to hold back. "That's it."

Lisa didn't believe him. "No ex-wives, no fiancées, no girlfriends calling your house and the fire station at all hours?"

He grinned. "No ex-wives, no fiancées, but I'm not a monk."

"But you don't believe in marriage," Lisa commented.

"Not for me."

Another one. Was that all there was in life? She closed her eyes and sighed. "Lord, deliver me from Peter Pans."

He didn't particularly like being lumped into the same class as her ex-husband. Although Bryce didn't know the man, he didn't like him. "I'm not Peter Pan. At times," he told her honestly, "there's nothing I want more than a wife and kids."

Yeah, right, Lisa thought. "Not believing in marriage makes that kind of tough."

"The reason I don't ask anyone to marry me is because—"

Lisa held up her hand, stopping him. "No, let me field this one." Passing her hand over her forehead, she pretended to divine his explanation. "Let's see, you don't want to do anything to spoil a perfect friendship. Or, you just haven't found that special someone, but she might be just around the corner, so you're going to keep looking and sampling." He began to interrupt, but she just plowed ahead. "Or, you just don't know if you could handle the pressure of

being a good husband so you don't want to put anyone through the torture of putting up with you." Finished, she scrutinized his face. "Any of that work
for you?"

Her ex must have really done a number on her,
Bryce thought. The urge to hold her came out of
nowhere. He let it go.

"What I couldn't handle," he told her slowly, deliberately, "is knowing that if something happened
to me, someone I loved would be in pain."

He could see she wasn't following him. He supposed it did no harm to tell her. It wasn't something
he was accustomed to talking about, but as she'd
pointed out, she'd bared some of her soul to him.
Turn about was only fair.

"My father died in the line of duty when I was
thirteen. I spent the next year not only grieving for
him, but watching my mother fall apart bit by bit,
withdrawing into a world I couldn't enter."

Instant empathy rose within Lisa for his mother.
And for him. Feeling guilty as well, she bit her lip.
"I'm sorry, I didn't mean to be so flippant. What
happened to your mother?"

It had happened so long ago now, but with very
little effort, it felt like just yesterday. "My mother
couldn't bear the pain, couldn't stand the thought of
what had happened to my father. Or of her going on
without him. She was in an institution for a while,
until she got better."

Without realizing it, Lisa lowered her voice.
"What about you?"

He tried to pass that part off lightly. "My brother

and I went to live with my father's best friend. A great guy named Sugar Riley."

"Sugar?" That didn't sound like the kind of name any man would tolerate.

"Yeah." He laughed. "It was a nickname pinned to him by some unthinking aunt when he was a kid. It stuck. Sugar became my uncle, his wife, my aunt. At least for two and a half years, until my mother came home from the hospital."

Were there scars, she wondered, left in places he didn't visit emotionally anymore? To look at him, she would've said no, but then, to look at him she wouldn't have guessed that he'd suffered any sort of emotional trauma to begin with. The look in Bryce's eyes now told her differently.

"What happened after that?"

He contemplated the liquid at the bottom of his glass for a moment, then finished it. "I'd like to say she made a full recovery, but she didn't. She was never quite the same, though she tried." Too painful to dwell on, he banished the memory. "The upshot of the whole thing is that I don't think it's fair to put someone you love through that kind of pain. The way I see it, you have to make responsible choices in life." There was one slice of pizza left and he silently offered it to her. When she shook her head, he slid it onto his own plate. "And I made mine. I became a firefighter, something I always wanted to be." Even if he tried, he couldn't imagine himself being anything else.

That sounded a little drastic to her. Was it an excuse he used to hide behind? "So, in your opinion, firefighters should be like priests."

Given his lifestyle, the comparison amused him. "In a way."

The expression on his face pretty much said it all, but she pursued the topic a little further. "Celibate."

Bryce laughed then, wiping his mouth. "No, not that far."

She figured as much. Leaning back, she slowly wiped her fingertips. "Just romance without ties."

Bryce watched her movements. Funny, when she did that, he could almost feel her fingers brushing against his skin. The thought made him warm. And curious. "You make it sound cold."

There was something in his gaze that was definitely getting to her. "Isn't it?"

"Doesn't have to be." Leaning over the table, he got to the heart of what was really on his mind. "I'd like to keep seeing you."

She felt her heart hitch. Damn, why did he have to be so direct, so honest? She preferred the word games to facing something right now. Trying her best to remain aloof, she asked, "To what end?"

The question amused him. She sounded as if she was reviewing a job application. "Mutual enjoyment."

There was a wisp of hair falling into her face. He gently moved it behind her ear. The startled look that came into her eyes reminded him of a puppy he'd once found, a puppy that had been mistreated and was suspicious of kindness. He dropped his hand.

"From what I gather, you're not exactly in the

market for marriage, either. And I did enjoy that kiss in your kitchen.''

She blew out a breath and hoped it didn't sound as shaky to him as it did to her. "I've misjudged you.''

"Good misjudged or bad misjudged?'' Bryce inquired gamely.

That, she thought, depended entirely on your perspective. She wasn't altogether certain of hers. "I didn't think you were an honest man.''

He laughed softly under his breath. "I've got to remember to leave my black cloak at home more often.'' He moved his plate toward the empty pizza tray. "So, what do you say?''

Moving her chair back, Lisa tossed her napkin onto her plate. "For now, I say that I have to get back to the shop.''

He rose and she noticed that he left a five-dollar bill on the table as a tip for the boy who bused the tables. Kyle, she recalled, liked to hoard every dime, saving it to spend on himself.

She had to stop comparing the two men, she upbraided herself. There was no reason to compare Bryce to anyone who had passed through her life, especially not Kyle.

"And later?'' he pressed when she said nothing.

"Will be later.'' Her tone was flippant and noncommittal. The response didn't feel right to her and she added, "We'll see.''

*Yes,* he thought, *we will.*

With his hand at the small of her back, he guided her to the door as if this was a routine they'd been comfortably following for a long time. "Nothing I like better than a challenge."

Lisa bit her lip and remained silent. That was exactly what she was afraid of.

"What's this?" Bryce found himself looking into the animated face of the stuffed animal that Lisa held up in front of him. They'd put in three more hours since they'd returned from the pizzeria, working diligently to transform the store into something that would charm both parents and children. He'd never seen a woman work as hard as Lisa. He was surprised when she'd abruptly announced a couple of minutes ago that they were through for the day and that he was welcome to leave.

"It's a porcupine." She looked into the face of the toy she'd just spent the last twenty minutes searching for, trying to remember which box it had been packed in. Its soulful expression made her smile. She figured it would warm the heart of any stuffed animal aficionado. "At least, a cute, cuddly version of one." She offered it to him. "I thought that maybe Lanie didn't have one in her collection."

"She doesn't." Taking the stuffed animal from her, he looked it over. His niece was going to fall in love with it. Bryce took out his wallet. "How much?"

She pushed the wallet back at him. "Call it payment in full."

"Long name." He pretended to consider it, then grinned. "Maybe 'pay' for short." Bryce flipped open his wallet with one hand, taking out several larger bills. "Seriously, you can't make a go of the store if you give things away."

She ignored the money. Instead she took out one of the bags she'd had made for the store and, taking the porcupine from him, tucked it inside. She held the bag out to him. "I like to pay my debts."

He'd never found stubborn an appealing trait before. Maybe, he thought, it was the way she raised her chin that did it. The word adorable filtered through his mind. He knew she wouldn't have been happy at the description.

"You paid for lunch," he pointed out.

Why did he have to give her an argument about this? She was trying to do something nice, she thought in suppressed frustration. "If I'd had someone helping me, they would have charged a lot more than eight dollars for the day."

He thought about that for a second. "The pizza and beer came to sixteen."

"I had half," she reminded him.

Taking the forest-green bag from her, he peeked inside. The porcupine was looking up at him with the same soulful eyes. "So this is to make up for the rest."

"Yes." The word reeked of frustration.

"Okay." He inclined his head, surrendering. And then he placed the bag on the counter, his eyes remaining on her face. "Any chance of a tip?"

She wasn't sure she followed him. "Tip?" Lisa looked around the store. Had he seen another toy that caught his fancy? "You want something more?"

He liked the choice of words. "Yes."

The way he said it had her turning around to look at him again, knowing what he wanted.

The same thing she did.

But she'd been wrong before. Maybe she was wrong now. Maybe she misunderstood everything. Her breath suddenly coming to a halt within her lungs, she raised her eyes to his. "What?"

The smile that bloomed on his lips teased her. Pulled her in. Just as his arms did. A flush of warmth followed swiftly in their wake.

"Guess."

Because her lips were suddenly unbearably dry, she moistened them. And saw desire flare in his eyes. "The emu?"

Slowly he shook his head, his eyes never leaving hers. "Not even warm."

But she was warm. Warm, bordering on hot. Hot arrived the instant his mouth touched hers.

She would have liked to have said it was the beer she had at lunch that made her head spin, but it had only been a single mug and besides, lunch had been hours ago. It might have been a tad more accurate to blame her condition on the fact that the store, though not airless, was still pretty stifling.

But it had nothing to do with beer, or stagnant air and everything to do with the deep, tangy flavor of Bryce's mouth. Everything to do with the stirring excitement of his breath as it caressed her face. And everything to do with the hardness of his body as it gently pressed against hers.

Giving herself up to the sensation, to the desire

that sprang forth, full and fresh, she leaned into his body, wrapping her arms around his neck.

The kiss deepened, as did her reaction. She felt herself tumbling into a whirlpool and sliding there willingly.

It had been a long time since she'd wanted a man.

The abruptness of the thought had her pulling back, pulling away so quickly, that, caught by surprise, Bryce almost stumbled into her, falling forward before regaining his balance.

The smile was rueful, the recovery quick. One look in his eyes told her that she hadn't been the only one to have felt the jolt or experienced the exhilaration. Knowing didn't help one bit.

Clearly shaken, Bryce laughed, picking up the bag again from the counter. "I guess maybe I was overcharging you."

Lisa cleared her throat. Everything within her felt as if it was about to go up in flames at any second. She tried to tell herself that it was the novelty of a man, not the man himself, that was creating this reaction, but she wasn't very convincing.

"Maybe," she agreed hoarsely. Clearing her throat again, she turned away, fumbling for the purse she had tossed in a corner. "I've got to get home. I promised CeCe I'd be back in time to play a game with her before she went to bed."

He wanted to explore what had just happened a little further. "I'm good at games."

Turning around again, she slid her purse onto her shoulder. "I bet you are." It was so tempting to ask him to come along. She knew that CeCe and her mother would be happy to see him.

But that was just it. She didn't want to give in to temptation. The man had been utterly up-front with her, and she was grateful to him for that, for telling her that there wouldn't be any ties between them. And he was right, she didn't want a husband or marriage. Ever.

She stopped. If she felt that way, what was the harm in having him come over? What was the harm in spending a little time with a man who made her blood heat if they both knew this wouldn't go further?

The trouble was, she knew, that heated things had a tendency to catch fire when you weren't paying attention.

The tug-of-war she felt going on inside confused her. And irritated her. She took her irritation out on the source.

"You told me at lunch you didn't want a family. You can't have mine."

He was about to tell her that the thought hadn't even crossed his mind, but then he realized that maybe it had. Maybe the way he sated his sublimated desire to have a family of his own was to borrow others' for a little while.

He wasn't the type to press. "Fair enough," he allowed.

Damn him, why did he have to be so reasonable? She'd just acted like a fishwife, after he'd spent the day toiling in a stifling store, helping her. Guilt had her calling out to him.

"I didn't mean to sound like a shrew."

He turned around at the door. "You didn't." An enigmatic smile tugged on his lips. "I just wouldn't try out for the town welcoming committee anytime soon if I were you."

She opened her mouth to say something, then decided that maybe it was for the best, for both of them, if she didn't. If she just let him walk out the door.

So she did.

# Chapter Seven

To her relief—and disappointment—Bryce didn't stop by the store to offer his services the next day. Or the day after that, either.

Feeling a little let down, Lisa told herself she was being ridiculous. This was just what she wanted. To be left alone, to get her store ready in peace and to keep her life moving along the track she'd taken. A track that exclusively involved her daughter, her mother and her business. If there was any time left over, well, a woman could do with a little of her own space now and again, too. Nothing wrong with a little alone time. There was absolutely no need for a man with wavy, dark blond hair and eyes the color of wild shamrocks in her life. None at all.

Still, every so often over the course of those next two days, she found herself looking over toward the front door. Just in case Bryce decided to launch another invasion. After all, it never hurt to be prepared.

With each passing hour of each day, it became increasingly apparent that there was nothing to be prepared for.

The only people who arrived at her shop-in-progress had deliveries to make, except for the manager of the mall and he only stopped by late the second afternoon to see how things were coming along.

Struggling to maneuver yet another large shipment of toys to the rear of the shop, Lisa realized she missed Bryce. Or at least his muscle. She decided, slashing through the cellophane tape at the top of the box, that maybe she'd actually finally succeeded in getting her message across to him. The one that said she wasn't interested. Nope, not a whit. With a yank, she opened the box. Stuffed animals came pouring out.

If she were being honest with herself, there was a small part of her that was irritated that Bryce had given up so easily.

With a sigh, she ran her hand through her hair. "Damn it, Lisa, make up your mind. Either you want him interested, or you don't. If you do, you'd better get your act together and if you don't, well, congratulations, you've won."

The odd thing of it was, she didn't feel like much of a winner.

She forced herself to focus on her work and not the man who'd inadvertently—or possibly on purpose—messed with her mind. She worked steadily, finding places to house the latest shipment of toy citizens to her store. By the time the last stuffed animal had found housing, it was half past seven.

Tired, looking at her watch, Lisa decided to call it a day. The store, thanks to her own industry and the one whirlwind day that she'd spent working side by side with Bryce, was really getting in shape. She was ahead of even her own far from conservative estimates.

Locking the door, she looked at the sign in the window proclaiming the grand opening date. If things kept going the way they were, she'd be ready before then. Maybe she should see about moving ahead the opening date, she mused.

The ringing sound coming from her purse had her putting her thoughts on hold as she rummaged around through things she meant to throw out, looking for the elusive object. Finally getting her hands on it, she pulled the cell phone out and flipped open the cover.

No one had her number here except her mother and her mother never called it just to "chat." She felt nervous as she put her ear to the phone.

"Hi, Mom, what's up?"

"CeCe's temperature," came the terse response. "It has been high all afternoon. I think you had better come home, Lisa."

Her mother was not an alarmist by nature. Lisa could feel her stomach tightening into an unmanagable knot. She was already striding through the mall's west end, intent on getting to her car. "How high is it?"

There was a slight pause, as if Cecilia was worried

about telling her. "A hundred and four. I just took it."

The knot in her stomach turned to pure lead. Lisa lengthened her stride. "I'm on my way."

With fear impeding her, it took Lisa a few minutes to locate her car in the large parking lot. When she did, she strove to make up for lost time. She drove the speed limit all the way home. Several times, when there were no other cars around to get in the way, she knew she went over the limit. It didn't matter, her little girl needed her. Weaving in and out of traffic, she covered the distance from the mall to her house in record time.

Until they reached the age of seven, Lisa knew that children's temperatures fluctuated wildly, knew that children could seem deathly ill one minute and almost completely recovered the next, with theme and variations occurring in between.

But it was one thing to know about these things academically and another to experience them first-hand. Quite another to have it happening to her daughter. She couldn't calm down. Half formed fears rose up to torture her.

Any way she looked at it, Lisa didn't like CeCe's temperature climbing that high. The little girl had seemed a little listless this morning when she left but Lisa had just chalked that up to a reaction to the heat. While the weather in Southern California was far drier than what they'd left behind in Dallas, after a certain point hot was still hot and today had been a particularly brutal day. Thank God the air conditioner was finally working in the store.

But her mind wasn't on the air conditioning in the store just then. It was on her daughter. Pulling up askew in the driveway, she threw up the hand brake, raced out of the car and burst through the front door.

Her mother was just coming out of CeCe's room. One look at her face had Lisa's heart freezing. Cecilia's face was ash-gray. The last time Lisa remembered seeing it that color, her father had just died.

Lisa was halfway up the stairs before her mother could come down. "How is she?"

Cecilia shook her head. Her voice quavered when she spoke. "Not good. Still a hundred and four. I have been bathing her in cool water, but it does not help. We need to get her to a doctor, or a hospital emergency room as soon as possible."

If this had been Mesa, Lisa would have already been on the phone to CeCe's pediatrician. Or bundling her into the car to drive over to the hospital in Dallas. But the comfort of the familiar was absent here, adding another layer to her dilemma. She had no doctor to turn to in Bedford, knew of no reliable hospital.

Finding a doctor or hospital was an easy enough thing. She could just look through the yellow pages of the phone book. But the phone book couldn't tell her who the best doctor was, which hospital had a better reputation than another, all the important things that mattered in moments like this. Only experience or word-of-mouth could and she didn't know of anyone to ask.

Except, she realized, someone with a niece who collected stuffed animals.

"What are you doing?" Cecilia asked when Lisa headed for the living room instead of up the stairs.

"Getting help. Go back to CeCe, Mom. I'll be up as soon as I can."

Cecilia nodded, leaving. Lisa pulled out the residential phone book from inside the cabinet beneath the wet bar and turned to the front of it.

On the stairs, Cecilia turned to see what she was doing. "Who are you calling? You know a doctor?"

Lisa tried to remember where the listings of city facilities were kept. "No, but I might know someone who does."

Paging quickly through the government pages, she found what she was looking for. Cradling the receiver between her head and shoulder, she dialed.

The deep voice that answered the telephone on the second ring informed her that she had reached "Orange County Fire Station 6."

"Hello, is Bryce there? Bryce Walker." She realized belatedly that she didn't even know if today was one of his "on" days to work, or how to reach him if it wasn't. Mentally she crossed her fingers, waiting.

The person on the other end paused, as if debating giving out that kind of information. "Who's calling, please?"

"Lisa Billings. If he's there, please tell him it's an emergency." Several agonizing minutes passed before she heard someone picking up the receiver again.

"Lisa?"

It was Bryce. She didn't have time to make excuses or apologies for calling him at work like this, didn't have time to deal with the audible bewilderment she heard in his voice or the sense of tentative relief that washed over her.

"Yes, it's me. Bryce, is there any way that you would know the name of your niece's pediatrician?"

"Yeah, as a matter of fact, I do. His brother works with my brother." Concern edged out bewilderment in his voice. "Why?"

"It's CeCe. She's running a hundred and four temperature." Lisa struggled to keep the hysteria out of her voice. She wasn't going to do CeCe any good falling apart. "My mother says she's been like this the better part of the day and I don't know anyone here besides you. What's the doctor's name?"

"Rafe Saldana. Hold on, I'll be right over."

A sense of gratitude, immense and nearly overwhelming swept over her, surprising her by its appearance. She didn't try to analyze it. All that mattered was CeCe. "Aren't you on duty?"

"Just getting off. If you'd called ten minutes later, I would have been on my way home."

Rummaging through the cabinet, she searched for a pen and something to write on. She settled for a pencil and the margin of the phone book. "How do you spell Saldana?"

He gave her the spelling, adding that the doctor was located in the Newport Beach medical complex. "Tell the nurse it's an emergency, they'll fit you in," he promised before he hung up.

* * *

He was at her doorstep just as she was ending her call. She opened the door, the cell phone in her hand. Her eyes didn't seem to focus on him as she stepped back, allowing him in. "Yes, doctor. And thank you."

One look at her face and he knew that Lisa hadn't used the word emergency carelessly when she'd call the station.

Disconnecting the call, she looked at Bryce for the first time. "That was the doctor on the phone. He said to bring CeCe right over." Lisa tossed the phone in her purse, relieved to see him and flustered by the feeling. "I'm sorry. I didn't mean to put you out like this."

He paused a moment to pass his hand comfortingly along her cheek. "Hey, emergencies are my line of work, remember? It's not all fires. I've got paramedic training, too. Where is she?"

"Upstairs, in her room. My mother's with her."

Not waiting for her, he strode up the stairs. Walking into CeCe's room, he nodded at Cecilia, but his attention was on the little girl.

"Hi, short stuff," Bryce said softly, coming to stand over her bed. "I hear you're not feeling too cool right now."

The small, flushed face brightened only marginally when she saw her visitor. "No," she moaned. "Bryce, I feel hot."

"I know you do." Cecilia rose and moved out of his way. As gently as possible, Bryce scooped CeCe up in his arms, blanket and all. "But we're going to have you feeling better in no time."

The small, delicate form nestled against him, giving him all her trust. "Really?" she asked. He felt his heart twist inside his chest.

"Really. It's my job," he told her solemnly. Moving swiftly, careful not to jolt her, he carried CeCe down the stairs. Lisa and her mother followed directly behind him. "I'll drive. I've got the car right out front," he told Lisa.

Instincts of self-preservation, honed so sharply in the past five years, rose automatically within her, prompting Lisa's protest. "So do I."

His eyes narrowed as he glanced at her. "You're in no condition to drive. It'd be better for CeCe if you stayed in the back with her." He knew that right now, CeCe needed as little turmoil around her as possible. Turning toward Cecilia, he tried to be reassuring as he silently instructed her to remain behind. "We'll call you as soon as we know anything."

Cecilia nodded, understanding, as she accompanied them to the front door. She held it open for them. "Thank you. And God bless you."

Following him, Lisa saw that Bryce had driven the red paramedic car over rather than his own vehicle. She looked at him questioningly.

"We'll make better time," he told her. He waited as she buckled CeCe into the back seat. She moaned, protesting the change in position. "You'll be better soon, CeCe," he promised her softly, masking his own concern.

His arms felt hot from carrying her. The little girl was burning up.

Lisa climbed in quickly as he got in behind the wheel. Common sense told him it was going to be all right. But emotionally, he felt there wasn't time to waste. Driving to the medical complex, he used the siren. Evening traffic was thick with people trying to get home after a long day.

Cars moved out of their way, pulling over to the right. Bryce got them there faster than Lisa had driven from the mall. The tires screeched in mingled protest and relief as he pulled up in the near empty parking lot before the center building within the medical complex.

Dr. Rafe Saldana had seen his last patient and was about to go home to his own wife and daughters when he heard the telephone in the front office ringing. His office manager and nurses had already left for the day. Ordinarily, he would have let his service pick it up since it was almost an hour after his regular hours. However, he was glad he picked up the receiver because there was nothing Rafe hated more than knowing a child was suffering.

His examination concluded now, he removed the stethoscope from his ears and offered Lisa an encouraging smile.

"I know it's scary from your end, but it's not nearly as bad as it looks." Pulling his prescription pad over, he wrote out a prescription for a common children's antibiotic then handed it to Lisa. "Have this filled as soon as possible and make sure she takes it until it's gone. The fever should go down soon. I'm going to give her a double dose to start her on her way."

Preparing a syringe, he slanted a glance at Lisa. "This is the part I hate. Roll her over on her tummy, it'll hurt less going in her bottom than her arm."

Bryce saw the look on Lisa's face. "Want me to do it?"

She shook her head. "No, I'm her mother, I should be the one to do it," Lisa said. But there was gratitude in her eyes at his offer.

Lisa held her breath as she watched the needle go in, feeling it every bit as much as CeCe did. Rather than scream, the little girl whimpered, rolling up into a ball as if trying to elude the pain.

Disposing of the syringe, Dr. Saldana stripped off his rubber gloves, tossing them into the wastebasket after it. "Good thing you brought her in when you did. Fevers that high are nothing to fool around with, even if they are fairly common. My office manager is going to have my head for not getting you to fill out the new patient forms. If you wouldn't mind stopping by tomorrow and doing them for her—"

"Absolutely," Lisa promised enthusiastically. Gathering CeCe into her arms, she stroked her daughter's small head lovingly. "Anything you want, you've got it. And thank you again for seeing her."

He smiled, stroking the little girl's head. "Don't mention it. And don't forget to have the prescription filled." He nodded toward the paper she had clutched in her hand. "Amoxicillin. One teaspoon, three times a day until it's gone." He lowered his head to

CeCe's level. "You'll like it," he assured her. "It tastes just like bubble gum."

CeCe murmured something in response just before she fell asleep in her mother's arms.

"I like him," Lisa told Bryce as she stepped out of the elevator. Walking ahead of her, Bryce reached the door first and held it open.

She'd get no argument from him. "Yeah, my sister-in-law swears by him. Lanie says she's going to keep going to him forever." He grinned, remembering how vehement his niece had sounded, making her announcement at the dinner table when his brother, knowing of her crush on the doctor, had teasingly suggested that it was time she began going to a regular general practitioner. "He's got a way with kids." He glanced at Lisa. "Parents, too. Makes them feel confident that things'll be all right. And they will be," he added, unlocking the passenger door of his vehicle. He opened the door for her, then stepped back. "I'll take you home and then get that prescription filled."

He was putting himself out. Guilt nibbled at Lisa for the way she'd treated him the last time they'd been together. If CeCe hadn't gotten sick, she'd had every intention of never seeing him again. "I don't know what to say, Bryce. You've done so much already."

Getting inside, he started the car, then glanced over his shoulder at her. The smile he gave her was warm. "Just say thanks and we'll call it even."

She stroked CeCe's head. The little girl was still sleeping. "Doesn't seem like enough."

"It is if you say it right." He pulled out of the parking lot, heading toward MacArthur Boulevard. He ventured a glance into the rearview mirror. "She asleep?"

"Yes."

"Now might be a good time to call your mother. She's probably sitting by the telephone, worrying."

Lisa flushed. She'd almost forgotten. Leaning over, she began to dig through her purse for her cell phone. "Good call."

He turned his attention back toward the road. Twilight was just beginning to set in, brushing the countryside beyond with darkness. He felt oddly content and satisfied. "Thanks."

As soon as he saw them safely home, Bryce, armed with the necessary information about CeCe, went to the local pharmacy and got CeCe's prescription filled. By the time he returned, Lisa had gotten CeCe settled in. The little girl's forehead felt cooler to her already.

Lisa's relief was immeasurable. "I don't know how to begin to thank you for what you did tonight," she told Bryce as she accompanied him to the door. Upstairs, her mother had remained by CeCe's bedside to make sure the little girl was resting comfortably.

Bryce paused at the door. "I might have a suggestion."

She was far too exhausted and far too relieved to be leery. Besides, the man had ridden to her rescue like a white knight. No matter what, there would always be a soft spot in her heart for him. Leaning against the doorjamb, she looked at him, curious.

"Such as?"

Did she realize that, with her eyes half closed like that, she looked incredibly sexy? "I'm having a barbecue this weekend."

Right now, it was hard for her to think. Too much had happened in too short time. "You need a cook?"

"I need a guest." He took her hand. Despite the exhaustion she was battling, it felt right somehow, having her hand in his like this. "Actually, three guests. You can bring your mother and CeCe."

Uncertain, Lisa glanced up toward the ceiling. "You really think she'll be well enough to come?"

"Kids notoriously bounce back a hell of a lot faster than adults do." He'd seen it happen with Lanie and Ethan more than once. "She might be well enough by morning to make you think you were only imagining things tonight. My advice is to keep her in bed for the day just to make sure."

She made no effort to hide the amusement that rose at his words. "What makes you such an expert on kids?"

He pretended to consider her question. "Well there's Lanie and Ethan. And the Rileys had seven kids of their own. I put in a lot of baby-sitting while I was with them. Besides, you tend to pick up things along the way if you're paying attention."

And there was no doubt in her mind that he paid attention. She couldn't help wondering if there had been a particular woman in his life he'd applied that attention to.

But for now, she just smiled at him. "And I bet you did."

He grinned, feigning being affronted. "I'll thank you not to think those kinds of thoughts about me." And then he sobered, drawing closer to her. Close enough to feel her breath on his skin. "You'll be okay?"

"I'll be fine." But she liked the fact that he asked. "I'll probably drop right off to sleep by the time I close the door."

He lingered, unwilling to leave just yet. Knowing he should. "I could volunteer to stay over and catch you before you hit the ground. As you might recall, I do a pretty good fielding job."

She laughed. "I recall. But I really think you should go now." *Before I do something stupid,* she thought, *and ask you to stay.*

Cupping her face with his hand, he lightly brushed his lips over hers. And felt the intoxicating kick of excitement. He savored it a moment before drawing away. "I'll call you tomorrow to see how you're both doing."

"Okay."

Lisa was too tired not to allow his words to remain with her, comforting her, long after she'd closed the door behind him.

# Chapter Eight

Lisa woke up the next morning expecting to be drenched with regrets. They didn't come. She wasn't sorry for agreeing to attend the barbecue. Oh, there was a butterfly or two hovering around, but nothing like what she expected.

Maybe attending the barbecue would be a good thing, she thought, hurrying through breakfast and then driving to her shop before eight. Bryce had given her the impression that there would be a lot of people there and if nothing else, it would give CeCe and her mother a chance to meet people. As for her, well, it wouldn't really hurt for her to get out, either.

She didn't let herself examine the fact that Bryce had somehow managed, by his kindness to her daughter, to quickly, effectively erase her desire to say no. No to the barbecue, no to him.

She wanted to see him again.

Maybe it was knowing ahead of time that whatever

happened between them was only going to be a pleasant interlude in her life. That she was to enjoy it—not nurture it—took away any pressures that could be associated with a would-be relationship, draining it of problems and leaving behind only pleasure. Only the good parts.

Good parts that Lisa found herself looking forward to.

Or maybe it was knowing that her heart was safe that freed her of her own bounds. But whatever it was, she heard herself humming through her work, going over the last of the inventory and making notes as to what she still needed to stock.

And while she hummed, every so often, she glanced toward the door. Each time, she expected to see Bryce tapping on the glass door, waiting to come in.

But he wasn't there.

And she had to admit she was nothing short of disappointed.

Lisa had just assumed he would come because she knew that, adhering to the two days on, two days off policy, Bryce was off today and tomorrow. And because, since she'd made it rather obvious that she was in his debt, he'd take that as a signal to want to hang around her a little. Maybe help her with the last phase of getting the store into shape.

As she worked, she tried to tell herself that this just went part and parcel with the idea that there wasn't going to be a relationship between them. What there would be was time spent together, nothing more. After all, that was what she wanted. She was the one who had made it abundantly clear she didn't want any sort of a relationship, wasn't about to start one or be drawn into one.

It should have helped ease her restlessness at not finding him at her door. It didn't.

To get her mind off something she shouldn't have been dwelling on in the first place, when noon finally rolled around, Lisa locked the store and took off for home again. She wanted to see for herself how CeCe was doing. The call she'd made to her mother at ten had reassured her that CeCe was definitely on the mend. Her mother said she was having trouble keeping the little girl in bed.

It looked as if Bryce was right. CeCe would be able to make the barbecue.

This time, the thought of the barbecue caused her stomach to tighten.

God, what had she agreed to in a moment of weakness? Other than occasionally mingling with her friends and their spouses back in Texas, she hadn't really socialized in a very long time. Certainly not as a single woman, wandering through a crowd of people she didn't know.

Nerves pressed themselves against the knots in her stomach.

This was silly. Lisa didn't like being held prisoner by her own emotions. She had said yes to Bryce and couldn't go back on her word. She was going to attend. And she wouldn't be wandering through a crowd of people she didn't know, she'd be going with her mother and her daughter. Going with her daughter and her mother and having a good time with them.

If there was anyone else there to have a good time with, that would only be a bonus, but not a primary ingredient. The only primary, necessary ingredients in her life were CeCe and her mother.

She felt better for her pep talk by the time she reached home.

There was a car in her driveway. A shiny, black, open Jeep. It made her think of sitting parked at the beach on starlight nights, gazing into forever and making silent promises.

She blinked, rousing herself. The thought had come out of nowhere. What was going on with her? Anyone peeking into her mind would think she was in the market for a relationship instead of being an independent woman who just wanted to continue the way she was—self-sufficient and content.

Pulling up next to the vehicle, she hurried out of her car to the front door. It wasn't locked.

"Mother, what did I tell you about locking the front door?" she called out, walking inside.

Two steps into the house, Lisa stopped short. Bryce was sitting on the edge of the sofa where her daughter was supposedly resting.

Except that she wasn't. With the blanket that should have been covering her small body dribbling down onto the floor, CeCe was sitting bolt upright. There was a lunch tray tented over her little legs. On the tray was a checkerboard complete with sliding checkers. A few had pooled onto the floor, using the blanket as a long, baby-blue slide.

Turning at the sound of her voice, Bryce grinned at Lisa as if it was the most natural thing in the world to find him there like this. "That's exactly what I told her. Bedford isn't exactly the big city yet, but it doesn't hurt to be just a little cautious."

It was only because Lisa made the concentrated effort that her jaw didn't drop open like some gaping fool. "What are you doing here?"

"Checking in on the patient." Very carefully, he moved one checker forward. "It's something we like to do from time to time. Gives that small town feeling to the department that the chief likes." He watched as CeCe jumped the checker he'd just moved, then jumped another for good measure before she stopped.

Moving closer to the duo, Lisa looked at the board between them. She'd been meaning to show CeCe how to play, but she just hadn't gotten around to it. Obviously now she didn't have to. "Is teaching a patient checkers included in the package?"

"It is when the patient seems to be bored and about to launch herself like a rocket at the first available target that comes into range." Leaning over, he tousled the little girl's hair. She retaliated by taking another checker he'd just moved. "Although I have to admit I've never been greeted with so much enthusiasm before. It's kind of nice." This time, Bryce managed to jump one of CeCe's checkers and retire it. Watching, Lisa couldn't help wondering if he'd done that just to make the little girl think he wasn't purposely losing to her.

He startled Lisa by asking, "What are you doing here? I thought you'd be busy working at the shop."

So he hadn't come by the house, assuming she'd be here instead of working. He'd actually come to see her daughter. Maybe there was a lot more to the man than just a keen smile and a hard, sculpted body.

"I was." She perched on the arm of the sofa directly behind CeCe, resting her purse on the floor. "I thought I'd come home and give Mom a break for a little while. I see you beat me to it."

"He is not beating anyone," Cecilia informed her, walking in the room. Coming from the kitchen, she was carrying a tray loaded down with a platter of cookies and some of her homemade twisted bow-tie crisps snowed under by powdered sugar. "Cece is beating him. He taught her how to play," she said, setting down the tray on the coffee table by the sofa, "and now she has won three games. You should be very proud of your daughter, Lisa."

Lisa stroked CeCe's silken head. "I am." The little girl flashed her a quick smile before blissfully announcing, "King me," to Bryce.

He placed another checker on top of the one that had reached the opposite side of the board. "You might have yourself a prodigy on your hands, Lisa. Your daughter's the smartest little girl I ever ran into. Smarter than some adults I know, too."

Warning bells went off in Lisa's head. She stole a glance at her daughter before saying to Bryce, "Um, could I see you for a minute?"

It was obvious that CeCe was anxious to move in

for the kill. "Mommy, wait until I finish winning," she pleaded.

"This'll only take a second," Bryce promised her. Coming to the far end of the room, he waited until he and Lisa were sufficiently far away from CeCe so that their lowered voices wouldn't carry. "Did I inadvertently bump up against some rule?"

It wasn't so much a rule as a gut feeling. Without meaning to, Lisa leaned into Bryce, inclining her head. "I'd rather you didn't praise her so much. I don't want her to get an overblown sense of what she can do."

He could smell Lisa's shampoo on her hair. Something herbal and musky. It made him want to run his fingers through it. And his hands along her skin. Slipping his hands into his pockets instead, he looked over at CeCe. She was explaining the rules of the game to her grandmother. He grinned.

"From where I stand, that little girl will be able to do anything she sets her mind to." His eyes shifted to Lisa. "And it isn't praise that's harmful to a child, it's the lack of it. It's feeling that you're never good enough to measure up, or to count that's destructive."

She paused a moment, taking in what he was saying. "I take it you're not speaking from firsthand experience."

He'd been lucky that way. Both his own father and Riley's had always had a good word for him. And an encouraging one when he needed it. He leaned against the fireplace, studying her. Wondering about her. Wondering if asking things would make her put her guard up again. "I wasn't, but what makes you say that?"

That was a rhetorical question from where she stood. "Because I don't think I've ever run into anyone as confident as you before."

The inflection in her voice told him that she didn't mean that as a criticism. Still, he figured he needed to define the difference for her.

"Oh, but I'm not. At least, not about things I have no firsthand control over. The only thing I'm confident in is my own ability to deal with things as they come. The good and the bad," he added pointedly for her benefit, thinking of the husband who had walked out on her. "The rest is very much out of my hands."

"Mommy, are you through talking to Bryce yet?" CeCe called out to her impatiently. "My legs are getting twitchy."

"Twitchy are they?" Crossing back, Lisa leaned over the sofa and nuzzled the little girl's neck. CeCe giggled. "Well, we certainly can't have that, can we?" She kissed CeCe's forehead, unconsciously checking it for a fever, grateful to find it cool. "Go ahead, get back to your game. I have a shop waiting for me." Picking up her purse, Lisa paused a moment longer to drink in her daughter's contentment. And her own. "Be sure to listen to G-mama while I'm gone."

"Okay, Mommy."

One look at her daughter told Lisa she was already forgotten as the little girl settled in to trounce Bryce for another round of checkers. Lisa exchanged looks with her mother and smiled.

"I'll see you all later."

Bryce caught her eye just as she turned to leave. "Count on it."

A warm shiver went through her. It sounded like a prophesy. She tried not to think about how she felt about that. Instead she concentrated on what he was doing for her daughter.

She thought it very sweet of Bryce to allow CeCe to win. Some men had trouble with that, with not being the zenith to which others strove and looked up to. But Bryce didn't appear to be like that. He seemed too relaxed and comfortable with who he was to worry about having his identity sapped away by a pint-size checkers champion in the making.

That said a lot about the man, she allowed, walking outside.

"You really didn't have to bring anything with you except for these two."

Coming up to the backyard entrance, Bryce took the large bowl of potato salad from Lisa's hands. Cecilia and CeCe were standing behind her and CeCe was peering around her mother's legs, trying to see everyone.

There were an awful lot of people here, Lisa thought, feeling her nerves beginning to pinch. "I didn't want to come empty-handed."

His eyes met hers for just a second. "Not possible." He looked over her shoulder, smiling a greeting at her mother. "Hello, Cecilia." His eyes lowered to CeCe's face. "Hi, short stuff."

"Hi!" To say that CeCe was fairly bouncing up and down was an understatement. She was extremely pleased to be brought into a social situation. CeCe thrived on meeting people, especially, but not exclusively kids. Her eyes wide, she panned the area. "Is Lanie here yet?"

Setting down the bowl on the nearest available table, Bryce lightly placed a hand on the little girl's shoulder and directed her toward the back.

"She sure is. And she can't wait to meet you. Lanie, CeCe's here," he called.

A little girl who looked for all the world as if she could have been Bryce's daughter rather than his niece, flashed a bright smile at his summons and came hurrying over. In her wake, but not so closely as to be teased about it, came her younger brother, Ethan. Also another miniature copy of Bryce. Lisa wondered just how much Bryce and his brother looked alike.

The two children surrounded their uncle's newest guest. Lanie had the same easygoing smile as her uncle. She took charge immediately. "Hi, you want to come play on the swings?" she asked CeCe.

"Sure." Excitedly, CeCe took the hand that was offered to her.

"I'm Ethan," the boy told her, not to be left out.

"I know," CeCe responded. "You're Lanie's brother."

Ethan looked pleased to be recognized. Seconds later, the children burrowed their way through a sea of bodies and disappeared, presumably on their way to the swings.

Turning away from them, Bryce read Lisa's expression. "She'll be okay," he whispered against her ear. He missed the shiver she tried to stifle but couldn't. Bryce turned toward Cecilia and slipped his arm through hers. "There's someone here I'd like you to meet." He began drawing the older woman away, leaving Lisa to follow behind them. "He's the father of one of the guys I work with. Immigrated to this country from Poland when he was thirty." He knew how much Stash hungered to talk to someone from his native country. He had a hunch it might be the same for Cecilia. "I thought the two of you might enjoy having a conversation."

Cecilia's face lit up. She stopped walking and drew Bryce aside for a moment. "You are a delightful, thoughtful young man and on behalf of my granddaughter, my sometimes stubborn daughter and myself, I thank you." She brushed her lips against his cheek. "Be patient with her," Cecilia whispered in his ear. "It will be worth it for both of you." Straightening, she smiled innocently as if she hadn't said anything. "Now, show me this gentleman you have found to make me fondly remember my homeland."

There was no two ways about, Bryce definitely got a kick out of the women, pint-size or regular, in Lisa Billings's family. With blatant pleasure, Bryce introduced Cecilia to Stash Waslowski, a gray-bearded, distinguished-looking widower. When introductions were made, Stash gave a small bow and kissed Cecilia's hand. If possible, the light in Cecilia's eyes grew brighter.

A barrage of foreign words flowed in the background as Bryce left them by the pool and turned his attention to Lisa.

Bemused, she could only shake her head at what she'd just been party to in the past few minutes. "Well, you've effectively paired off my daughter and my mother, did you have someone in mind for me?"

His smile was warm and all encompassing. It effectively cut them off from the crowd of people who were attending, muting them into the background. "What's wrong with me?"

For once, she cut through the wariness, decimating it. She concentrated on the man in front of her and what he had just done for her mother and daughter: made them feel a part of things, made them feel at home. More than that, he'd made this place feel more like their new home.

She smiled at him, slipping her arm through his. Surprising him, she noticed. That made her feel even more satisfied. "Absolutely nothing from where I'm standing." Playfully she cocked her head. "Which makes me a little suspicious."

His expression was exaggerated innocence as he fought off the sudden urge to kiss her mouth. Instead he drew her over to a side table sporting a punch bowl. "Oh? Of what?"

He was good, she thought. "Of my own perception, for one."

"Don't."

For a second, he sounded so serious, it made her wonder if there was something else at play here. Something else other than her own heightened awareness of how close he was standing. Of how much she remembered every detail of the way he'd kissed her. "Don't what?"

"Overthink things." And then the easy expression was back, along with the smile that could so easily turn her bones into liquid. "I didn't think you were going to come."

She'd fought that battle in her head over and over again. Each time she lost—and won. "I couldn't exactly go back on my word after you came to my rescue like that with CeCe. And then went out of your way to entertain her the following day. You're all Cece talks about." Lisa glanced toward where her mother was. Cecilia looked positively radiant, laughing over something Stash had just told her. Lisa was grateful to Bryce for finding someone who could allow her mother to remember she was a woman and not just someone's mother or grandmother. "You made a pretty good impression on my mother, too."

He moved so that he blocked her view of the pool. Of everyone but him. When she raised her eyes to his face, he felt as if his stomach flipped over. "How about you? Did I make a good impression on you?"

"Yes." Why should the admission make her throat feel so dry? "You did."

"Good." He took her hand, slipping his fingers through hers, banking down urges that couldn't be met. Urges that rose so strong, they surprised him. He didn't surprise easily. "Why don't you come and enjoy the party? I've got some people for you to meet.'' Looking at her over his shoulder as he led her to a group, he winked. ''They all have children. They'll need toys, what with Christmas just around the corner.''

She laughed, looking around at the colorful array of summer clothes his guests were wearing. ''It's barely August.''

He liked the easy feel of her hand in his, liked the sound of her light laugh as it followed him. ''December'll be here before you know it.'' He scanned the crowd, wondering where his brother and sister-in-law were. ''You know how fast time goes when you're busy.'' Passing the barbecue, another thought occurred to him. He stopped, turning to face her. He continued to hold her hand. ''By the way, how do you like your steak?''

There was no hesitation. ''Rare.''

He grinned. ''Hey, we've got something in common besides being crazy about CeCe.'' Because the din around them was growing, he leaned into her and said against her ear, ''This looks like the start of a beautiful friendship.''

Another wave of warmth bathed over Lisa at the feel of his breath, at the promise, careless or not, of his words. She didn't want to go there, didn't want her thoughts, or worse, her heart, to go there.

For her own survival, it was best to keep things light and superficial. A smile quirked her mouth as she looked around at his guests. There had to be at least thirty people here.

"You're feeding this crowd steaks? Just how much do firefighters make, anyway?"

"Enough to get by," he told her honestly. "And I'm getting the steaks at cost. Besides, what's money for if you can't use it to bring your friends pleasure once in a while?"

This had the earmarks of far more than just an impromptu party. He even had streamers strung and paper lanterns hung. "Are you celebrating something?"

He followed her gaze. "Yes. Summer." And then he began to lead her off as he finally located his brother. "And the opening of your store."

She stopped suddenly, forcing him to look at her. She looked at him uncertainly. "You're kidding, right? About the second part?"

But he wasn't.

It took her very little time to discover that almost everyone at the party knew about Dreams and Toyland and were looking forward to coming by with their children. He had very effectively acted as her public relations man.

As he drew her away from the latest group, she could only laugh. "You ever think of leaving the fire department and starting your own advertising firm?"

"Just trying to help a friend." Passing the punch bowl, he snagged two glasses. "Here." He offered her one, a tall, frosty-looking glass filled with a light yellow liquid.

Her eyes on his, she sampled it gamely and liked what she tasted. "What is this? It's tart, but sweet and it's got a kick to it."

"I couldn't have described it better myself." He grinned. "It's my own take on lemonade. Tart, but sweet, with a kick. Kind of like you," he observed.

He was making her warm again. She pretended to study the glass. The sides were less frosty where she had touched it. "What's the kick?"

Lisa could feel his eyes on her. "That's what I'm exploring right now."

She cleared her throat, knowing her voice would crack if she didn't. "In the drink."

"Rum."

She tasted it on his lips when he kissed her.

# Chapter Nine

"Hey, break it up, you two. This is a G-rated bar-becue."

Startled, less than seconds away from sinking softly into what had all the earmarks of being a mind-numbing kiss, Lisa drew her head back. It took her a moment to catch her breath and another moment to be grateful for the interruption.

Riley, with a hand firmly clamped on each of their shoulders, stood grinning like a Cheshire cat. His comment was directed at Bryce. "You want to be-have like that, take it inside." The grin had spread to his eyes as he looked at Lisa. "In fact, I insist on it. You're making me jealous. By the way, I'm Ri-ley."

"Nice to meet you," Lisa said.

Leave it to Riley to read his mind, Bryce thought. There was nothing he would have liked more than to take what was going on between Lisa and him inside.

Inside to the bedroom. Just being near her had him fantasizing what it would be like to make love with her, to be with her in every sense of the word.

But there was a yardful of people here, people he'd invited, and whatever he was feeling was going to have to be put on hold. Bryce glanced at Lisa. He could see she was already distancing herself from what had happened. He only hoped that the moment wouldn't be irrevocably lost when he tried to take it up again.

Lisa ran her hand through her hair. The strap on her sundress dipped, falling from her shoulder. She readjusted it, feeling just this side of flustered.

"Um, I'd better go see how CeCe is doing," she murmured, backing away before she turned and worked her way through the crowd. She'd lost her head there for a second, and allowed her feelings and the moment to get the better of her.

Even with no relationship on the horizon, she was going to have to watch that, she told herself.

Bryce turned straight into Riley's wide, smug grin. He was more than passingly acquainted with that look. "She had something in her eye."

"And you were what, trying to suck it out through her mouth?" Riley hooted, helping himself to a glass of lemonade. "If you'd been any closer into her space, we would have gone right past PG to R without breaking a sweat—or maybe, in this case, you would."

Bryce wasn't about to stand here and let Riley get carried away. "Anybody ever tell you you have a big imagination?"

"Yeah." Craning his neck, Riley tried to catch a glimpse of Lisa in the crowd. "And right now I'm imagining that little lady with nothing more than a bow in her hair—" Failing to see her, he turned around and saw the look in Bryce's eyes. Riley held up his hand to his eyes, pretending to get a vision. "Wait, wait, there's more than a ribbon. She's wrapped up like a Christmas present, heavy-duty foil paper and all." He grinned at Bryce. "Just for you."

"Better," Bryce told him. "The operative word here, my friend, is lady," he reminded him. "And don't you forget it."

Riley looked at him thoughtfully, a trace of surprise in his eyes. "No, I don't think so. I think it's more like 'private property.'"

The observation was so absurd, Bryce wasn't sure just where to begin. Sure, Lisa was pretty and he was attracted to her. Who wouldn't be attracted to a woman with light blond hair and honey-colored limbs? He was, after all, only human. Damn, Riley had just admitted being attracted to her himself.

"You're talking through your fire hat, you know that, don't you?" It was time, he decided, to get busy with the barbecue—before he was tempted to skewer Riley. Bryce strode toward where the barbecue was set up. "We haven't even been on a date yet, unless you call rushing her daughter to the pediatrician a date."

Riley picked up the bag of coals and handed it to Bryce. "I call it a lot more than that. I call it instant closeness. And as for that so-called 'first date' thing—"

Emptying the coals beneath the grill, Bryce set the bag down on the ground. "Yes?"

"There's a surefire remedy for that sort of problem," Riley told him glibly. "Ask her."

Bryce waited until after everyone had gotten their steaks. He used the time to figure out just what he was going to say to Lisa. By the time he was finished, he was really no closer to the answer than he had been at the start. He decided that the best approach was an honest one.

Finding her in the center of a group of his friends, he waited a few more minutes, then stole her out of the crowd.

Curious, she let him lead her to a corner of his yard that wasn't crowded before asking, "What's up?"

Why was he having trouble getting this out? He'd never had any trouble asking anyone out before. "Riley thinks I should ask you out."

Bemusement highlighted her face. "Oh, he does, does he?"

"Yeah." Leaning his hand just above her head on the fence, he created a small alcove for them as he talked. "And here's the thing. He's my best friend even though he can be pretty much of a pain in the neck sometimes. I'd really hate to disappoint him by saying you turned me down."

She had to admit his approach was unique. "And Riley's happiness is somehow tied up in our going out on a date?"

Bryce nodded his head solemnly in response. "Pretty much."

Humor curved her mouth. "Don't you find that just a little odd?"

The scent of her perfume was beginning to weave its way into his senses, making him just a wee bit dizzy and unsettled.

"Hey, I never said Riley was all there, although I have to say he has his moments of insight." Bryce smiled down into Lisa's eyes. "Like now." Very lightly, he ran his hand along her cheek. "How about it? I've lugged your boxes, introduced your daughter to a pediatrician and found someone for your mother to talk to in her native tongue. Doesn't that qualify me as a good candidate for a date?"

Was that what he was auditioning for? "Date," she repeated. The word felt strange on her tongue. "Why does that sound as if I'm suddenly back in high school?" And why did it bring a flurry of fresh butterflies to her stomach?

He paused, thinking. "We could call it a clandestine meeting if you like."

She nearly laughed at the absurd proposal. "That would make me feel like a spy."

"Oh good, I've always had a weakness for sexy women with long lashes, long legs and secrets." His eyes teasing hers, Bryce smiled. "So, can you do a good foreign accent?"

Lisa began to laugh. He looked at her quizzically. "Oh boy, have you ever come to the right place for that." Glancing first to see where her mother and her mother's new friend were, she proceeded to recite

*Mary Had A Little Lamb* in a Polish accent so thick it could only be cut with a well-sharpened ax. Finished, she told him, "I used to tease my mother like that when I was a kid."

He bit back a laugh. "And how'd she react?"

"She'd retaliate by doing me one better. My mother's sense of humor is alive and well and she knows I don't mean anything by it." Looking over toward one of the tables, she smiled fondly at her mother. From all appearances, Cecilia was still deeply engrossed in conversation with the man Bryce had introduced her to. "It's because I love her that I can do it."

He was curious. "So why did you just look to see if she was around anywhere before you went into your little act?"

"Don't miss much, do you?"

"I try not to." Especially not, he realized, when it came to her.

"To be honest, I didn't know how her friend would take it and I didn't want to offend him."

He liked that she was thoughtful of others, but then, given her nature, he wouldn't have guessed that she would be any other way. "Trust me, Stash is the first one to join in on a joke."

She spared the couple another glance. Her mother was being fairly animated. So was the man she was talking to. "Well, then, I suspect my mother is having a fabulous time."

"How about you? Are you having a fabulous time? Or should we downgrade that to something a little less overwhelming?"

Overwhelming, yes, she thought, that just about summed it up as well as anything. *Careful, Lisa, you know what happens when you let yourself get carried away.*

Trying to seem nonchalant, she said, "My daughter's laughing, my mother's smiling and if I'm the trusting sort, I'd say that I've just made enough connections at your party to assure my first and second month's rent payment at the mall. So, yes, I'd say that I'm having a pretty fabulous time all right."

It wasn't what he was trying to find out. "I noticed that you didn't mention your personal feelings in that little litany."

Remembering what he'd told her the other day, she raised her eyes to his. "I thought we weren't going to get personal."

Oh damn, but he wanted to get personal with her. Very personal. "Even fruit flies get personal."

Her heart suddenly began to hammer, but she managed to appear unaffected. There were things she couldn't bring herself to admit to yet, not directly. "Were you there for that kiss earlier, or was that a stand-in?"

The corners of his mouth lifted. "That was most definitely me."

"Then I think you know where my personal feelings are in the scheme of things."

The footwork was fancy. Mentally he took his hat off to her. "Getting back to the original question—"

She looked at him innocently. "Oh, was there an original question?"

He grinned, enjoying the wordplay. Enjoying her.

"There was. And it was—Will you go out with me?"

She slipped into the accent again, narrowing her eyes and seductively hooding them. Somehow, it felt safer that way, as if it wasn't really her saying yes, wasn't really her admitting that she wanted to go out with him. Very much.

"Yes, my friend, I will go out with you on this date you are talking about." She tossed her hair, sending it over her shoulder. "You will tell me when, I will tell you if."

"If?" He raised an inquiring brow.

She waved her hand vaguely. "Perhaps it will not fit with my schedule. One does not know, these things, they happen sometimes."

Laughter echoed and died in his throat. He couldn't resist kissing her again. He cupped the back of her head and, tilting it up, he lightly brushed his lips along hers, taking care not to linger there the way he very much wanted to.

It couldn't have been more casual. So then why was her heart pounding as if she'd just run this long, wild marathon?

She tried very hard to focus. It wasn't easy. All she saw was him. "What about Riley?" she breathed.

"I don't want to kiss Riley, I want to kiss you." But he let out a breath and backed up. Backed up before he let himself kiss her again.

And again.

Taking her hand, he led her back to a more populated area. "Maybe we had better join the others.

Before I do something I'd infinitely enjoy but would make me a hell of a poor host.''

She couldn't keep the smile from her lips. "And that being?"

"Run off somewhere with you."

Cocking her head she looked at him, playing along. "And if I didn't want to go?"

He winked at her. "You forget, I know how to carry people fireman style."

No, she hadn't forgotten that. The problem was, she was beginning to have trouble remembering why she was resisting so hard.

Biting her lower lip, she surveyed herself in the mirror, turning very slowly. Indecision hovered over her like a dark specter.

The dress she had on, formfitting and red, dipped low in the front, lower in the back and while the hem was several inches above her knee, the side was slit up high on one thigh.

She glanced toward her mother. "What do you think?" She presented herself squarely in front of Cecilia. "Too much?"

Cecilia laughed shortly. "I would say that the words 'not enough' come to mind. It must have been a hard year for the dressmakers," she commented, "working with so little." And then she smiled her approval. "But on you, it is beautiful."

Lisa was accustomed to making split-second decisions with no hesitation. Why was deciding what she was going to wear to a place that probably had dim lighting to begin with so damn difficult for her? "Then you think I should wear it?"

Cecilia ran her hand over her daughter's hair in an old, familiar gesture. "It has my vote."

"Me, too," CeCe piped up, scrambling off the bed where she had been sitting patiently for at least two minutes. Standing next to her, she looked up at her mother. "You look pretty, Mommy. Just like Bryce's fire engine."

"Like his fire engine," Lisa echoed. She stared at herself. Too red. Oh God, why hadn't she realized that? "The man'll think he's still at work." She looked over toward her closet. An array of dresses were flung onto her chair, disqualified candidates from her search for the perfect outfit. "Maybe I should—"

Like a reading on the Richter scale, her indecision multiplied tenfold.

Reading her look, Cecilia commandeered her daughter's arm. "Too late for 'should,' Lisa. The young man is already here. He is waiting for you downstairs."

"It'll just take me a minute to—"

"No, it would not. It would take you a long time. It has already taken you a long time." Cecilia frowned. "I do not want him to think you are being, how do you say it, a stereo?"

Lisa laughed, the tension breaking, at least for a moment. "Stereotypical's the word you're reaching for, Mom, not stereo." Pulling herself together, she blew out a breath. "Okay, I won't be a stereo, or any other part of an entertainment unit." She smoothed down her hair, wishing she could do the same to her case of jitters. "I'll just be a really nervous woman."

"Why?" Cecilia looked at her, puzzled. "Nervous is for people who have no confidence."

Finding the shoes she wanted, Lisa slipped them on. The matching high heels made her four inches taller than her mother. "Bingo."

Cecilia raised her eyes to Lisa's face, mildly confused at the word. "We are not playing Bingo here, we are playing Life and Life has been very nice by bringing a nice man to you."

She didn't want her mother having her hopes raised unnecessarily, or CeCe's, either, for that matter, she thought, looking at the little girl's face. "Mother, we've had this talk before. Bryce and I are just going to have a nice time, nothing more."

Impatient, Cecilia tugged a little on her arm. "Well, you cannot have a 'nice time' standing here like this in your bedroom." She thought her words over, then amended them. "At least, not with CeCe and me standing in it, too." With both hands against Lisa's bare back, she gave her a little push toward the door. "Go, say hello. Begin your evening together."

Grabbing her purse, Lisa made her way to the door. "Yes, Mother."

"Ah, obedience. Music to my ears." Cecilia bent over to her granddaughter, saying, "Now, if she only listens to all my other advice, it would be a symphony to my ears."

"I heard that," Lisa tossed over her shoulder as she left the room.

"You were supposed to," Cecilia called after her.

Bryce was at the bottom of the stairs, waiting, when she finally emerged. All doubts about her choice of dress dissolved when she saw his face. An appreciative glow came into his eyes as she came down.

He let out a long, low whistle. "Wow." Bryce took her hand. "All I can say is that it's a good thing I'm a firefighter."

"Why?" she asked, puzzled.

"So I can put out any fires that spontaneously combust in your wake when you pass by." He had to stop and just look at her before they went out into the evening. If there hadn't been a smattering left in his lungs, he would have said she took his breath away. "Do you have any idea how good you look?"

She was afraid that the blush that crept up her cheek was the same color as her dress. "None whatsoever."

"Terrific, we'll have something to talk about on the way to the restaurant." Opening the front door, he looked back to Cecilia standing in the living room. "Don't worry, I'll have her home early."

Cecilia waved him out the door. "Keep her as long as you want."

Bryce was going to think that her mother was trying to get her married off, Lisa thought. That it was true only made everything worse. Embarrassed, Lisa could only manage an impotent, "Mother."

Cecilia merely offered an innocent shrug in her

own defense. "What have I said wrong? Americans like honesty." She splayed a hand across her breast. "I am being honest."

Lisa rolled her eyes, knowing better than to get into a debate with her mother over semantics, especially in front of Bryce. Wanting to leave before her mother had a chance to say anything else embarrassing, she turned to Bryce. "Let's just go."

"My thoughts exactly." But he still paused at the door to look back at CeCe. "See you, short stuff."

The little girl beamed over being remembered. "See you," she echoed. "Bye, Mommy. Have fun."

"I'll do my best," she promised.

"Me, too," Bryce chimed in. He was looking at Lisa when he said it.

The night air was balmy as they went to his car. "That was nice of you, saying goodbye to CeCe like that."

"Not exactly a hardship." He opened the passenger door, waiting for her to get in. Despite her independent streak, it never occurred to him to think the gesture might offend her. Some things a man just instinctively knew. "I like her," he told her, rounding the hood to the driver's side. "And your mother." Getting in behind the wheel, he strapped in, then started the car. "Your family seems to raise a nice crop of ladies."

"I'm not sure what I'm supposed to say to that."

He glanced in her direction before backing out of the driveway. "Thank you might work. Try it."

"Thank you."

He grinned. "You're welcome."

* * *

Lisa looked around inside the building Bryce had just brought her to. Overhead lights were flashing, creating an almost surreal quality, as if she had stepped onto the set of an old silent movie in progress. Except that silence was the last thing available in the packed building. Music and noise filled every crevice.

She turned toward him, raising her voice. "Dancing?" He'd just sprung the purpose behind this second pilgrimage less than a minute before they entered the building.

Holding her hand, he brought his lips close to her ear. In her heels, she was far easier to reach. "Yes, it's when your feet move but you really don't go anywhere." He turned her to face him, taking her other hand as well and, covering it with his own, placed it on his shoulder. "You might have heard of it. It's catching on in some regions."

"I know what dancing is." She was already doing it, swaying to a beat that invaded her body. Burrowing in next to another, far more primal beat that was beginning to take root inside of her. "I just didn't think, that is, when you said dinner—"

"I said date," he corrected. "Dinner was assumed, but it wasn't implied exclusively." Because of the lack of space, her body was pressed against his as they danced. Not a bad thing as far as he was concerned. Still, he didn't want to force her to do anything she didn't want to do. "Would you rather not?"

"No, that is, yes, I mean—" This was coming out really badly, she thought in frustration.

"I always liked multiple choice in school, it gave me a fighting chance of being right." He searched her eyes for his answer. "How about now?"

Defeated, Lisa started over again. "Yes, I'd like to go dancing with you." Which was a moot point, since they already were. "It's just that I didn't expect it."

Someone bumped into them, pressing her farther against him. His arm closed protectively around her. He never lost step. "I figure it's a good way to get you to let me hold you without spooking you too much."

She raised her chin defensively. "I do not get spooked. Much," she added when she saw the amused look on his face.

The din within the club rose, vying with the music, and the press of bodies brought the temperature up by a good ten degrees. Fifteen if she were going by her own heat. But that could have been a result of being held close in his arms. She could feel herself almost melting against him.

"Um, Bryce?"

"Yes?"

She drew his attention to the barely audible music. "They're playing a fast song."

He pretended to listen for a second, then nodded and continued dancing very slowly. "That's okay. They'll catch up." He saw the quizzical look in her eyes. "They're bound to play a slow one sooner or later. We're just getting a jump on them, that's all."

"Oh." She felt a smile form, taking hold of her from within. "Okay."

Lisa hid her smile in his shoulder as she pressed her face there. The smile widened as she felt his heart rhythm match her own. Just for now, she wasn't going to think, wasn't going to take this beyond the moment. Because the moment was warm and comforting. And he was in it.

# Chapter Ten

$A$s the days of summer moved languidly along toward September and the fall, Bryce found himself thinking of Lisa more and more often.

He liked seeing her.

Liked looking forward to seeing her.

If there were danger signs hidden just beneath the surface, he didn't stop to unearth them. He was having too good a time with Lisa, with her daughter, even with her mother who reminded him so much of the way his own late mother had been before his father's death had taken away her smile and her grit.

Over the course of the past six weeks, ever since he'd held Lisa against him in that dance club and pretended to dance, they had gone to a slew of movies, amusement parks, museums and restaurants. They went as a duo, a trio or a quartet, depending on whether or not they were taking CeCe and Cecilia with them. There were even times when Bryce didn't know if he was having more fun with all of them or alone with Lisa.

And then he'd go out with just her and have his answer in front of him, all done up with a bow.

There was just something about Lisa that got to him. That stirred him as it anesthetized his normal ability to back off whenever he thought himself getting the slightest bit involved.

He became involved without realizing it. It happened when he wasn't looking.

Her store seemed to be on its way to becoming a success. Bryce liked to think he had a little something to do with that. He'd gone out of his way to spread the word among his friends and acquaintances he frequently exchanged only a few words with, telling them about the new toy store that catered to the imagination of a child rather than to the latest action figure on the market.

Parents showed up at her store in increasing numbers as word got around. She gleefully gave him a progress report every time they got together. She had someone working full-time for her now, as well as a high school student, Alessandra, coming in part-time.

It was nice knowing she was settling in, really making Bedford her home.

It was nice seeing her smile.

Everything about Lisa lingered on his mind. Whenever his attention wasn't absorbed by an immediate emergency unfolding before him, Lisa was there, whispering along the outline of his day. At times, it was her smile, at others, her laughter, that seemed to consume his every thought. And then there was the way she kissed. As if each time was her first after a very long exodus.

He tried not to think about what that did to him. And how much he wanted her. But there was no getting away from the fact that he did. Badly.

"Hey, you in there, Walker?"

Startled, he looked up to see Riley standing over him in the fire station's tiny kitchen. He hadn't even heard Riley come in.

"I was just thinking," he muttered, shrugging carelessly.

Riley looked at him knowingly. "You looked like you were a million miles away. I called your name twice, didn't you hear me?"

"If I would have heard, I would have answered." Annoyed with himself, Bryce steered the conversation away from any speculation Riley might feel called upon to make. "What's on your mind?"

"Seeing as how we're both getting off at the same time for a change, you want to go out and snag a couple of beers at Vitale's?"

It had been a while since he and Riley had gone out one-on-one. He hadn't really gotten together with him since the barbecue. But he shook his head. He had other plans.

"Maybe some other time." Bryce finished putting the groceries away. It had been his turn to do the shopping. "I told Lisa I'd stop by when I went off duty."

Riley watched him thoughtfully. "You know, if I didn't know any better, partner, I'd say that you've got it bad."

Bryce stopped bunching the empty bags together and looked at his friend. "Got what?"

The shrug was wide and exaggerated. "I dunno, what would you call it? Lisa-itis? The settling-down-with-one-woman look?"

Bryce set his jaw hard. "You don't know what you're talking about."

"Don't I?" Riley hooted, feeling as if he'd just been challenged. "Hell, Bryce, I've got four brothers, remember? I can draw that look on a piece of paper with my eyes closed—and I can't even draw."

Bruce stopped walking away from him and looked at his friend seriously. "You know how I feel about commitment."

"Yeah, I know how you feel about it. Up here." He flicked his fingers at Bryce's temple, then waved them at Bryce's midriff. "But a better question would be how does your gut feel about it?"

Irritated, Bryce batted away Riley's hand. He didn't like the direction the conversation was going in. Didn't like that Riley was giving voice to questions that had been hovering just out of reach in his own mind. Questions he didn't want to deal with.

"My gut doesn't have any feelings, it just gets hungry three times a day." After he had finished unpacking and clearing away the bags, he crossed his arms and leaned against the pantry. "All this because I won't go out for a beer with you?" And then, to prove to Riley and himself that he hadn't fallen victim to any malady that rendered him incapable of walking away from the situation at anytime, Bryce changed his mind. "Okay, Riley, tell you what, you're on."

Surprised at the abrupt change, Riley looked dubious. "What about Lisa?"

"I'll just phone her and postpone," Bryce said casually, more for his own benefit than for Riley's. Riley's expression remained unchanged. "Hey, it's not as if we're seeing each other exclusively."

"Oh? Who have you been seeing lately?" Riley asked.

Ambushed without a proper answer, Bryce scowled. "I'm seeing you, isn't that enough?"

Riley laughed shortly, shaking his head. "Well, I gotta tell you, you're going to have to brace yourself to be disappointed—I don't look nearly as good in shorts and a tank top as Lisa does."

Laughing, Bryce hit him on the back of his head with the flat of his hand. "Shut up and wait in my car, I'm just going to make a call."

Riley stopped, looking serious. "Hey, I didn't mean to break anything up."

Bryce looked at him pointedly before he reached for the telephone. "You didn't."

Wiping her hands on the apron, Cecilia walked out of the kitchen into the living room. The telephone had rung and she'd refrained from answering it, knowing that it would be Bryce calling Lisa. Watching the romance between the two unfold made her heart swell. Having her own gentleman caller these days didn't hurt things, either, she thought, smiling to herself.

"So." She nodded at the telephone Lisa had just hung up. "When is he coming?"

Lisa let out a long breath before answering. "He's not. Something came up."

The edge of the apron slipped from her fingers. Instinctively she glanced toward the window, as if that would give her her answer. "A fire?"

Lisa shook her head, feeling unaccountably lost. "He's going out with Riley."

Lisa knew that nothing permanent could form between them. Hadn't she been the first to say she didn't want anything to take root?

So why did she feel so disappointed?

It wasn't even as if they had been planning some big evening out on the town. They hadn't. There were no hard and fast plans. Bryce had just mentioned coming over, perhaps watching a video with all of them. And then maybe, later on, they'd take a walk under a darkening sky, the way they had several other times in the last few weeks.

No big deal, really. Certainly no big loss that he'd canceled.

Lisa pressed her lips together. So why the hell did she feel as if someone had just propelled a cannon ball right through her and left this big, gaping hole in her middle?

If she wasn't careful, she warned herself, she was going to start crying. Without a clue as to why. Trying to outdistance the feelings that were nipping at her heels, threatening to overtake her, she suddenly turned to her mother.

"Mom, you want to go out for a pizza? You, CeCe and me?"

The suddenness of the request took Cecilia by surprise. She'd just spent the last hour and a half preparing a special meal. Even now, the aroma was seductively drifting in from the kitchen.

"But dinner—" The protest died as she saw the expression on her daughter's face. "Of course." In a smooth movement, she untied the apron and tossed it over the back of the sofa. "My hips could spread out a little farther in the name of a family evening out. Just let me shut off the stove and get my purse." Crossing to the banister, she leaned and called up the stairs. "CeCe, come down. We are going out."

The words were no sooner out of Cecilia's mouth than the little girl came flying out of her room and down the stairs. Coming to a halt in front of her mother, CeCe's head swiveled as she looked around the room.

"Oh boy, with Bryce?" CeCe asked.

The question pushed a sharp pin into Lisa's chest. "No, honey." Lisa rested a hand on CeCe's shoulder. "Just the three of us."

A frown puckered CeCe's lower lip. "Why not with Bryce?"

Lisa cupped the small face in her hand. She did her best to sound upbeat and cheerful. "Well, for one thing, he's not here."

CeCe still didn't understand. "But he will be, right, Mommy?"

Lisa dropped her hand. "Not tonight."

"Is there a fire?" Without waiting for an answer,

CeCe ran to the window to see if the fire truck was still visible in the fire station driveway.

"No," Lisa told her quietly.

Perplexed, CeCe looked at her mother over her shoulder. "Is he mad at us, Mommy?"

Anger scrambled through Lisa, rallying her. Dissolving her disappointment in its flash of heat. This was it, this was why she had resisted getting involved with a man, because it affected not only her, not only her mother's mute and not-so-mute hopes, but her daughter's heart as well. And there was no way Lisa was going to stand by and watch CeCe get hurt.

"No, baby," she told her brusquely, "he's not mad at us. He's just busy."

"Too busy for us?" CeCe asked her mother.

"Apparently so." Purse in hand, Lisa saw that Cecilia was emerging from the kitchen. They were ready. Lisa took CeCe's hand firmly in hers. "But we can have a good time without him. We did before we met him, remember, CeCe?"

"Yes." But the answer was given without enthusiasm. Breaking Lisa's heart.

Riley pulled out a five to cover the two beers the man behind the counter set down in front of him and Bryce and reached for his own mug. "Look, I was just kidding, Bryce. I didn't mean to make you change your plans for the evening."

Bryce stared at his beer. He was feeling bad about what he'd done already. Paradoxically, because he was, he knew it had to be done. "Hey, it was nothing written in stone. And maybe you're right." He lifted his mug, taking a deep swallow. "Maybe I was see-ing too much of Lisa lately. Maybe it's time to just step back and let things slide for a while."

"Why?"

Bryce shrugged. "Before it gets too serious."

"Gets," Riley repeated thoughtfully. "Hell, man, you're a few miles past 'gets' don't you think?"

Bryce frowned, contemplating the bottom of his mug, trying not to think about the fact that he felt like a heel. "Shut up and drink your beer."

Riley drained his mug, then signaled for a refill. "You know, Lisa's a great woman."

Bryce wished his friend would talk about some-thing else. "Nobody's arguing with that."

The bartender took Riley's mug and filled it with the beer on tap. Riley nodded his thanks, shelling out a few more bills. "And the parcel she comes with is pretty great, too. Kid's cute and I heard Dean's dad, Stash, talking about the grandmother. I think the two of them might be getting cozy pretty soon." Riley raised his mug in a silent salute before sampling the second serving. "Nice to know there's life after fifty. Gives me something to live for." Setting the mug down slowly, his eyes shifted toward the front door as it opened. "Speaking of something to live for, head's up."

Caught up in his own thoughts, Bryce looked at him. "What?"

Riley inclined his head toward Bryce. "Subjects approaching, nine o'clock."

Confused, Bryce turned to look in the direction Riley indicated.

*  *  *

Vitale's was the closest pizzeria to her house that Lisa knew of. She'd also heard from some of her clients that they served the best pizza west of New York. She had her doubts, but anything was worth a try. Right now, she could do with a little mindless noise and loud chatter.

The place appeared to be doing a lively business when they arrived, so much so that the parking lot was packed. The first spot Lisa found was a fair distance away from the pizzeria, in front of a clothing outlet store in the outdoor strip mall that had closed for the night.

As they walked back across the lot to Vitale's, just before she came to the entrance, she could have sworn they passed Bryce's black Jeep.

But that was just her imagination, working overtime, she told herself. Besides, this was Southern California, land of the perpetual vacation site. At any given moment, there was more than just one black Jeep in close proximity on the road.

Looking at the license would have taken the guesswork out of the situation, but she refused to do that, even just to satisfy her curiosity. He'd told her he was going out with Riley. He hadn't said anything about getting a pizza. Besides, she was doing this to get her mind off Bryce.

"Let's go inside," Lisa urged, opening the door for CeCe and her mother.

It was as if CeCe had radar.

If nothing else, she definitely had eyes like a bat. The moment they entered Vitale's, she seemed to hone in on Bryce and where he was sitting at the modest bar.

Her small face was wreathed in smiles as she excitedly pointed into the crowd. "Mommy, look!"

"Look at what?" But by the time she looked, CeCe was already darting away from her, leaving her behind, stunned. "CeCe, what have I told you about running off?" she called after the little girl. "Stay here," she instructed her mother, hurrying after CeCe before she lost sight of her in the crowded restaurant.

Finally managing to catch up to her at the bar, Lisa grabbed CeCe's arm. "Don't scare me like that. What's come over you?"

And then Lisa saw him. The answer to her question. Her attention completely focused on CeCe, she thought she was just imagining seeing Bryce out of the corner of her eye.

But there he was.

Surprise pulled the words away from her. But only momentarily. "Oh…Bryce." For lack of anything else to do, she blew out a breath, stalling for time. "I'm sorry, I didn't realize that you were coming here." Flustered, not for the world wanting him to think she had come here deliberately looking for him, she drew CeCe to her. "Come on, CeCe, let's go."

Torn, CeCe made her choice and dug in as best she could. "But we just got here, Mommy. Can't we stay with Bryce?"

That was the last thing Lisa wanted to do. Stay with a man who didn't want to be in her company. "No, honey," she said tersely, "we can go someplace else."

Even in the dim light, Bryce could see the flicker of hurt in Lisa's eyes. No matter how much she was attempting to mask it.

Hating himself for having done this to her, Bryce was on his feet immediately. "No, don't go. There's no reason to leave."

What was he doing to her? He'd called her not more than half an hour ago, canceling. Now he was rescinding that? What was his motivation? Pity? The thought galvanized her.

"Yes, there is." She tried very hard not to sound as if this mattered to her one way or another. "You're having an evening with your friend and we don't want to intrude."

Cecilia came up behind them. Bryce wondered if he'd just gained an ally. Seeing her here so suddenly, he knew he didn't want Lisa leaving. He nodded at her mother. "Hello, Cecilia."

Cecilia returned the greeting, inclining her head. "Hello, Bryce. I did not realize that we were meeting here."

Still holding CeCe's hand, Lisa turned toward her mother, and the door. "We're not, Mother. We're leaving. Now."

CeCe's lower lip began to protrude like a perch intended for sparrows. "But I don't want to leave, Mommy. Can't we stay? Please?"

Bryce put his hand on her arm, lightly restraining Lisa. "Please?" he chimed in, adding his voice to CeCe's and gaining a sunny smile from her in return.

"Stay," Riley coaxed, coming around to her other side. "He's been miserable company so far. Can't tell him apart from all those other guys they make up all those country and western songs about.''

''Oh?'' Lisa looked at Bryce innocently. ''Someone steal your Jeep?''

Riley leaned his head in close to hers. ''I'm talking about the part about the girl walking out on him,'' he clarified.

''Shut up, Riley. Stay,'' Bryce entreated Lisa, trying to sound as sincere as he could. ''Rescue me from him.''

''Yeah, stay,'' Riley echoed. He turned toward her mother, an engaging smile on his face. ''You'll talk to me, won't you, Cecilia?''

''If you wish.'' To make good on her word, as Lisa watched, Cecilia made herself comfortable on the stool next to Riley's. ''What are we having?'' Cecilia glanced at his mug. ''Boiler Preparers?''

''Makers, Mom. Boiler Makers,'' Lisa corrected automatically. ''And no, we're not having that. We're having pizza.''

''Sounds good to me,'' Bryce told her. He slipped his arm around her shoulders, silently coaxing her onto the stool he'd just occupied. Then, scooping up CeCe, he planted her on the stool next to her mother's. He took his post behind her to keep her from falling off.

Lisa began to soften, though she knew she shouldn't. ''I thought you wanted to get a beer with Riley.''

Lifting his more than half filled mug, Bryce nodded at it, then at the man sitting beside her mother. ''Beer. Riley. Requirements fulfilled. Besides, you're a hel-heck of a lot—'' he glanced at CeCe ''—prettier than he is.'' His look swept over the two women and the single woman-in-training. ''You all are.''

Giggling, CeCe turned on her stool and looked up at Bryce as if he were made entirely of her favorite kind of chocolate. ''Can't we have pizza with him, Mommy? He can have my share.''

Why did such a simple offer from a pint-size human being twist his heart?

*Mayday,* something cried within him, setting off an alarm, *you're getting in too deep.*

But just for now, he blocked out that warning. He'd much rather listen to the soft voice of the woman in front of him.

''That's okay, CeCe,'' Lisa said. She knew that she was going to regret this waffling, this retreat. But fighting the look in CeCe's eyes as well as the one she saw in Bryce's was more than she could successfully manage. ''We'll get an extra-large one.''

''Yeah, Mommy!'' CeCe cheered, clapping her hands together enthusiastically, then hooking them around Bryce's.

''Yeah, Mommy,'' he echoed.

It was the wink that undid Lisa. And tipped the scales entirely in his favor.

What did one more evening matter, she told herself as she waved to a waitress. She knew where she stood with him. On temporary ground. Which, Lisa reminded herself, was just fine with her.

## Chapter Eleven

Bryce watched the moonlight dance along her skin as they stood inside the white-framed gazebo that jutted out onto the waters of the man-made lake. The small structure, with its serene view, was quickly becoming his favorite place in Bedford. At least, when he was with Lisa.

She was so beautiful, she made his heart ache, Bryce thought. It wasn't the kind of beauty that seized you, unannounced, but rather the kind that crept up on you slowly, quietly. Lastingly.

His mind wasn't on the conversation and it had slowly died. Because he couldn't resist, he silently turned her to him and trailed his fingers along her throat, bringing them softly to rest along her cheek. The look in her eyes delivered a one-two punch to his gut he hadn't been prepared for.

Tilting her head, he pressed his lips against hers, thinking himself fairly safe. He only risked kissing her when they were out in public. When circumstances were such that things couldn't escalate into something far more intimate than a kiss. He only kissed her then because he knew that if he did it when they were alone and he made love to her, this woman would linger on his mind far longer than any ever had before. She would leave an indelible mark on his soul, making him want more than he had ever wanted anyone before. And that was bad.

Bad for him. And most especially, bad for her.

Despite all his mental precautions and self-cautioning, the kiss was intimacy personified from the moment his lips brushed against hers. It sank deep into his soul, nudging it, arousing it.

For a second, he forgot himself, forgot vows and drew Lisa into his arms. His heart hammering, he deepened the kiss. Or perhaps, the kiss deepened itself. He wasn't sure. Wasn't sure of anything.

He caught himself absorbing everything about Lisa. The feel of her body against his, the scent of evening in her hair, the taste of her lips pressed so ardently to his. Everything.

He wanted more. Needed more.

Shaken, Bryce pulled back abruptly, his hands on her arms now as if to safeguard the distance between them. He really wasn't sure if he could hold himself in check if he didn't.

He wasn't so sure he could even if he did.

Very slowly, he took a deep breath. His hammering heart downgraded to frantic. "Maybe I'd better get you home," he said quietly.

Lisa felt her heart racing as longing sprang up,

longing that ran so deep, it threatened to almost consume her. The degree with which she wanted him startled her.

She hadn't been with anyone since CeCe had been conceived. Hadn't wanted to be with anyone. Until now.

"Yours or mine?" she heard herself asking.

Despite her zest and her verve for life, it was the most brazen question she'd ever asked. He held her confidence, not to mention her future, in his hands. Without realizing it, she held her breath, waiting for his answer.

Bryce masked the wince as best he could. He smiled into her eyes, wishing for the first time in his life that he hadn't chosen the path he had. But he had and veering from his promise wasn't right. But doing what was right sure wasn't easy.

"Yours," he told her. "It's getting late and I'm on duty tomorrow."

It felt like a cold slap in the face. She told herself that he didn't mean it that way. That it was just circumstance that had him drawing back. After all, it was late and he did have to get up early.

She tried not to think about the fact that she had just thrown herself at someone who had very neatly sidestepped the pitch.

"Sure." Lisa was vaguely aware of nodding. "I understand."

But she didn't. Not really. Not any of it. Not in her heart, where all important things counted. All she knew was that she felt very, very hurt and not altogether sure why.

* * *

In the days that followed, Bryce felt like he was unwillingly involved in a dance that was beyond his control to end, or even to modify the music being played. The closer he got to Lisa, the more he knew he should pull away.

So he did. But not very effectively. Something was always pulling him back at the last moment.

When he was with her, he was where he wanted to be. When he was away, he knew that was where he should be. Away. Away so that no more bonds could form between them, no more binds could creep out over his feelings.

He was already in far deeper than he had even intended on being. Far more involved with her and her family than he had ever been with any woman before.

Because he wanted her, he told himself he didn't. And knew he was lying.

But ultimately, it wasn't supposed to be about what he wanted. It was supposed to be about what was right. And it wasn't right to tangle her life up in his when at any given moment, that bond could unravel because he wasn't there anymore.

Just like it had with his father. And his mother. The look in his mother's eyes the day she received the news about his father's death had haunted him for a long time, outweighing the pain and loss that existed in his own heart. He didn't want that look to ever be in Lisa's eyes.

Because he cared about her too much.

Lisa stared at the dark cordless telephone on the kitchen wall. The silence was deafening.

Going through the motions just to have something to do, she poured herself a cup of coffee from the automatic coffeemaker. It was cold. She'd inadvertently turned the machine off earlier.

Making a face, she poured the contents out, shaking her head at her foolishness.

She wasn't sure she could take much more of this. She was beginning to firmly believe that it was better being alone than living in this strange limbo she found herself in. When she'd started seeing Bryce, everything had been brought out in the open. He'd told her his position, she'd told him hers. Everything had been so nice and clear. Well, at least for him, it was still going along according to plan.

So how did it get so miserably tangled, so complicated for her?

The answer was simple. Because he'd stuck to the plan, and she hadn't. Somehow along the way, she let her heart do the thinking for her.

And now look at her, she was sitting on a kitchen stool, drinking cold coffee and willing an inanimate object to do her bidding. What was worse, it wasn't. The telephone just continued to silently mock her.

"Money for your thoughts," Cecilia said brightly, coming around the counter.

"That's a penny for your thoughts." The correction was automatic.

"A penny?" Cecilia repeated, laughing. "What can you possibly get with a penny except annoyed that it is not more?"

"It's a very old saying," Lisa assured her, "when

pennies counted.'' She sighed deeply, hating the way she felt. ''When feelings counted.''

Cecilia frowned. ''Feelings still count.''

Yeah, they do. And they're making me miserable, Lisa thought. ''Well, they shouldn't.''

Cecilia looked at her daughter thoughtfully. ''He has not called, eh?''

Lisa opened her mouth to deny the thought behind the question, or at least feign innocence. But what was the use? Her mother had always seemed to know her deepest feelings.

''No, he hasn't.'' Getting off the stool, Lisa went to rinse out the cup.

Cecilia shadowed her every move. ''So, why don't you call him?''

Lisa hadn't seen that one coming at all. She placed the cup onto the drain board, shutting off the water. ''Mother.''

The look on Cecilia's face was innocent. ''The telephone is rather an amazing invention. It works both ways, you know. You can dial out as well as have calls come in.''

''Why aren't you more old-fashioned?'' Lisa asked her mother.

Cecilia slipped an arm around her shoulders. ''The times change, you have to go with them or remain behind. Maybe Bryce just needs a small nudge. Maybe Bryce has what they call cool feet.''

''Cold feet, Mother.''

''Cool feet, cold feet. Same thing, a temperature irregularity.'' Her eyes softened as she looked at her only child. "I know he cares for you, Lisa. I see it in his eyes."

She'd thought she had, too, but they were both obviously mistaken. Restless, Lisa began to clear away the last of the dishes out of the dishwasher. "Apparently not enough to pick up the telephone. Except to cancel on me."

Joining in, Cecilia took a large pot from the rack and began to wipe away the last few drops of water on it. "You think it is another woman?"

Frustrated, Lisa raised a shoulder, then let it sink again. "I don't know what to think."

Cecilia tucked the pot away in the cabinet. "Well, if it were me—"

Lisa's head jerked up, a warning look in her eyes. She didn't want to discuss this any further. And she didn't want any unsolicited advice. "It's not."

Cecilia ignored the vehement bite she heard in Lisa's voice, allowing her leeway because she was hurt. "Well, actually, it is, in a way. Everything you feel, my darling, I feel. Right here." Cecilia splayed her hand over her heart. "And I cannot do anything to make it hurt any less, or be any better," she admitted truthfully. "But if I were in your situation, I would go to him and ask what was going on."

Lisa threw aside her towel. "I know what's going on. He said he didn't want to get involved."

Cecilia looked at her, confounded by this latest news. "When? When did he say this to you?"

"When he asked me out the first time."

Relieved, Cecilia nodded her head, pleased at the information. "Ah."

Lisa's eyes narrowed as she felt her back going up. "What 'ah'?"

"Men say a great many things to—how shall I say this—'protect' themselves in the beginning," Cecilia commented. "In case things do not work out."

Lisa could feel her mood growing darker with each passing minute. "Well, they didn't."

But Cecilia was not as sure as her daughter. Her expression indicated as much. "There is only one way to know for sure."

Why was her mother putting her through this? Why couldn't she just accept what was right there in front of them? He'd changed his mind. However much time he had allotted to their relationship—just enough to make her care—it was up. Over. Finished. And he was out of here. Out of her life.

"I know for sure," Lisa retorted angrily. She could feel tears beginning to form, beginning to demand release. "Look, I know you mean well, Mother, but can we just drop this discussion for now, okay?"

"Mommy?"

Startled by CeCe's voice, Lisa wiped away her tears with the back of her hand and pulled herself together before she turned toward the doorway. She had no clue if CeCe was drawn by her raised voice or not.

It quavered slightly as Lisa said, "Yes, honey?"

"When is Bryce coming over?" CeCe held aloft the red fire truck he had presented to her at the annual firefighters picnic last Sunday. It was an exact miniature of the one sitting across the street at the station. "I want him to play fire truck with me again," she said, despite the warning look in her mother's eyes.

"Honey, Bryce might not be coming by anymore," Lisa said.

Anymore sounded like a long time. Maybe like forever, CeCe thought. But Mommy couldn't mean that. CeCe's brow puckered as she tired to make sense out of the words. "Why?"

"Because, well, because—" Lost, Lisa looked toward her mother for help, but Cecilia left her freefalling in the wind. She looked back at her daughter. "Because he's very busy right now and might be for a very long time to come."

CeCe's chin trembled slightly. She dug in stubbornly as tears shimmered in her wide eyes. "No, he's not too busy to see me. You'll see. He said so. He said he'd always have time for me," she insisted.

Lisa hated this, hated having her child hurt. Now Bryce was making promises to CeCe he had no intention of keeping. "When did he say this?"

"The last time he read to me."

The night after the picnic. The last time he'd been here, Lisa thought.

"And he wouldn't lie, he wouldn't!" CeCe insisted. Then, defiantly, she backed away from both her mother and her grandmother. "I'm going to my room now. When he comes, call me."

"CeCe—"

But the little girl spun around on her heel and raced up the stairs to her room without a backward glance.

"Okay, that does it," Lisa announced angrily to the room at large. Or perhaps it was to herself, to signal an end to her passive period.

Turning on her heel much the way CeCe had, Lisa marched out of the kitchen.

"Where are you going?" her mother called after her.

"To give someone who needs it a piece of my mind." Barefoot, she looked around for the shoes she'd kicked off as soon as she'd walked into the house. "It's one thing to pull a disappearing act on me, it's another to do the same thing to CeCe."

Finding her shoes on the opposite ends of the sofa, she put them on, shoving each foot in with a vengeance.

Cecilia began to follow her, then stopped. Initially she wanted to tell Lisa not to say anything to Bryce in the heat of anger she might regret. But even anger had its place at times. And who knew? A display of justified temper might just nudge things along.

Besides, Cecilia smiled to herself, remembering, it was so very nice, making up again after the shouting was all over.

Her thoughts colliding into one another, Lisa wasn't thinking very clearly as she quickly made her way across the street. There were only a smattering of cars out. Rush hour traffic was over and dinner, for the most part, wasn't yet. People were in their homes, sharing precious time. A hint of envy flickered through her soul.

She had to do this now, while she was still angry

enough to carry it off. It wasn't as if she wanted him back in her life, she told herself. After all, what did she want with a man who made promises to little girls he had no intention of keeping?

But she did want to tell Bryce Walker what she thought of him. That she regretted the day she ever laid eyes on him. Regretted every unbidden dream she'd ever had of him.

She just wanted to tell him that he had gotten his wish—he was out of her life and out of CeCe's. But before she told him that, she wanted to tell him what a miserable rat he was for toying with CeCe's hopes the way he had.

The firehouse seemed deserted when she entered it, although the truck was still there. She knew Bryce was on duty because she had seen his black Jeep parked in the lot to the right of the station house. All she had to do was keep her anger wrapped around her long enough to find him.

Lisa took the stairs on the far side and made her way up to the living quarters. Several men she recognized from the barbecue and the picnic were engrossed in a poker game.

Riley was the first to look up when she approached.

Lisa could feel her courage flagging. "Hi, is Bryce around?"

The rest of the men all turned and looked at her in unison.

Riley took the unlit cigar out of his mouth and set it on the empty ashtray as he rose to his feet. "Hi, Lisa. You don't know?"

There was something in his voice that alerted her she wasn't going to like what was coming. She suddenly remembered that this was fire season in Southern California. The population held its collective breath, waiting for the cooler weather to arrive. Until then, the possibility of devastating fires hovered over all of them.

Lisa looked at Riley warily. "Know what?"

"Bryce and most of the crew are down by Lake Elsinore," one of the other firefighters, Joe Donnellson, told her.

"There're three major fires going on down there and the area put out a call for any firefighters who could be spared. I thought he called you," Riley said.

"No." The wind had completely gone out of Lisa's sails. "No," she repeated. "He didn't. When did he, when did they," she amended, "leave?"

Riley could see why his friend was so affected by this woman. He felt something protective stirring within himself as well. Damn Bryce and his stupid edict. He should have said something to her.

"They went this morning. Early," he added, as if that somehow excused Bryce's sin of omission. "They're still all down there," he said hurriedly. "I really don't know how long they're going to be there." Riley shook his head, mystified. "I thought for sure he told you."

She shook her head. "No, maybe he just didn't stop to think of it."

Didn't stop to think that when she found out, she'd be terrified for him. Didn't stop to think that maybe she would have liked the chance to talk to him before he left. In case…

Lisa pulled her thoughts up sharply. She refused to let her mind go there. Bryce was a firefighter, had been one for over eight years. He'd survived fires before he ever met her, there was no reason to think he wouldn't go on doing just that now that he had.

Plenty of firefighters lived to retire from their jobs.

So why did she suddenly feel as if her insides had all turned to gelatin?

She searched Riley's face and saw kindness there. He understood what she was going through. Too bad his friend wasn't as insightful. "Is there any way to contact him?"

Riley shook his head. "Not really. There's a command post set up down there, but getting a call through to him that isn't an emergency—" He stopped abruptly, his eyes washing over her and coming to rest on her abdomen. "It's not an emergency, is it?"

Lisa knew what Riley was thinking. "No," she replied quietly. "It's not an emergency. If Bryce calls in by some chance…"

"Yes?" he coaxed encouragingly.

"Don't tell him I was here," she said, edging her way out of the communal room. Out of Bryce's way of life.

"Whatever you want," Riley replied.

That was just the trouble, she thought, hurrying from the station. It wasn't what she wanted. But apparently, it was what Bryce wanted. Why else would he have answered the call for volunteer firefighters at Lake Elsinore without so much as calling her to say goodbye? Because she didn't matter to him, that's why.

# Chapter Twelve

Lisa felt like throwing things, preferably breakable things that made loud noises when they crashed against hard surfaces.

The man was despicable, absolutely despicable. She hated Bryce for having toyed like this with her emotions. Hated him for making her care. For making her feel isolated from him, not because of the miles that separated them, but because of the feelings that kept him distant from her.

With all her might, Lisa tried to hang on to her anger. Anger was her glue, it was what kept her from falling apart. But it was slowly being dissolved in the wake of a very real, cold fear. She'd never had a personal stake in watching a disaster unfold before. She had one now.

The Lake Elsinore fires were in full swing, in their third day, with no containment in sight when Lisa found out Bryce was there. She immediately began watching the cable station dedicated to broadcasting the Orange County news twenty-four hours a day.

The set droned on in the background no matter what Lisa was doing at home. At work, she had a small set tuned to the station under the main counter. She needed to remain connected to what was going on. Just in case.

"You are making yourself crazy," her mother said the second night of her vigil. But Cecilia sat with her and watched.

Only CeCe was kept in the dark as to why something so boring as news was on constantly.

And then, on the afternoon of the fifth day, it happened. The story Lisa had been praying not to hear. She'd just finished ringing up a huge, grinning teddy bear for a man whose wife was expecting their first child when the newscaster announced, "This just in. Two Bedford firefighters were rushed from the site of the largest of the Lake Elsinore fires and flown by medi-vac to Harris Memorial Hospital."

Transfixed, unable to breathe, Lisa stared at the television screen. She barely remembered to hand her customer back his copy of the charge receipt.

She turned up the volume.

"…the second firefighter was injured when he went in trying to save his fellow fireman who had been pinned by falling debris in this terrible blaze. Names are being withheld pending notification of the families. On a brighter note, two of the fires appear to be under thirty percent containment, while the third is more than fifty percent contained…"

Lisa knew it was Bryce.

While she fervently prayed it wasn't, in her heart, she knew. The second fireman was Bryce. It was the kind of thing Bryce would do without thinking. Put himself on the line for someone else, disregarding his own safety.

When the telephone rang as the scene on the screen turned to local sports, Lisa jumped. But it was only her mother on the other end of the line, not anyone official. As if they would call her if something happened to Bryce, she mocked herself. She'd made it clear to everyone that she wanted her space, not Bryce.

Her mother's voice was filled with emotion. "Lisa—"

Lisa held the receiver against her ear with both hands. There was no need for her mother to elaborate. Lisa knew her mother was keeping vigil, same as she. "I know, I just heard."

There was a pause, as if Cecilia was searching for the right words. "They gave no names. We do not know that it is him."

"We don't know that it's not."

Cecilia continued pragmatically. "I have just called the hospital. They will not tell me anything," she said, frustrated.

Lisa knew her mother was as worried as she was. And not just because Lisa's own heart was tangled up in this situation, but because her mother genuinely liked Bryce. He'd made a place for himself in all their lives—which was why his abrupt withdrawal this way didn't make any sense.

Lisa made up her mind. "I'm going down there

myself to get someone to talk to me.'' There was no way she could remain here, waiting for word, or arguing with a disembodied voice over the telephone. She'd go out of her mind within ten minutes. "I'll call you when I know something.'' And then she paused as a thought struck her. "Mom, don't let CeCe know.'' The little girl would be devastated if she knew something had happened to Bryce. There was no point in telling her and getting her alarmed until all the facts were in.

"I am already leading the way there.'' Lisa guessed that her mother meant she was way ahead of her there, but didn't bother correcting her. "Do not worry. I have her playing with the girls next door. Just go. And if it is him, give him my love.''

And mine, Lisa thought. "Don't worry, I will. Just before I read him the riot act.''

"There is a riot along with the fire?''

"Never mind, Mom. I'll call you as soon as I have anything to tell you.'' She hung up and pushed the telephone back on the counter.

Leaving the three customers in the store with her assistant, Lisa was in her car and driving toward the hospital within seven minutes of hanging up the telephone.

The trip from the mall to Harris Memorial was a blur of traffic lights she just managed to squeak through and lanes that she wove in and out of, trying to gain a few yards, a few precious seconds.

Her mind was focused only on one thing. She hoped that if it *was* Bryce in one of the two hospital beds, he would be all right.

And when he got well, she thought, brushing away with the heel of her hand the tears that insisted on falling, she'd strangle him. Strangle him for leaving to fight this huge disaster without telling her what he was doing. Without even saying goodbye.

Lisa parked her car and rushed inside the hospital entrance. Following the signs, Lisa found the emergency admissions desk just beyond the emergency room itself. The nurse was about to call over the next patient, but Lisa reached her desk first.

"Can you tell me if you've admitted a Bryce Walker here in the last hour or so? He was one of the two firefighters flown in from the fire out at Lake Elsinore."

The pleasant-looking woman in the pink smock looked genuinely sorry. "I can't tell you—"

Lisa cut her short. "Please," she said, anguish in her eyes.

A wealth of feeling and information reverberated in the single word. The woman hesitated, then moved her chair to face the computer monitor on her desk. "What was that name again?"

"Thank you." Lisa's sigh of relief was audible. "Bryce Walker."

Keying in the name, the receptionist pulled up a screen and then nodded. "Yes. He was admitted about ninety minutes ago."

Admitted. It was serious. Lisa wanted to ask how he was, what they had done to him, but those were questions she could answer for herself once she saw him. "Where is he?"

"Third floor," the woman read out loud. "Room 312."

A second "Thank you" hung in the air in her wake as Lisa dashed down the hallway to the elevators in the rear of the building.

Once inside the elevator, she jabbed the button for the third floor. ICU was located on the first floor. That meant Bryce was stable, didn't it? She wondered.

She wrapped her mind around the thought and hung on to it for dear life.

Not wanting to waste precious time by stopping at the nurse's station, or risk being sent away from a room that allowed no visitors, Lisa hurried down the hall, reading off numbers to herself, looking for his room.

She found it soon enough. And Riley who had gotten there ahead of her. The latter shot to his feet as she rushed into the room.

"Lisa."

Weak, with his right hand bandaged up to his elbow and sporting a large dressing just over his left eye, Bryce was just as startled to see her as Riley was.

"Did you send for her?" he accused Riley with something that would have passed for anger had it more verve.

Riley raised his hands in protest. "Not me. I wouldn't have 'sent' for her. Not without specific instructions."

Lisa wanted to fling herself into Bryce's arms, bandaged or not, and cover his face with kisses. She wanted to scream at him for shutting her out.

Instead, as both emotions warred inside her, she forced herself to remain as cool as she could.

It lasted all of three seconds.

"No, he didn't summon me," she told Bryce tersely. "No one summoned me." Her eyes, like twin blue flames, bored into him. "Just like no one thought to tell me what was going on in the first place."

Bryce had wanted only to spare her, and he'd apparently managed to do just the opposite. "Lisa, I—"

Riley knew when to make a timely exit. "I'll see you later, Walker. Lisa." He nodded at her, backing out of the room.

With barely a nod, she hardly spared the man a glance. Her eyes were focused on Bryce. The instant the door closed, she approached his bed with small, sure steps, like a puma stalking its prey into a dead end. The flames in her eyes rose.

"How dare you?"

He couldn't take his eyes off her. "You're going to have to be more specific than that."

Specifics? He wanted specifics? She'd give him specifics, all right. A ton of them.

"How dare you just go off like that? How dare you make a place for yourself in our lives and then just vanish as if you'd been some sort of dream we all mass hallucinated? And then to find out—" She stopped abruptly, her voice hitching. She wanted to pummel him for the scare he had given her. "Do you have the slightest idea what I've been through these past three days?"

He set his mouth grimly. "Yeah, I do. And that's exactly why I tried to 'vanish' out of your lives the way I did."

She didn't want to hear it, the sterling sentiments that had nothing to do with the flesh and blood feelings that existed between them.

"Oh, please, spare me the I-don't-want-to-hurt-you-so-I'm-out-of-here speech." She struggled to keep her voice steady, to keep the tears she felt back. "Don't you get it? It's too late for that. Too late to try to run for cover or throw protective stone walls back up. I'm here, I'm invested. And damn it, you did this to me. To all of us."

He saw the tears shining in her eyes and ached because he had caused them. Ached because despite it all, he still wanted her more than he wanted anything else. Ever. "Yeah. I know. I'm sorry."

He still didn't get it. Frustrated, she sighed and dragged a hand through her hair. "You're being sorry for the wrong thing, don't you understand that?"

Bryce understood. He understood a lot of things. He'd had a great deal of time to think, both while he was lying exhausted in his cot during the enforced breaks he'd taken while fighting the fire, and while he was lying here. He looked at her now, perhaps seeing her for the first time. Seeing her with his heart. He couldn't keep the words back.

"Lisa, I love you."

She opened her mouth and then closed it again. Her eyes narrowed as she looked at him. "What?"

"I love you," he repeated. And he did, he realized. With all his heart.

She stared at him for a moment, flustered and at a loss as to what to say. What did he mean by springing something like that on her just when she'd worked up a full head of steam?

"Is that supposed to keep me from yelling at you?"

Smiling, he moved his head from side to side. But not too hard because it still hurt like hell. "No, I just wanted to let you know where I stood."

Now he said it. But then, she admitted to herself, had he said it earlier, maybe she would have run for the hills. It took something like this to make her realize where she stood herself. "You mean, instead of wavering in the shadows?"

He grinned now. "Yeah, instead of that."

She sighed. "You took all the wind out of my sails, you know that, don't you?"

Bryce laughed shortly. "God, but I hope not. I really like that wind. You really are magnificent when you're angry, you know. C'mere," he coaxed, holding out his one unbandaged hand to her.

Lisa pulled a chair over to his bedside, and took the hand in both of hers, grateful to be able to be here with him like this. Grateful to be anywhere with him.

"My life literally did flash before my eyes when I was inside that inferno, trying to get Jim out—they say he's going to be okay, by the way," he interjected.

She hadn't stopped to ask about the other firefighter. All she could think of was Bryce. But now she nodded, relieved. "I'm glad." Her eyes encouraged him to continue.

"But I realized that I'm not going to be all right." He saw her eyes widen in concern and he hurried to make her understand. "Not without you. You and CeCe and your mother." This wasn't exactly coming out right. Determined, he gave it another try. "I realized, in that split instant when I didn't think Jim and I were going to make it out of there alive, that you were the best part of my life. And that going on without you wasn't really going to be life at all. I always knew I wanted a family, but the idea of a family was something abstract. You know, the way you want something you don't really have. I never realized just how much I wanted a family until I found myself enfolded in yours." Despite the pain, he squeezed her hand lightly in his. "And now going on without it just wouldn't be the same."

Her eyes held his, love welling up within her. "Who says you have to?"

To shackle her with his love still wasn't fair. He wanted her to think this through very carefully. "What you said you just went through—the fear, the terror, that's not an isolated incident. In one form or another, it'll happen over and over again. I'm a firefighter, Lisa. It's who and what I am."

If there was an argument, she wasn't the one creating it. "I know that. Did I say I wanted you to be a plumber?"

"No."

"Then what are we talking about?"

He looked at her earnestly. "We're talking about you living with fear."

It was still no contest, she thought. "Better with fear than without you."

She'd hit the nail right on the head. There were no guarantees in his profession. They were as careful as they could be, taking all the necessary precautions. But death rode on every trip. "There's that, too."

She knew what he was saying to her. Knew, too, that it didn't matter. Not the way he thought it did. She wasn't going to let fear stop her from enjoying his love. Not anymore.

"Are you familiar with Milton? *Paradise Lost?*" she added in case he didn't understand her reference. "He said something to the effect that it was better to rule one minute in hell than to serve all eternity in heaven."

His grin was wide. "Are you by any chance equating me to the devil?"

The man could be difficult when he wanted to be. "No, I'm saying that there are choices in life, choices that, because of what they are, are far better risking than going with a peaceful, sure thing."

He sat up, his hand curled around hers. "So I'm your one minute in hell?"

He was fighting her, she thought. "It loses something in the translation."

He reached for her face, caressing it. "As long as you don't."

She thought if she loved him any more, her heart was going to explode. And to think, she'd almost lost this without ever finding out how much was at stake. "Not a chance."

"So you're determined? To stick by me?" he added in case he wasn't making himself clear.

"Yeah."

He wanted to give her every opportunity to back out. Because once the words were out, they were binding. "And I can't talk you out of it?"

She moved her head from side to side, her eyes on his. "Not a chance."

It was all he wanted to hear. "Then I guess I'd better make an honest woman out of you."

She blinked, afraid she was taking too much for granted, afraid that she was somehow misunderstanding what he meant. "Are you asking me to marry you?"

"Yes." Was she going to turn him down after all? Bryce wondered.

Dazed, she swallowed. "Unless I'm mistaken, the term making an honest woman of someone usually applies after the couple's made love."

"I have. In my mind. A hundred times."

She grinned, feeling her body heat already. "Reality is much better."

"I'm counting on it." He linked his hand with hers again. "Then it's yes?"

"What do you think?"

He drew her over to the bed and she sat down beside him. "I think that I have a hell of a lot to get well for now."

Her eyes twinkled. "Yes, you do." Getting comfortable beside him, she took her cell phone out and began to press a key.

"What are you doing?"

"Calling Mother and CeCe to tell them you're all right. And that there'll be one more to dinner." She looked at him significantly. "Permanently."

He put his hand over the keypad. "Call them in a few minutes."

She flipped the cover shut, looking at him. "Why?"

He shifted so that he could slip his good arm around her. "Because right now, I'd like to kiss the woman I love."

Lisa grinned, setting the cell phone aside on the table. "Best offer I've had all day."

His eyes were already making love to her. "Best offer you'll ever have."

She knew that it would be. "You've got that right," she whispered softly just before his lips met hers.

\*    \*    \*    \*    \*

0502/51a

# DESIRE

**AVAILABLE FROM 17TH MAY 2002**

## HER IDEAL MAN

**A LOVING MAN** Cait London
Rose had denied her fiery, forbidden thoughts for Stefan because she knew he wouldn't be satisfied with small-town life. Except her resistance seemed to be dwindling with every spine-tingling kiss...

**THE BARONS OF TEXAS: TESS** Fayrene Preston
Tess Baron knew she was in trouble the second she laid eyes on the mysterious—and oh-so-sexy—stranger. But just what was it about Nick that made Tess long to be in his arms?

## SECRET CHILD

**HIS BABY!** Maureen Child
*Bachelor Battalion*
Marine Jeff Hunter couldn't believe Kelly had kept his baby a secret! But once he held his little girl in his arms, he knew he'd do anything to keep sexy Kelly and their child by his side.

**THE SULTAN'S HEIR** Alexandra Sellers
*The Sultans*
Marriage was the only way Sheikh Najib could protect Rosalind and her son. But with every night in the arms of her sheikh 'husband,' Rosalind's secret threatened to surface...

## BUSINESS OR PLEASURE?

**THE AMERICAN EARL** Kathryn Jensen
Giving her virginity to Matthew Smythe, her sexy boss, was a special moment for Abby. But how could she convince the aristocratic bachelor to exchange his single life for marriage?

**BEAUTY IN HIS BEDROOM** Ashley Summers
A house-sitting service was all Regina had offered. Except when Clint Whitfield came home unexpectedly, she couldn't suppress the fiery attraction between them—dare she hope for more?

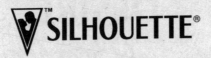

Fortune's Children™
THE GROOMS

# *Welcome back to the Fortune dynasty*

The drama and mystery of Fortune's Children continues with a new 12-part book continuity series.

**Fortune's Children: THE GROOMS**
**and**
**Fortune's Children: THE LOST HEIRS**

The drama, glamour and mystery begins with Fortune's Grooms, five strong, sexy men surrounded by intrigue, but destined for love and marriage!

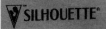

# SILHOUETTE® SUPERROMANCE™

*is proud to present*

**nine months later.**

*Friends... Lovers... Strangers...*
*These couples' lives are about to change*
*radically as they become parents-to-be*

## AND BABY MAKES SIX
Linda Markowiak
May

## THE FRAUDULENT FIANCÉE
Muriel Jensen
June

## SNOW BABY
Brenda Novak
July

## THE FAMILY WAY
Rebecca Winters
August

Join us every month throughout the
whole of 2002 for one of these dramatic,
involving, emotional books.

0502/SH/LC29

**SILHOUETTE® INTRIGUE™**
*is proud to present*

# TOP SECRET BABIES

*These babies need a protector!*

## THE BODYGUARD'S BABY
### Debra Webb - January

## SAVING HIS SON
### Rita Herron - February

## THE HUNT FOR HAWKE'S DAUGHTER
### Jean Barrett - March

## UNDERCOVER BABY
### Adrianne Lee - April

## CONCEPTION COVER-UP
### Karen Lawton Barrett - May

## HIS CHILD
### Delores Fossen - June

*Unwrap the mystery*

## 1 Book
### and a surprise gift!

We would like to take this opportunity to thank you for reading this Silhouette® book by offering you the chance to take another specially selected title from the Desire™ series absolutely FREE! We're also making this offer to introduce you to the benefits of the Reader Service™—

- ★ FREE home delivery
- ★ FREE gifts and competitions
- ★ FREE monthly Newsletter
- ★ Books available before they're in the shops
- ★ Exclusive Reader Service discount offer

Accepting this FREE book and gift places you under no obligation to buy; you may cancel at any time, even after receiving your free shipment. Simply complete your details below and return the entire page to the address below. *You don't even need a stamp!*

**YES!** Please send me 1 free Desire book and a surprise gift. I understand that unless you hear from me, I will receive 2 superb new titles every month for just £4.99 each, postage and packing free. I am under no obligation to purchase any books and may cancel my subscription at any time. The free books and gift will be mine to keep in any case.

D2ZEB

Ms/Mrs/Miss/Mr ................................................................Initials ....................................

BLOCK CAPITALS PLEASE

Surname ...........................................................................................................................

Address ............................................................................................................................

..........................................................................................................................................

..............................................................................Postcode ..........................................

**Send this whole page to:**
**UK: The Reader Service, FREEPOST CN81, Croydon, CR9 3WZ**
**EIRE: The Reader Service, PO Box 4546, Kilcock, County Kildare (stamp required)**